I0726446

MONARCH
OF
LIGHTNING

Titles By Danith McPherson

<u>Cassie Windom Mysteries</u>
Averted Vision
Not Her First Murder

<u>Speculative Fiction</u>
Monarch of Lightning
Lightning World Book One

Blade of Mad Vision

Roar at the Universe

MONARCH OF LIGHTNING

LIGHTNING WORLD
BOOK ONE

DANITH MCPHERSON

This is a work of fiction. Names, characters, places, events, and dialogue are either the products of the author's imagination or used in a fictitious manner. Any resemblance to actual people, living or dead, or to actual places, events or dialogue is purely coincidental.

MONARCH OF LIGHTNING
Copyright © 2017 by Danith McPherson

All rights reserved. No part of this publication may be used, reproduced, distributed, transmitted or stored in any format or manner whatsoever, without the prior written permission of the author, except in the case of brief quotations included in critical reviews and certain other noncommercial uses permitted by copyright law. No part may be incorporated into or used in any way in artificial intelligence without prior permission. Printed in the United States of America

Wayward Serpent paperback second edition, April 2020
ISBN 978-1-950506-02-6 (print 6x9)
ISBN 978-1-950506-20-0 (print 5.5x8.5)
ISBN 978-1-950506-03-3 (ebook)
Library of Congress Control Number 2020935035

Published by Wayward Serpent, Farwell MN
Up to no good but means well

For Don, who knew the job was dangerous when he took it
For Matt, my much appreciated first reader
For Aaron, who is quick with witty banter

We breathe in the written word like air, and it becomes part of us.
We inhale the stories and make them our own.

D.M.

PROLOGUE

Nevran, forced from the monarchy by his madness, held the small girl in his arms and walked the battlement of Aerrion Fortress. At this height she should be afraid, but she always felt safe snuggled into her great-grandfather's arms. Besides it was daylight. The vast expanse of sand they gazed at was rippled with heated air but was calm.

They'd been speaking in their secret language. Now Nevran spoke in Lorchan.

"Leave from the little fortress. Travel with first light. Give Fujin his head."

It was a lesson. She repeated the words as she had often done before.

Nevran kissed her forehead. "The half-moon mirage will be before you." He could only tell her the bones. Giving her the whole fish was dangerous. He hoped, wished, prayed to the old, absent gods that this would be nothing more than a pretending they shared. But, like most things on Alchorel, hopes, wishes and prayers found it hard to survive.

Nevran switched back to their secret language. "What do you want, stranger?" he said in a comically gruff voice.

Mimicking his funny, deep tone, the girl said the foreign word. "Sanctuary."

~

CHAPTER

ONE

Aerrion Fortress crouched high on the craggy bank of the river like a wary beast, as if the entire realm depended on its vigilance. A massive stone array, it spanned the ruins of crumbled battlements where tyrants once perpetuated clan warfare. Before that, so the older than old stories told, the site had been sacred to machine users, who long ago had been lost in myth.

Janvian joined her husband Rojelon at the railing of a protruding balcony. Heat of the fading day radiated from the heavy structure, as if the stones breathed, warding off the spreading coolness of a harvest evening. Thunder churned in the distance. Dressed for the celebration already underway in the hearth hall, they were an elegant couple in their formal robes.

"The ambassadors are on their way back to the *skyship*," Rojelon said.

"*Skyship*," Janvian said. "You say the foreign word as if it were your own." She didn't want to talk about the strangers from the United Trade Worlds, who seemed more predators than ambassadors. Private moments had been scarce of late. She wished, at least for a short time, they could just be any married couple and not the monarchs of Lorcha. But he was Rojelon of the Felcon Clan. Tall and handsome, he wore his dark curly hair pulled back from his angular face in accordance with his family's tradition. Schooled in history, duty and protocol, he'd been raised to handle any diplomatic challenge, even the rare appearance of alien visitors.

And she was Janvian of the Druetens. Slight in stature, she had the combination of blue eyes and copper hair that only showed itself in her clan. With her own hereditary ties to the throne, she'd also been trained in responsibility and leadership. Their match had been almost inevitable.

"We've given our final refusal," Rojelon said. "They're gone. We'll have no more of them, or their talk of how much we would benefit from trade with machine-using otherworlders."

Janvian wasn't convinced they would go away just because they'd been told to. She feared what they could see from above the clouds with their mechanisms, but she didn't dare voice her concern here. Some things should not be so much as whispered in an unprotected place, even one as secluded as their personal balcony.

"Their devices are crutches," Rojelon said. "These people are incapable of thinking and making decisions on their own. They frequently had to go back to their ship to consult with gears and cogs. Their machines will tell them there is little potential for profit here."

He and Janvian had analyzed the situation together. Although the visitors had praised Alchorel as if it were a precious jewel, the planet must look like an insignificant rock to them. Its population was too small for trade across galactic distances. The land would appear too inhospitable and void of natural resources to be a temptation. The purpose of the delegation had probably been more to judge the planet's progress than to establish commerce.

Janvian wished they could have sent the ambassadors away when they'd first arrived. That wouldn't have been very diplomatic and it might have appeared suspicious, as if they were trying to hide some treasure.

The real danger was not from the outside but the inside. Some Lorchans were curious about what the United Trade Worlds had to offer, and how it might be used for their own gain. She feared that even lor, the loyalty that held them together, would not prevent someone from betraying the secret at the core of the planet, if the personal benefit seemed great enough.

"I think we handled them very well," Rojelon said. "They went away satisfied that we have nothing they want."

"Yes, we did well together," Janvian said. As they always did. But she was not as convinced of their success as her husband.

To the west, the first flash of lightning ripped the red sky and spiked the great Bewailed Wilde, bursting a boulder to rubble. The rock's surprised cry rumbled across the desolate plain and faded as the next strike exploded sand to dust. She turned a shoulder to the nightly tempest and gazed north, preferring the calm grays slowly deepening to black. She had enough turbulence in her life.

Laughter echoing up through the fortress from the hearth hall was rough, not the easy music of companionship but a hollow bellow that vibrated tensely through the stone. She almost preferred the storm to the veiled hostility below.

When she was young, the vast Wilde had seemed a place of adventure. Great-grandfather Nevran was the only one ever to claim he'd journeyed across the deadly expanse. On many unsettled nights, she had huddle with him under the massive table in his workroom. While she had nibbled treats snatched from the kitchen, he had spun exotic tales of the Mirage people living at the center of the turmoil.

Janvian felt she dwelled in a storm of a different kind. There was love in her marriage, but too often she was reminded that its purpose was to guarantee an alliance between two powerful families. Until recently Rojelon's sister Lelian had served as blood heir, preventing other clans from thinking about their own possible claims to the throne. When the quiet, thoughtful woman had died in a hunting accident, which may have been no accident at all, the line of succession had suddenly turned murky, causing dormant ambitions to wake.

Duty required Janvian and Rojelon to assure the lineage. Their lovemaking had become a scheduled chore instead of the passionate pleasure it had previously been. They were both relieved that Janvian had finally conceived.

The full moons Pypeed and Noalgaz moved closer together in the sky, casting double shadows. Within the hour quick Noalgaz would cross its larger sibling, signaling the start of a fresh year and a new century.

"We can make the announcement tomorrow," Janvian said. "Tonight, let the baby be ours alone."

"It must be now," Rojelon said. "No one will dare break lor at the time of a new heir." He put his arms around her. "Whatever this child is to the country, it will always be our personal joy."

He always knew the perfect thing to say, publicly and privately, slipping between monarch and husband as if there were no difference between the two roles. Janvian leaned against him. Perhaps the time would come when she would have an isolated life all her own, but it would not be tonight.

They left the intermittent glow of the lightning and passed through their rooms to a passageway. A waiting mystic followed them down the staircase. The silent being, anonymous in its hooded robe, moved like an empty shadow.

The hearth hall blazed with thick candles. Rojelon and Janvian entered through the high arching doorway. Benches scraped the slate floor as guests rose to give the hand to shoulder salute, palm forward to show it held no weapons.

Out of habit Janvian flexed her wrists to feel the pressure of the blades strapped to her forearms. The pleated sleeves of her pale green gown fanned from the shoulders, giving enough freedom to swing a sword, should the need arise. The fine fabric was gathered into bands embroidered with the Drueten crest set below the elbows. From there, smooth fabric fell straight, concealing the weapons. Her collar stood high to protect her neck. An overlay from shoulder to waist, beautifully stitched with a delicate pattern of lliwant leaves, was thick enough to weaken an enemy's blow.

Rojelon's deep green robe fit him as easily as the monarchy. Similar to Janvian's in style, it allowed movement yet gave protection. His overlay of tooled leather displayed the Felcon emblem—a keen-eyed phianj in flight, sharp talons ready. The motif was repeated in gold on his armbands.

With pleasant smiles the couple surveyed the assembly, noting the location of enemies and allies. Each clan occupied its own island of tables. They were as separated in this room as within their own borders—the Felcons from the wooded north; Drueten Clan from the eastern highlands that stretched through mountains to the ocean; the Joachs from the southern river valley; the Walbasks from the mountains to the far south; the Tskants, host to Aerrion Fortress, from the western bend of the river and land bordering the Bewailed Wilde.

The families arrogantly thrived despite the planet's

harshness. They were competing vines of the same weed, sending roots and runners to anchor into the rocky crags and burrow into the wet clay. They reached out in every direction except one. They pulled back from the barren plain of the Wilde as a leaf curling from a flame.

Mystics formed dark spots among the colorfully dressed revelers. Merchants mixed with clans other than their own for the good of their commerce. A few of the guests crossed boundaries for sport or other reasons.

In a corner Janvian's sister Rozel, wearing a gown so scarlet it threatened to pale her long red hair, joked with the musicians. Their Uncle Benoc sternly stood where he could survey the entire room. Janvian nodded formally to him, showing the respect he deserved as tarryn, the leader of her clan. He locked her in a steady gaze and slowly returned the greeting. His graveness told her he understood there was more to the festivities than the beginning of another year.

Other clankin, their armbands alive with the burly mountain rask rearing on its hind legs, were scattered throughout the gathering. During the announcement, they would not have their eyes on the rulers but on selected guests, those whose reactions would display their lor—or betray their lack of it. Like the Drueten tarryn, they knew only that a declaration of importance would be made. They didn't know its nature, but they could guess.

The monarchs strolled toward the double throne set on a raised platform at the far end of the room. Rojelon continued to scan the faces, some already blurry-eyed with drink. He had always sought out his sister's presence in the crowd. Perhaps he searched for her still out of habit and loss.

If Janvian had been raised to worship the old gods, she might have been inclined to think that Lelian's death and the new child's life were linked by some deity's plan. She was not always sure of her beliefs, but one thing she had learned young: Whatever power had created this harsh planet, it had long ago turned its back on the mistake. It was nowhere close by to hear prayers or to answer them.

Skaln stood to their left, wearing a robe of subdued yellow that fell elegantly to the tops of his soft boots. Rojelon stopped and clasped wrists with his cousin. "Fortune to you in the new year."

Janvian stiffened. Physically the two were alike. Pronounced cheekbones and a strong jaw gave Rojelon a bold appearance, while on the Felcon tarryn those features seemed harsh.

Skaln gave a smooth smile. "Fortune and a long reign to you." As the leader of Rojelon's clan, he was responsible for fortress security and for the safety of the ruling family. With Lelian dead, he was also a potential heir. When the announcement was made, Janvian's eyes would be on him.

The monarchs continued to the dais and stood before the assembly. A mystic presented the ceremonial goblets, crafted with the insignias of the five clans. The dark robed figure was skilled at detecting poisons. Its function was to assure that food and drink were free of others' ambitions.

Janvian didn't know if the same hooded mystic presided over their safety each day or if different ones attended them. Their faces were always sheltered. With the strange multiple-voice effect in their speech, they were neither male nor female sounding.

Rojelon lifted his goblet. Arms encircled with the signs of every clan raised mugs in a single movement.

Janvian held her cup high, hand quivering at the power that suddenly charged the air. This was the Lorcha that could be. United. Loyal to the land and to one another. She and Rojelon would make it happen. They would bring the clans together. Not as Druetens or Felcons, not as Joachs or Walbasks or Tskants, but as one people.

"Welcome, Lorchans." Rojelon's rich voice reached to the high ceiling.

Lorchans. Rojelon felt it too.

"Good fortune to you in the year 401 of the Age of Order, the beginning of the new century," he said. "As the two moons meet, it's customary to drink in honor of Relacav, the greatest leader we have ever known. But first, tonight I have an announcement, one important to our present well-being and future prosperity. Janvian and I share with you our great joy—"

A whistle cut the air. A chalice clattered against the floor. Spilled wine sparkled with candle flame. Rojelon staggered. He clutched the jagged metal protruding from his chest.

Janvian slid a wrist blade from beneath her sleeve. Her eyes followed the path the weapon had traveled to the Walbask tarryn, arm still retreating from the throw. The assassin's chin was tilted high. Janvian flung the thin knife, piecing the exposed flesh of the neck above the collar of her gown. The woman's eyes showed no fear or surprise, only recognition of her own death. The puncture in her throat bubbled red and she crumpled to the floor.

Benoc and Skaln shouted orders. Felcon and Drueten clankin surrounded the platform, blades suddenly appearing from hidden sheaths.

Janvian grabbed Rojelon as he fell, collapsing under his weight. The spikewheel stuck grotesquely from his leather vest. The image of the phianj had suffered most of the blow. There was blood, but surely it could not be a killing cut. It would heal badly, as all wounds from a tearing weapon did, but he had suffered worse. This would be one more scar to add to the others.

Rojelon's dark eyes showed no fire. She had seen enough

cold death to recognize its chill. She reached to wrench the blade from his body. A faint flowery odor warned her and she drew back her hand.

"Poison, My Liege." The mystic stood calmly at her side. Its whispers seemed pulled from a dream. "The edges are coated with polumia, the sweetness that kills. The Baerryns must contemplate why we did not detect its presence in the room."

A hand pressed her shoulder. "You know your duty," Benoc said. Yes, duty before personal need. The lessons instilled deep in her from childhood were hard but necessary. She would have to grieve later.

She rose with her uncle's help. Crimson streaked her pale robe. She signaled the mystic to wrap the assembly in a blanket of stillness. Shouts and confusion tapered to tense silence. In the distance the storm crashed mercilessly against the dead sand bordering fertile land.

She and Rojelon had shared the leadership. Suddenly the throne was her responsibility alone. Many would be quick to place their petitions of lineage before the Baerryns in hope of being proclaimed ruler instead of her. She must make it clear her position was secured by the strongest rope. And she must do so now before potential challengers started gathering support.

"I claim the monarchy three-fold," Janvian said. She wanted to sound steady and controlled, but there was anger in her tone. "I claim the throne as spouse of Rojelon, murdered monarch of Lorcha.

"I claim the throne in my own right as great-grandchild of Nevran, past monarch of Lorcha.

"I claim the throne as bearer of the blood heir, the future monarch of Lorcha." Waves of startled gasps, cheers, and dark murmurs washed the room. The mystics could not hush the tide.

Janvian turned to the impassive hooded figure near her. "I ask audience with the Baerryns to make formal petition." It showed no sign of having heard her request, but she knew it mentally communicating with the others. After a moment the covered head nodded. "It is granted. You will be summoned."

She again faced the crowd, but her stare purposefully locked with Skaln's across Rojelon's fallen body. "Those who think they have a right to challenge my claim should give grave consideration to the consequences."

Skaln returned her gaze without a flinch.

CHAPTER

TWO

"It's true then about the babe," Benoc said, confirmation rather than doubt in his grizzled tone.

Janvian sat stiffly. She nodded, fingering the drying blood that marred her skirt. They had withdrawn to a smaller, more easily secured room used for conducting daily business. A single candelabra cast uneven light over the heavy table and simple chairs. The mystic was exiled to the hallway to stand with the Drueten guards.

Benoc had led his niece here and had ordered the preparation of Rojelon's body for viewing before cremation. "I find no gain for the Walbask in this," he said. "They have a land dispute with the Joachs, but killing the person who was to judge the case doesn't get a favorable decision. The originator of the treachery, that's the one we want."

He returned his dagger, drawn and ready since the attack, to the secret sheath camouflaged by a fold in his robe. Carrying a weapon at a formal gathering was a serious breach of courtesy—officially. But the churning political stream made it inadvisable to mix with other clans unprotected. Slight bulges in vests, sleeves and boots were noted but not challenged. A practical philosophy was best: You can have yours as long as I can have mine. Who could predict when the rippled surface would erupt into white water as it had tonight?

Benoc thought through the puzzle, sorting known enemies and possible enemies into motives and plots. He scratched at his beard for inspiration. Once black it was now pierced with white. His thick mane, worn loose and past his shoulders according to clan custom, showed the same snowy mix. The growing silver was a badge of experience, as intimidating as his agile, muscular body.

When Lelian died, he had found it difficult to suspect Skaln of arranging the tragedy, as others immediately had. Trust within a clan was sacred and necessary. To breach it was like splintering the wood and still expecting the tree to stand. A tarryn against his own blood! It was too contrary to his beliefs to accept, so he had looked in other directions for the cause of the woman's death. That had been a mistake. Now, after this bold murder, he must seriously consider it, even though it shook him to the core.

"Rojelon asked me to set watchers tonight," Benoc said.

"You do that anyway," Janvian said, "asked or not."

"This is the *only* time he's asked," Benoc said. "He was giving me permission to act, if needed. Against Skaln?"

"Rojelon has never spoken against his cousin to me, but he's been more cautious around him of late. I don't know if he was reacting to my distrust of the man or his own."

"Skaln will have his own petition to place before the Baerryns," Benoc said. "The next one to wear the golden armband could guarantee the Walbask a generous slice of fertile Joach land. But is that a great enough reward for the tarryn to sacrifice her life?"

He slammed a fist into the polished table. The branched

candlestick shook, sending out waxy smoke. "An alliance between Felcon and Walbask," he muttered, "that won't hold. They're at the extreme north and south of the country. The Joach would join with us, and that would split Felcon land from Walbask no matter who the Tskant aligned with."

"Skaln is too smart to base a plot on a risky treaty." Janvian freed herself from the confining chair and paced, as if orderly steps could force orderly thoughts. "He's had several opportunities to speak privately to the envoy from the *skyship*. Perhaps his real alliance is with the United Trade Worlds. If he can promise the Walbask strength from the sky, geography becomes less important."

Benoc shivered, not just because the thought repulsed him but because he saw how easily it could be true. If the monarch's cousin could betray his own blood, he could betray the country as well. "His ambitions have always stretched beyond his talent. Still, it's nothing but tattle until we have some facts."

Gathering information would take time. Assuring succession for his clankin—for the child—was a more immediate matter. Clankin—that included the child. "Janvian, an unborn babe is a fragile heir. You must continue to press your own claim."

She would, as strongly as possible; but despite her confident declaration to the gathered clans, she understood her position. "My lineage alone is no better than Skaln's. Or Rozel's, although I'm sure she has no desire to do anything as boring as rule a country."

All three were great-grandchildren of Nevran, a bloodline Benoc didn't share. The great Felcon leader and his descendants had ruled Lorcha for over a century, and the clan had prospered in proportion to its power. His third child, with little prospect of inheriting the monarchy, had married a

Drueten with rights to a large section of land. The couple had then defied common wisdom and aligned with the wife's noble but less prestigious family. If they had chosen differently, their descendants, including Janvian and Rozel, might have been Felcon.

The unusual decision had prepared the way for a future alliance between the two clans. It materialized only two generations later with the union of Janvian and Rojelon. Sometimes in the complexity of the weave, Benoc thought he detected sly Nevran's influence. "Your marriage," he said.

"Is a very slim advantage," Janvian said. Only Rojelon's child held an indisputable claim.

Four patterned raps on the door disturbed them. Despite the correctness of the code and the safety it implied, Benoc's hand went swiftly to his hidden dagger.

"It's Rozel." The words were muffled by the thickness of the barrier but the brash tone indisputably belonged to Janvian's younger sister. Benoc unbolted the door and swung it open only wide enough to accommodate the woman and the tray of steaming mugs she carried.

He slammed the door and slipped the latch. "This is no time to give your sister warmed wine. She needs her wits if she's to get through this night."

"And don't I know that." Rozel pushed aside a pile of official looking documents with an elbow and set the tray on the table. "It's dillab with spices the way herders brew it, designed to keep the brain alert, not addle it the way wine does." She thrust a mug at him. "It'll do you some good too."

Rozel led Janvian to a chair and put a mug in her hand. "Sit and drink. I fixed it myself. And I insisted that *two* mystics check it, since they're not as perfect as they want us to believe."

Benoc sipped. The earthy herbal tastes held a bitter tang, which affected him much like the presence of his younger niece. She had only been in the room a few heartbeats and already he felt he had lost control. He often found it harder to manage Rozel than to order about an entire clan. She and Janvian were deceptively similar in appearance. Both had slight frames with strong movements developed through training with various weapons. Their piercing blue eyes were identical. The red in Rozel's hair was more intense, which provided an immediate clue to her personality. With the great effort given to Janvian's education, little energy had been left to channel Rozel's exuberance into acceptable lines. The younger sister seemed destined to test every rule and everyone around her.

"This isn't the time to anger mystics," Benoc said. "We need to be well in their thoughts when they consider Janvian's petition."

Rozel gave her head a quick tilt, her way of dismissing the insignificant worries of others. "They sulked at such a disrespectful order. At least I think they sulked, who knows what grimaces they're making under those hoods. But they did it. They weren't in a position to say no. And I told them to gather the Baerryns at once because Janvian wanted an audience before dawn."

Benoc slapped his mug on the table, sloshing liquid over the rim. "Your impudence compounds our troubles."

Rozel gave that tilt again, which angered him more. "I'll get away with it as long as they let me."

If she were his daughter! Had things been different, they might have been his children and not his brother's. He often saw their mother's likeness and intelligence in them. She glowed in Janvian's depth and sparkled in Rozel's defiance.

Old regrets must not be allowed to interfere with present duties, he told himself. This was not the time to stand alone. He needed promises of support from the other tarryns. Rozel could stay with Janvian. The young woman was impulsive, but dependable in defense of her sister. He was sure she carried an assortment of weapons. Having trained her himself, he knew her habits.

"I'm going to find Skaln," Benoc said. "The child is as much a Drueten as a Felcon. That forces him to include me in fortress security. Maybe I can get a public pledge of lor out of him, even if he doesn't mean it." As he slipped out, he gave his younger niece a serious look, which she ignored.

Rozel secured the door. "Skaln." She tossed out the name as if it were an old curse.

"Can the answer be that easy?" Janvian reviewed the maze of information—again. Again she found Rojelon's tarryn at the center. But the simplicity of the path that led there unsettled her.

"Why should it be more complex?" Rozel asked. "He wants to rule, so he plows a way to the throne." She pulled back a sleeve to reveal twin blades stuffed into a sheath made for one. She slid out the extra knife. "I brought you this. You can use it until you get yours back from the corpse of that sand-born assassin."

Janvian tucked it away. Since she wasn't allowed grief, she nurtured her anger. It coiled through her like a creature whose only thought was revenge. She would strike out now if she knew where to direct the blow. The feeling was more dangerous than an enemy. It lived only in the present without a thought for the future. Benoc would tell her to be patient. He would advise her to think of tomorrow and the tomorrows after that. And so she would. She would keep her beast on a short chain, and she would make her own plan.

Rozel pulled a chair close so she could sit facing her sister. She leaned, elbows on knees, and stared into the distracted eyes. "Janvian, I have confidence in Benoc, never doubt that.

But there are many ways to be killed. Whoever is behind the assassination, whether Skaln or another, needs you dead. We must go home to Drueten land." She suddenly smiled, as if planning a carefree outing. "We'll cross the mountains to the ocean. I can catch fish, and you can weave seaweed into baskets and"—she gave a shrug—"maybe a hut? And we can sleep on the beach."

"And what of Lorcha?"

"Hear this, sister," Rozel said, suddenly serious again. "The country means spit to me. I care about you. You'll be lost if you don't leave this place. Lorcha will have to survive on its own."

Rozel spoke treason, but in a way she made sense. Was anything more important than her child's life? Tonight Janvian had paid enough lor for a lifetime. She could withdraw her claim to the monarchy, say the baby was an impulsive lie created at a desperate time. She could sequester herself in the highlands and have the child there. She could live, selfish and secluded, without thinking of her duty to clan and country.

But danger lurked in denying the baby's existence and going into hiding. Friends and enemies alike would always wonder, and they would seek her out. When they found her, as they eventually would, they would watch the legal blood heir grow, plotting how the child could be used by them while afraid of how it could be used by others against them. Eventually fear would win. A child who was not supposed to exist was an easy target.

She asked herself her own question. And what of Lorcha?

If she disappeared, the present skirmishes would become out and out war as the clans pressed their tenuous claims to the monarchy. Violence would travel across the breadth and depth of the world like a fire. Only the Wilde, with its natural defense, would remain untouched. As it had in the past, the country might spiral into a state of wectulk, chaos so widespread that even the Baerryns could not contain it.

Janvian couldn't let that happen. She must stay to rule and trust that her clan would keep her safe.

Four soft raps thudded against the door. "My Liege," came a male voice, "it's clankin Filara with a message from Tarryn Benoc."

Janvian was reluctant to let anyone in for any reason. "Give it to the guard. I'm busy with important matters."

"Forgive me, My Monarch," the muffled voice said, "but I was also sent to relieve the guard. She's already gone. I could recite it for you, but it seems improper to shout Drueten business at Your Royal Self through a closed door."

Janvian and Rozel exchanged wary looks. They didn't need to be of one mind like the mystics to have the same thoughts. Rozel held up two fingers. Two guards should be in attendance at all times. The person spoke as if he alone stood on the other side of the wood.

A dagger appeared in Rozel's hand. She slid the bolt free from its socket then positioned herself against the wall beyond the reach of the door, so she could not be trapped behind it.

Janvian slipped the wrist blade Rozel had brought her partially out of its sheath, making it more accessible but still hidden. She stood beside the table, seemingly unprepared to defend herself. "Enter."

The young man, barely more than a boy, stepped in, focused only on the monarch. It was indeed Filara, one of Benoc's trainees. Clankin. Family. There was nothing to fear.

He dropped to one knee, head bent, tawny hair spilling across his shoulders. Such formality was seldom used between blood in private.

"Rise and give your message," Janvian said.

Filara put his weight on his forward leg to stand. It brought him close to Janvian. He raised his head. She recognized the resolve in his eyes before she saw the knife in his hand.

With a swift sweep of her blade she deflected his thrust. Filara had the advantage of height and zeal. Janvian was more experienced and possessed a deeper understanding of what she fought for.

Rozel moved quickly behind the traitor and shoved her knife between his ribs. The glow in his eyes changed from conviction to surprise. He went limp and thudded to the floor.

Rozel kicked away the fallen weapon. "Didn't anyone teach you to survey the entire room when you enter?" She bent to the body. "He's still alive." She searched the young man's clothing, tossing aside the weapons she found with a clatter. "Janvi" she said, using her sister's childhood nickname, "the fortress is filled with enemies. You must come home with me where I can protect you."

A moment ago Janvian had believed her only safety was within her clan. Now the blood of a Drueten assassin pooled at her feet. This scheme had something hidden about it, a shading she couldn't quite see. It seemed nowhere was safe.

"It's either the highlands or across the Wilde to mad Nevran's Mirage Clan," Rozel grimly joked.

Janvian nodded, "I've come to that conclusion too."

Rozel straightened and smacked Filara with the toe of her boot. "I'd carve out the traitor's heart except we need him to explain why he raised a blade against his own blood."

"Your control shows you've gained a small portion of wisdom with your years," Janvian said. In the midst of grim business, it felt good to fall into her usual banter with Rozel. They viewed life differently and were often at odds, but they were bound by a bond that could never be severed. "A short time ago you would have killed him quickly without a thought to his usefulness."

Rozel looked at her with relief, as if Janvian had just returned from somewhere far away. "It comes from spending too much time with my diplomat sister."

The passageway echoed with pounding feet. Benoc rushed in, sword in hand, followed by a hoard of kin, not all of them soldiers.

Janvian explained what had happened although she felt her words were unnecessary. The tarryn's practiced gaze showed him all he needed to know.

Benoc ordered Filara removed and his wound tended. He wanted the betrayer healthy enough for questioning. "There's a dead guard and a dead mystic outside. I've never known anything like this. Baerryns who can't detect poison or danger even to themselves. Blood against blood."

"You must have assigned new guards when you left. Was Filara one of them?" Rozel asked.

Benoc's face burned crimson. "With him not yet through his training and his mother a Walbask?"

"You're still a long way from being a diplomat," Janvian told her sister.

Rozel sighed and gave a slight bow. "My apologies, Uncle. I meant no challenge to your judgment."

Benoc hid his discomfort in brusqueness. "The other guard was Kaul. Filara told him I wanted him at the stable to assess the number of riding animals available should we need them. Kaul thought it an unusual assignment. He came to me to verify it. I hurried here with whatever kin I could find." His wrath was mostly aimed at himself. Filara had been under his command, so the treachery reflected back on him.

"Kaul did well," Rozel said. "I hope you tell him so."

Benoc dismissed the praise for his son. "He did his duty, same as you. Seems with traitors among our own, that isn't enough. Janvian, there's doubt about the pregnancy. Rumors buzz the fortress like flies around rotting fruit."

"Rozel," Janvian said, "Please take a message for me to the Baerryns."

"They're waiting," Rozel said. The delight at her previous affront to the mystics rang in her tone.

"Tell them I humbly beg their indulgence a while longer and that, with their permission, I'll present myself this very hour."

"As you wish, Your Royal Self," Rozel said, mimicking Filara. She gave the hand to shoulder salute and flashed a smile. "I'll fill in all necessary homage, so they won't think you're a rash mountain clod."

When Rozel was gone, Benoc moved close to Janvian and spoke softly in her ear. "The Baerryns are not the only audience you must attend tonight. And the other will be more dangerous."

CHAPTER

THREE

"You asked audience." The Speaker's words resonated as if many voices vibrated through the single set of vocal cords.

Nine robed and hooded Baerryns formed a semicircle of identical pillars decorating the expansive balcony that had been built to the mystics' specifications four hundred years ago at the beginning of the Age of Order. By that time, machines were forbidden, and the task had taken a decade. The platform jutted into open sky toward the Bewailed Wilde and had no railing to prevent a misjudged step from sending a careless soul plunging onto the rocks below.

Janvian stood at the focal point, aware of the edge behind her. The moons, having embraced to begin the new year, were now separate coins. Quick Noalgaz was lost behind tortured clouds. Bending toward the west, Pypeed cast single shadows. The air felt thick, as if concentrated. Each thunderous clash made her tremble inside, but she refused to show it. A somber gray cloak covered her blood-stained clothes. She had experienced the magnified multiple voice during other audiences. As always, the effect was eerie and unsettling. Until now she had never faced the Baerryns alone without Rojelon beside her.

The Speaker stood in the keystone of the mystic arch. "Before we hear your petition, we express our regret at the death of Rojelon. It is uncertain why we did not detect the presence of poison. Our current opinion is that the essence was blocked by one not of us. Although the existence of a solitaire is rare, it is not unknown."

The storm crackled at Janvian's back. A shiver ran through her spine. A solitaire, a rogue. She only heard of such a thing in tales children told to scare one another. They were often of parents hiding youngsters with mental powers in the hope of using them to gain land and wealth. The results were always disastrous.

Could one really exist? Without the mind sharing, could such a creature live without growing insane? So little was known about the mystics. Most of it was probably wrong. Examination for any reason was prohibited. The body of the one slain by Filara had been whisked away before anyone's curiosity overcame the threat of punishment.

A lightning strike spread red and gold across the worn granite and blushed the passive figures. The pillars faced the tempest without flinching, as if drinking in its energy. The Speaker barely moved, even to breathe. "We knew this information would be of value to you."

It was the closest to an apology Janvian would get from these beings who hid in folds of rough cloth, and who were so removed from humanity by the demands of their special abilities that they claimed blood ties to no clan.

The Speaker did not expect thanks for the explanation. Janvian offered none. Some courtesies had no meaning to mystics, while others were of great importance.

"You may now make petition," the Speaker said.

"Most honorable Baerryns," Janvian said, "in your wisdom you remain apart. You use your powers to intervene in the affairs of the five families only when necessary to protect the monarchy and to maintain the stability of the country."

She raised her voice, shouting above the staccato of cracked air and splintering rock behind her. "Due to the death of my husband, succession is in question and the country may soon find itself in a turbulence more terrifying than the one that tears at the Wilde this very night. Within me I carry the child I share with Rojelon. I petition that you confirm the baby's existence and identity, and that you declare it to be the blood heir." The linked minds conferred silently. Did beings truly reside in those robes or were they shells for bodiless spirits?

The Speaker's response was a whispered choral chant. "We will examine the child."

A magnificent calmness enfolded Janvian. A presence seeped into her. How peaceful to be joined with others. She felt released from the weight of personal grief, free from the burden of individual decision.

A pool formed before her. Petals emerged from its center, translucent, as if carved from soft ice. The dripping blossom pulsed with radiance. A velvety twin hung below it, beckoning like a dark entrance. Janvian dove into the still water. She stretched a hand toward the shelter, aching to reach the soft, comforting embrace.

A delicate restraint halted her. She suddenly wept. The water rippled where her tears joined the liquid. The flower sank into the cavern, and the shining fluid dissipated. She was again standing on the balcony. Sorrow and the future pressed upon her. She yearned for the presence to return. She wondered if the baby had felt it too. Gently, a false peace replaced the longing.

"The child does not know worldly pain, and therefore felt only a small and pleasant change," the Speaker said in answer to Janvian's unspoken question. "It cares little that we have come and gone."

Janvian feared she had behaved badly under the probing. In seeking greater contact with the mystics, she might have committed an impropriety. "Forgive me if I—"

"There is a trace of perception in you," the Speaker said, "far below our level, a snowflake to an avalanche, but enough for you to pursue a joining when the opportunity was close. As for your petition, we declare the child to be blood heir, first in line for the monarchy. We will publicly proclaim so."

A short time ago Janvian would have welcomed the assurance as a victory, but the night's bloody events had shown her that more active measures were necessary.

"I have another petition, honorable Speaker," Janvian said, "if you'll be so patient as to hear it."

"We will indulge this excess."

The Speaker meant to humble her, but she did not hesitate. "There are some who will not want this child to be born. They'll kill us for their own gain if they can. Pregnancy and birth are times of great vulnerability. I fear that even with your help I can't keep myself and the child safe within the fortress or even within my clan's boundaries." She did not remind them that Rojelon had been murdered despite their presence, that one of their own had died by a traitor's blade next to a fallen Drueten, or that an undetected solitaire might be in their midst. These were already known. Considering the mystics' failures, the Speaker was the one who should be contrite, not her.

"My intent," Janvian said, "is to leave for a place where the enemies of our country will not find me."

"We saw this place in your mind." The Speaker's voice carried a slight timbre of awe. "It has its own dangers. We had thought—" The Speaker hesitated, as if a disruption occurred in the joined minds. "There are those of us who had hoped to offer one of our abbeys as a refuge." The blended voice sounded less varied now, as if some of the chanters were silent.

Janvian suppress her surprise. She had never heard a hint of division within the Baerryns before. She had assumed that divergent opinions were impossible. And, as far as Janvian knew, no one outside of their community had ever been allowed to live within the cloisters. The compounds were hidden, their locations unknown even to the clans whose lands they occupied.

"Unfortunately," the Speaker said, "you've proven too sensitive to be among us. The peril would be greater in our midst than on your chosen journey."

Janvian thought she heard a twinge of individual regret, despite the choral voice. "I must know that the country is secure. Therefore, I petition the Baerryns to hold Lorcha in regency for the unborn blood heir until the child is presented for recognition."

Thunder filled the long silence. What Janvian asked had only been done once before. She wondered if they were startled or if they had seen this as well during their examination. She waited. The Speaker had given her an insight. Now she understood that it was not one mind of many parts but many separate minds working to reach a decision.

After what felt like a very long time the Speaker said, "Lorcha is held in regency." The sexless voice was now restored to fullness and its former detachment. "It shall remain so until the blood heir is presented to us."

A cool breeze of relief swirled around Janvian. It was not a perfect solution. Disputes would still flair among the clans, but no family would be able to gain an advantage. She felt free to abandon state concerns and concentrate on survival. The monarchy would be waiting when she and her child returned.

The Speaker continued, "Or until one year has passed."

A year! Janvian's shock flashed red and gold with the storm. So little time!

"Since, as you wisely recognize, pregnancy and birth are fragile events," the Speaker said, "and since the journey you've selected is dangerous, we cannot assume that the blood heir will survive. During the regency, we will accept petitions for succession. Sanctioned petitioners will present themselves at the selection ceremony commencing at sunset on the last day of this year. The monarch will be chosen from among those in attendance. No other candidates will be considered. The new monarch's reign will begin when the moons meet, signaling the year Age of Order 402."

"Speaker!" Janvian shouted in protest.

Unnatural multiple chords bellowed, silencing her. "It is for the good of Lorcha."

In unison the creatures turned their backs to Janvian. The rustle of heavy robes dragging across slate filled the silence between fits of thunder. Single file, the mystics flowed through an arch into an unlit passage. Moonlight failed to penetrate the black gap. The faceless figures passed through it and were gone.

Janvian sunk heavily to the floor. She had hoped to disarm her enemies. But even as she snatched a sword from their hands, the Baerryns handed them another. Skaln, and whoever else had designs on the throne, no longer had to kill her but only prevent her from returning before the year expired.

She had to concede that it was a necessary limitation

from the mystics' perspective. The route she chose was uncertain, perhaps even foolhardy. She might die before giving birth. The child might be stillborn or become ill. The Baerryns could not wait forever for a child that might not arrive.

Had she made a mistake? Her child had been granted the monarchy, and she had thrust it away.

No. She could not let the promise of a shiny jewel blind her to caution. The Baerryns had given her what she'd asked for. She would make good use of it.

<><><>

Long after Pypeed had followed its sibling west into the storm, the Speaker crossed the balcony with slow gliding steps. He leaned into the fury as if it might support the weight of his thoughts.

When the Sage returned from the separation of olax, the self-imposed withdrawal from the Unity to reflect inward, he would be reprimanded for his behavior tonight. The Prism, which advised the Sage, had already prepared recommendations for his censure. Offering the woman retreat in one of the abbeys had been his own idea. Such lone action was not allowed, even for the Speaker.

And he had done worse.

The Sage would be pleased that Janvian had asked the Baerryns, as clanners called the Unity, to rule in her absence; but he would be furious that a time limit had been imposed.

The Speaker pulled back his hood, exposing a short white mane. He no longer recalled his birth name, but he remembered that when he was young, his hair had burned with the same color as Janvian's. Stray wisps curled about the gem affixed to his forehead. Freed from the shield worn in the presence of those not of the Unity, the luminous stone glowed as it drank energy from the air.

In his mind he cleared a space for private thoughts. His impulsive, personal act could have destroyed the carefully crafted plan for the country's future. Designed and set in motion by the highest tier, the Sage himself, he had no authority to question it, let alone, to act against it.

As the only mystic below the level of the Prism entrusted with the knowledge, he had been directed to use his position to advance the program. At first he had been honored, and a bit proud at the implied promise of advancement that went along with being in the confidence of the leadership. Then he'd noticed a pattern of deaths. He'd examined old records and found accidents and sudden illnesses that went back for centuries. Did they conveniently fit the Sage's design? The Speaker had never doubted the Unity's actions or motives, not for one breath since he'd been welcomed into it, until that moment when he'd looked at the tangled maze of history and had suddenly viewed the path that had been created.

He had tried to put aside his concerns. Perhaps this manipulation was necessary and he was simply too young to understand. Perhaps the ultimate goal justified the methods. Perhaps. The clans were inferior, but that didn't give the Baerryns the right to breed and herd them as if they were animals.

Tonight the Speaker realized he could no longer ignore what was and what might come. He licked his lips and tasted the power around him. In the part of his mind still linked to the community it was difficult to keep his emotions subdued so they would not disturb the others.

"Speaker." The timid vibration irritated. He identified a novice who had stood with him during the session with the widowed monarch. The eight who had flanked him had been mere figurines, representing members of the Prism, who never physically attended audiences. Similarly, although he had spoken for the Unity, another held that role above him in the revered nine.

Unseasoned, the novice was barely a hundred years old. "She will truly go," she thought. "We sense it. Against all her terror."

The Speaker could have blocked the contact, but that was not the way. He had an obligation to teach. He stepped out of the privacy. "Yes," he replied.

The Speaker sensed that the novice had detected his mental separation and did not understand it. She probably knew that private thoughts were permitted at advanced levels but had not encountered the phenomenon before. The confusion broke her concentration and sent tiny ripples through the mental network. He muted the disruption she caused and gave a caution. At her level of development, a reprimand would be too harsh.

In his own early days, he could not imagine why anyone would want to keep a part of the mind hidden. The Unity was accepting of even the deepest, most hideous thoughts. It brought them to the surface where they could be purged. He had believed that a mystic who attained the high station of Speaker would no longer need to conceal any reflections. He was wrong.

Empathy for the novice was easy. The Speaker still did not comprehend olax. The idea of being completely severed from the community disturbed him despite his accomplished emotional control.

"Could we sway her to a different course?" the novice asked.

"Could we?" the Speaker repeated. "Are you concerned

only with our ability? What of the morality of altering another's decision?"

"Why consider the morality of an action if it is something we cannot do? When we know we can do it, that is the time to discuss the right or wrong of it."

The Speaker was too weary to debate theory. Reality was his immediate concern. "You monitored the audience. Did you detect any attempt to influence the woman's will—by anyone, mystic or clan?"

The novice had not.

"The decision to take the dangerous path is her own." The Speaker remembered the woman's fear. How could a lone person without the support of a structure like the Unity overcome such cold fright? "By your own argument then, we will postpone this discussion until such an event is proven possible."

"How will we recognize it?"

"A question to ponder."

The novice withdrew. An echo of their exchange remained with the Speaker.

The ability to do the action is tested first. The morality is considered later—if at all.

Doubt sat within him like a beast growling with hunger. He wondered what the Sage was doing during olax, as separated from the Unity as a solitaire.

~

FOUR

The staircase spiraled into the labyrinth, a black shaft pierced by cones of light from sooty oil pots in scattered niches. Somewhere a thin trickle of water splashed into a shallow pool. Janvian descended. Her short leather boots slid on the smooth steps, making progress slow. She pulled the gray cloak tightly around her pale green gown against the sour odor of mold. There had been no time to shed the fine fabric, made richer with Rojelon's blood, and change into more suitable clothes. It was her banner now, her mainstay while the Baerryns served her victory and defeat on the same platter.

The stairs branched and branched again, always plunging deeper below the fortress. Each barred chamber she passed was another secret on a planet that sprouted them like twisted thorns.

As a child, secrets had been exciting and exotic. Together she and Nevran had prowled these gritty passageways, visiting once sealed rooms where even the air was old. They had examined relics from the Lost Years when Relacav fought and won his campaign against wectulk.

And better.

Janvian's great-grandfather had shown her remnants of machines from before the time of legends. She had held smashed pieces, brought to the fortress and hidden in its depths along with drawings of how they fit together in complex ways. Nevran had taught her to see the flat drawings as he saw them, real and fully formed. There were marvelous devices that flew like winged animals and that crawled like insects. There were mechanisms whose movements she could envision but whose uses she could not guess. All banned now. All forbidden. All hidden.

To Janvian, the relics and the stories had been equal treasures. Crouched with the old man between carved posts supporting a slab of polished stone, she had listened carefully to her earliest and best lessons in politics and history. Above, the table had been laden with weighty petitions and decrees of state. In the private world below she had learned that government was defined by people, not paper.

Her favorite tales were of his flight across the Wilde and the strange clan he found living on the lightning plain. Banished by his mother, the Monarch Corella, on the false charge of plotting against her, he had undertaken the dangerous journey in a desperate attempt to stay free and alive.

Still tall and broad-shouldered in his advanced years, he had huddled close to her tiny figure in the cramped space. Again and again at her urging, he had described his faith in old records he had found beneath the fortress. They had guided him in his dash across the desert. There, in a half-buried moon nestled in the sand, the Mirage Clan had given him a special kind of shelter. They called it *sanctuary*.

The blue fire of youth had burned through irises clouded with age as he spoke. "They have many faces but are one clan. Their tarryn doesn't govern by right of blood but by right of skill. Any child with leadership talent might be trained as heir."

For decades Nevran had remained silent about his absence to everyone except her. Advanced years either made him forget that it should be secret or made him stop caring. By the time he died he was called Mad Nevran for his unbelievable ramblings.

Janvian wearily put a hand against the damp wall to steady herself. Secrets. She was a grown woman now and understood how heavy they could become. The stairs ended in a sharp turn. She followed a narrow hall to the archway of a chamber where many passageways converged. Voices echoed from within, distorted by architecture. Faces turned as she entered. Her presence smothered conversation.

Benoc and Kaul were waiting for her. Neither liked her arriving without them as escort. She saw it in the tight-jawed expressions they wore.

Assembled were the tarryns and their seconds. The last time she saw them, they had been draped in decorative clothing. Now they wore simple dress—plain, loose shirts; warm tunics; and long pants tucked into tall, hard-soled boots. Variations showed individual clan styles.

Gozax and her daughter Ellud sat at the stone-slab table. A ribbon of deep purple bordered the Tskant lightning bolts on their sleeves. Across from them Melaph of the Joachs and her son Ianz displayed the sign of mourning above a bundle of grain entwined with a river snake.

Janvian was touched by the respect it showed. The gesture made words of sympathy unnecessary. She had not added the purple to her own band yet. The cloth was in a cabinet in her room, where she had placed it when mourning for Lelian had been set aside.

Paulian, the new Walbask tarryn slouched at the fringe in disgrace, pale hand unconsciously kneading his insignia. Only a few hours before his predecessor had killed Rojelon and met her own death at Janvian's knife. There had been no time for him to declare a second.

Skaln impatiently paced, the only Felcon in the room. As usual his second was managing clan affairs at home.

An anonymous mystic stood against a wall. Useful to prevent violence when discussions became intense, its main purpose was to represent the Baerryns. Although not considered a clan, in this room below the fortress it held equal status with the five families.

"Forgive my being late," Janvian said. "I had an audience with the Baerryns." The mystic could have told them that, but she was sure it hadn't. Janvian watched the leaders' faces as the statement penetrated.

The room was free of the oily smoke that clogged the passages. Their features were illuminated by the glow from fist-sized lamprocks in stands fixed to the walls and scattered across the table. This was the only place where the lightning charged ore was used, and the only place where it was safe to speak of the planet's greatest secret.

"Then the child is officially confirmed as blood heir," Benoc said loudly.

"The child is confirmed." Janvian's gaze swept the room to gauge reactions. Melaph nodded slowly, as if she never doubted it. Gozax seemed relieved that the line of succession was clear. She saw no sly glances that might indicate a conspiracy.

Skaln addressed the mystic. "Is this so?"

If they had been in the hearth hall, Janvian would have challenged him for implying she had lied.

"It is a truth," came the soft, expressionless reply.

"Skaln." Benoc's gravel voice carried an edge. "You will be first to swear lor to the blood heir of course."

"That is for another time," Janvian said before the Felcon tarryn could reply. "The only lor sworn here is to the integrity of this forum." Relacav had established it to transcend allegiance to a clan or a monarch. The single goal was to guard knowledge of what the storm's power had done in the past and what it could still do. She would not let it become entangled in other webs.

There was a murmur of agreement. Those still standing joined the others at the square table. Four sides and four benches for five clans. "Not five sides, so they can separate themselves," Nevran had explained to Janvian when she was a child. "Not two benches so they can take sides against one another. Four, so they will be close when they talk."

Ellud made room for Janvian, who gladly accepted the spot. The girl was a younger, narrower version of her large, good-natured mother. Her yellow hair was swept into a knot at the nape of the neck and hung down her back. She put a hand on Janvian's where it rested on the bench unseen by the others and gave a gentle squeeze. For the death and for the new life, Janvian knew. For the grief and the joy.

All in attendance, including the mystic, sat elbow to elbow. There was no formality of position. Regardless of wealth and influence outside the chamber, each had a single and equal say within it.

Melaph asked to begin. Joach land bordered the Wilde south of Aerrion Fortress. "Five nights ago a strike at the edge cut a fresh cliff face on one of the pilings and exposed lamprock a good four arms high and two wide." There was a mumbling of awe at the size.

She brought out a tattered map and pointed with a hand rough from farm work. A thick braid of nut-brown hair looped her shoulder. "It'll burn for at least two passings of Pypeed, maybe more. Ianz and I smeared it with pitch, but an area that big is hard to keep masked. It faces the sand and can't be seen from any of our towns, luck of Lorcha. But you should know it's there, especially you, Paulian, since your journey home takes you through our land." The border dispute between the two clans would not be mentioned here.

"We'll follow the valley road to the east of the river," the new Walbask tarryn said. "There'll be little danger of my clankin noticing."

"I've something else," Melaph said. When she spoke so seriously, all listened. She was a grave-faced woman with somber brown eyes. "Children hunting bewak eggs saw the glow. They'd been warned not to climb the crags, but the young are more attracted by danger than put off by it." She rolled up the map, twisting it in her fists beyond the need. "I'm not one who fosters superstition, but I've let stories of dust daevas be spread without reprimand—as should be done when people tell such brainless tales. Your clans will no doubt be hearing some strange rantings from my people." Her downcast eyes showed she thought it shameful.

My people. Our land. Janvian frowned. Her hope for a unified country had died along with her husband. Even here where barriers of birth dissolved, outside divisions persisted in their minds.

Gozax chuckled and tossed her head. Light tangled in her silver hair and reflected the bright threads of the embroidered ribbon that captured it high on her head. She was a big, handsome woman with twinkling gray eyes. She startled Melaph with a friendly slap on the back. "The tales are harmless. Let them be told, if only because they're entertaining on a cold night."

"Distorted truth is dangerous," Melaph said. "One lie can lead to many—and to madness." She shot Janvian a firm look, gave her a short nod of apology and quickly looked away. She would say what she believed, yet regretted any pain it caused.

"Do you fear another mad monarch, Melaph?" Skaln asked.

"Someday our great-grandfather's stories will be proven," Janvian said, reminding him that Nevran was their shared ancestor.

Skaln twisted out a smile. "Even the *skyship* and its viewing machines couldn't find the lost clan."

"An ambassador told you this?" Kaul demanded and suffered the blow of his father's disapproving stare.

"We were discussing crops and grazing lands," Skaln said. "I was told much more land, twice what we know, is divided from us by the desert. Naturally I asked about the sand itself. I was assured there are no significant traces of life."

Janvian wondered if agriculture had really been the crux of the conversation. Was he telling the truth about there being no sign of the Mirage Clan? Janvian could only speculate about what the machines could do—and not do. A *skyship* orbiting Alchorel was very far away. Still, Skaln's words were like an itch in an open sore.

"Can we trust them?" Ianz asked.

"Or anyone who uses machines?" Benoc added. "Especially ones that spy on us from the sky."

Gozax leaned on the table, claiming considerable space. "And we can't even spy back. But speculation won't get us anything but headaches. And we've other business. Paulian, you had something to show."

The tarryn sighed and pulled folded papers from his tunic.

He had been an apprentice to his aunt for many years and had expected her to outlive him. Now he found himself catapulted by embarrassing circumstances into a role he never thought he'd have.

He wrestled with the documents, ripping a corner. "Never seen the like. We've only a spit of land up against the Wilde. An ironmaster watched tammat bats fly about between lightning strikes." He spread out the papers, patting the damaged spot as if he could mend it. A device was drawn from several angles. Rods spaced in a box were attached to a wide sail. Notations in the margin specified dimensions. "He built one and put it on the edge overnight. The next day he hooked it to a toy cart and"—he leaned over the drawings, voice barely above a whisper—"the cart moved by itself." He pulled back as if startled by his own revelation.

Gozax nodded. "Best to stop it now or it'll show up at every bazaar. Your ironmaster's clever and won't be satisfied just using it for toys. Soon he'd be making real machines."

"It's been melted down." Paulian poked the papers. "These are the only records."

"Except for what's in your ironmaster's head," Skaln said. "Can you be sure of his silence?"

Gozax spun to glare at Skaln, silver hair swinging. "He's tarryn now and will be obeyed by his clan, just as we all are."

The drawings were placed in a chest. The pages curled among similar papers confiscated from other inventors. Janvian never doubted the need to avoid repeating the destruction of the past, but she wondered how discouraging creativity might cripple their future.

Business concluded, the leaders drifted off through the many passages. Ianz lingered and put himself in Janvian's path. She gave Benoc a questioning look. He pretended not to notice her being trapped into private conversation by the apprentice tarryn, but he and Kaul stayed within sight.

"We've been friends since childhood," Ianz said.

Two years younger than Janvian, she remembered him as an amiable little boy she had played with a few times, but she only thought of him as Melaph's second. He had grown tall. In Joach style his curly brown hair was tamed into multiple braids. They framed his wide, weather-tanned features. His face was soft now, but she had seen it hard and determined when he and his mother had argued petitions for their clan.

She sensed an intensity that was almost a warning and felt the need to remind him of her position outside this chamber. "Pledging lor to the blood heir should take place in the hearth hall, not here."

"That isn't—. Janvi, you must marry me."

She stepped back in shock.

"The Joach are a small clan," he said, "but we're the best trained fighters in the entire country. I know it's a breach of protocol to wed so soon after a spouse's death, but it isn't uncommon with monarchs."

The commanding tone of his proposal enraged Janvian. She quickly moved forward and took back the ground she had surrendered. "Was that supposed to be charmingly persuasive?"

The earnest young man suddenly transformed into a practical and demanding leader. "You know how I've always felt about you. I could give you phrases dripping with sweetness, but we don't have time for romantic nonsense. Skaln is lor-bound to support Rojelon's child, but having him at your back is more a worry than a comfort. With two clans for support, Benoc and I can keep you safe—and away from Skaln."

Janvian flashed a fiery gaze at her uncle, who was

intentionally ignoring her. "You and Benoc worked this out together?"

"I asked permission to speak to you, nothing more. I realize I should have discussed it with him in more detail, since he is your tarryn."

"This is the only solution you see?" She was supposed to know how he felt about her? She had never given him a thought.

"It would grant me the right to be at your side. As I should be. You would have only had to wait another year. I could have married by then. How could you have wanted to be monarch so much that you chose Rojelon over me?"

Tears burned at her eyes but did not fall. Rojelon belonged at her side. This head-strong, conceited child could never match him.

Ianz put a firm hand on her arm. "Have you thought about after the baby is born? What will happen with a child ruling the country?"

She wrenched herself free. "The Baerryns will—"

"Mystics! They couldn't save your precious Rojelon. I've no confidence in anything but this kind of strength." He made a fist and put it close to her face. It brought a flash of her father's cruelty. Blind with rage, Janvian made her own fist. With all her strength she slammed it below his rib cage.

Benoc quickly moved behind Janvian and turned her away from the doubled over form. "Come along, Sweet Niece." He propelled her toward the arch. "We've other matters to attend to." The arrogant young man would be fine as soon as he could draw a full breath.

"You're lucky." He called back over his shoulder. "She's adept at far more damaging moves. I know. I trained her. She appreciates your offer. Truly, she does. She'll realize it once she's calmed down." Ianz was not a bad lad. With experience he'd be a good tarryn. Although he hadn't been threatening Janvian, he shouldn't have made such an aggressive move. Despite his claim of early friendship, he knew nothing of her childhood.

Benoc kept her in his arms as they climbed the stairs. "He had that punch coming, so don't you regret it."

The mystic stood serenely while the folded-up man struggled for air. It had watched the interaction and had anticipated this result. It was obligated to intervene before an event such as this one became violent. On rare occasions, however, punishment for failure to perform one's duty was worth enduring.

~

CHAPTER
FIVE

tars adorned the sky to the south and the north. The
Speaker faced the west, letting the storm's energy seep
into the oval on his forehead and ease his weariness.
He had been wrong to suspect the Sage of manipulating the
clans. The pattern he thought he'd discovered was no more
than the shadow of tree branches that resemble a beast. The
Baerryns protected Alchorel and guided the people they shared
it with for the welfare of all. They clarified, they suggested, and
they acted within their own rights and freedoms.

They did not interfere beyond the scope of written
agreements. They did not meddle in clan affairs. They did not
kill.

He meditated on the monarch's assassination and the
death of the mystic who had kept watch over the widow.
Poison and murderous intent had not been detected. The
orbiting *skyship* might have machines that could distort the
mental network, but that would have been felt by all.

This deadly interference was focused and controlled. The
entire community contemplated the possibility of a solitaire.

The Speaker had indiscreetly relayed that information to the widow, and it was now one of the complaints against him. Could a rogue develop such advanced ability outside of the Unity? Could it exist undetected?

He wanted to consult the Sage, who, unfortunately, was still enduring olax. He also wished to confess his previous suspicions and purge himself of shame.

"You are troubled."

The Speaker recognized the presence of the Prism. He was welcomed into the private space. The nine cradled him in their minds as a child in arms.

"All are here to help you return to a place of peace. Give form to your distress. We'll examine it with you. A boulder seen from all sides is often not as large as first imagined."

"The monarch's murder with mystics in attendance is troubling," the Speaker said.

"That is as it should be, but calm is still possible."

"I've studied the histories."

"This we know."

"If there is a rogue, it may have been active for many years."

"You are uncertain."

"The evidence is not clear."

"You have considered possibilities."

He hadn't wanted to reveal his ridiculous theory to anyone except the Sage. Under the Prism's gentle probing, it leapt into his mind. He flushed with embarrassment. "It was an exercise," he explained, "a conjecture I have discarded." But he hadn't. It still festered within him, and the Prism sensed its intensity. "Help me be rid of it," he pleaded.

A silence deep as deafness hovered in his thoughts while the Prism made a decision.

"The storm will calm you."

The power of it was before him, velvet and silver. Silver and crimson. Crimson and velvet. Unthinking, he rushed forward and suddenly teetered at the balcony's edge. A lightning flash showed rocky crags far below.

"The storm will give you peace," the Prism urged.

He staggered backward. A chill gripped his heart. Sharp beaks snatched at him from swirls of gaudy colors. Talons raked away bloody fragments of his flesh. He flailed his arms to beat at them but felt nothing.

A multiple whisper burned in his brain. "Seek the storm!"

He remembered huddling in his mother's cottage, tortured by voices he couldn't suppress, plagued by loneliness and the turmoil of his strangeness. Dizzy, he spun away from the assault of talons and beaks toward the comforting rumble of thunder. He stumbled, face smashing against worn stone. An arm and a leg hung into nothingness. A roaring wind of pain momentarily cleared his head.

He concentrated on the agony in his jaw and transformed it into a hot, white light that challenged the barrage of spinning colors. His gemstone vibrated against his skull with the force of the Prism. It urged him toward the comfort of oblivion. He need only let go. He lifted a dangling hand and grasped the jewel. He tore it from his forehead and flung it toward the storm. He felt it arc and fall. The terrifying images dissolved as it descended. He shuddered and cried out as it smashed against jagged rocks.

A breath away from the same end, he struggled to dig his fingers into pits and crevices in the cold stone. Blood and grit mingled on his tongue. His jaw throbbed and his body ached, but the pain was nothing.

His mind was empty of everything except his own thoughts. He was no longer of the Unity. He had no position, no home, no one. From this moment he was the most detested of all mystics, a rogue. His life seemed a small thing to be left with. He tucked his head into the crook of his arm and sobbed. For the first time in over three and a half centuries, he was completely alone.

<><><>

Janvian pawed through a trunk of clothes. Her private room suffered for the haste. "What made Ianz think I would marry him under any circumstances?"

Rozel wrapped food in bits of cloth and stored them in a pack. Crescent shadows sagged under her tired eyes. "You're the only one who didn't notice him acting like a courting lover since the day he turned thirteen. All the unwed men will propose marriage now if they get the chance."

"They'll have to find me first." Janvian discarded her bloody gown. She pulled on a loose shirt, pleated riding pants, and a belted tunic. She exchanged short boots for tall ones tied with leather strips above the knees.

"You're committed to a crazy course," Rozel said. I won't try to persuade you to change your mind. I can see it won't do any good. That's why I'm coming with you."

Until now Janvian hadn't noticed her sister was dressed for hard riding. "I have a different task for you. Something no one else can do." She opened a cabinet and pulled out a bundle. A Drueten crest embroidered in gold rested on folds of deep purple cloth.

Rozel groaned.

Janvian grinned. "I knew you'd hate it."

<><><>

The old man hunched over his flagon of tepid ale and listened.

He needed current information, and the Split Hoof tavern was the best place in Aerrion City to get it.

The establishment was full tonight. The new year's banquet at the fortress meant travelers from every part of Lorcha laden with coins and finery to impress the royal pair and one another were in the city. So as dung can be found behind a line of slow-moving clobben, thieves followed the procession of the wealthy and ended up here with their profits for their own celebration.

Insignias might be worn elsewhere, but there were no clan armbands in the room. Thieves belonged to their own tribe that had nothing to do with birth or blood, only profession. They worked independently or with allies of their own choosing. The old man envied no one and nothing, except the freedom of thieves.

The rough benches were crowded. They ran the length of a long, scarred table. He pretended to watch the antics of a trained eipy. The furry animal capered among tankards to a whistled tune. Its owner, agile and cautious-eyed as the spindly-limbed creature, begged coins between songs.

The old man's real attention hung on four patrons more interested in their own conversation than the entertainment. It must be fascinating talk indeed. The three scruffy ones carried most of the chatter and the gesturing that went with it. The fourth turned quiet about the time he took a slanted interest in the group. Sitting at an angle across the table from him, the silent man passively drank ale from a tall clay mug and watched his companions, his expression as unreadable as a mystic's.

The table played out, the whistler hoisted the critter onto his shoulder and moved on to what he hoped would be more profitable territory, shifting melodies without a pause.

"And what if he be dead." The large, ruddy-cheeked man

sat on the far side of the quiet one. "One ruler or another—makes no differ to me."

"Well, Uz," the woman sitting across from him said, "so's I agree. But having no monarch brings slippery times." She wore her dirty blonde hair twisted back and pinned. Pale blue eyes were set in a narrow face deeply marked. She'd been unlucky enough to get the pox but lucky enough to survive. "Makes people feel wary. Bad for business. Even makes me feel itchy." She scratched at her neck with a thumbless hand. Apparently, her luck hadn't always extended to her thievery.

"I say he be better than most," the one sitting next to the old man said. "I'm sorry to think him dead." Past thirty years, he was skinny as a youth. A mass of black curly hair appeared too heavy for such a slight body. If it became unbalanced on top of the long wobbly neck, it might easily flip the whole man upside down

"Ahhh, monarchs ben't good for much but decoration." It seemed the one named Uz hated to be contradicted, especially by his own companion. But he was unwilling to press an argument with a partner who might be guarding his back during the next business transaction. He chose his opponents carefully. His quick eyes went to the stoop-shouldered old man and judged him a safe old hive to poke a stick at. "What do you say about it, ancient one?"

"I be called Orioph, when I be called anything at all," the old man said in a wizened voice.

Uz laughed loudly at what sounded like it might be a witty reply. "Give us your opinion, and my friends and I'll let you buy us more ale."

"You're quick to place all the giving on me," Orioph said. "Tell me what occupies your thoughts this night. If it be worth putting up with noisy companions, I'll gladly supply the drink and maybe a thought or two of my own."

Uz roared. The old hornet still had a few stings left. "Oh, it be. It be." He introduced skinny Yadul, itchy Ham, and quiet Amud.

"You haven't heard then," Yadul said, afraid the topic might roll away if he didn't scoop it up. "The rumble be that Rojelon's dead."

"But he be a young man," Orioph protested.

"Murdered." Yadul glanced around as if expecting to be accused of the crime.

"That be rumble worth a round," Orioph said.

The tavern owner suddenly jangled behind him, having a business sense second to none. An iron ring strung with keys bounced on her hip. She leaned over and poured brown liquid from a fat pitcher. The towel slung around her neck stank of aged spirits and threatened to slap the old man in the face.

The barkeep jangled off. Orioph was minus more coins than he'd expected. Prices rose when demand was brisk.

"What of Monarch Janvian?" Orioph asked.

"She sliced up the old Walbask tarryn like a roasted beast," Ham said. "That's who struck Rojelon the deadly blow, the Walbask tarryn. Two corpses right in the center of things to start off the century. Wish I'd been there. Then Janvian made a speech about how she be having Rojelon's babe soon."

"Babes never come soon," Uz said. "They always come late."

"Oh, and when did you ever have a babe?" Ham asked.

Orioph impatiently took a bitter swig and let them spar. Over the mug rim he observed Amud. The thief's shirt and tunic were cleaner than those of his friends. In his left earlobe he wore an earring cleverly shaped like a lliwant flower. He ignored the light barbs tossed his way. Instead, his penetrating brown eyes were on Orioph.

The old man set down his tankard and shifted square to

the thief. He pushed up his sleeves and leaned his right arm on the table. Let him have a good look.

Openly Amud studied the cascading scars on the right side of Orioph's neck. They flowed into the shirt collar, as if some bursting river had carved the skin like a flooded field, then they reappeared, encircling the arm and trickling onto the wrinkled hand.

Most people turned away from the heavily etched reminder that suffering comes with the speed of a flame. Amud examined the ridges and valleys as if they were a disguise. An uncommon thief, Orioph decided. One who sees that I am an uncommon old man. "Monarch Janvian be well?" he asked.

Yadul bent his unbalanced head toward the stranger. "Almost got the blade by one of her own clan."

Orioph shook his head as if amazed. "Now why would kin do that do you suppose?"

Ham's face twisted in contempt. "There be no mercy in clan blood." A fact apparently discovered through experience.

Yadul poked Orioph with a sharp elbow. "You can bet that old warrior Benoc will wring the reason out of the traitor."

Orioph raised his tankard in salute. "Praise to the long-gone gods that a monarch still lives." He smiled crookedly, pleased with the rumors his companions had absorbed along with their ale. So Rojelon and the Walbask tarryn were dead. Good. And Janvian was alive. Good. But she had not killed Filara, and that could be a problem. He drank. The four joined him, Amud slower than the others.

Yadul wiped his mouth on his sleeve. "The throne's cursed."

"Cursed!" Uz's chest rumbled with laughter.

Yadul was not put off. "When be the last time we had a ruler lived near as long as old Orioph?"

Orioph chuckled. "Oh, I don't know anyone's ever lived as long as me."

"Mad Nevran be almost ninety when he died," Uz said.

"And since then?" Yadul asked.

Uz had no answer.

"Heirs too," Yadul continued. "Once there be more than the Baerryns could sort out—"

"Thanks to Corella's five children and their offspring," Uz interrupted.

"Only Nevran's line counts for anything," Ham said.

"And how many of the madman's descendants be alive?" Yadul asked, planning to answer the question himself.

"After him the throne went to Taznia, now dead," Ham recited, "who had one child, Judsant, now dead." It was clear she had not been born to thieves. She was clan educated, most of the knowledge useless in her current profession. "There be two children, Lelian and Rojelon—"

"Dead and dead," Uz added gleefully.

Yadul grabbed for attention again. "That be the end—"

"Except for the babe." Uz rounded his chest, showing how proud he was of his quickness.

"Doesn't count." Yadul's patience had been drained along with his tankard. "It ben't born yet. And with a curse ready to pounce on it, best it never be born."

Ham slapped the table. "The woman can't stay pregnant forever, with or without a curse!"

"Where did this curse come from?" Orioph asked. Ham and Uz did not notice his increased interest in their friend's babbling.

Yadul leaned over the table confidentially and motioned for the others to do the same. He'd thought it all out by himself and was impressed with his own theory. When their heads were clustered together and Orioph could smell their stale breaths and gauge how long it had been since they'd last bathed, Yadul pronounced his conclusion. "The mystics, I say."

Ham and Uz exploded in guffaws. Ham slammed her mug into Yadul's. "That be a good one."

Orioph searched the skinny man's features. This was not just speculation to get his friends' attention. He believed his own conclusions and was genuinely hurt by their reactions.

The old man traced a groove in the table with a cracked fingernail. Just words. But words spoken often enough spawned a life of their own. When he looked up, he discovered Amud staring thoughtfully at him.

The conversation slipped easily into less intense topics. Yadul pouted while the tankards were refilled. One swig was enough fortification for him to charge back into the banter.

The crowd dwindled along with the blaze in the fireplace. The eipy curled into a shadow in the rafters and slept while its owner spent his earnings.

Orioph stiffly rose to leave. Uz protested, unwilling to let a soul who bought ale escape so easily. Yadul and Ham added their own objections. They hated to see a good audience walk away.

"My coins now be few," Orioph said and wished them a good night.

Yadul watched the old man's hunched figure hobble out the tavern door. From a fold in his tunic, he pulled out a small leather pouch on a thong, the kind some folks wore around their necks to keep valuables close. He coaxed out the contents. A jewel, clear and dazzling as spring water glistened in his palm. He curled his hands around it so only his companions could see. "Now where would a geezer get such a pretty piece?"

Uz was entranced. "That be a clever bit of snatching. I sat right here and didn't see the move."

"Did you grab his coins too while you be about it?" Ham asked.

"You don't pick coins from the one that buys the ale," Uz said. "He might not have enough for the next round."

Yadul tried to appraise the gem's value but had nothing to compare it to. "Amud, you be the brainy one of this motley bunch. Ever seen the like?"

Reluctantly, Amud took the teardrop, keeping it sheltered. The stone was perfectly cut and polished. It splintered the smoky tavern light into reds, blues and golds. A crystal of this quality should hang from an embroidered ribbon or a chain of tiny links, not be held in grimy leather. He balanced the weight of it in his hand, and the look of the old man in his head. "I say this be a very dangerous sparkle to've snatched."

CHAPTER

SIX

Ⅱll was in shadow, the shade of deep water, the
shelter of night. The moons were lost to the storm,
blocked by the towering walls of the fortress. A
mound of debris from previous structures supported the
edifice like a dried out, crumbled loaf of bread. The meran
expertly picked its way along the eastern base where the river
swung south. Rozel dismounted beside a clump of scraggly
brush.

Quiet now, the animal had snorted and stomped in the
courtyard at her encouragement. Fujin belong to her sister, but
it was known that she sometimes rode it. She had kept the
hood of her sleeved cloak around her shoulders, even though it
was a chilly night, so there would be no mistaking her identity.
Servants and stable hands had watched her swing up into the
saddle. They had seen her face clearly in the torchlight as she
had leaned down to exchange easily overheard words with
Benoc. They would meet soon in homeland. Accommodations
for Janvian's comfort would be ready.

Rozel listened to the racer's soft breathing, the gurgling

water, and the calls of nocturnal birds. Stars provided the only light. If a spy or an assassin waited and watched, it would be here, but all seemed well. She scrambled over rubble to the chunk of quarried stone that served as marker.

A snake dangled in her face. Quickly she stepped back and pulled her dagger. The black line in the black night hung limp, unimpressed by her swift blade. The relaxed serpent was what she sought. Her gaze followed the dark trail upward. It disappeared into an expanse of stars cut off by the outline of the fortress. *So that's where I'm off to*, she thought.

She sheathed her knife and tugged on her gloves. They were stiff, not properly broken in. Her uncle would be furious if he knew. As long as she succeeded, he'd never find out. Nor would Benoc ever learn how often, in what way, and for what reasons she used the skills she'd gained in the rope training he'd insisted she endure when she was a child. Mostly, she repelled down to get out of places, including the fortress. Climbing up to get in was a far more difficult application.

She left her cloak on the ground and grasped the rope. Hand over hand, she ascended, twining her legs around the braiding for support. The Drueten tarryn had better appreciate this service to the clan. She looked down and saw nothing. She looked up to a more promising view.

I'll just shinny right into the sky, Rozel told herself, settling into a rhythm. *See if it's true that the old gods are gone. Maybe they're just floating around on clouds laughing at us. Maybe I'll climb up into that skyship and tell them to—*

Loose gravel rained down. Someone concealed above had slipped. She almost called her sister's name but paused. She felt a quiver, a gnawing or—. A blade sawing slowly, carefully through the hemp above her, severing it strand by strand.

Had the spy she'd been expecting discovered the rope? Had it grown tired of waiting for someone escaping the fortress to appear? Bored, had it climbed up in pursuit of a victim and found Janvian?

This wasn't her usual point of egress from the fortress, so she wasn't sure of the vertical territory around her. The scree of previous architecture jutted out in places forming ledges. During one of her top down excursions, she had discovered a sizeable strip. It should be to her left. If the rope was long enough—. If she had enough time—.

She pumped her legs, becoming the weight at the end of a pendulum. Right then left, right then left, building up an arc. She thought she saw a thin line of variation in the rock just out of reach. It was too dark to be sure, but it was all she had.

The rope jolted as more strands gave way. There was no time to gain length by sliding lower. She swung toward what she hoped was the ledge and kicked hard. She stretched to extend her flight, straining the rope. It went slack. Momentum carried her to the apex. She hung suspended in darkness. She floated, no longer tethered to the earth. Then she plummeted.

Rozel tried to be philosophical. There were advantages to living a reckless life and dying young. She just hadn't expected to die *this* young. Her reflections were interrupted by hard ground slamming against her back.

The landing had come too fast. She should still be falling. And she seemed to be alive. She certainly hurt enough. If this was death, why did pain shoot through her head, and why did she gasp for breath? She must have landed on the ledge. Success!

The assassin would be listening for a body. Breathing was difficult; standing impossible. The rope, still clutched in one hand, flopped like a dead vine when she tried to release it. Her fingers were frozen tight. It seemed she would carry the useless twine for the rest of her life. At least there was a rest of her life. So far.

Rozel explored with a foot and found an irregular block. It might have been a gargoyle with a broken wing that had fallen from a battlement above. She put her feet against it and pushed. The uneven chunk rolled to the edge. It tipped forward, wavered back, then found a balancing point. Rozel reached with her toes but couldn't touch the uncooperative rock. Frustrated, she pounded a heel into the slab that supported her and winced at fire jolting through her body.

Encouraged by the vibration, the rock teetered and fell. The timing was wrong. The bouncing and thudding came from the wrong place and didn't sound like a soft, squishy body. At the moment she was glad she had managed that much. She hoped the assassin had heard what it expected to hear.

Rozel convinced her sore hand to unclench and surrender the rope. She tied it around the bone of an old tree clinging to eroding soil, not that it helped in any way. The part she needed dangled somewhere overhead and to the right.

She took a small amount of pleasure in knowing the assassin was stuck on a ridge above with a rope that no longer reached the ground. She could hear it shuffling about. It didn't seem too far away. She must be closer to her goal than she'd thought.

There were plenty of protrusions and cracks in the stones. She ached but nothing seemed broken. She started to climb. The assassin might have been fooled by the tumbling gargoyle, but it would soon understand the deception. It would hear her, and it would be ready.

Slowly, slowly, she crawled upward. All was silent, except for distant thunder muffled by the massive structure. How close was she now?

A figure blocked the star field above. A hunched bulk with a raised blade, it held motionless on the ribbon of land that hugged this part of the wall. The silhouette waited for her to rise above the edge so it could strike.

Rozel found a firm grip. She pulled her legs under her and felt solid purchase. *I am your nightmare*, she thought. She bolted upright, grasped the raised arm and pulled, collapsing back into a crouch against the cliff. The surprised shadow catapulted over her, knife slicing through the back of her leather vest. She released the weight before it wrenched her with it.

Almost immediately she heard the body bounce on the slope where the rubble fanned out to meet the meadow. There was a thud as it reached the base. That's what it was supposed to sound like. The assassin now had first-hand knowledge.

She eased over the rim and rolled away from the edge, glad to be on the shelf that marked the separation of the fortress walls from the rubble. Cautiously she stood, hugging her ribs. She had felt worse. Many times. Once on the Cadaca River she'd decided to navigate through the rapids instead of taking the trouble to portage around them. Benoc had ordered her to clean the stables for a week when she'd told him the boat had experienced worse injuries than she had. For a moment she'd thought he was going to even up the damage.

Rozel felt around for her sister's body. She hoped Janvian had followed their plan exactly. After securing the rope and tossing it over the side, she was to wait inside the hidden passage. Satisfied, Rozel shuffled north on the narrow path.

The wall was overgrown with rough branches. Twisted thorn trees hid a door. Rozel wished she'd known about the secret access before. It would have made slipping out of the fortress for an evening's adventure much easier. She suspected several such entrances existed. Did Janvian know them all? Despite their closeness, Rozel understood her sister would never break lor and share such information with her. It didn't matter. Windows were more fun, and Rozel preferred to find her own secrets.

She gave the coded knock. The door creaked and groaned. Stale, damp air tainted the breeze. Sword ready, Janvian emerged, her gray cape a pale shadow in the hollow.

"Are you all right?" Janvian asked.

Rozel realized she was standing stiffly and holding her sides. "I'm fine. It's cold out here." Janvian wrapped her cloak around her sister, knowing Rozel's waited for her below.

Rozel explained about the assassin. "I hope you have more rope. I'll pull it up when you're gone."

Janvian showed her sister how to release the door's lock from the outside. She took her hand and pressed her fingertips to a carving in the stone on the inside. Rozel explored the indentations. A circle held an arrow that pointed toward the depths of the labyrinth.

"You won't have to stay in the dark for long," Janvian said. "I left a torch a few corners back. Follow the circles, not your curiosity. It's easy to get lost if you don't know the tricks."

"When you get back you can teach me all about it," Rozel said.

"Yes," Janvian said. "When I get back."

<><><>

At the base of the mound Janvian hunted for the assassin's body. She wanted to check the insignia on the armband and would not have been surprised at any emblem she found. The ground was scattered with brush and rock piles from landslides, complicating a search in the dark. She soon abandoned the task. There was little time to devote to the dead.

Janvian knew Rozel was in pain. Whatever the injury, it

wasn't the young woman's first and was unlikely to be her last. She had placed an enormous burden on her marginally responsible sister and trusted her to meet the challenge. Rozel must look after Lorcha now instead of herself.

"Fujin," she crooned softly. The meran snorted a greeting, leading her to him. She affectionately stroked his white blaze and checked that the bridle was all leather. Her departure did not need the jangle of metal to draw notice.

She swung onto the animal's back and directed him across the field toward a stand of trees and underbrush. A seldom used trail angled west and south. The fortress no longer provided protection from the rumbling red glow of the storm. Its fury would ease as day approached. When the first finger of light stretched over the horizon, she must be at the Bewailed Wilde's edge or she would have already failed.

Orioph missed the crystal before he stepped outside the Split Hoof. The subtle vibrating of his companion dimmed the moment he rose and crossed to the door. He knew the skinny one, Yadul, had snatched it while he'd been distracted by the tale of a mystic plot against the monarchy. He could not shuffle back to the table now and demand the return of his property. That would attract too much attention and foster too many questions.

Outside wood smoke floated on the cool night air, a change from the heavy closeness of the tavern but not a pleasant one. "Careless fool that I am," he muttered, straightening from his well-practiced stoop. Hunched shoulders accentuated his stocky build and gave him a slow, vulnerable appearance he found useful when collecting information.

He ducked through a space between a bakery shop and a

gambling establishment then turned back toward the tavern. He enjoyed thieves' company for their tricks and cleverness just as he enjoyed the antics of the eipy tonight. He had forgotten that an animal followed its nature indiscriminately, not judging whether it was a safe time or a dangerous time to perform a trick.

A thief must steal. Others had tried to mine Orioph for treasure, only Yadul had succeeded. He was skilled at his profession, although unwise when to practice it.

The one with the lliwant earring was an exception. Intelligence governed his thieving instinct. His cool brown eyes and controlled expression told nothing, except that more went on in his mind than Orioph would ever know while in his current state. Amud was not as inferior as his companions. But he was still a thief, Orioph concluded.

The stench behind the Split Hoof was enough to make a brave soldier faint. The long building was not flush with its neighbors but stuck out several arm lengths into the narrow alley, forcing the structure across from it to shrink back to compensate. The jog interrupted airflow that would have carried away the foulness.

Orioph kicked at a scavenger, sending the animal scurrying. Although Yadul possessed the crystal, it was still under its owner's control. In a way the theft made Orioph's task easier. Yes, Yadul must die for stealing the crystal, but Orioph had to kill him anyway for his theory and his eagerness to spread it. Ham and Uz had laughed at their companion's speculation, as most listeners would. But even a crazy conjecture got believed if told often enough with sincerity, especially if a few events seemed to support it. Fear of mystics persisted even now, centuries after Relacav condemned the purging.

Orioph had lived at Vetra Abbey for some time when it was

attacked. He'd been placed in the mystics' care at the age of four by a mother who thought him a monster and a father worried about the prejudice of the village.

During the Lost Years, the outside world raged with ignorance, while he had happily studied and learned and become skilled at using his mental abilities. Superstition and terror soon evolved into savage violence that swept the country. Robed figures were slaughtered as they peacefully walked the roads.

It was inevitable that the frenzy would reach Vetra. The mystics thought the gate would hold. They thought they could fend off an insane mob with their few minds. Most of them were quickly slain. Many more died in the fires that scorched every building to ash and cracked stone. Their screams pierced Orioph's mind as he ran from the destruction, his clothes dripping flames. He carried away burns that scarred but never healed. They became rivers of twisting flesh running the length of his body.

The moons crossed the sky many times while he tended his wounds and fought the pain. He charted their orbits and meditated. Clearly mystics were superior to the mad creatures who had devastated the abbey. It should be their responsibility to manage the country and the planet as good stewards of the land.

He proclaimed himself not one of the sages but the only sage. He formed a focus of thought that called the scattered survivors to him. At first small in number, they created a community that operated in secret until they convinced Relacav to grant them the protection of the throne. In return they offered services to the monarchy that made them indispensable and forced the clans to accept them as necessary and almost normal.

Now through the stolen jewel, Orioph gave Yadul an urgent

need. He chuckled at the easy response. Drunk, the unbalanced thief stumbled out the back door of the tavern and prepared to add his urine to the filth in the alley.

Orioph drew a blade. Silent as a breeze, he moved behind the skinny man. In a neat, single stoke he slit Yadul's throat. His other hand lifted the leather pouch from a pocket.

He drifted around a corner and was gone before the head of heavy curls tipped to the side of the scrawny, gashed neck and thudded to the ground, pulling the rest of the lifeless body with it.

CHAPTER

SEVEN

Squinting against the last tremors of the storm, Janvian sat astride Fujin facing west in a shelter formed by a jumble of slate slabs. She eased the meran from the towering protection to where she had a view of the east through a gap between natural walls. The sun would send shoots over the horizon soon.

"Leave from the little fortress," Nevran had said, holding her in the crook of an arm and pointing from the battlement toward the blue-black barrier that separated quivering cream from cool green vegetation. He had directed her eye to where the irregular line was broken by vertical peaks that mimicked the spires towering above Aerrion Fortress. Despite the dizzying height, she had felt safe snuggled against her great-grandfather's shoulder.

"Travel with first light," Nevran had said. "Give Fujin his head."

Her ear had pressed against his chest. She had heard the vibrations of his voice as if the words were inside her own head. "But Fujin is yours," she had said.

"Someday I'll give him to you as a present."

Young as she was at the time, Janvian had known the value of the gift. Merans were leaner and more elegant than sturdy, plodding clobbens. They were racers with great endurance, long-lived and rare. And they remembered.

He had brushed back her hair and noticed the yawn she had tried to hide. They had spent a long day together. It was past time for a meal and a nap. "When I no longer need him," Nevran had said, "he will be yours."

In the false light before sunrise Janvian put a hand against a cold, smooth slab. Its surface seemed sliced and polished by a skilled cutter. "Leave from the little fortress. Travel with first light. Give Fujin his head." She chanted the litany her great-grandfather had taught her.

By the time Nevran died, he had little left to bequeath to one heir among so many clankin. Forced from the monarchy years earlier, he had lost most of his valuable possessions along with the royal position. Still, he had Fujin to leave to Janvian as he had promised, angering other relatives who had hoped that the animal would be their own.

A probe of light from the east explored the land. A golden arc prepared to rise from the horizon. The storm rolled back against the west and dissipated, a temporary retreat. Every moment was precious. Janvian nudged Fujin onto the sand and urged him into a gallop. The meran responded eagerly, as if excited by the adventure. He pounded across the Wilde with the confidence of a sprinter who knew where to find the finish line.

Janvian's spirits climbed with the sun. She clung to the meran's back and kept a gentle hand on the reins. Behind her the little fortress dwindled to a collection of thin black spires. She desperately hoped she'd not been seen against the flat, featureless plain. The deception she had planned depended on a clean disappearance.

She should be no more than a speck now to anyone gazing across the desert. She slowed Fujin to a brisk walk, a pace he could maintain all day.

From the edge, the Wilde appeared flat and featureless, but the landscape was subtly varied. There were stretches of hard-packed dirt. In places fine gravel shifted into hills and valleys. Fujin dodged among them, choosing his own course. Prickly plants nestled into small mounds. Rough-skinned animals the color of the land, invisible until they moved, disappearing into hiding places as she approached.

She stopped to share water with Fujin and to shed the warm cape then continued on. A rushing wind carried sharp grains that stung her eyes, and she worried about the meran's sight. The sun slid over her shoulder and into her face. Despite Fujin's steady stride, it seemed the bright star would reach its destination before she found hers.

Ahead was sand and more sand. She observed Fujin for signs of fatigue. She would have halted immediately and continued on foot to spare him. Speed was absolutely necessary, but so was a healthy mount. The animal kept up the gait without any indication of exhaustion.

An emotional night. Heat. Rhythmic hoof beats. Janvian slipped into a waking sleep. She shook off the lethargy. The sun was straight ahead, dipping to the horizon, and still there was no sign of the half-moon of the Mirage Clan.

A fear crept out of its hiding place and forced her mind alert. If Nevran had truly been mad, then his childish game with a trusting little girl was about to become a cruel joke that would end her life and throw the country back into the Lost Years.

The great crimson clot bled streaks across the sky as it

collapsed into the earth. A prickly charge scraped Janvian's spine. To her right, lightning cracked through a tumbling mass of clouds. It was impossible to turn and dash for the edge. She could only go on—and die bravely. She swallowed in a dry mouth and pushed Fujin into a hard gallop aimed directly at the fading scarlet.

Fujin swerved sharply almost unseating her. She clutched at the reins, steadied herself and was about to pull him back toward the west when she realized that every direction led to death, making all paths equal. What did it matter that the meran was a little crazed from the growing thunder and explosions?

The animal charged up a drift and leapt. Janvian's cramped and sore muscles were too slow to respond. She tumbled from the saddle. She rolled up onto her knees, trying to sort out which aches were caused by the fall and which ones she had brought to the ground with her.

A perilously close strike illuminated a dark hollow in the side of the pale mound. Fujin poked his head from the hole and snorted as if telling her how silly she was to sit in the open when shelter was near.

Janvian crawled into the strange cave.

Rojelon's body shrouded in a golden robe seemed to float above the long table draped in black and purple. One tawny armband bearing a phianj, talons flexed to snatch up its prey, laid at his side. The other circled a sleeve. Rows of tall candles served as sentries at his head and feet. The warm light lent a softness to the severely arranged figure. It seemed absorbed by the bright garments, giving the unnerving illusion that the body glowed with an internal brilliance.

Deliberately away from the light, Rozel sat with what she hoped appeared to be mournful serenity. In her sister's solemn robe and layered veils, she felt restless and vulnerable. She'd never imagined herself in golden armbands, certainly not ones trimmed in purple. Janvian's mourning clothes had gotten a lot of wear lately. First Lelian's death, now Rojelon's.

Rozel was glad for many reasons that she had not been so unwise as to fall in love with a monarch. She was not in love with anyone, and that suited her well. Love was a battle she planned to avoid. Look where it had placed Janvian. She wondered if that was an inappropriate thought here, and quickly decided it didn't matter since no one knew what she was thinking, not even Benoc who stood beside her, for all his uncanny ability to guess what was in her mind. And his great capacity to be constantly shocked by it.

She was sincerely sorry that Rojelon was dead. He'd been a good spouse for Janvian, as spouses went. And he'd been a good monarch, as monarchs went. But, sitting like a statue in an overly ornate chair, Rozel could not manage to concentrate on grief for very long at a time, no matter how padded and designed for comfort the furniture was.

After her fall onto the ledge the previous night, she felt as if her body were one large bruise, an image her black and purple clothing reinforced. Breathing put pressure on her aching ribs. Her head throbbed as if clumsy wine daevas danced through it. She wished she had at least had the pleasure before the punishment.

She stiffly faced the body and tried to distract herself from pain, and other things. At dusk the first lightning crack had jolted her from a fitful half-sleep, sounding like a heavy lock slamming into place. Janvian was safe. Or she was dead. Either way, disguised as her monarch sister, Rozel's future was one of waiting, just like a prisoner, either for sentencing or a pardon.

Behind the veils she shifted her eyes to the mourners who paid last homage from the brightly lit hall on the other side of the massive, arched doorway. Some bowed or gave the hand to shoulder salute. All were uninteresting. She searched the solemn faces for a small twist of a smile or a hint of victory gleaming in the eyes, any sign that might betray a connection with Rojelon's murder. Anything that might relieve the boredom.

Only those with close blood ties were allowed to enter the room. All others were barred by the need to keep the surviving royalty alive. The exception was the mystic. It stood like a black candle beside the arch. Considering the circumstances, Rozel was not comforted by its presence. She gave it a glance whenever the line of mourners grew thin, but there was no change in its posture, no stirring, no more sign of life than in Rojelon's corpse.

The mystic probably knew a counterfeit Janvian wore the golden armbands. Rozel wished she could see its face to try to read its emotions as she was certain it read hers. Did it recognize the irony here? An ineffective protector guarding the results of its failure: a dead ruler and a mock spouse.

A woman appeared in the archway, wrapped in extravagant white fur that brushed the floor and was too warm for the weather. The hood circled Calliud's lovely, pale face. The daughter of wealthy Tskant merchants, if she'd had her way, she would have been sitting in the chair Rozel now occupied.

Rozel had always believed her sister's rival had been more fascinated with the monarchy than with the young monarch, and had been driven more by status than by love. Indulged by her parents, Calliud expected to get whatever she decided to have. Rojelon's disinterest in her had increased her demand for attention, costing her family dearly in gems and gowns—and fur.

Rozel wondered if she had misjudged the depth of Calliud's affection for the dead monarch. The woman had not married, although offers were plentiful—which confirmed Rozel's belief that beauty, coin and advantageous ties could outweigh major personality flaws. She could almost pity her. Almost. Calliud had behaved badly toward Janvian at every opportunity. If she thought herself in love with Rojelon, it was only because she desired a country to adore her. Perhaps the two wants were one in Calliud's mind. Whether the mourning figure knew it or not, she grieved only for herself.

Standing straight, chin high, Calliud unfastened the clasp at her throat and let the rich cape fall to the floor where it was quickly retrieved by a scurrying servant. The change was from snow to storm cloud. Beneath the cape she wore a flowing robe of deep reddish blue, only shades away from purple. The hem and sleeves glittered with thin lines of gold. Her yellow hair was tied with ribbons embroidered in amber thread. The woman was dressed as if she were the grieving spouse. The entire costume was an affront to Janvian.

"Easy," Benoc whispered. "Remember who you are."

Or who I'm supposed to be, Rozel thought. What would Janvian do? She would do—nothing. Not now. This was a matter between clans. Later a formal complaint would be made to Gozax, and Calliud would be reprimanded.

The process seemed a lot less satisfying than knocking her on her butt and ordering her to shed the insulting clothes. At the thought of one pretender challenging another, Rozel's anger slipped into laughter that she suppressed at the expense of her aching ribs. If fraud were the offense, they would both have to disrobe. And wouldn't that make Rojelon's wake the most memorable in history!

Skaln entered the frame of the mourner's arch. Calliud turned to leave without a bow or salute. She gave the tarryn a sideways look of satisfaction then glided away. So much for grief.

There was planning and timing here. Calliud's performance was designed to enrage the widow, leaving her vulnerable prey for the real predator who entered now.

Skaln gave the hand to shoulder salute. By blood he had a right to enter. He picked up a chair from across the room, purposefully set there to discourage any confrontation, and carried it toward Rozel.

Benoc stepped forward and blocked his path. "Surely this is not the time to disturb my niece." Niece. It was not a lie. He couldn't keep the man away, but he didn't have to make the situation easy for him. "Please respect her grief and sit over there," he gestured toward the body, "nearer your fallen clankin."

"Your concern is nobly meant, I'm sure," Skaln replied, "but I must speak with her." He took long strides around the Drueten tarryn and put the chair next to Rozel's, facing the body as was proper. Benoc moved behind the two, within hearing and within reach.

"We share a loss that should be mourned without distraction," Skaln said, "but other matters must be settled. You've met with the Baerryns. Although they continue to accept petitions, I believe succession has already been decided in the baby's favor. Perhaps you will be named regent. Perhaps not."

Rozel kept her eyes straight ahead, focused on nothing. Had the mystics told him about the conditions they'd put on Janvian? She twisted the iref ring round and round a slim finger. A wedding present from the monarch to his spouse, it was part of the deception.

"You and Rojelon kept your own clans when you wed. Now there is a child, and a choice must be made. With all due respect to your Drueten tarryn who stands at my back with a hand on the hilt of his knife, I urge you to join the Felcons."

"It is wrong to speak of this here," Benoc growled.

"It is necessary," Skaln said without turning to look at him. "Janvian, a simple agreement between us will ensure stability. At Rojelon's cremation, you will pledge lor to the Felcon Clan for yourself and the child. In return I guarantee we will support you as regent."

And what if the offer is rejected? Rozel wanted to ask but couldn't. She had never been able to imitate her sister's voice. If she responded, he would know she was not Janvian. She clenched her hands, bit her lip, and tried to meditate on the benefits of self-control instead of on plunging a blade through Skaln's heart.

Her silence irritated him. He turned to her, trying to see the face beneath the layers of cloth. "Think carefully about this. Whether the babe is declared Felcon or Drueten, it must be obvious to the Baerryns that *I* would make an excellent regent."

"You act like a traitor before your murdered clankin!" Benoc's thunderous voice made the candlelight flicker. "See how you've upset the mother of the blood heir!"

Rozel lowered her head and choked out heart-wrenching sobs.

Shocked mourners clustered at the arch. Skaln rose. Twenty-five years younger and considerably taller than the tarryn he faced, he spoke softly. "You are a reasonable man. Our two clans would still hold power together. Surely you see the logic."

Neither height nor youth intimidated Benoc. Fighting skills were what mattered, and Skaln would never be a challenge for him in that area. "You've made your proposal. My niece and I will discuss it and give you a response—at a more appropriate time."

<><><>

Eyes followed Skaln as he strode purposefully, but not too quickly, from the ceremonial chamber. He had not learned the identity of the mourner, as he'd hoped. Janvian or an imposter? Hair could be tinted to appear red. Looped up under the veils, no telling how long it was. The loose gown could conceal almost any shape, wide or thin.

He knew for certain it wasn't Rozel. She had ridden out last night, supposedly headed for Drueten land. It was unlikely she had doubled back and slipped unseen past his guards. And she never would have sat silently through Calliud's theatrics.

Was Janvian still in the fortress, still within his control?

It mattered little if he had put the proposal before her or another. Benoc had heard his conditions, and the threat that went with them. If they wanted Felcon support, Janvian and the baby must become Felcons.

EIGHT

The steamy mineral pool in the abbey garden supported the meager flesh clinging to the Visionate's brittle bones. She contemplated the nature of patience. It was a useful quality. One to be cultivated.

Lightning flashes penetrated her closed eyelids. The storm had been lovely tonight. Now it dwindled with the coming dawn. Soon she would have to leave the comfort of the pool for her interior rooms.

Centuries before she had rejected the sunlight, choosing to venture out only after sunset when the storm could provide the strength her body lacked on its own. The abbey sat north of Aerrion Fortress, in an excellent position to collect the rolling power.

She knew where the Sage spent olax, not through spies or any special ability but because she was familiar with his disgusting habit of frequenting taverns and mixing with its patrons. The Visionate had minds she visited to collect information, but she was not bold enough to do so too closely to old Orioph for fear of detection. She was the second most powerful mystic on the planet. Still, he eclipsed her.

With street skills to rival any urchin, the Sage was entirely too independent. His times outside the community had increased in frequency and length. His obsession with privacy had flourished like a noxious weed until he trusted no one except himself. The great plan for the future of Lorcha, formed and executed as much by the Visionate and the Prism as the Sage, had become his personal crusade. But he rushed when he should pace himself. His manipulation had become far from subtle. He was no longer guiding the clans along a gentle stream but shoving them over a waterfall.

Dangerous. Dangerous. The Sage's eagerness would ruin the progress that had already been made. Whether disciplined mystics or barbaric clanners, people under pressure were not predictable. That single factor made the Visionate's function complex and imprecise. The future was like rain falling from the turbulent clouds over the Wilde. Too often the dry air drank it back into the sky before it touched land.

The motion of the pool soothingly massaged the Visionate's weak muscles. She felt the presence of the Sage drifting back into the community, the change unnoticed by any but the most watchful.

She secluded him in private thought and relayed the distressing departure of the Speaker. "We offered warnings about the hasty death of the monarch so soon after the sister's. It was predictable that one with knowledge of selected sections of our plan should conclude the obvious."

"You needn't be so formal," the Sage thought. "Appropriate action was taken?"

"Efforts were made," the Visionate thought. She knew the Sage disliked her use of the plural when they communicated privately. The Visionate hoped to diffuse her implied accusation that *he* had caused the loss of the Speaker by avoiding direct reference to herself.

Unfortunately, she was at fault for the man's escape. Admitting it could not be avoided. "The Prism—and I—mistakenly interpreted the shattering of his gemstone as an indication that his life had ceased. He survived the loss of the jewel and now lives rogue."

"I want him dead," the Sage thought.

"I gave the orders myself." She might as well get some credit along with the blame. "There is a search."

The Sage pulled into personal meditation. Finally, he thought to the Visionate, "You've been away from the fortress a long time."

"I find the abbey necessary for my health." She had outlived other ranking mystics. Knowing the Sage's preferred method of resolving conflicts, she remained physically removed from him. In several possible futures he was the cause of her death.

He thought he hid things from her. He did not. He was executing his own personal twist to the great plan. In most futures it led to a clan uprising against the Unity. The Purge rekindled. Abbeys burned. Mystics publicly beheaded. In every one of the visions, she died in the first wave. She could not tell the Sage any of it because the futures in which she did were worse.

This was not the babe. This was not the time. In several futures a better opportunity would present itself. She had explained that to the Sage, but he would not wait. She had tried to remove a critical event by placing the one-year time restriction in the Speaker's mind and making it seem logical and necessary. Once said, it could not be revoked, even by the Sage. The Baerryns must always be decisive and absolute. Any inconstancy would erode their image and power. It had been a desperate effort, but in several futures it had delayed the Purge.

"The fruit of our work ripens, my friend," the Sage thought. "I want you near me for the harvest."

"Travel is difficult." She was not fooled by the warm tone, nor was she meant to be. His confidence in her had waned.

"You'll come to the fortress," he thought, as if it were an invitation to a feast, "and so will the Prism."

"With pleasure," she replied. Patience she reminded herself.

Janvian drowsily awoke from a pleasant scene of water and a boat and Rojelon. Fujin stood at the cave entrance sniffing the wind and restlessly pawing sand. Janvian brushed the tears and dreams from her eyes. Outside the storm receded with the coming dawn. A chunk of lamprock she'd snatched up last night still glowed.

Tight muscles made her sluggish when she needed efficiency. She forced herself to work through an elementary training routine every child learned. Gradually her arms and legs became her own and not some stubborn creature's resisting her will. She did not have time to exercise as she should. Another day of hard riding would leave her knotted beyond movement.

She almost laughed at the thought, for the end of the day might bring her to the stiffness of death. A breakfast of dried bread and cracked cheese choked down hard with only a few sips of water. The rest of the liquid she gave to Fujin, who would need the moisture more than she.

The small, hastily gathered supply of food was almost gone. She would have been dead last night except for this cave, which Fujin found by accident. She rolled up her cape and put it in her pack. Outside the pre-dawn light grew. There was no sign of the Mirage Clan, and she could not expect destiny to thrust another convenient refuge in her path.

She would go back. It had been a foolish journey from the start.

Janvian hoisted the bundle onto the back of the saddle and secured it. She checked Fujin's hooves for rocks. A metallic crescent gleamed in the sand. She stooped and brushed it clean. The spread wings and flexed talons of a phianj glittered on the coin. Individual clans had not minted their own money since early in Corella's reign a century ago.

She imagined the child Nevran would have liked the shiny coin with the brave bird on it and would have kept it into his youth as a lucky token. And then he had dropped it here.

She clenched the disk in her fist. It was proof her great-grandfather had not gone mad and she was not a fool. The Mirage Clan was out there in the Wilde if only she could find it.

The meran stomped, ready to be off.

Leave from the little fortress, travel with first light, give Fujin his head.

Merans remembered. The animal had found the shelter not by chance but because he had been here before. If he could find the cave again after the passing of so many years, then he could find the Mirage Clan.

She tucked her new treasure into the pack. Fujin rushed from the hollow into the early light. He whinnied for her to hurry, flinging his dark main. Dots of bright rock faded, dimmed like stars by the rising sun.

The coin lightened her. Joyfully she mounted and released the eager meran to chase its own shadow across the wind-ribbed sand.

<>< ><>

Skaln awoke late and in a bad mood. He scowled at the brightness flowing through the fortress window across the functional furnishings of his room. He dressed in plain, unpretentious clothes. Muted colors formed a better background than bright finery for the purple addition to his armband. The details had to be right. He was the leader who worked hard to hold a fractured country together, and he needed to look like it.

His cousin's murder puzzled him. There was little to gain for the Walbask tarryn and much to lose, as the woman had discovered when Janvian's knife lodged in her throat.

Calliud rolled over in Skaln's bed and smiled. Loose waves of yellow hair framed her features. Cheekbones, nose, and chin seemed balanced by a sculptor for the perfect proportion of angle and curve. She was beautiful, but she was not a beauty to be remembered through the ages. Her features lacked the small incongruity that startled and pleased at the same time. There was no natural ease in her expressions that brought loveliness to life. She was not exquisite as Lelian still was in his memory.

He could not accept that Lelian's death had been an accident, even though he'd examined the body and the location.

The only marks in the soft ground were the sharp hoof prints of the clobben. It appeared the ill-trained animal had been startled—perhaps by a low-flying bird—and had reared onto its hind legs, unseating the young woman. Her neck had snapped like a dry twig, turning his bright Lelian into a cold portrait of horror. It could have happened that way. There was nothing to contradict it.

All of Lorcha had rushed to comfort Rojelon at his sister's death. No one had comforted Skaln. No one knew he loved her.

It was a weakness he had learned to hide while still a child when he, Lelian and Rojelon had played together. She had been his when they were alone. Rojelon took her from him whenever he appeared. Her brother had her affection while doing nothing to earn it, just as he had everything else because he was the blood heir. Skaln, as apprentice tarryn, had the honor of watching Rojelon enjoy his life and the privilege of ensuring that he kept it.

"I played my part well last night, didn't I," Calliud said. She retrieved her cape from the floor where it had been abandoned and wrapped herself in white fur.

She was pleasing. So were others who required less attention.

"I told you I could find out if it was Janvian or not," she said. "And it was. Who else would sit passively while I stood there in a purple gown far more elegant than hers? Anyone playing the part would have felt obligated to have me forcibly removed. Instead, she had Benoc wage a complaint with Gozax."

Skaln was not convinced of the logic or the outcome, but he kept his doubts to himself. One of the assassins posted outside the fortress to prevent Janvian's escape could not be found.

Benoc continued to guard his "niece." He was taking her to Drueten homeland to the comfort of her clan until after the baby was born. The company would leave today.

As the tarryn responsible for the safety of the heir, born or not, Skaln had the right to demand that Janvian remain at the fortress. He had planned to keep her here by force if necessary. The mystics were obligated to assist him, but their actions last night had caused him to change his strategy.

While the flames of Rojelon's pyre roared, the Baerryns had announced their confirmation that Janvian carried the blood heir. Along with the other tarryns he had sworn lor to the child, saluting whoever hid behind the mourning veil, as anonymous as the hooded mystics.

Then the Speaker, who seemed shorter than he remembered, had proclaimed that the Baerryns would rule until the child was presented for recognition. Mystics on the throne of Lorcha! Skaln could feel the ashes of his royal ancestors stir. The terms were ridiculous. A time limit probably seemed logical to the mystics, but he found it naive. The coming year would be a free-for-all.

Skaln had made certain assurances to the *skyship* ambassadors and received certain assurances in return. The deal was dependent upon his controlling the monarchy. When Rojelon died, the victim of someone else's plot, it had been like receiving a gift from an anonymous benefactor. Now the Baerryns had added a complication that he would have to turn to an advantage.

In the old carvings chaos and opportunity were the same rune. He no longer needed Janvian. Let her leave and take all the Druetens with her. The countryside was full of thieves, and traveling served up many dangers. Her own clan was best blamed for whatever might happen to her.

Without the authority of the throne and the strength of the Druetens, he had to generate support in other ways. The ship would return in less than a year, expecting his part of the bargain to be in place. The key lounged in his bed.

Calliud petting the pelt as if it were a live animal draped over her bare shoulder. "I'll have a matching cape made for you when you become ruler. You can wear it to our wedding."

Skaln continued his preparations without a glance toward her. He knew it infuriated her when he would not act as audience to her every move. "We could be married now." He was meeting with her parents today to discuss an arrangement. Negotiations with the successful merchants would not be easy, but he did not tell her that. A beautiful woman wrapped in white fur was unlikely to believe that the world would not present her with whatever she requested and thank her for the honor of indulging her.

"I'll be married in the hearth hall or not at all," Calliud said. "To a monarch, not a tarryn."

Calliud made it seem simple. Just rise in the morning and be enthroned before breakfast. "That's what you truly want?" Skaln hoped for a better answer than the one he expected. Perhaps a longing for love and happiness, contentment and joy.

"I want you"—she stroked the fur the way she moved her hand across his skin when they enjoyed each other's bodies— "once you're the monarch."

He could not be disappointed by her reply. In a way they had the same goal. Skaln wondered, when the throne was his, would he want Calliud?

CHAPTER

NINE

The undergrowth was thick in this part of the hills. Oktria stooped to sneak closer to her prey. The rich flavor of roasted doph filled her mind. She had not seen the bird but it had to be there. Her long, dark hair tangled in a low bush as she tripped on a fallen branch. A muscular woman, she usually moved with a grace that identified her as a warrior. Her skill seemed to have abandoned her, and she fumbled through a cluster of skinny saplings.

The craving was completely unreasonable. She had eaten a filling meal, but the sameness of soldiering food had not satisfied her appetite. This absurd obsession with doph meat was an insect buzzing in her head. She tugged at the earring she wore in her right lobe, a skillfully carved lliwant flower. Then she pulled at her bare left lobe. She could not dislodge the pest.

Instinct told her a plump doph lurked in the next patch of grass. She could not give up now. She held her handbow notched and ready. When the fat, feathery creature stuck up its head, she would transform it into a savory supper.

The day drifted toward the early darkness of the season. If she did not find her quarry soon, she would be forced to return to camp with her desire unappeased. She did not know if she had the will to turn back empty-handed.

Benoc would have noticed her absence from camp by now. Everyone had been ordered to stay close, and she had traveled farther than she'd expected. She could not hold onto the thought. The vision of a succulent doph crowded out everything else. She knew one was near.

Oktria slowly pulled back a thickly foliaged branch to reveal a small clearing, knobby with the roots of trees that circled it.

In the clearing a campfire burned.

On a spit over the fire hung a plucked doph seared to perfection.

A man bent over the bird. He poked it with the tip of a knife, releasing fragrant juices that rolled down the browned skin and dripped, sizzling, into the flames. "You're Oktria. I've been waiting for you."

She feasted on the overpowering fragrance. It pulled her from the protective cover into the open, an unwise position. The man might have companions hiding behind the trees ready to ambush her. She did not look for them. Her eyes were on the roasting bird.

The man straightened and blocked her view. Only slightly taller than Oktria his short silver hair curved around a wide, bony face heavy with wrinkles. The creases seemed more a sign of character than age. There was something wrong with the breeches, shirt and tunic he wore that went beyond their being too large for the narrow body.

A warning bell pealed in Oktria's head. She shoved aside the thought of food. She was acting foolishly and fools got killed. Benoc would be bloody angry if she got her throat slit because she could not control her hunger. She realized what was missing from the oversized clothing and leveled the handbow at the man's heart. If she died, she would not do so alone. "You're not wearing an armband."

"I have no clan." The man did not seem disturbed by the weapon pointed at him. He had none of his own beyond a small knife held limply at his side.

Nearby a clobben whinnied. Just one. The man was alone. There was no gear. The camp was bare, except for the hot, delicious, aromatic bird roasting over a low, smoky fire. Oktria saw it clearly as if the man were transparent.

She shook her head violently and forced her focus on the alert blue eyes. "Then you're a thief, and I should kill you for the crimes you've already committed." But she did not release the arrow.

"I've stolen, I admit that. These clothes and the animal to get me here. But I'm not a thief by profession."

"An amateur thief is just as guilty." This conversation was frustrating. She could barely follow the thread of it. "What's your profession then?"

"I have none."

"You're a riddle." Oktria's bow hand shook. "That's all I know for sure. At least tell me your name."

The man smiled and turned his back to the wavering arrow. "I've no name to give you. I suppose I shall have to find one." He shifted to the side so she could watch him slice a strip of tender flesh from the bird. "Instead, Oktria, I offer you a meal. And a story."

Oktria's mouth watered. The bow was too much trouble to hold level. She let it drop. She did not wonder how the stranger knew her name but not what to call himself. Nor why smoke from the fire had not warned her that this camp was here.

<>< ><>

"You wish to marry our sweet Calliud." Artulk was a flabby man lost in a robe of flowing folds. A fringe of white hair circled a growing bald island on top of his head. His watery eyes were translucent in a pale face that seemed to have never seen the sun.

"If a satisfactory arrangement can be made." Skaln thought it would be more accurate to say that Calliud wanted to marry him, and that he was not opposed to acquiring a stunning spouse from a wealthy and powerful family if provided with sufficient compensation for tolerating her personality.

Plain clothes would not do here. He wore an expensive and stylish formal robe and vest. Twin gems linked by a thin chain adorned the collar. The purple stripe above his clan insignia ruined the overall effect but was a reminder of his closeness to the empty throne.

A stoic servant added a drop more wine to the goblet on the table at his side although he had barely taken a sip. Trays of delicacies were replaced as soon as a removed sweet broke the pattern of the arrangement. All the trays were within an arm length of Artulk. He studied each carefully before making a selection. They were, however, beyond Skaln's reach. He would have to rise from the chair to retrieve a morsel. He would avoid the wine to keep a clear head and refrain from the treats to show there was nothing here he found irresistible.

The refreshments were as extravagant and expensive as the spacious room. Paintings, rich ornaments and thick wall hangings never allowed the eye to rest. Each moved the viewer to a new, unexpected delight. Flower arrangements added a natural perfume that enhanced the odor of wealth.

The house was surrounded by manicured gardens. The estate dominated the most desirable part of Aerrion City.

Calliud's parents owned other homes, plus farms and shops. They controlled most of the legal trade, and perhaps some of the illegal as well.

Diakt, Calliud's mother, dismissed the servants with a small gesture. Business was about to begin. Tall like her daughter, she had the same attractive confidence. Her thick gray hair was pulled back from her face and fastened at the nape with tiny interwoven golden chains. The details of her robe were most flattering when in motion. She strolled slowly about the room, as if appraising its contents, both inanimate and animate. Her gaze seemed adept at detecting deception. "Calliud has intelligence, wit, beauty, and the high spirits of a superior lineage. She deserves to be at the highest level of society and power. How do you propose to ensure this?"

"Forgive my spouse's directness," Artulk said. Where Diakt's talent was laying out the terms, his was negotiation. "It springs from great love and concern for our daughter. But perhaps you'll answer the question."

Calliud had been sent to one of the gardens on a pretense that Skaln recognized for what it was. Artulk and Diakt did not want their petulant child's eagerness to cheapen the terms.

"You've heard that the Baerryns will rule for one year," Skaln said.

"Shocking," Artulk said in his mild voice.

"Unexpected," Skaln agreed. "If Janvian and the baby were, perhaps, detained by some unforeseen event and unable to attend the selection ceremony, both of their claims would be nullified."

"That would be tragic of course," Artulk said.

"In their absence, I am the blood heir," Skaln said.

"There will be other petitioners." Diakt turned a vase to show it to more advantage in the afternoon light. The painted porcelain was finely crafted. When the market was right, it would be sold for a profit and another investment would take its place.

"None as strong as mine," Skaln said. "Rojelon and I share the same royal lineage. As tarryn of the ruling clan, I've proven my skills. Who better to assume leadership of the country with the least amount of disruption?"

Artulk consumed several sweets from a silver tray and leaned back into the large, soft chair he amply filled to recover from the exertion. His physical weakness was real, which made it all the more useful for strategy. "Possible. But we cannot rely on possibilities, even strong ones. I must know that Calliud's happiness is guaranteed." His posture implied that he might not be around long enough to guarantee it himself. "When Janvian and the baby do finally arrive, what will happen then?"

The chair that had been set out for Skaln carried deep carvings that poked him through the padding of his thick vest. "They will never arrive."

Artulk and Diakt let silence drift through the room while they pretended to be repulsed. They were civilized people after all, gentle merchants not accustomed to talk of treason.

"What would you require to advance our daughter's position?" Diakt spoke stiffly, careful to keep the blood from her own hands.

Skaln had already gone too far to be coy. "I need money to hire soldiers who will not be recognized and who hold lor to no clan."

"Clanless thieves?" Artulk wrinkled his flat nose as if a sugary taste had turned to vinegar.

Despite the reaction, Skaln suspected Calliud's parents sometimes used such people for special tasks of their own, although they would never admit so to Skaln. He picked up his goblet and fingered it but did not drink. "My kin are known and would attract attention and suspicion. Those without a clan are anonymous and skilled at deception."

"How much?" Diakt asked. She seemed surprised at his boldness and uneasy about some hidden leverage that fed it.

Skaln named a high figure.

Artulk physically shuttered. "Surely Felcon resources—"

"Are available to me," Skaln said, "but a sudden drain of the clan treasury would be questioned. I'd be hard pressed to find reasonable answers."

Diakt strolled to a window and adjusted the fold in a drape. "Money is always the easy part of the price. Most deals have greater costs in other ways. Only the foolish evaluate a proposition on coin alone. What else?"

Skaln matched her bluntness. "I require the support of the Tskant Clan for my claim to the monarchy." The contest was between the two of them. Diakt was after what he held in reserve, trying to force him to reveal what lay behind his confidence.

"You realize that it's not exactly ours to give." Artulk diverted Skaln's attention to himself to cool the game as the importance of the issues increased. "Gozax is the only one who can grant that."

"I'd hoped she would be here, so we could discuss it," Skaln said without meaning it. He had no interest in presenting the topic to the tough tarryn. She was likely to slice his head off.

"It's best if Diakt and I handle the persuasion on that delicate matter." Artulk leaned forward to entice Skaln into a feeling of intimacy. "But I must say, honestly, that I'm reluctant to approach Gozax on the subject when there might be a question of broken lor."

Skaln heard the clink of the stakes being raised as clearly as if a coin had been tossed on the floor. He had come prepared for the sport with gold of his own. Without it he would never be a match for these two. With it, he could purchase the world. If he used it carefully.

He held it in his fist a moment longer. Let them wonder. "Gozax need not formally offer support until after Janvian and the child are no longer of concern."

Diakt continued her slow tour of the room. "But you expect her privately to agree to your claim before such an event occurs. Convincing her to do so would place Artulk and myself in a treasonous position. Gozax would be within her right to sanction us."

"Then you'll have to be very careful how you go about it," Skaln said. He saw Diakt's shoulders tense, but her facial expression was unchanged. She was not used to being spoken to in a commanding and arrogant way. That was for her to do to others.

Artulk smiled. The more intense negotiations got, the more amiable his manner became. "It seems a disproportionately precarious position to be in just to have our child married."

"Very well married," Skaln reminded him.

"Even so." Artulk spread his arms and shrugged in hopelessness.

Skaln judged the time was right to show the glitter of his gold. "I've had several conversations with an envoy from the *skyship*." Diakt finally became still. "Trade with other worlds could be a great boost to our economy." Avarice glowed in his adversaries' eyes. "A monarch would have little time to manage an enterprise as huge as the importing and exporting of goods with other planets. Advisors would be needed to conduct the actual business."

"How interesting." Artulk picked up a silver tray and cordially extended it to Skaln. He selected the choicest confection. Maneuverings were over. Only a few details remained to be settled.

<>< ><>

Janvian kept her head pressed against Fujin's neck. Her face stung from the wind and the sun. Her thighs were damp with sweat. Fatigue and crippled muscles made her riding sloppy, putting added strain on the meran.

Fujin plodded along, his head wearily hung low. After two days of travel across the Wilde with insufficient food and water, his energy was almost gone. Only his spirit kept him moving.

Janvian felt suspended, as if in her dream from last night. The boat gently rocked with the comforting motion of tiny ripples. Surely Rojelon was near.

Before her a red sun eased into the sand. A dark moon rose slowly to eclipse it, an ebony curve rimmed in fading crimson. It moved toward her, growing larger with each sway of the boat. She would glide straight into it, crossing into a place of dreams.

Her balance was suddenly gone and she toppled onto hard water. She sank, exhausted. Fujin snorted and nudged her, urging her to swim.

The ocean swirled over her in billowing waves. It roared and crackled. Fire shot through it like iridescent spider webs. A blast, very near, deafened her. The flash made her blind.

CHAPTER

TEN

Benoc sat by the fire reading the small book of verse he always carried. Out of habit he kept an ear to the noise of the camp, alert for any change in the usual activity.

Around him kin with a few moments of their own before stretching out to sleep lounged around the fire joking and telling lies. Benoc enjoyed a good joke—and sometimes a lie if well said—but told neither himself.

Most of the idle soldiers were young, giving service to their clan before returning to other professions. The farmers were especially eager to get back to the fields for the harvest. Benoc preferred the occasional company of older warriors like Oktria, career fighters who knew what soldiering was and what it was not.

Usually poetry was all the companionship he needed. The imagery and rhythm relaxed him after a day of examining every twist in the trail and clump of trees for an ambush. He had watched for signs of Janvian's passing on her way to the safety of the homeland. He saw none. Not a hoof print or a broken twig. He took some pride in that. He had trained her well.

Tonight his thoughts wandered from rhymed words to his interrogation of Filara. The prisoner remembered killing the guard and the mystic. He described how he'd entered the room and lunged at Janvian. He had no explanation for his actions and seemed not to understand them himself. He claimed he held no grudge against her and nurtured no malice. Again and again he swore he had no alliance with the Walbask.

"I've gone mad!" Filara had cried just before he'd died from a wound that should have stopped bleeding but had not. Benoc was inclined to agree. It seemed the entire planet was daft along with the reluctant assassin. He did not know if he could hold on to his patch of it long enough for the rest of the world to regain its sanity.

On the other side of the fire Jedrut tossed a log onto the flames, sending up a swirl of sparks. Two riders had shadowed them all day. Ordinarily Benoc would not have allowed a fire that showed where they were. But their large number could not be hidden, and he wanted their location known. No need to eat cold rations on a chilly night when they could have a hot meal.

They had camped early on the shore of the Aerrion River where it swung east toward Drueten land before snaking southwest. Small boats and rafts sailed past by day. Boulders made the bend unnavigable at night.

An unhappy Rozel was secluded in a tent ringed with guards who thought they protected Janvian. The deception kept her swathed in veils when riding and caged up while camped. Her black and purple clad figure was a silent spirit that sobered the company. Only home could lighten the camp's mood.

Benoc heard his son mildly give an order that should have

been firmly delivered. Kaul was just past his twentieth year and more interested in the injured animals he took in and nursed back to health than in working at the skills that made a good tarryn. Benoc had turned over the routine duties of the camp to him, but he would have to check behind the boy to be certain all was secure.

Oktria entered the sphere of the campfire's glow. "Shall I read you some verse?" Benoc asked. They'd often shared a poem beside a warm fire as comfortably as other soldiers exchanged battle tales.

Oktria crouched beside him and poked at embers with a weathered stick. "Where's the mystic?" she whispered.

Benoc stared at his book and answered in kind. "Stationed by my niece's tent."

"Send it somewhere else, as far from your niece as possible." Oktria put a hand to her mouth as if to wipe away grime left from the dusty trail. The gesture concealed her words from everyone except Benoc. "I must speak to you and Rozel."

<><><>

Benoc did not like tents. They were too vulnerable to attack by fire or by a blade thrust through the fabric. They required guards stationed within sight of one another to the left and right but far enough away for private conversation within the flimsy walls.

The cramped interior, damp with the smell of the river, was lit by a single lamp hanging from the center post. Gear was stacked to the side. Rozel greeted her uncle. She nodded to Oktria, offering no explanation as to why she was there instead of Janvian, and asking none as to why the solider was privy to the secret.

"There's someone you must meet," Oktria said.

A breeze brushed Benoc's back. Before he could turn to the swaying tent flap, a silver-haired man stood with them.

"I come as an ally," the man said.

Benoc cursed, knife in hand. He could handle the seemingly unarmed stranger, but a fight would be difficult in the crowded space.

The man met Benoc's appraising stare. "I snuck between the guards." He thought it unwise to explain he had told their minds to see what they expected to see, and that didn't include him. "I have important information."

"We have our own sources," Benoc said.

"I bring you what no one else can. As confirmation that I have special knowledge I will tell you where Janvian has gone."

Benoc scoffed. "She is safe. I won't be tricked into saying more than that."

The man looked from the tarryn to Rozel's guilty expression and understood.

"Go ahead," Rozel said.

"On the Bewailed Wilde."

"I've no time for games." Benoc grabbed him by the wrist and twisted an arm behind his back. "Oktria, get some rope. We'll tie up this fraud for the night and question him in the morning."

"Uh, Uncle," Rozel said.

Benoc and Rozel sat with the silver-haired man in a tense triangle on the tent floor. Oktria had been sent to check on the guards. It had taken some time for Benoc to calm down enough to listen to the stranger.

"As Speaker, I conducted the audience with Janvian. I saw her plans. Rozel's impersonation, the risky journey."

"You don't sound like a mystic," Rozel said.

"I'm no longer of the Baerryns."

"A rogue masked the poison that killed Rojelon," Rozel said, implying it could have been him.

"I did not become a solitaire until after. I've no letters written in code or strips of cloth caught on thorns to support my suspicions. I've pieced together scraps that form a pattern. The pattern is the evidence." The Prism's trying to kill him would add to it, but he would rather not reveal that.

"You think the Sage made the Walbask tarryn kill Rojelon?" Benoc asked. "That's possible?"

"I think he arranged events in such a way that the tarryn felt compelled to do so." Unfortunately, the assassin was dead, so that could not be verified.

"Could the Sage cause one clankin to attack another?" Benoc asked. "Could he cause blood to flow from a wound until a man was dead?"

"Possibly," the mystic said. "The attack could be a compulsion through the mind, although it would be recognized as such if the person paused to examine it. The bleeding would be done through a certain substance in a drink. It is my belief that is what happened. It fits the pattern."

"And the pattern is the evidence," Rozel said. "I still think Skaln is the designer of the plot and not this Sage guy."

"Whether Skaln is or not, he'll take what advantage he can from it," Benoc said. He had picked through the bones the man had tossed out and had found more flesh than he was sure the man meant to expose. A mystic could stroll through a line of soldiers unseen. A mystic could manipulate a mind. A mystic could compel others to do its bidding. All confirmation of old myths and superstitions the Baerryns had tried hard to stamp out. Such a person, one who was independent, could be a danger or a weapon of great value. He could think of many ways to use such talents. "I don't know if there's truth in what you say, Rogue, but it buys your life—for the moment."

<>‍<>‍<>

Rogue. The word had not been said with contempt, but the former Speaker felt its sting. They might believe him. They definitely didn't trust him. Oktria would never forgive him for planting a desire for doph meat in her head.

He should have just gone off and lived as a hermit in the hills. The clans were like scrawny bushes clinging to the cliffs. They would survive no matter how harsh the weather.

Yet, here he was. He had revealed only as much as was necessary, feeling like a traitor for even those pebbles in the great mountain of Unity. There were many things they hadn't asked, so he hadn't answered.

He had told them the Sage planned to control Lorcha and let them conclude how that might be accomplished. He wasn't sure himself. He hadn't said that he suspected it was important to the Sage that Janvian cross the Wilde. He didn't know why or how that fit into the pattern.

The Baerryn traveling with the company was on the other side of the camp. Rogues were difficult for the Unity to detect. If the former Speaker was careful, he might not be discovered. Still he worried. He knew nothing about defending himself on his own. With a crystal, nearer to the storm where he could gain its energy, he might defeat a lone mystic. But here, with a bare forehead, he could not hope to survive an attack by one linked to the strength of the Unity.

He could not sleep in the camp. He'd persuaded the guard who'd brought his supper to retie his bindings with a bit of slack after he'd eaten. He shed the ropes and rode a docile clobben to a den where he curled up in his cape with a family of rudiuls for the night.

<><><>

Jeremy and Dougal were late. They were so late. The cart whined across the sand going slower and slower. It rolled to a stop and would not be coaxed back into motion. Light was almost gone. Dark clouds roiled and spit sparks. They were close but they couldn't carry everything in one load and there would be no time for another. Jeremy opened the cages. It had taken all day to catch the specimens that vanished in a blink.

The two young men gathered up as much of the equipment as they could carry. In the diminishing light their visors had turned clear. Jeremy rolled up his cap and shoved it into a pocket on the leg of his jumpsuit. They did a running-walk back toward the complex. Some of what they held attracted lightning, making it dangerous to carry; but it was too valuable to leave in the cart. The sand was beginning to sparkle with a scattering of the glowing particles Dougal was fond of collecting.

They rushed around the side of the dome to the entrance and collided with a horse. It almost definitely was a horse. Or at least horse-like. It had things strapped to it, so they couldn't see the entire beast.

A figure on the ground groaned, human, just as strange a vision as the animal.

A bolt struck close. They had to be quick. The automated systems had already secured the door for the night. Dougal used the emergency override. They dumped their loads in the garage where the metal on some of the devices would not draw lightning. They rushed back into the thunder.

"Sanctuary," the woman murmured. "Sanctuary." Jeremy carried her to the airlock. He estimated she was a few inches shorter than he and of a slight build. Not sure how to get the animal inside, Dougal tried to encourage it toward the opening with outstretched arms. It ignored him and followed its fallen rider.

Jeremy left Dougal to deal with the shields and the large, rolling door. He hurried straight to medstat and placed his burden on the exam table in front of a shocked Merede, the senior medic. "We found her outside," he said, helping to set up the monitors that would assess the woman's condition. "She's an outsider. From—"

"The outside?" The medic watched the oxygen exchange and the heart rate come up on the screen. An inch taller than Jeremy, she had shadow-tinted skin and bold features. "And I'm supposed to know what's normal?"

Jeremy sobered. He was still dressed for harsh sunlight and wind. His shoes shed particles on the sanitized floor. Merede was angry at him, but not for dumping sand and a foreign patient in her clinic. "The cart broke down. But we made it back."

Again, Merede thought, *the cart broke down again*. He and Dougal were going to get themselves killed going so far from the dome. Jeremy had assured her the benefits from their experiments would be worth it. She wasn't convinced. "Cradle six has an abnormality in the right atrium."

"Can it survive?" Six was their best incubator. Months of work had gone into preparing the fertilized egg, nurturing it into an embryo, and installing it in the artificial womb.

"I'll know in a few days."

"Genetic defect?" Jeremy asked, already knowing the answer.

"I've ruled out other causes."

Jeremy ran a hand through his bristly brown hair. In contrast to Merede, he had pale skin and unintimidating features. Another failure and it was his fault. He'd selected a flawed donor and hadn't noticed the damaged code.

Merede pulled an examination panel down from the ceiling and moved it over the body. "This is interesting. Our visitor is pregnant."

Jeremy examined the visual. This was even more exciting than the horse. Which, he realized, was still in the garage.

ELEVEN

F ew in the camp by the Aerrion River spent an easy night. They rose in the cool half-light, shaking wet beads of dawn from their blankets. A low, velvety mist swelled over the bank and swirled away on a slow breeze.

Benoc had no spare moments to dwell on the merits of the morning. After a hasty meal he thanked the Baerryn for its assistance and released it from its duties, using the excuse that they would soon be in Drueten territory and no longer in need of extra defense. The mystic accepted the dismissal with a nod. If it was confused by the unexpected removal, it gave no sign.

Since the meeting last night in Rozel's tent, Benoc thought differently about Lorcha's protectors. He sent Jedrut to follow the figure. It would know the watcher was there and not dare do anything but return to the fortress. So Benoc hoped. He already had two Felcons at his back; he did not need another tail. He warned Jedrut to stay clear of the riders. The stocky soldier accepted the warning one would give an inexperienced child without a flinch.

Benoc listened carefully to the muddled reports of strange

thoughts from the guards who had surrounded Rozel's tent last night. He gave them vague assurances that they all looked fit then sent them off to their tasks.

The silver-haired man had been well trussed up when the tarryn had left him. This morning he rested in the same spot unencumbered. The company broke camp and continued east along the shore. The aged stranger rode beside Oktria as if he had been with them all along and had just become visible with the dawn.

The soldiers murmured among themselves but did not challenge him. Tasseled cords dangled at the throat of his baggy shirt in Tskant style. What of it? Perhaps he had a relative of that clan who'd made it for him. If he dwelled in the city where clans mixed more freely, he'd think little of wearing it. And his hair could have been cut due to an illness.

He wore Drueten armbands and the tarryn spoke directly to him, that was good enough. They didn't know the insignias had been stripped from Filara. "So you won't be mistaken for a common thief," Benoc had told the rogue as he'd thrust them at him. The clans displayed a pride in blood the mystic had no empathy for. He remembered little of his life before the Unity. His abilities had been evident early, so he had been sent to the abbey before memories of kin had taken root.

Without being asked, the former Speaker assumed the duties of the dismissed mystic. He didn't have a gem to enhance his abilities but he could still scan the land. Beside him Oktria babbled about people, places and events—some interesting, some not. The constant words were surprising after the mental communication the former Speaker was accustomed to. Had she forgiven him for the doph obsession?

They were in Tskant territory. Farmers and animal herders who lived in the low hills they passed watched them to make sure they moved along taking nothing but wild game. He reported so to Oktria. He had only a vague concept of property and homeland—the physical things clans fought over. "The more distant images are dim. My power is not as strong as when I was of the Baerryns." Immediately he regretted the slip and was relieved that Oktria did not probe. Let the warrior think he referred to the loss of linked minds and not something else. He must not forget the Drueten was his guard.

"We've sent out scouts," Oktria said. She rode a broad animal two hands taller than any other clobben in the company. "We're not helpless, just lazy from depending on the unnatural powers of mystics for too long."

"A master sword smith fashions a blade with what seems to be unnatural cunning," the former Speaker said. "To the sword smith it's simply the use of a talent that's been developed into an art. Mystic abilities are just as natural."

"Not everyone is born a mystic."

"Not everyone is born a sword smith. Or a warrior like yourself."

"Mystics were created by Cyran-ozel during the last destructive years of the Machine Age to show us the way of mind over mechanics." Oktria gave the cupped-hand gesture of a true believer. "They are not unnatural because they are mistakes, as some proclaim, but because they were made long after the Origin when the planet was shaped and life was placed on it."

The former Speaker knew the myth. Once numerous, disciples of Cyran-ozel were now rare. "A soldier who worships a peaceful god?"

"I believe in many things, not all of them consistent with one another. But that's a good discussion to continue over a large tankard of ale." Oktria pulled strips of dried meat from her pack and offered the mystic a salty chew. "You haven't remembered your name, have you? It's awkward not knowing what to call you."

The former Speaker gnawed at the tough meat. "Any will serve. I don't have a fondness for one over another. I don't even know many names."

"Then you're Lnez." Oktria bit off a chunk of jerky.

"If you wish." He tugged at the meat, but a bite would not come free. He spent most of the forenoon grinding the strip between his teeth.

Newly named Lnez watched the countryside with part of his mind and directed the rest of it to what Oktria had said about the scouts. When you depend on something, it is easy to forget your own resources. For centuries he had relied on his jewel and the power of the Unity. Before the link he had been untrained but strong. He should not think of himself as crippled.

Lnez chewed. There had been an incident that had caused a novice's gemstone to fractured. He would review every such event that had occurred during his three-hundred-and-seventy-some years in the Unity. This might take a little time.

Lines of data froze, faded, returned, froze again then faded. Jeremy was using the genetics station's most reliable monitor, such as it was. He performed the routine Dougal had shown him, pressing the spots for controls not currently visible on the misbehaving screen. They were still there and functioning even though he couldn't see them.

Dougal had repaired the unit many times, using parts from machines beyond resurrection. He had talent and the advantage of a full tech team to support him. The equipment had been designed and built to last centuries, but it was not immortal.

The display of DNA sequences returned. Jeremy had neither gift nor guidance. Revelation came to him slowly, gleaned from the journals and notes of Senior Geneticist Marla and First Assistant Nicholas.

The hour was late and his work was futile. A whisper of conditioned air was the only distraction in the soundproof biome. Layers of plastic skin, neofabric, and insulation abated the noise of the storm. He knew how flimsy they were. Only the magshield protected the structure from the lightning.

Eight years ago the generator in this section had failed. Marla, Jeremy's mentor and friend, had died along with Nicholas and others in a blast that had ripped through the fabric lung. Fire had added to the damage. Jeremy remembered little of the event and his being rescued, but it was always with him. At strange moments he would again experience the flash of the explosion in stark black and white, or he would suddenly smell ozone.

The generator and shell had been repaired, but the intellectual loss and equipment damage were permanent. The error in cradle six would not have happened before the accident. Reproduction had been done through genetic selection from the large bank of genomes. Every section had been thoroughly examined before it was used. Marla had been a genius at manipulating human codes. With a snip and a patch, she had corrected most defects. If one slipped through, it was identified and recorded for future scrubbing.

That was all gone in seconds—most of the stored genomes; the readers, splicers, and sequencers; the records, notes, and instructions. Worse, the people with the knowledge and experience to use those resources, the only ones capable of regaining at least some of what had been destroyed, were dead.

Jeremy now held Marla's title and position not because he'd earned them, but because there was no one else. He and the staff he was still rebuilding had been forced backward to replenishing the population through basic egg and sperm selection.

He spent most of his spare time trying to replicate Marla's work. He had taught himself to perform some genetic procedures on animals, where mistakes could be mercifully disposed of. But human genes were not for experimentation.

He rubbed his aching eyes. How could he hope to rediscover even half of what his mentor had known? There were children who would not be born because he could not solve the genetic puzzles.

A killer lurked somewhere in cradle six's code. All he could do was search the genome a few sequences at a time, hoping to find the criminal. Then backtrack to identify which of the donors he'd selected had contributed the deadly trait. Perhaps it was a combination. He'd had to tag all of the contributors as unusable, shrinking the community's gene pool until he had the answer. If he could find the answer.

For now, he marked where he was in his analysis. He needed a break, and he didn't want to miss the council meeting about the outsider.

<><><>

Rozel paced the small fabric prison. She felt like poking the rough cloth and watching it ripple. Rozel might do that. Janvian would not, so she kept her hands tucked into her cloak. If only she knew that her disguise did some good and her sister was alive and safe, then the confinement would be easier to endure.

The tent did little to keep out the cold of the foothills. She did not look forward to it getting worse as they climbed higher into the mountains. The chill seeped into her healing ribs. She wrapped a heavy blanket around herself over the cape and wrinkled her nose. Everything smelled of animal sweat and the trail.

Rumors leaked through the woven walls along with the cold. Caravans had been attacked by thieves. Travelers were set upon by other clans within their own borders. Entire villages were terrorized. Sorting out the facts was impossible by the time the stories reached her ears. They had been told by too many tongues and were now too far beyond reason. In her private cocoon she realized what the tellers did not. A clever enemy need only stage a few raids then let the growing tales feed the anger and suspicion like a twisted tree yielding rotten fruit.

Benoc announced himself and entered, stubborn determination in the furrows between his eyes and the set of his jaw. "We'll not argue about this again, Niece."

"We will, Uncle, if you insist on discussing it."

Benoc put his hands on his hips. "No discussion. I'm the leader of your clan. You will obey me."

"You're ordering me, Tarryn Benoc?"

He gathered his composure. He could settle land disputes, resolve grievances, and send soldiers into a bloody fray, but he could not force Rozel to accept a mission she opposed. "You have a responsibility—"

"To my sister." Rozel crumpled up the blanket and threw it on the floor. She was no longer cold. They had debated this issue during each brief rest most of the way to the Drueten town of Melltona.

"—to Lorcha. If the rogue is to be believed, we must put up as many barriers to the Baerryns' plan as we can." Benoc turned his back to her and massaged a throbbing temple.

"Lorcha can turn to sand for all I care," Rozel said.

Benoc spun, arm raised to strike with the back of his hand. Rozel stuck out a defiant chin. She had endured enough beatings from her father to be unafraid of a single blow. It was quickly received and quickly gone. Only memories stung forever, and she had learned to manage them.

The hand halted, suspended at the apex of the swing. She saw the muscles unknot and the breaths become controlled. Slowly her uncle lowered his arm. She knew the technique. He had given her instruction in it, but she rarely cared to practice.

If only his brother had learned the calming routine, Rozel thought. If only Benoc had done something to stop him. Instead she was the one who had accepted that duty. She was the one who had stood between Janvian and their father's temper. Now Benoc, the man of great lor, wanted her to publicly renounce her support for her sister and to petition the Baerryns on her own behalf. "I'll not betray Janvi."

Benoc's stance was rigid, but his voice softened. "You'd only be holding the throne for her, not taking it forever. We must be prepared in case she doesn't return within the year."

Rozel could not look at him. It *might* be forever. Janvian might never returned. Benoc could not ignore that possibility any more than she could. They left it unspoken, a silent sword between them. Her thoughts caught on the sharp edge of that blade. She held back tears. She would cry later.

This ploy of Benoc's might trap her in the monarchy for the rest of her life as securely as she was now confined in this cursed tent. And all for a hunk of dirt as politically scarred and eroded as the soil beneath her feet. She could never be a true monarch, never rule as well as Janvian. If placed on the throne, she might cause more damage than Skaln. Despite her efforts, tears slid across her cheeks.

Benoc put his arm around her shoulders and set her down on the discarded blanket. "She'll come back." His eyes filled with his own unspilled tears.

"You're sure I won't get stuck ruling until my hair turns white and I'm forced to abdicate like Mad Nevran?"

"The old gods help Lorcha if you do," he said. He brushed wetness from her cheek. "I'll establish proof that you're acting under my orders, that you're not breaking lor. It'll have to be a secret until the right time. Publicly it will look as if you've turned against Janvian and that will be hurtful, but there'll be evidence of your real intent."

"I'll listen," Rozel said, "but I don't promise to agree."

Benoc's expression told her that was as he expected. He folded his legs under him and sat facing her. "I'll warn you, this will be more dangerous than anything you've ever done."

Rozel suppressed a shrug. Her uncle knew little of the things she'd done.

CHAPTER

TWELVE

The habitat station was crowded. Dougal's account of finding the "red-haired beauty" and, more importantly to some, the horse had generated a lot of curiosity. Jeremy grabbed a pillow and took his place on the floor at the low council table. A dull-gold coin rested on the shiny black surface, casting a half-moon reflection. Beside it three unusual looking knives and a double-edged sword were metallic shafts with their own pale echoes. He faced the transparent wall that looked onto the waterfall in the next biome.

Merede addressed the group. It was her turn to sit "center cushion" and manage the agenda. The meeting was for information and discussion only. No business would be conducted.

"The woman appears to be a native. She has extended mobility in the wrists and elbows. Certain indicators of diet are consistent with consuming organic grains, meats and fish. She's obviously been breathing the planet's air for years and been exposed to the weather. Trace elements in her system correspond with what could be predicted given the outside environment. A DNA sample will be analyzed, although we've not much to compare it to. She is dehydrated and her glucose is low. Both are being corrected. Her clothing is being examined." She gestured to the coin and weapons on the table. "The personal items she carried appear to be of clan origin."

Mayor Sasha picked up the coin and examined the markings. Once a tall woman of five feet eight inches, the mayor was now a hunched figure. In contrast to the short sleeves, knee-length pants and sandals worn by those around her, she was bundled in long pants, sturdy shoes and a quilted jacket. Her failing body would soon take her keen mind from them. "There's been unfounded speculation that the woman has been sent by the Tynat craft that recently orbited the planet. There appears to be nothing to support that conclusion."

"The Tynats could still be there," Tamaki said. Senior teacher, he was in charge of the children's general education. "Maybe they can mask their ship, and they haven't really left. They could have detected our shields and sent a spy."

The thought had never occurred to Jeremy, but apparently it had to a few who spoke up.

Other concerns surfaced. The woman was dangerous. She carried four weapons. Wasn't one enough?

She might have already infected them all with a disease— not intentionally.

A full-grown adult, she was a strain on their resources. Jeremy found that one tragically laughable. They had fallen behind producing replacements for the population they already had, and the biomes could easily support at least twenty more beyond that. He realized in some people's minds this was a gathering to decide if the outsider would be allowed to stay.

"There is another important aspect to her physical condition," Merede said. "She is approximately fifty days pregnant."

Bartholomew laughed and scratched his large, round nose with a stubby thumb. Senior agriculturalist, he ran the agristat. "I don't think the Tynats would send a pregnant spy."

"What better way to make sure we'd take her in?" Yakov said. He was senior technician. Dougal served on his team. "We can't toss a pregnant woman out into the desert."

"We wouldn't toss out anyone," Sasha said.

"An implant into the womb is awfully risky," Leslie said. She ran the garage and was in a foul mood. One of her vehicles was stuck out in the storm overnight and a strange, pooping beast was in its place. She'd have to deal with the inconvenience and the smell until a quarantine location could be set up.

"It's apparent she's been carrying the fetus since inception," Merede said.

Everyone was suddenly still.

"You mean—"

"She's been carrying it since fertilization," Merede said.

"You mean—"

"Fertilization took place in the womb." Merede had never seen a case before, but there were records of it happening. Questions flew at her from around the room, most of them unanswerable at the moment, but the senior medic did her best.

"I heard her say 'sanctuary,'" Dougal said.

"Are you sure you didn't imagine it?" Yakov teased. "Perhaps your hearing was affected by her 'outsider beauty.'"

"She definitely asked for sanctuary," Jeremy said.

Tamaki sat glumly beside Bartholomew. "Only a Tynat spy would know what that means to us."

Outsiders and Tynats. *We are so afraid of anyone who isn't us,* Jeremy thought. *Sanctuary* was the ship that had brought their ancestors here when they broke away from the Tyllur Nations. Sanctuary II was what those settlers named the complex of biomes that became their new home. They were Tynats before they came here. When they landed, they were outsiders. They'd brought the belief in sanctuary with them in name and in spirit; yet, some of their descendants in this room thought it only applied to them and would deny it to others.

Sasha held up the coin. "My predecessor Mayor Thomas had a good luck piece. He told me it went with the position. When I became mayor, it was waiting for me on my desk. It looks exactly like this. It was a gift from the outsider who lived here for a while. You all know the history. He returned to his clan and brought us no harm. He knew the word and could have shared it with others."

The story of the stranger Nevran was taught as a curious side note in the dome's past. Jeremy thought it should be given more emphasis. The meeting ended but the discussions carried on. He grabbed Dougal and pulled him away from a knot of people who wanted to hear his account of rescuing the woman one more time. "I'd like your opinion on something," Jeremy said.

"Sure, where're we going?"

"To look at the horse."

<><><>

On one side of the winding thread of riders an irregular wall swirling with pink, gray and black jutted toward an overcast sky. On the other side land dropped away to nothing. Rozel kept her eyes on the back of the rider ahead of her. She was bored with picturesque rock, and her last experience with a cliff had not been a pleasant one.

Scruffy bushes tenaciously clawed at cracks and managed to draw out enough sustenance to survive. Their branches were bare in the early winter caused by the altitude. Rozel ducked below a branch, but not low enough. A twig plucked at her veil. Her muscles had gone to sleep, and she had to push them to do the simplest tasks. She felt fat and lethargic from days of inactivity.

The rogue rode at the front of the party ahead of Oktria. Rozel didn't know if she trusted the man—or any mystic in or out of the Baerryns. Oktria behaved as if they were old acquaintances. That was her way, part of her easy calmness that masked the ever-alert soldier. Rozel saw Benoc's hand in the companionship. While the warrior showed friendliness toward this Lnez, she also kept him away from the others who might ask questions just to make conversation.

Kaul appeared at a twist in the trail. The rock wall curved inward, widening the path enough for two animals to stand together. Kaul waited in the niche for his father as the others filed by. Rozel lowered her head as she passed, only giving him a gesture of greeting with her ringed hand. She had to be careful. He knew her well enough to guess who she was from small clues.

Benoc reached his son and ordered the party to halt.

"A message from Rozel," Kaul said.

Rozel's ears strained at the sound of her own name. She turned in the saddle to see Benoc reading. "There's a herder's compound in a valley ahead. Rozel arranged for us to camp there tonight. We should reach Nept in three days."

"Tarryn," Kaul used the formal address, "I could catch up to Rozel and help her scout. She isn't far ahead. I can tell by the tracks. If I start now and travel all night, I can reach her sometime tomorrow." Kaul's back was to Rozel so she could not see his face, but she heard sincerity in the offer.

"You're needed here." Benoc shoved the paper into his vest.

Rozel felt sorry for Kaul. He didn't understand his father's rebuke to his brave offer. Apparently, he did not know the rider who left messages and purposely did not concealing her tracks was an imposter Benoc had arranged in Melltona. Clankin of the right size, the girl knew the mountains well and was comfortable traveling them alone. Rozel doubted the explanation that would come later would compensate her cousin for this moment.

The circle of deception spread outward like the sound of a bell through the countryside. Part of it would be over soon. Three days to Nept. Benoc ordered them to move on. Rozel gave him a glance over her shoulder. He answered with a small nod. She stifled a whoop of joy at the real information encoded in the message.

They followed a shadowed pass as the sun hid behind a white-capped peak, traveling the last slow miles by the swing of lantern light. The air smelled laden with coming snow. This time of year mountain travelers pushed on until they reached shelter. Even a pleasant day became a bitter night. Blizzards killed those lulled into camping in the open.

The herder's hut and sturdy sheds were nestled in a valley against a hill. The ground showed signs of sharp-footed grazing animals. The place was deserted, its summer occupants having left for lower pastures and warmer temperatures.

"Lnez."

Hearing the word that identified him, the mystic turned to Oktria. He was startled by how quickly it had become a reflex. It grasped his attention even when he was deeply within his own mind. A single word that had no meaning for him until a few days ago now had power over him. The clans were awe-struck by mystic abilities, yet oblivious to the wonders in their own lives.

Oktria dumped her gear beside the borrowed odds and ends Lnez used. "You're to concentrate on the trail behind us. The Felcon riders are sure to follow into the shelter of the valley."

Benoc's orders always came through Oktria in a quiet voice so the others would not suspect his role. Necessary secrecy aside, the tarryn could not get past his discomfort at having a rogue around enough to speak to Lnez directly.

No matter. Oktria was more than a sufficient companion. He continued to scan the area as he had before. Oktria and Benoc thought of his ability as if it were a shaft of sunlight through an open window, a beam set to a single direction, striking a small space at a time. He could use it that way if needed, but it was more like a campfire, luminous in all directions.

He watched the movement of the camp with his eyes and felt it with his mind. Tired travelers prepared a meal. Others led clobbens from an icy stream that sliced the valley to a weathered corral meant for smaller beasts. He saw Rozel and Benoc walk past the fierceness of freshly kindled flames. Mentally he followed them through the darkness. If he hadn't seen them and noted their location, he wouldn't have been able to distinguish their identities. One went on alone. One returned to camp. He watched Benoc stroll to the fire and warm himself.

It was not so strange that the young woman would desire a little freedom and exercise. Perhaps Rozel went out every night and Lnez had not noticed until now, thinking the person he detected was a soldier on patrol.

A crescent Pypeed cleared an edifice, casting light filtered by flat clouds. Lnez went to the stream for a taste of fresh water. The flowing liquid made noises he found disturbing. Or was it something else that unsettled him? The two Felcon riders were in their expected place. Could there be another? He wandered upstream away from camp through lush grass that burst from the ground along the bank.

Rozel was just ahead. Someone moved swiftly toward the pretend monarch.

Lnez ran. There was no time to alert Benoc and Oktria. The attacker would soon reach Rozel. If he could intercept—

He had the advantage of knowing exactly where the enemy was. He stumbled forward, unable to sense the terrain as he did living things.

His path converged with the stranger's. A startled figure drew a blade. Lnez forced snow and ice into the mind. The small woman with long, loose hair shivered. Still she gripped the trembling blade and stood her ground.

"You're a Drueten," Lnez said.

"And w-w-what are you?" his adversary stuttered through chattering teeth. "You w-w-wear the armband, but s-s-seem to be s-s-something else."

"Quiet, both of you." Rozel reached them. "Do you want to alert the entire valley?"

The stranger managed a tight grin. "C-c-clankin Rozel, I'd know you anyw-w-where."

Rozel turned to the mystic. "It's all right. This is Hannen."

He removed the freezing thoughts from the girl's mind. "I'm called Lnez." The two women were almost identical. Hannen's stance under attack had a calmness that reminded him more of Janvian. "My apologies," he said. "I thought you were going to harm Rozel. Now I see that you've come to change places with her."

Hannen's blade disappeared. "How is it you attacked my mind?"

"Lnez is a rogue," Rozel told her. "Don't tell anyone. Don't let anyone know you know, especially Benoc."

Lnez was still a rogue. His presence required an explanation and a pledge of silence. He was as separate as a thief, and just as clanless.

Rozel and her kin exchanged clothes in the night chill. Hannen still shivered. Her abdomen showed the small bulge of pregnancy. The impersonation would be most accurate.

This was why Benoc had ordered Lnez to concentrate on the riders behind them. He was to be occupied in the other direction when the exchange took place. The tarryn would not be pleased that Lnez knew about the switch.

"I'm afraid my hair is too red," Hannen said. "I guessed at the amount of cambre root to use." She adjusted the sleeves over her wrist blades and smoothed the robe. On Rozel the skirt showed a bit more boot than it should have, and the sleeves showed too much wrist. Slightly shorter, Hannen fit into the costume perfectly, a well-tailored monarch.

Rozel removed Janvian's iref ring. She put it on the younger woman's finger as if her sister's safe keeping went with the gem.

Hannen squeezed Rozel's hand. "Follow the stream through the split in the rocks. Your mount is tethered in the shelter of an overhang. There's a map in the bedroll showing where the company should camp for the next two nights and where you should leave the messages for the scout to find. You can easily reach Nept ahead of us."

Rozel slipped away. Hannen stared after her through light whirls of snowflakes. Lnez suspected each young woman thought the other had the more dangerous task.

The uneasy feeling that had followed him from the stream still haunted him.

THIRTEEN

The Drueten caravan followed the stream through the valley. Here traveling was easier than clinging to a narrow path bordered by a cliff as they'd done the days before. Last night's flurries melted in the sun but kept the mountain shadows white.

A mist curled around the woman dressed in grief. She looked as she always did—veil concealing her face, hair tucked into the collar of her cape for warmth. No one seemed to notice any change.

Oktria gave Lnez concerned glances as they rode. "The altitude's getting to you. You were already pale. Now you look like snow. Some never can live this high up."

"You seem robust enough." Lnez gripped twin hooks on the front of the saddle. Yesterday's uneasiness had grown. The jagged peaks taunted him to lose himself in them, to belong to them when he belonged to no one. The call was a distorted whisper. Rough. Askew. Demented. Pulling his thoughts in a thousand directions.

Oktria seemed to thrive on the atmosphere. "I spent some time in the Walbask range before I took to soldiering."

"A Drueten in Walbask land?"

"It worked out as well as you might expect," Oktria said. "I was involved in a bit of private enterprise."

Lnez could guess what that was. Illegal mining. Amicysk most likely, but there were other gems and ores, all valuable because the mountains were prone to quakes. Many fortune seekers had lost their lives in landslides and cave ins. The Walbask would be the richest clan on the planet if their resources were easier to mine.

"Thought I would own the world," Oktria said, "or at least I would be able to buy most of what was in it with the bounty. Before I found a single stone or nugget, I was attacked by sand-blasted thieves." Oktria spat on the ground for emphasis. "They took my supplies and left me to freeze to death or be eaten by faezads. But not before I sliced off the leader's ear. That's how I got this." She tugged at the single lliwant flower earring she wore.

"You didn't die." Lnez felt as if he would die soon from the motion of the clobben.

"A crazy Walbask miner decided I was worth saving or I wouldn't be here to tell about it." Oktria laughed. "I worried quakes were going to get me and instead it was bandits. There was a shaker near here a winter or so ago. It added a new feeder to the river. You can see how the increase in flow has cut into the banks."

Word traveled through the line that the company would halt for a short break. Lnez heard the order but was unable to do anything about it. Oktria reached over and tugged on the reins of his animal. "You get a drink and rest. I'll tell Benoc the scouts will have to earn their supper."

Dizzily, Lnez half climbed, half fell off the clobben. He

hardly noticed Oktria's leaving. He knelt and splashed freezing water onto his face.

Eyes squeezed shut he saw a milky stone in the stream bed. He opened his eyes to nothing but dull rocks and silt. He plunged a hand into the prickly water and dug into the bed. An oval seemed to jump into his palm. Nausea pitched his stomach as if he were once again on the balcony with the storm pounding in the distance and a fall to a battered death only inches away. He vomited what little was in his stomach and wished he could wretch out more.

A hundred, a thousand sparks called out along miles of the winding river. He jerked back as if from fire and dropped the stone. Nestled in blades of grass, it sang to him as if it owned him.

<>< ><>

Hills became a mountain. A mountain became a tropical forest. Janvian felt as if she'd spent months riding through the southern territory instead of only a few minutes strolling inside a bubble. The concentrated terrain changed with each step. General shapes and structures of the trees and plants were familiar. Odors and the textures of barks, leaves, fronds and flowers were foreign.

The lack of sky betrayed the setting. Artificial light mixed with filtered sun cast undefined shadows. Colors were a shade away from what Janvian's mind told her they should be. The greens held a tint of blue. "So much in"—she cupped a hand and traced a finger across the palm—"a small space."

Jeremy walked beside her on the path, selecting their course at each junction. He seemed to have a destination in mind. His cropped hair made him look almost bald. "It doesn't feel small to me. It feels very big. You're used to outside, which is definitely bigger."

Janvian understood most of what he said. At first, stretched out on a strange bed suffering from heat sickness, she had thought she was in a dream. The strangers moving around her spoke words from the secret language her grandfather had taught her. Some of it she did not know or had forgotten, but a slice of it was familiar.

A woman with dark skin tended her frequently. Janvian was initially alarmed. Some of the Walbask had similar tones, and their tarryn had killed Rojelon. But she was not at Aerrion Fortress. She was somewhere else and Nevran was nearby. The woman had used reassuring tones that transcended translation. All was well and sleep was best.

Two days later when Janvian was stronger and alert, she'd been moved from the medical station to her own room in the habitat. The circular stack of identical living quarters seemed an imaginative variation of the fortress. It occupied the center of the complex with biomes like this one circling it as petals on a flower.

Jeremy led her through hanging vines to a secluded spot. Water tumbled freely over a pleasing arrangement of stones and splashed into a pond. He slipped off his sandals. "This is the only open water for personal use. Do you know how to swim?" He pulled his shirt over his head and stripped off the rest of his clothing.

This morning the topic of Janvian's language lesson with Senior Teacher Tamaki, who sprouted stubby yellow hair, had been water. Either the teacher knew of Jeremy's plans or he was the one who'd suggested this activity. "Yes, I learned to swim when I was young," Janvian said proudly, exactly as she'd practiced only a few hours ago.

Janvian removed her shirt. The exceptionally soft fabric

was tightly woven yet stretched without tearing. She was increasingly aware that much concerning her was discussed and arranged without her direct involvement. She was treated with suspicious politeness. Something tainted the explanations she received, the teaching, and the careful guidance along paths they had already chosen for her.

Her rescuer-guide knew what was being kept from her. He carried it like a burden, tangled in words he did not say, questions he fought not to ask. The young man did not have the discipline to keep them subdued for long. Soon they would escape.

He stood naked in shallow water. Ripples lapped at his ankles. Janvian examined his pale, muscular body. A realization burst into her thoughts. Her diplomatic training abandoned her, and she could not hide her reaction. Nevran had told her about this strange behavior in the Mirage people, but she was still surprised.

Jeremy bent down and flipped a fingertip of water at her playfully. Then he saw her expression. "What's wrong?"

She struggled with the foreign words. Tamaki had not prepared her for this. "Except for clankin and spouse, I have not seen a person without—"

"Without?" Jeremy looked to her for a clue.

Janvian rubbed her exposed forearm.

"Without clothes!" Jeremy said in revelation. "I've broken a custom about clothes. I should've realized. We have them too —when to wear them, when you don't have to." He jumped over the pond's rock border, grabbed his pants in one hand and his shirt in the other. "What do I put on? Or do I put on both?"

At the sight of the sincere young man standing naked before her asking her to choose which part of his appealing body to cover, Janvian collapsed into laughter. She tried to explain that clan customs regarding clothing had little to do with modesty and everything to do with concealing— What was the word? Merede had used it when she'd asked Janvian about the things she'd brought with her. "Weapon," she said. "You are without weapon."

<><><>

"Tell me where they are now." Benoc rode beside Lnez. He knew where the Felcon riders hid. His own scouts had signaled their location. He wanted to hear the rogue's reply to find out if he would answer true.

Lnez stared straight ahead, pale as a corpse. "Two on the left." He couldn't verify they were Felcon, but they were the ones who'd been following the company. "Above the village in the crook between the hills behind the boulder that looks like an angry old man."

Nept was a collection of thin lines of smoke and patches of roofs snuggled together. Benoc purposely searched the terrain to the right. The mystic was correct. In every test he'd devised, the man had proven his worthiness. Still, he was not blood.

An experienced soldier watched for expressions. A poetry book in Benoc's pack held the lines

> *My enemy's jaw shifts;*
> *I know a death daeva*
> *rides Noalgaz through*
> *shadow clouds this night.*

He'd based entire battle strategies on shifting jaws. The blanched face at his side give him nothing to decipher. "Our Felcon watchers are fools. They should split, one on each side."

Oktria guided her animal around boulders at the edge of

the narrow trail so she could stay beside her tarryn. "They'll have a clear view of the performance."

"From one angle only," Benoc said. "We can use that. Don't show surprise when Rozel greets us at the village."

"I wondered how this would play," Oktria said. "That was a slick switch."

"Not slick enough." Benoc adjusted the reins twined in his large fingers. "The rogue detected the substitute's arrival, thought she was an enemy and tried to stop her." The man had behaved well even when there'd been no test, Benoc admitted to himself. Hannen had relayed the event to him, though Rozel had told her not to. Still it proved nothing.

Oktria turned in the saddle and gave the mystic an awkward bow. "Sounds as if you've earned that armband."

Benoc scowled. Oktria showed trust too quickly to the stranger who had tampered with her mind. "It takes more than a single brave act to make a Drueten." He spun his animal toward the troops and shouted orders for their entrance to Nept.

The high mountain village secluded deep within Drueten land was a good choice for a refuge. During the warm months, frequent rain kept the vegetation full. A recent killing frost had withered away the foliage, leaving skeletons that provided little shelter for attackers.

Rock slides from each side of the valley walls sloped to touch the only road, making the entrance easy to defend. A solid slab closed the far end of the oval bowl. Benoc's experienced eye saw the vulnerabilities—the possible arrow assault from the advantage of height, the inability to retreat if defenses did not hold at the barrier he would erect connecting the rock slides. A dark cloud heavy with snow labored over a jutting peak. Nature would protect them until spring. Then they must move.

After the hard journey he ached for the welcoming smell of hearths consuming slabs of strong wood, instead of the camp fires of the past days, made from brush and near rotted deadfall that gave quick, hot heat without lasting warmth. All he could smell right now was his own sweat gone cold.

At Benoc's command the road-weary troops shook themselves to attention and formed a double line along the main street. Villagers stood among the solid stone and wood buildings, giving the hand to shoulder salute. Benoc cursed himself for having to deceive them. People here lived their entire lives never knowing anyone who was not kin. They embraced their duty to a monarch they had never seen.

Many gathered at the far end before a low house, larger than the others. A small figure with flaming hair stood on the raised porch. Oktria stifled a laugh at seeing Rozel finally back to being herself.

"This is a small village," Lnez said to her.

Oktria thought she caught disappointment. The former Speaker held his place in the procession with the stature of someone used to ceremony. Since his illness had set in, he had been reserved and tense, as if a breath from losing control. "Some of the herders take their stock to lower villages for the winter," Oktria said. "We'll be using their homes."

"Can so few people be self-sufficient?"

Oktria shrugged. "They've done so for a long time. They store plenty of food and have a good water supply that doesn't freeze."

"Crafters?"

"All they need. Even a healer." Oktria looked for a response to her hint and saw none, but she'd gotten used to that.

Benoc escorted the purple-clad woman to the platform. Rozel rushed forward and hugged her. "Sister."

The crowd cheered. "Long live the monarch." "Health to the blood heir!"

The veiled figure nodded her appreciation and waved, a water-colored gem sparkling on her hand.

"Long live Janvian!" The crowd carried the chant like a banner. "Long live Janvian!"

Rozel ushered the woman into the house.

Benoc stepped forward to thank the village for its hospitality. Oktria gave Lnez a wink. That ought to give the spies something to report.

Lnez wondered what the wink meant. Perhaps it had something to do with Oktria's starting the cheers for Janvian. He would ask about it later. The milky oval secured in a leather pouch pulsed. He wished Benoc would finish the speech so he could dispose of the churning contents of his stomach. Again.

Apprentices scurried about the shop, collecting scattered tools and covering sculptures at varying degrees of being recognizable forms with thick cloth. A youngster brushed rubble from a workbench to the floor. Another, identical to the first, attempted to sweep with a straw broom and screeched a complaint. They tossed insults as if one person argued with an alter self.

Lnez stood at the doorway, understanding why his scan had made no sense. The image had not prepared him for the raucous darting and bumping and yelling and laughing.

"Come in, come in." The older apprentice pushed the door closed behind him. "Master Tlorieger," she shouted, "an honored clankin is here."

Lnez rubbed the armband on his sleeve. The girl dashed away.

A man sat hunched over a small table by the fireplace. His gray hair spread across bulky shoulders and into a thick beard so that it seemed one continuous growth. He did not look up from his work. "Ah, you arrived with Benoc and little Janvian. Villet, bring a stool for our guest."

Lnez stepped closer to examine the tools in the man's large hands. The carving blades were delicate, miniatures of those a limping boy with a crooked foot carried past. The table held a candle and a disk of swirling green. The beginnings of an etched pattern showed in the jade, faint in the lamp light. "Thank you, but I don't—"

"Villet! Where's that lazy child! The best apprentice I ever had, but don't go telling her that. Villet!" The stonecutter alternated between shouts and mumbles that seemed more comments to himself than to his visitor.

The girl pushed through a curtained doorway carrying a round slab supported by three legs. "I was getting our guest something to sit on."

"Well, then bring it here!" The stonecutter put down his tools and rubbed a thumb across the disk.

Villet set the stool by the fireplace across the table from Master Tlorieger. "I'll fetch hot wine."

"You give away my profits before the deal is struck," Tlorieger said. He bent close to his work, a strand of silver hair teasing the candle flame. "Bring two mugs!"

The apprentice smiled, not the least bit disturbed by her master's sharpness or the threat to his hair—in fact, rather delighted by both.

A small girl stacked wood on a pile by the hearth with a loud clomp as each log fell into place. The twins explored new ways to insult one another. Lnez feared he might faint from the noise and disorder. His legs collapsed. He found the stool under him and the boy who limped easing him onto it. He wanted to express his thanks, but the child was already off to another task.

Villet placed steaming mugs on the table.

Lnez inhaled the sweet, moist aroma. "Master Tlorieger, I am—Lnez. May I speak to you alone?"

"Alone? My worthless apprentices put you up to this so they could leave early. Ah, but very well, a customer is a customer." He flapped his hands at the children, as if a grandfather brushing them away. "Out then. All of you, out."

The apprentices of various ages, five in all, bundled into cloaks. The twins could not agree on who owned which gloves. Villet shoved hats on the little girl and the lame boy. "Goodnight, Master Tlorieger," the group chorused before tumbling out the door.

"Yes, yes, goodnight, goodnight." He called each by name. "Goodnight, Villet, my dear."

Lnez sipped wine and enjoyed the sudden stillness. He touched a curve carved into the green disk, unable to guess what twist the line would take next. Only the master knew the heart of the stone.

"Now, what's this business you bring to me in the middle of the night when most people are relaxing with their close kin?"

Apparently the stonecutter saw nothing strange in his comment, despite Lnez finding him and his apprentices still working. Perhaps this was how he relaxed, and perhaps the youngsters were his equivalent of close kin.

Lnez was the master's senior by a few centuries, but he felt he had lived a shallow life compared to the man. "Do you work with gems?"

"We're a poor village. Where would a simple stonecutter such as I get gems?"

From what Lnez had seen, the village might function

simply, but it was not poor. He pulled the pouch from a cape pocket. He had not dared tuck it closely into his tunic. He dumped the white stone onto the table without touching it. It wobbled between the mugs.

The master put his hands on his knees as if centering himself and stared at the egg. "Hardly a gem."

"There's a clear crystal inside," Lnez said. "I want it cut in a design of symmetrical facets and hung from a chain without piercing the stone. Can you do that?"

Tlorieger picked up the oval, judging the weight of it in his scarred hand. He held it between thumb and forefinger and watched the candlelight roll across the curve. "So deceptive. Who would guess at the beauty within."

Lnez shivered, as if the cutter spoke about him. But he was sure there was no beauty, not in a traitor who belong nowhere and to nothing.

The master shifted the stone from hand to hand, as if testing its balance. "This is a good one. Yes, I can release the crystal. My fee will be high."

"As long as it includes your silence." Lnez had no way to pay.

Tlorieger pulled a scrap of brown paper and a charcoal stick from a pocket and shoved them at him. "Show me what you want, a picture."

Lnez created a vision in his mind of what he hoped would be a functioning crystal and translated it into a drawing as best he could. It would have been easier to place the image into the man's thoughts, but he would not give herself away so completely. Let the crafter guess what he could from what he obviously already knew about crystals. Lnez would not supply him with extra information.

The stonecutter scrutinized the drawing and nodded. "Come back tomorrow night."

Tomorrow night. Lnez dared not probe the man's mind to discover if he was honest. He thanked him and left. It was not far to the cottage that would be his home for a while. The deserted street relaxed his mind, and the cold air made him hungry.

Tomorrow he would have a gemstone again. He hoped it wasn't a mistake. He had done well without one, increasing his skill with each exercise. There was a pride in relying only on yourself and not on some device, no matter how much a part of you it seemed to be. But to be honest, he didn't know if he could survive on his own.

Tlorieger rolled the smooth oval in his hands. A fine stone, rare in its symmetry and inner balance. It would make a powerful crystal. The door opened, allowing in a hint of winter along with Villet and Benoc.

He held out the stone. "My old friend, who've you brought to our little village, eh?"

Benoc took it with a puzzled look.

"Villet, fresh mugs! Quickly! An old story should always be told by the fire with hot wine."

The apprentice had anticipated her master's order, just as she had his wanting to report the stranger's visit to the tarryn. The two men were soon settled before the last embers of the day with steaming tankards. Villet curled up on the warm hearth stones and rested her head against the stonecutter's knee.

Tlorieger began, "Longer than long ago, when I was an apprentice—"

FOURTEEN

"Pregnant." Senior Teacher Tamaki pointed to the illuminated drawing of a woman in profile, her abdomen rounded. The word flashed on the screen beside the drawing as the machine spoke it.

Janvian smoothed a hand over her own bulge. "Pregnant."

The learning center was cluttered with things of varying colors, textures and sizes. The students who manipulated them were equally diverse. Skin tones ranged from pale to tree-bark brown. Hair, never longer than just below the ear, went from sunlight to the black of a cave. Eyes, noses, chins, cheekbones were as different as if they each came from a separate clan. Old, middle and young mingled together. Clan children attended school until they found apprenticeships. Here a student could be any age.

Tamaki worked the learning machine's controller. On the monitor the woman's flesh became transparent, showing the baby head down in the birthing position. Janvian understood the cut away style. The master healer used the technique to explain illnesses, and Benoc used it to show the most vital organs to attack

Fetus.

Janvian touched the controller in a specific spot, as Tamaki had taught her. F-e-t-u-s flashed in blue and an arrow connected the letters to the curled form of the baby. Janvian had requested this lesson so she could communicate better with Merede and Richard, who now conducted her examinations. There was much the medics had tried to explain using these same moving pictures. What she thought they said made so little sense that Janvian was sure she'd misunderstood.

She had assisted at births since she was a child. It was part of the clan way. She'd stood guard when they were on another clan's land. She'd prepared teas and helped the baby struggle free of the womb. There were no Druetens here to perform those functions for her, so she hoped to ask Merede, Tamaki and Jeremy to act as clankin. It was not unheard of. Babies came when they were ready, whether blood relatives were available for protection and assistance or not.

Tamaki moved the controller. Red arrows along the walls of the abdomen indicated pressure from muscle contractions.

Labor.

The diagrams were not completely accurate. The woman's face did not show pain as her body momentarily become her enemy.

The figure of the woman stiffly rotated to a horizontal position as if she were on a table. A red line appeared across the abdomen like a wound. The skin separated, and the baby emerged through the gap.

Delivery.

Delivery? Janvian knew it as forennton, the forced removal

of a baby. The lesson made it appear simple and clean, but it was complex and bloody. The procedure was only performed when normal birth might kill the woman or the child. It left the mother weak for a long time. Sometimes she died, during the operation or afterward, from loss of blood or infection.

Janvian reversed the lesson and reviewed it again. The woman was standing. The baby's head was toward the ground, as it should be. The upright posture helped the child through birthing and allowed the mother to protect them both from attack. She put a finger on the baby and showed it traveling through the birth path and into life. "What is this called?"

Tamaki wrinkled his forehead and studied the screen with bright green eyes. He advanced the motion. Again the woman tilted onto her back. Janvian did not understand the teacher's puzzlement. Were Mirage women incapable of giving birth naturally? Was there a physical defect that always made forennton necessary? There was nothing to indicate that in the drawing.

Tamaki made another attempt while the process repeated. "This is done by a medic. Like Merede or Richard. A cut is made. The baby is taken out. This is called 'delivery.'" He had Janvian repeat several words then build them into a phrase.

"Is the problem with the mother or with the baby?" Janvian asked.

"Sometimes there is a problem," Tamaki said.

That was not what Janvian thought she had asked. They spoke in the formal style. Janvian preferred the condensed format usually used in speech. She pointed to the prone woman, slit open, her child still connected to her by the birth cord. "In this picture. What is the problem?"

"There is no problem," Tamaki said. "That is normal birth."

Janvian felt panic rise up. They wanted her to think this

was normal because her baby was damaged and could not handle the stress of birth. They could not expect such deceit to be successful. She was a grown woman. It was language she lacked, not knowledge.

These people were not used to secrets. They wore even the smallest avoidance in tight lines on their faces. Tamaki's expression held no more than concern for the progress of a student. He had shown Janvian the reality of birth as he knew it. In this land there was no other way.

"Is this what you needed to know?" Tamaki asked.

Janvian nodded, smiling, not allowing her face or breathing to betray her thoughts. Merede and Richard would place Janvian on a table in an unnatural position. They would cut her open and make her as defenseless as the woman in the pictures. They would make her weak, not just for the hours of birth but for days afterward.

Her safety here suddenly felt very fragile. Benoc could not keep Skaln following a false trail for long. The Felcon tarryn would look to other hiding places. Janvian had found her way across the sand, so could Skaln's troops.

She thought of Jeremy standing in the pool, weaponless. These people had never experienced threats from other clans or raiders or thieves. They were incapable of protecting themselves. She could not expect them to defend her and the baby. They were not clankin.

Yes, this was what she needed to know.

She began her own plans for the birth of her child. Alone.

A rainbow flared within the white fire. A golden cage held it, dangling from a thin chain attached to each side. Master

Tlorieger twirled the mesmerizing gem before Benoc. He blinked to break the spell and looked at the stonecutter to see if it had the same effect on him.

Tlorieger calmly fixed his work with an appraising squint. He had labored last night and through the day to coax this masterpiece from the misty stone.

There were no apprentices in the shop when Benoc arrived. The one from Nept lived with his parents. The others, from villages scattered throughout the mountains, were lodged in various homes. It was a privilege to have one's talent shaped by the master. He chiseled raw youth into skilled crafters as carefully as a boulder became a graceful bird at his hands.

Benoc had been an apprentice himself when he first came to Nept, in training to his mother who'd been called upon to settle a dispute over grazing lands with the village to the east. Torn between the scholarly profession of his father and the physical action of his mother, he'd seemed to balance on two logs in the middle of a river, unsure of which one to abandon.

Instead of riding the disputed land looking for old markings as his mother had instructed, Benoc had sat at Master Tlorieger's side. Sneezing from the powdered rock that clouded the air, he'd watched the stonecutter sculpt an irregular chunk of black obida marble into a living rask. The animal's snout pointed into the wind and a front paw was raised in frozen motion.

While Tlorieger worked, he had talked of the picture in his head, showing him the shape that lived inside the stone. Mind and hands had worked together, intelligence and action in tandem. Two logs could be strapped together to better ride the water's current.

Benoc thought of that sculpture now as he watched the necklace spin.

The door opened, chiseled dust sifted across the floor with the bitter night breeze. Lnez stepped in. His eyes flicked to Benoc, registering no surprise. Then his gaze locked on the spark gently swinging from Tlorieger's hand. He walked toward it as if it pulled him in, eyes ablaze. "Benoc, I should've known the second soul I sensed was you and not Villet. Master Tlorieger, is this how you keep a secret?" He reached for the white flame, fingers trembling.

Benoc snatched the jewel from Tlorieger and held it encased in his fist. "What goes on here is rightfully mine to know."

Lnez squeezed his eyes shut. "Am I not allowed a trinket for my own enjoyment?"

"A trinket or a weapon?"

Tlorieger put an arm around Lnez. "I told him because he should know your strength so he can make use of it. But he seems to think you'd wield the stone against your own clan instead of for them."

"He's not kin." Benoc shook his fist. The facets cut into his palm.

"You told me he rushed to protect Rozel," Tlorieger said. "Sounds like a hot-headed Drueten to me."

Benoc took a calming breath. He knew who was really being called a hot-head. "He's not blood. That can't be changed."

Lnez opened his eyes. "I am a rogue. I claim to be nothing more."

Tlorieger released Lnez. "Make a man a tarryn and he loses his eyesight," he half grumbled to himself. "Benoc, you've spent too much time among foreigners." The stonecutter stomped across the workshop and through a curtained doorway.

"I've no way to convince you of my intentions," Lnez said.

The rogue's health seemed to have improved in the past day. His creased cheeks, so pale during the last part of the journey, held a tint of red. The dark crescents below his eyes had receded slightly. But he'd lost much weight since Benoc first saw him in Rozel's tent, as if the flesh had been sliced from him.

Shuffling and scraping came from behind the curtain. Benoc wondered how Tlorieger could defend this stranger, this rogue. And what did he mean by attacking Benoc's eyesight? It was as good as when he was a youngster. Others might have had their vision dimmed by age, but his was still as sharp as a phianj's.

Tlorieger emerged through the flapping fabric, huffing under the strain of a bundle wrapped in cloth. Benoc quickly cleared a space on the crowded workbench, although he felt the effort the stonecutter showed was more pretend than real. No doubt the bundle was heavy, and the master was an old man; but he had carried boulders most of his life. Muscles bulged in his large shoulders and forearms.

The crafter hefted the burden onto the splintered wood with a thud. He ran a sleeve across his forehead and looked from Benoc to Lnez to make sure he had their full attention. When he was satisfied that they were sufficiently curious, he pulled off the wrappings with a flourish.

The sculptured face of the woman was lined by a long life. Large, wide set eyes looked with anticipation. High cheekbones slanted toward a long, thin nose. Her small mouth was a breath away from a smile, and her narrow chin tilted at a slightly mocking angle. A small scar twisted along the jawline. The face seemed pleased with the many years in her past and eager for those yet to come.

Tlorieger put a knuckle under Lnez's chin and lifted his

head to duplicated the angle. Firelight put the faces, stone and flesh, half in shadow.

A pricking crawled up Benoc's spine. He gave a long whistle. They were the same face—one relaxed and eager, the other tense. The carved one seemed the most alive.

"My father's work." Tlorieger ran a proud hand over the ripples of hair twined along the neck. "The model was his grandmother, my great-grandmother. A Drueten from her father's and mother's lines back through spoken records."

Lnez broke the pose. "Is that how I look?"

Benoc scratched the skin beneath his silvery beard. He should have recognized the features. Lnez was kin who had proven his lor, though Benoc had not recognized it at the time. Mystic or not, honor was due him. And privileges. The rogue's behavior had been exemplary, while his had been disgracefully.

"I apologize for my behavior." Benoc held out the crystal by its yellow chains.

Lnez looked at the gem with hungry sadness. "I'm still a mystic."

"You're Drueten." Benoc took his hand and put the necklace into it.

"Sandblasted snakes!" The stonecutter took the jewel from Lnez. He put the chains around his neck and fastened the clasp. "Most inconvenient to be clutching it in your hand all the time."

The magnificent crystal set in the golden spiral rested below the collarbone, clashing with his simple shirt. He shivered and calmed. "Perfect."

Benoc turned to Tlorieger. "Thank you for correcting my grave error."

"Don't get all tarryn-noble on me," Tlorieger said. "You would've noticed yourself if you had a crafter's eye."

Lnez pulled a pouch from his belt and dumped the contents onto the bench beside the statue of his kin. Coins rolled and bumped along the rough wood. "Is this enough to pay for your splendid work? If not, I'll get more."

Benoc watched the pieces find resting places in the multi-colored dust. "I didn't know rogues were rich."

"This came from your soldiers," Lnez said.

Tlorieger picked up a shiny circle, flipped it into the air and snatched it in flight. "I've never known a soldier yet who handed over coins without an argument."

"Oktria showed me how to play cards and roll dice," Lnez said.

"And you won all this?" Benoc asked.

"I have certain advantages," Lnez said.

"You cheated clankin?" Benoc bellowed.

Lnez looked blankly at the tarryn. "Did I do something wrong? I've never had need for money. I didn't know how to get any to pay Master Tlorieger until I saw the soldiers betting."

"That'll teach them not to gamble!" Benoc grumbled.

Tlorieger scraped the coins into a gritty pile and counted them. "Benoc, haven't you paid this man for his services?"

"I've never had a mystic within my troops." The realization hit Benoc. A rogue mystic was one of his clankin, one of his soldiers, his to command. The weapon he had speculated about was now tied to him by blood. "You're on the payroll now." He would still have to be cautious. The man did not think of himself as a Drueten. Not yet. Bonds could be forged that would make the rogue useful in the move that must be made next.

Tlorieger scooped a few pieces back into the purse and handed it to Lnez. "This is what's left of your spoils after paying my fee."

Lnez felt the weight of the bag. "Did I give you a fair price?"

"More than fair. You're a most generous customer. I wish that all who came to my shop were so appreciative of my skills."

Benoc directed the mystic toward the door. "Come, Lnez." For the first time he used the name Oktria had given the man. "We've important matters to discuss."

FIFTEEN

Thick layers of gray gauze hung low over jagged peaks. Rozel inhaled a moist, heavy scent. She urged her meran to a quicker gait. Oktria and Lnez matched the pace with their clobbens. The animals snorted protests. A two-hand depth of white already on the ground obscured the trail's uneven terrain and made progress tedious. Since leaving Nept, snow had teased them. What she now saw in the clouds and smelled in the chilled air was more menacing. They needed shelter before the blizzard hit.

Behind them the high mountains had turned solid white. Nept was surely snowbound. Too early. They should have reached the foothills before winter gales set in. At least the lie about Janvian's location would hold until warm winds tore down the natural barrier.

Rozel had decided to believe what she needed to in order to agree to Benoc's plan. Janvian was alive with the Mirage Clan and would return soon. For now, she would play the rebel. She would ride straight down the enemy's throat, march into

Aerrion Fortress and plant herself before the throne. Let Skaln and the Baerryns choke on that. And let them try to dispose of her. She had an experienced fighter and her own personal rogue to help her through their games.

Rozel chuckled. She had one old warrior and one outcast mystic of uncertain loyalty. Having an army at her back would be much better. But even if Benoc had troops to spare, he could not assign them to her. Drueten Clan supported Janvian as the rightful monarch. Rozel and those with her would be labeled traitors the moment she presented her petition. They might be killed by their own zealous clankin.

Rozel shrugged off those thoughts for more immediate concerns. If the storm closed the passes ahead, they would be trapped, unable to go forward or backward. They would be stranded with limited supplies and no hope of rescue.

There's only one way it could be worse, she told herself. *I could be stuck in Nept behind a veil.*

Oktria watched the weather as closely as Rozel. She had more experience with the route they took. "Around the bend the trail narrows. Just beyond there's a cave we can use."

"Three waiting ahead. To the right." Lnez spoke with a new confidence. His mystic duties seemed to need less concentration. Although often silent, he sometimes participated in conversations, usually by asking questions. From what Rozel had pieced together, Lnez's life as Speaker had been as isolated from the normal world as Rozel's had been while disguised as Janvian.

"All on the same side?" Oktria laughed. "They must be Felcons. The two who followed us to Nept have a friend."

All right, Rozel acknowledged, there were other ways the situation could be worse, and one of them had just popped up. "Maybe the cold keeps them together. They probably had a fire until they saw us coming."

Their Felcon shadows had disappeared soon after the company had set up a permanent camp in the valley town. It could be them. The conditions were too bad for thieves to be about.

Oktria flipped the corner of her cape back to reveal a sword. "In this country they can see us from far off and pick the right spot for an ambush."

Rozel surveyed where the trail bent close against a mountain wall then narrowed into a gorge. Riders would have to enter single file. That's the place she'd choose.

The wall would hide them from view for a while, giving them maneuvering time. They could abandon the well-worn trail and make one of their own, but the only alternate route was up. And to the right. And straight into the ambushers. "We can't slip past them," Rozel said, "so we'll give them a surprise."

Most of the stations hummed with the sound of machinery. In contrast the agristat dripped and swished with the constant movement of liquid. Hanging plants formed a canopy of green leaves and white roots that sucked nourishment from moist air. Long rows of narrow tables supported shallow tanks filled with plants, their roots immersed in a nutrient solution.

Janvian stuck a fat probe into the liquid equidistance between roots as she had been taught. The box connected to the rod beeped and registered a series of lighted symbols. She copied the foreign numbers onto the paper that was not paper with the pen that needed no ink. Then she checked again to be certain of her accuracy.

The box almost tingled in her hand. She was surrounded by real machines. They were not the flat representations on parchment stuffed into trunks in the bowels of the fortress. They had curved surfaces, flashing bumps, and changing symbols. They were constructs alive with their own energy. And Janvian currently lived inside the most complex one of them all.

Senior Agriculturalist Bartholomew shuffled over and held out his hand for her slate. He always moved as if his sandals were too big for his feet. She handed him the rectangle that was stone but not stone. After working in agristat for almost a quarter month she could distinguish between acceptable numbers and ones that indicated adjustments were needed. A quarter of an Alchorel month, she reminded herself. A Mirage month was shorter.

Bartholomew scratched his large nose and held the slate at arm's length. "Umm." The numbers were within the target range. He handed back the slate and patted her on the back. "Umm."

Janvian felt as if she had received abundant praise. Her first attempts had met with "humphs" from Bartholomew and lengthy instructions from Senior Student Rasch that were full of words she did not know. A scrunched-faced, serious woman, Rasch disapproved of anything less than perfect. She watched Janvian's every move as if an action might destroy the dome. In fairness, the advanced student treated everyone with equal intolerance.

Sometimes Bartholomew's "humphs" were not directed at her work but at the numbers. He would scratch out calculations on his own slate and order alterations in the gizmos that managed the hydroponic tables. But all was well today.

Janvian pointed to long, tapered leaves extending from a single core. The root immersed in liquid had a central tuber surrounded by a tangle of spindly offshoots. "Senior, what's the name of this plant?"

Bartholomew stretched his thick neck and tucked his chin into his chest. He squinted at the greenery and answered with a string of syllables she could not follow. "That's the Latin name, Student Janvian. Old language, Latin. Only used by crusty scientists such as myself. Usually called munch, although I can't think why. Something Senior Geneticist Marla created, when such things could still be done."

Student Janvian. The title was honorary. She hardly deserved it. She had not done the hard study the others had to earn their positions. Her presence here was a courtesy because she insisted on doing a share of the work for the hospitality she received.

Most people wanted to treat her like a pampered curiosity. She knew her pregnancy had much to do with it. In any clan town at any given time there were many pregnant women going about their normal routines. Here she had seen none. It was a strange village. There were so few children. No wonder they treated her with the care given fragile things. Merede had reluctantly sanctioned her firmly stated request to do more than take walks and study the language.

"Please tell me what munch is used for," Janvian said.

"You probably ate some for supper last night. And you'll probably eat some tonight too. Now enough. Your shift is over. Go do something frivolous. Humph." Bartholomew walked away, sandals scrapping.

Janvian turned in her slate under the suspicious supervision of Senior Student Rasch. The readings would be taken to a room protected from the humidity and transferred to permanent records.

She exited through the green airlock. Every section had the

special tiny room separating it from the whole. She followed a corridor to the blue entrance of the habitat. A waterfall cascaded down the high court and splashed onto jumbled rocks. Real rocks. The only things Janvian had found that came from outside. The area was surrounded by clear fabric that was not woven. It formed windows for the stacks of private rooms.

Jeremy was waiting for her. "Today we'll visit the prairie." He led her to a section marked in orange. In the double airlock he examined the floors, walls and ceiling. "Some of the animals are small. They can get out if you aren't careful. The loss of even one can change the balance."

The balance of what? Janvian wondered.

The final door slid open to a stream meandering through flat grassland. Low hills sloped to a horizon of bushes. Scattered workers tended plants or handled creatures with unfamiliar markings and almost-familiar shapes.

Jeremy and Janvian took a gravel walkway, joining other strollers enjoying a free shift. A breeze swirled a skeleton of dried brush across their path. Jeremy snatched it and handed it to a worker for recycling.

Janvian's grasp of the careful management here was growing keener with these excursions. People's behavior told her more than the explanations of how air and water were purified and recirculated. The complex grew or manufactured every new thing it needed. Jeremy, her other rescuer Dougal, and a few others were experimenting with what they could glean from the Wilde, hoping to add fresh resources.

The expanse of waving grasses appeared removed from anything mechanical. "Are there machines here?" Janvian asked.

"Mostly in the floors and along the walls," Jeremy said. "I'll show you."

They climbed over a fence and hiked to the far perimeter

of trees. Janvian smelled blossoms and observed changes in the varieties of foliage, from green to gold to blue. Over a hill and behind a cluster of bushes a metal box rested on a floor void of dirt and vegetation. The rectangle was as tall as Janvian. A huge tube protruded from the side and arced upward along the sweep of the biome where it disappeared into the wall.

"There're similar units camouflaged at regular intervals around the circumference. Each biome has them to circulate air."

The light dust on the floor had not been disturbed for some time until they arrived. The tube was cool and flexed inward at Janvian's touch. She put her hand on the metal box. It was warm and solid and hummed like Bartholomew. "Do the workers need to tend these often?"

"I think they run by themselves."

Janvian did not want to seem too interested in this spot. "Machines. If you lived on a real prairie, you wouldn't need them." She returned to the path, making note of a slight irregularity in the terrain that placed one bush askew from the others. She checked the angle and distance to the airlock.

"This *is* a real prairie," Jeremy said.

A herd of animals Janvian didn't recognize grazed nearby. Two larger beasts galloped together in the distance. One turned its head, displaying a flash of white. "Fujin!" Janvian gave a whistle. The meran beside it tossed its mane, also showing a white blaze. The second animal rushed to her, skidded to a halt and thrust his muzzle against her neck. He smelled of soap and sweet grass.

Jeremy kept his distance. The horses were why he had brought her here. "They're identical, right down to their genes. I've been waiting for you to learn more words before I told you. And for yours to be released from quarantine. They're clones.

I'll explain that later." He gestured to the duplicate. "That horse is very old. It's one of Marla's creations."

"Horse," Janvian said. "In my language it's a *meran*." She cooed to Fujin in Lorchan. The animal pressed against her. Janvian closed her eyes and stroked the soft fur, feeling less alone.

"I thought it was a *fujin*," Jeremy said.

"Man, Jeremy." Janvian pointed to him, as he had pointed to objects when he first struggled to explain his world to her. Then she pointed to herself. "Woman, Janvian." She rubbed her cheek against the white blaze. "*Meran*, Fujin."

"Understand. Yes," Jeremy said as she had during those first conversations.

Janvian bent and touched a long, tapered leaf, one of many protruding from a central core. Fujin followed her hand and sniffed at the plant. "Bartholomew said Marla created this plant and you said Marla created a *meran*. Is created a way of saying found?"

"Created is more like made or built."

Janvian shook her head. "How do you built a *meran*?"

"Build," Jeremy said automatically. "We used to be able to build animals and plants. That is, Marla and seniors before her could. They all died before anyone else could learn the process. The documents that explained it were destroyed in the same accident." He grieved for the loss of knowledge as much as for the loss of friends. "The horse is controversial. Some people think an animal that large takes too many resources. But it's important for research." He didn't say there was a faction that thought it should be dissected and were eager to do it.

"You've told me about Nevran," Jeremy said. "Did he take a horse with him when he left here?"

"Yes," Janvian said. "He took Fujin. The same horse he

bring." She did not understand 'created.' These people were not gods. Not Alchorel gods anyway.

Jeremy frowned as if he could not accept what he heard. "Do you understand the difference between 'take' and 'bring'?"

Janvian cupped her hands and pushed them toward him as if offering something. "Bring." Then she pulled her hands back. "Take." She thought that was correct. Although she learned Mirage words that were equal to Lorchan ones, they did not always carry the same scope or subtly.

She realized Nevran had tried to prepare her, giving her puzzles in their secret language. "Tell me," Nevran had said, "what is a mountain?" And she had spoken of rocks piled to the sky. Nevran had interrupted, "What is sky?" And she had said sky was where rain and snow came from. Nevran had asked, "What is snow." And so the game had continued.

But she had been a child then. The important nuances were yet to be learned. She would discuss "created" with Tamaki. Right now she had a different objective.

Janvian again bent and fingered the long leaves of the plant Bartholomew called munch. "Plants like these grow near the dome, where I live. During the cold time of year, we put them in pots." There was no word here for winter or season.

"Munch grows where you live? For how long?" Jeremy asked.

"If watered and in sun, a long time."

"No. That isn't what I meant." Jeremy paced away from her and then back. "Have these plants always grown where you come from? Before you were born? Before Nevran was born?"

"They are in drawings and writings before Nevran's mother." If she failed and brought up the munch again later, Jeremy might guess how desperately she wanted it. "We put them in pots and keep them inside."

"Inside what?"

"Inside a room." Inside-outside, another complicated language problem. "Is it allowed to have this plant in my room here?"

"Sure. Some people do that. I'll arrange it."

"Thank you for bringing me to Fujin." She ruffled the dark mane. The munch must not seem too important.

Jeremy looked from the plant to the meran as if he saw something else entirely.

~

CHAPTER

SIXTEEN

"**A**storm be coming. Best do this quick and get to camp." The thin voice held little enthusiasm for the enterprise. "Not much of a way to make a living."

"Not much of a living to be made," a deep voice grumbled. "Hard times for honest thieves when clans be squabbling like honking fowl."

Thieves. Rozel had hoped they were Felcons. She knelt below the crest of the ridge, sword ready. The legs of her breeches were tucked into her boots and the boots tied closed above the knee to keep out the snow.

Oktria's sword rested on a shoulder. Lnez carried no blade. When quizzed he could not recall ever using one, although he confessed to poking a kitchen knife at a furry creature who'd threatened a vegetable garden in his care some uncountable years ago. Rozel was not concerned. The rogue's mind was weapon enough.

Rozel held up two fingers to Lnez. The mystic did not understand the gesture. She pointed toward the two voices they heard with a questioning look then held up two fingers again. She pointed again and showed three fingers. Lnez watched the pantomime without expression. Rozel resisted making a rude gesture that conveyed her frustration.

Then Lnez grasped the meaning and responded with three fingers. Although one was silent, all of the watchers were together.

The animals had been left a distance away. Oktria had led the climb to high ground and had found a spot where brush hung with fat blossoms of snow covered their crossing over the ridge. Through the increasing wind and icy flakes, they had crept below it to a good position.

"They be so slow," Deep Voice said.

"Should be back in sight by now," Thin Voice said.

Rozel signaled and they rushed into the clearing. "And here we are."

The three sat on folded blankets before the charred remains of a fire. They reached for weapons. Their bodies suddenly jerked with uncontrollable shivering. Horror froze the faces of a dark, ruddy-cheeked man and a pox-marked woman. Curling into their cloaks, they searching for warmth that was not there.

The third thief fought a frigid gale racing through his head. He stretched a shaking hand toward a waiting handbow, cocked and ready. He grasped it and pointed it at Lnez. Sweat beaded his face and turned to frost. With great effort he thumbed the trigger. The arrow went astray, whooshing past the solitaire into the snow.

The thief flung himself forward, grabbing cloth at his opponent's neck. Lnez stumbled and fell, taking the man with him. The thief rolled clear, agile now that he was free of freezing thoughts. He got his feet under him and found himself against Rozel's sword. Defiantly he smirked at the blow that would cut him down.

Rozel did not swing the metal. A whimpering coward she could lay open without a thought, for that was the kind who begged mercy then slide a blade into your back. Sword to sword, she could run an opponent through without splashing blood on her cloak. A fighter accepted the possibility of that fate with the heft of the hilt. But a weaponless soul who spat in the daeva's eye deserved more. Wind stirred the thief's hair, exposing an ear. Rozel realized this was not her battle.

Oktria held the other two at sword point, a collection of confiscated weapons at her feet. She did not agree with Rozel's restraint. "He would've shot us down from here."

Deep Voice seemed recovered from the cold blast. "We would've told you to put your valuables on the ground and be on your way."

"At arrow point," Oktria added.

Deep Voice shrugged. "That be how it's done."

Lnez gasped and wheezed. Rozel would have gone to him, but she felt it healthier to watch the thieves. She preferred a fair fight, but she was not foolish. Oktria gave the mystic a quick glance but held her ground.

"Your friend used a strange weapon." Deep Voice appeared a lot braver now than a few moments ago. "I've still got the raging shivers. Seems I should check for frostbite. You too, Ham?" He laughed and slapped Thin Voice's arm. The woman smothered his roar with a look.

Panting, Lnez staggered to his feet. He wiped slush from a scraped cheek. The tasseled tie was ripped from one side of his cape and dangled, still knotted, to its twin. He straightened the covering about his shoulders. A swatch of torn cloth hung from the neck of his shirt, exposing the crystal at his throat.

"Blast me to sand." Deep Voice said, expressing everyone's

surprise. "It's another one of them sparkles what look like ice. Never seen one in my whole life, and now I seen two in less days than it takes to die of thirst."

"For a clobben to die of thirst maybe," thin-voiced Ham said. "Uz, your tongue would've blackened twice between now and then."

Lnez pulled his cape over the jewel. "You've seen one before?"

"And had a friend killed for the owning of it." Ham's tone conveyed her loss.

"I realize you're the one with the sword," the third thief said to Rozel, "but since you're not going to kill me and the storm might, we could declare a truce. We'll provide shelter if you'll tell us what you can about the jewel your kin wears."

"Thieves' trick," Oktria snapped.

"Think about the truce you offer and the place of shelter," Lnez said.

The man gave his head a shake.

"What be this?" Uz, the deep-voiced man protested.

"I seen a mystic do that once." Ham reached to her belt for a knife that was not there. It rested in the pile at Oktria's feet. "He be a rogue! Sand! Get out of Amud's mind!"

"Quiet," Oktria ordered. "He'll do no harm in there. Might even do some good."

Lnez blinked and looked at the ground. "He believes he offers honest terms. But there are others at the camp."

Snowflakes clung to one another and swirled around them, a promise of what was to come. Right now Rozel would snuggle up to a lice-ridden, one-eyed hermit with swamp breath if it meant a fire and hot food. But Amud the thief did not have to know that. "Are you the leader? Can you speak for them as well?"

"What Amud says be for all," Ham said.

Amud smiled as if he knew the deal was already sealed. "I'm listened to and no one will cross me in this even if they disagree."

A curtain of snow swept over the ridge. Amud put up an arm for protection. "Whatever else we've done, we've never left a soul to the winter mountains to die."

Not this time anyway, Rozel thought.

The volumes were neatly bound. The paper covers were only slightly heavier than the internal pages. Jeremy spread the manuscripts across his bed. He had resisted opening them on the walk from the archive to his room. Teacher Isabelle had protested his strange request, but she could not deny records to a senior. The quiet keeper of Sanctuary II's archives had sighed and sent Student Raji scurry to retrieve the requested journals. She had released them into Jeremy's hands with an unnecessary lecture about their value.

These may be more important than you can imagine, he'd wanted to tell her. Instead he'd thanked her and promised not to spill anything on them.

Printed records spanned less than eighty years. When the storage cubes became unreliable and the comps that deciphered them started to fail, a change became imperative. They learned to make paper and ink, and they revived the ancient art of cursive.

Jeremy ran his hand over the standard information on the cover of the oldest: name, year of birth, biome, journal classification, time span. Student Marla, 285, Genetics Station, Personal Journal, 9.7.303 to 8.7.304. It was thick for only one year. The handwriting was small and precise with a curvy flair. Marla had been 18 when she had started this record. Newly accepted as Senior Geneticist Ambrose's student, she would eventually advance to take his place, and she would bring new plants and new animals into the stagnant biosphere.

Jeremy hadn't studied this early part of Marla's career. He had read and reread the journals and notes from when she was a teacher and then a senior. He had memorizing long passages and had copying sections into his own journals. They chronicled many of her great accomplishments; but important parts, including the munch and the horse, were not among the detailed drawings and careful descriptions. He had finally concluded that the precious information had been destroyed in the accident. Along with vital equipment. And vital minds.

The explosion had left genstat limited in what it could do and how much it could do. Jeremy and the students he taught and supervised had resources for nothing beyond the priorities: Improving the food stock they already had, and making people. They'd been reduced to almost mindlessly following set procedures.

The ability to clone was gone, and there were not enough spare materials and research time to reconstruct the equipment and the process. The same was true of identifying and correcting genetic defects.

Plants and animals were easy. Less than satisfactory products were discarded. There was no margin for error with people. Jeremy had too few sets of genes in the library to begin with. Every flaw that showed up meant the elimination of at least two donors. Sometimes the genetic relatives had to be marked as unusable too. Cradle six was now empty because he'd chosen the wrong combination.

We maintain, Jeremy thought. *We no longer discover.*

Since his walk with Janvian earlier today, the munch and

the horse had obsessed him. He assumed Marla had produced them by manipulating and combining the genes of similar plants and animals. His efforts to reverse engineer them back to their source materials had been inconclusive.

Munch had been her most valuable creation. The greens provided key nutrients that had almost disappeared from their diet. It had been constructed here, in this sealed environment. It couldn't possibly grow where Janvian came from.

What about the horse? The most reasonable explanation was that Marla had made two. One must have escaped, although Jeremey couldn't image how. It could have found its way to the land where the clans lived. That was possible. The confusing conversation with Janvian about the plant and Fujin must have been what Dougal called a 'language malfunction.'

The pages fluttering through his fingers suddenly changed. The paper and ink were definitely of a higher quality. The cursive, still neat and familiar, now formed strings of unknown symbols. Inserted into the middle of the journal, this section was not part of the original.

Intrigued, he skimmed the volume for the next year. Again the beginning read easily then was transformed, as if to a different language. What knowledge required such secrecy? Jeremy followed the strange writing line by line. Familiar words were embedded in the code—technical equipment, terms specific to genetics.

It wasn't Latin, which was only used for scientific classification. There were many languages in the universe, but they were not used, or even studied, in Sanctuary. Only Amersan had every been spoken here.

And Lorchan.

<><><>

The cave was long and narrow, little more than a bulge in a network of twisting tunnels that spread through the mountain like the burrowing of a large animal. Smoke from a fire burning in a stone-lined pit clogged the air before escaping into a blackened crevice in the high ceiling. Amud sipped hot soup—melted snow, meat of a local critter and spices. After days and nights of this capricious mountain he feared he would never be warm again. He was not a soul to worry about dying; but after the rogue's frigid attack he hoped that, whatever death was, it was not cold.

Amud watched the visitors quietly eat the meal Propaulnem, the mother of his daughter, served them. Then the woman returned to the large cave room where the rest of the company passed the time. Her parting look told Amud she was ready if he needed more assistance than Ham and Uz could provide.

The band should have been south by now at their winter campsite in Walbask territory. Or at least in Aerrion City. But clans fought and raiders crossed borders, making travel dangerous no matter what armband a soul wore. And the fortress city was full of the worst kind of thieves.

The Druetens sat on boulders around the fire pit with Uz and Ham. The rogue was a stranger, but the other two Amud recognized before they introduced themselves. Any thief worth half a coin knew the red-haired sister of the monarch and the warrior closest to the Drueten tarryn.

The thieves knew of the royal escort to Nept. Why had these three left the village? Amud tugged at his ear and paced. Whenever he moved, Oktria tracked him.

Rozel, put down her bowl. "We thank you for your hospitality." Amud appreciated her neither falsely praising the soup nor justly belittling it.

Uz wiped a sleeve across his chin and plunked his bowl to the floor. "Now then, let's talk about those sparkles. I figures our side of it be worth some coin."

"Possibly," Lnez said. "You say your friend has one."

The mystic had tied up his shirt to hide the gem, but Amud could not forget it was there any more than Uz and Ham could. He was not what Amud expected of a rogue. On the ridge his probe for the truth had been gentle, pleasant in a way. He had explored only the surface thoughts of the cave and the offer of a truce. He had not delved deeper where he had no license to go. The thief took it as an assurance that the three could be trusted among his own companions, whatever their mission.

Amud had learned to distinguish between honest souls and honest business. The first were not always engaged in the last, nor the last always performed by the first. He judged people and left them to judge their actions for themselves.

"Not *has*," Uz said. "It be *had*. Yadul had it then didn't. A dangly thing, a big drop of water stretched all out." He elongated imaginary liquid with his fingers.

"Or one of them icicles what hang from rocks when the sun melts the snow," Ham said. "Only fat and sliced smooth down a side. More like half a 'cicle."

Uz leaned toward the rogue. "'Course, Lnez, if I could see yours close up, I'd be able to tell if that one be like it or not."

The warrior Oktria made a hardly noticeable shift. A weapon was ready. Amud resisted the instinct to protect his friend. Uzec would have to handle this one himself.

The rogue did not seem threatened. He diffused the pointed request with a question of his own. "How did your friend get this jewel?" He was fairly certain the size of the gem was being exaggerated.

Uz could not resist a willing audience, especially when he

had a good story to tell, sad as it was. He rolled his burley frame away from Lnez. "I'll not forget any of it. Not with a dozen tankards of hard ale in me."

Oktria moved slightly and the hidden weapon was at rest.

"We be in the great center of the monarchy, Aerrion City. In the Split Hoof, an establishment of uncertain repute." Events magnified under the lens of Uzec's talent. He recounted the trained eipy's tricks and the appearance of the old man. Ham embellished the tale with her own details.

Oktria scowled, tight as a strung bow. Lnez sat calmly, giving no clues to his thoughts. Amud concentrated on Rozel's reactions. She probably was familiar with the tavern. The monarch's sister was known to gamble and carouse in such places. She raised her eyebrows at Yadul's speculation about a mystic plot against the monarchy but did not seem shocked.

Uz described finding Yadul, both the crystal and his life snatched away, in the mire behind the Hoof. "Imagine, our old friend and the monarch both sliced on the same night."

The three guests seemed to stop breathing. To Amud, the glance between Oktria and Rozel was louder than a dozen exclamations. He scratched the beginning of a beard. He was no longer in a center of commerce where many styles were accepted. This was Drueten land, and it required that he looked as if he belonged. He was letting his hair grow, but it barely fell to his chin. "Might the crystal have something to do with Rojelon's death?" he asked.

Oktria locked her dark eyes on him. "You were in the city. You're better able to answer that."

"You were in the fortress," Amud said. "I know who you are."

"I don't think you do." Oktria's black hair, free of silver despite her age, swooped to her waist. "I must know how you came by that earring."

Amud's hand went to the miniature lliwant. "That's best left for another time."

Oktria turned her head and pushed a wing of shiny strands behind her right ear, revealing her own bloom. "We'll speak of it now."

~

CHAPTER

SEVENTEEN

Oktria had waited through the courtesies of a sparse meal served with cautious glances. The leanness of the tattered thieves told her they had little to share, yet share they did. She was not fed bland soup while roasts sizzled in another chamber. All ate the same. Amud and his pack were good hosts—for thieves.

Amud sat on a flat-topped boulder. During the meal, he had kept as careful an eye on her as she on him. He was a fighter, this one, able to offer you soup or put a dagger in your throat with the same calm. Someone had trained him young and trained him well. If, as he said, he truly knew who they were, then despite all the hospitality, Oktria needed an answer. Yes or no, did an enemy fill her bowl, share his fire with her, give her a place to lay her gear? Tonight while she slept, it would make a difference in how many eyes she kept open.

"I hold my oath binding whatever your tale," Oktria told Amud. "If there's a feud between us, we'll settle it when we're free of the truce. And I declare to you and to all that this matter doesn't concern my kin, only me. I've so sworn before Tarryn

Benoc of the Drueten." She would not say if the man she'd left with one ear had been friend or enemy, so Amud would not slant his tale to appease her.

"Most here know the story," Amud said.

Not from you, Oktria thought. She doubted the thief told much about himself.

Amud rubbed his forehead with his knuckles then began. "Some years ago six of us went into the Walbask mountains in search of whatever precious ore we could find. Our sweat brought the reward we'd hoped. We found a small deposit of amicysk, valuable enough by itself. As sometimes happens, it also held a dull blue eye of gaedennen."

There seemed no joy in remembering the great wealth. The Walbask mountains did not gradually rise and fall as those enclosing them now. They were unstable crags and narrow ledges that shook with sudden tremors.

Blustery Uz stared at shadows, a twitch in the hand gripping his knee. Ham backed away from the flickering light until the rock wall supported her. Amud, Uz, and Ham. They were bound together by this tale. Oktria wondered who the other three in the expedition had been.

Amud said, "We made our way down the high mountains and had almost reached the low ones when the largest man I've ever seen blocked our path. He had yellow hair, a handsome face, and a wicked smile. His only ear was adorned with this." Amud touched the blossom on his own lobe. "He feigned friendship and used his clever tongue while the rest of his company circled us. Two of us were killed in the attack.

"Thieves might lift a coin or two from one another, but only scum behave as they did. They took the fortune in ore we'd wagered our lives to get. They could have done it simply, taken what we had and been gone. Instead they wounded us for sport and left us, thinking we'd soon be dead."

Ham came from the shadows and placed a hand on Amud's shoulder, tears sliding down her cheeks. She seemed unable or unwilling to wipe them away. Uz rose and moved behind them, putting an arm around Ham's waist.

Amud took strength from his friends. "We don't die easily. One comrade walked a long road before her daeva came. The three of us patched up our slices and tracked the scum. We gave them clean deaths, unlike what they'd left us to. I'm not a soul for trophies. True friends were gone and no gesture could bring them back. I took the token to remind me of what a thief should never be."

"Whose hand swung the sword that struck down the one-eared man?" Oktria gave no hint of her own feelings.

"Mine," Uz said. "If that don't please you, I'll fight you right now."

"My hand," Ham said. "Your scuffle's with me."

"I have loyal companions," Amud said. "Truth, it was my sword and my hand. If that makes us enemies, so be it. The truce remains, but I ask you leave as soon as the weather allows. We'll find one another later. It would give me great pleasure to cleanse the world of a friend of the yellow man."

"We'll know your side of it now," Uz's said.

"I, too, gained my earring in the southern mountains," Oktria said. "The large man had two ears then. Foolishly I traveled without companions. I was young and in search of quick wealth, sure I could scoop up enough raw gems to support lazy habits for the rest of my life. I found nothing but hardship.

"The giant walked into my camp asking only a little company and a place to spread his bedroll. When he was certain I was alone, he signaled and his band appeared. Disappointed I'd nothing of value, they took my clobben, gear, food. Then beat me and left me to the mountain. I would've frozen to the stiffness of death that night if a miner hadn't thought there was enough spirit left in me to save.

"Through a winter my bones and flesh healed. When spring came, I retrained my weak muscles, all my thoughts on revenge. The old miner convinced me I could search the mountains for a lifetime and never find a trace of the beasts. He showed me what he'd found at the bloody scene. A large ear pierced by a carved lliwant blossom. Although I don't remember, I'd gotten in at least one good blow before they brought me down. I took the earring and left the mountains, hoping the giant and his band would meet a fitting end to their honorless lives.

"I owe you a debt," Oktria said, "and I'm glad we didn't kill you back on the ridge."

"Glad you didn't kill *us*!" Uz released Ham. "Why, I be getting ready to kick the sword from your hand. Another breath and your face be pushed into the snow by my boot."

Ham shoved Uz with her elbow. "Our Uzec, what a brave soul he be—at a warm fire, after he's eaten."

Uz protested with a returning shove. Shouts and laughter echoed through the cavern.

Marla had penned her first entry in Lorchan two years after the date on the journal that contained it. Jeremy and Janvian worked on the translation together. They began with erasable slates—leaving gaps, multiple words, or question marks if they were not sure of a meaning. As they completed passages, Jeremy wrote them in Amersan on paper. The radical path his hero had taken quickly became clear, and he could not stop.

* * *

12.7.305

I am now a Teacher. Officially I'm allowed to pursue my own research, but my proposals are ridiculed and rejected. My perspective is considered dangerous. I've been warned to keep my thoughts to myself. Since I find that impossible, I will disguise them in a language not my own.

We've been on this planet for 172 Sanctuary years. Still, it's foreign to us and we're strangers to it. We've enclosed ourselves in a manufactured bubble, not possessing the land as our ancestors did Earth or the colonized worlds, not taking from the soil and enriching it in return. We live as if we continued to travel, as if we were not yet home.

Thirty years ago the bubble was pierced by an outsider named Nevran, a true native of this planet called Alchorel. Through his writings and recordings I learned his language. I use it here for protection.

He speaks of this single world as if it were all the universe. To him it is. Knowing what I do of stars and the vastness of space, it is small to me. But he has seen more of it than I, and more of life than I.

He brought us opportunities that have been ignored. We are one disaster away from collapse. But more likely slow deterioration will cause our doom.

Am I the only one who foresees this?

* * *

2.8.305

My proposal to create a new plant has been approved! Ambrose is relieved I have come to my senses and given up all that outsider crap. He doesn't know the genetic foundation was brought here by Nevran. I found it a year ago, preserved and cataloged. My requests to experiment with it were denied, so I swapped it with the genome of another forgotten flora we have never grown. The data bank is full of them. They are of no interest to Ambrose. Like so many, he is focused only on what he already knows.

My hand shakes as I write this. I don't know what will happen to me if the deception is discovered, but now I have done worse. I have long petitioned to clone the horse. I understand the concerns of ecological balance in maintaining a large animal, but I see a future where such an animal will be useful. Equipment dies hard deaths daily. Techs revive the devices for a few last gasps without understanding what they do, without thinking, without questioning if there's a way better suited to this world. Horses could be renewable engines to do the heavy work. They might even help us transition to the outside. Perhaps that is what scares those around me the most.

The last time I brought up the subject Ambrose ranted about the danger of undesirable traits. He ordered me to destroy every bit of genetic data on the foreign animal. I disobeyed. I hid the genome, hair, tissue samples, everything where it will not be discovered, so I hope. I fear my delicate lab instruments will fail from exhaustion before I can accomplish my goal.

I would clone Nevran the man, too, if I could. What might we become with his spark, inventiveness, and love of adventure scatter among us? I would like to find out.

<><><>

"Where are they?" Skaln crouched in a circle of skeletal trees overgrown with vines to form a living cave. His breath became fog. A single lantern spread cold light. The storm was a muted rumble and distant flashes of white. Skaln was furious that both trackers had returned and one had not stayed to watch as he'd ordered.

"Nept is in the high mountains," the taller one said. Skaln thought of him as a tree of a man, even hunched over, elbows on knees for support. He described the location, elevation, and distance into Drueten land.

Skaln was too impatient to let him complete the details. "Did you see Janvian?" He expected independence from the hired thieves and mercenaries he used, but these were clankin. Their disobedience was inexcusable.

"Yes, Tarryn," Tree said, "and Rozel right beside her."

"Are you sure it was Janvian?" Skaln knew she had not left with Benoc. The missing assassin that had been stationed outside the fortress on the night Rojelon died proved that. She probably joined the Drueten party on the trail. She had nowhere else to go except to Benoc's protection. Skaln's spies had searched and found no sign of her elsewhere.

"She wore mourning clothes and a veil. I didn't see her face, but it was her all right." Tree talked and the other nodded. "No one has hair that color except those two."

Skaln gouged at the dirt with a stick. "Have you seen every red-haired Drueten? Are you certain there's no one else with that particular shade? If it was her, can you be sure she didn't leave the moment you were gone?"

The trackers exchanged looks. If one was a tree, then the other was a stump.

"Tarryn," Stump said, "as we were explaining, the blizzard stitched the valley closed. We barely made it through the passes alive. No one's getting in or out of there 'til spring."

The talk of snow and mountains finally reached Skaln. He jabbed the stick into the ground with a force that snapped the wood. The squatting trackers rocked back on their heels in surprise and plopped into the dirt.

Skaln had everything arranged to make an attack on Nept look like a random raid. He could fight anything except the weather.

He worked entirely with verbal orders and reports. If ink splashed on paper, there was evidence. As long as he kept everything in his head, only the Baerryns could discover the extent of his actions. And they would need good cause to force him into an examination.

These two in the dirt, who stared at him as if he were a wrathful daeva, did not know about the four separate forces he had spread across the country. Likewise each pack did not know about the others. At times they attacked one another out of ignorance, not realizing they had the same employer. Perhaps that would not matter to them any more than it did to Skaln.

The raiders were equipped with armbands. Drueten, Walbask, Tskant and Joach, but not Felcon. He would show the Baerryns that his superb leadership kept his clan controlled and civilized while all around chaos ruled. He would remind the mystics that Janvian and Benoc hid while he fulfilling his duty. A convincing argument. He planned to reinforce it by eventually defeating his own hired thugs with Felcon troops.

But mercenaries would not wade through snow-packed mountain passes to attack a village. He had to maintain the forces and continue the skirmishes through the winter, stirring the unsettled pot of clans as much as possible. It would be expensive. Skaln would have to extract more money from Calliud's parents, if they were not already bankrupt from the extravagant wedding arrangements.

His hired bands were not the pickpockets and petty snatchers of the marketplace; they were bitter bandits who dared to swoop upon heavily armed travelers. They had no respect for lives, sometimes not for their own, and no ambition past the next raid. He despised them, not for the stealing and killing—both were useful and necessary—but for their inability to think into the future. They dealt only in days. In two days attack this village. Then travel south for three days and raid a caravan. Camp for a day then . . .

Still he found them a fascinating challenge. Alone with the scum of the scum, his will dominating theirs not because he held a longer knife or a sharper sword and not because he would soon wear the golden armband but because he was Skaln.

He dismissed the trackers. There was no challenge in a tree and a stump.

"Tarryn?" Tree uneasily shifted back to a more dignified crouch.

"Yes, quickly, what is it?"

"They sent their mystic away. On the trail. Before they reached the Drueten border." Tree and his companion looked to Skaln as if expecting some indication of what it meant.

"Anything else?" Skaln had more important matters to mull over than the movement of one mystic.

Tree shook his head, disappointed. "No. Nothing, My Tarryn."

The two left the arbor, disappearing beyond the cloudy lamplight. Later if they survived the missions ahead, Skaln would have them punished for their disobedience.

Lantern swinging in his outstretched hand, Skaln walked along the cliff to the hidden door. He knew of three such ways in and out of the fortress. There were more. He wasn't sure anyone alive had knowledge of them all.

He tried to stayed in the middle of the musty passageway so his clothes would not brush the close, moldy walls. Light rhythmically slid from side to side with his steps. Black corridors branched away. One led to the room where the tarryns gathered to protect the storm power. He cursed having to use this route, but the commander of Aerrion Fortress could not shuffle back and forth through the gate after dark without inviting suspicion.

Moisture beaded his forehead. He forced himself to draw breaths of sour air. The walls, the dripping ceiling, the entire tunnel suffocated him.

Skaln felt like a child again visiting the fortress. His father had shown him the sliding panel in the records room that led to the labyrinth and had sworn him to secrecy. He hadn't understood that the burden of trust prepared him for the responsibilities of a tarryn.

Soon after, a servant's boy had beaten him at wrestling, pinning him and his pride to the dirt while older clankin and Lelian and Rojelon had cheered and laughed. Skaln had brushed mud from his breeches, new for his stay with royalty. He'd kept his head down until the tears had dried on his flushed cheeks.

Later he'd privately revealed the secret doorway to the gloating winner and had dared him to explore beyond the shadowed entrance. Skaln had meant to frighten him, to humble him, to make him cry as he had. The boy had snatched the candle from young Skaln's hand and had swaggered into the gaping hole. Aftnoon passed to night and the child had not returned.

Ashamed, Skaln had confessed to his father. The tall, dark man with a jutting jaw had moved away from his son. For an eternity he'd stared at nothing. Then he'd turned back to Skaln and placed weighty hands on his shoulders. His eyes seemed to ache in a heavy face. "We'll not speak of this again."

No search party was ever sent into the labyrinth.

That was long ago but it seemed like now as the shadows swung, as the damp seeped through him and he smelled mold. At any moment he expected the boy to step from an archway, still a child in breeches worn through at the knees, still forcing a bravado to mask fear.

Skaln reached what appeared to be a dead end and pulled a lever. Fresh air tinted with wood smoke pulled away the dampness. His breath settled into an easy rhythm. He ruled here.

He walked through a series of rooms to the hall. A servant wearing the Felcon insignia moved aside the moment he appeared. He had replaced most of the local Tskant workers with his own clan. He thought Calliud might object, but she was too occupied with arrangements for a wedding that was at least a year away.

She had urged him to move into the royal chambers as a sign that they were rightfully his. She understood symbols, but she was weak on strategy. He would remain in his own unadorned rooms until the title and the trappings and the power were laid at his feet.

For now the weather delayed his plans. Come spring thaw, Nept would be in flames.

~

CHAPTER

EIGHTEEN

The boy's stubby fingers moved the needle in a stitch. The heavy fabric of the torn tunic bunched and puckered against the thread's tension. Rozel nudged the boy's knees, shifting them to support the cloth. She adjusted the tunic's position.

The boy tried again with more success. "Uz says you know where the monarch be."

"Yes, but it's a secret." Sewing required patience, as did being snowbound inside a mountain. Patience was not Rozel's strength.

Throughout the connected caverns it was eternal night. The thirty or so men and women, plus children of various ages, followed a routine of work and leisure as if the sun rose and set before them. Rozel helped where she could.

"Then I won't ask about it," the child said. "Secrets be not for sharing."

No doubt the boy had his own, living as he did outside of the protection and assistance of a clan. A vulnerable existence. At the moment it was life-threatening.

Snow drifts gained depth while food dwindled. The sparse meals increasingly left Rozel's hunger unsatisfied. A dull ache held permanent residence in her stomach. How much worse must it be for this boy? Every morsel she put in her mouth was one taken from him and the other little ones.

A small portion of relief was close by, in the packs bulging with supplies from Nept. Again, Rozel debated whether or not to turn over the food to Amud. She had her own mission to accomplish. Without the dried meats and fruits, traveling would be suicide. She, Oktria and Lnez would have to stay here, and the strain of feeding them would continue, perhaps to the point of starvation. They might have already doomed these people with their presence.

Each day Rozel hoped that they could be on their way, but the weather alternated between blinding snow and bitter cold. Every day brought less chance of leaving.

Oktria and Amud played twigs, their matching earrings giving them a strange link. Uz and Ham treated Oktria with the jovial back-slapping of an old friend. Amud was reserved but less guarded since discovering he had a bond with the warrior.

Lnez hovered over the arranging and rearranging of the sticks, trying to follow the intricacies. Rozel and the mystic were treated formally, as the strangers they were.

Rozel had been taught that all thieves were untrustworthy and dishonest, traveling in murderous packs like the giant who originally owned the earrings and his companions. Everything she saw here contradicted that.

These people did not wear armbands and were not connected by blood. Yet wasn't this a clan huddled together, sharing duties for the good of the whole? And wasn't Amud a tarryn of sorts—making decisions, discussing serious matters, offering truce? He seemed honorable enough to lead a clan. More so than Skaln.

But why were the thieves in Drueten land? In the mountains? In the winter? There were milder climates available for souls who had no aversion to crossing clan boundaries uninvited.

Tap. Tap. Tap.

She had studied Amud closely while he told Oktria of his encounter with the giant. Amud called him scum, giving the word the slight inflection of a casual curse, as Rozel might say "thief." He referred to his own people as thieves with a touch of affection, as Rozel might say "Drueten." He'd told the story straight, not for self-glory or the excitement of the telling. The loss suffered was too great for him to take pride in the victory.

Rozel had thought a thief was a thief. She realized she was wrong. Some were honorable; some were scum. Fortunately, on the mountain trail with a blizzard wind on the back of her neck she had met the former and not the later.

Tap. Tap. Tap.

"You be doing it again," the child said.

Rozel folded her arms to still her fingers. The drumming annoyed everyone, mostly herself. She had never been plagued by a nervous habit before. The unconscious display of frustration and restlessness angered her. She sighed and examined the boy's sewing. The cloth was worn smooth but still strong. The fairly even stitches adequately held the rip. "Very good. You should apprentice to a tailor."

"Me?" The boy crumpled his sewing into a ball and slammed it to the ground. He laughed, his young features proud and bitter. "I'm an apprentice thief."

Rozel's face stung. Life here was so like that in a Drueten village, the boy so like a clan child, she'd forgot he had no chance to learn an honest skill.

The boy ran off, leaving Rozel searching for a way to repair the damage. It was not as simple as stitching together frayed cloth. The boy knew his position would never change.

The discarded tunic lay at her feet. Just as she had not realized there were different kinds of thieves, Rozel had not considered the children of thieves until a little face with curious eyes had peeked through the curtain at the archway to a chamber. Or until several had charged through the cavern to the next, their shouts lingering. Or until she had volunteered to help a boy with his sewing. These children had been judged before birth, condemned by their parents' actions.

Rozel acknowledged that her quick temper was a legacy from her father—curse his memory—but she'd escaped the deep streak of anger that had ruled Cimtale. Janvian had inherited nothing from the man. Judging either of them by their father's behavior would be an injustice.

She looked at those laughing, working, and playing games around her. How many were second generation, or third, fourth? How many were thieves because of the crimes of ancestors long ago?

Rozel pledged to herself that if circumstances placed her upon the throne, she would find a way to halt this perpetuation of criminals.

Tap. Tap. Tap. She frowned and shoved her hands into the pockets of her tunic. A short time ago she'd denied interest in being monarch. Now she thought of it without prompting. Hunger had scrambled her brain. She was not ready to give up her freedom for a lifetime of service. She would not allow herself to start believing in her own petition.

At the moment she felt a need to act for the boy's benefit, if only in a small way. She interrupted the twigs game and brought Amud, Oktria and Lnez to the chamber where their gear was stored. "Amud, we're turning over our food to you. I know it won't go far among so many, but it will add a little variety."

"Then we have to stay," Oktria said. She bent over her satchel with her back to them, disappointment in her slumped shoulders.

Lnez picked up his pack and handed it to Rozel. "I've nothing personal in here."

Rozel transferred cheese and dried meats from her satchel to Lnez's. Oktria silently added more to the cache.

"Amud," Rozel said, "my meran's value goes beyond what it would fetch at market."

The thief helped her with the loose bundles. "We've had to start butchering animals. I'll make sure yours is last, if it comes to that."

Rozel searched the thief's face for gratitude, approval, even mockery at the small contribution of food not likely to make a difference in a desperate situation. Perhaps there was a flicker of warmth in his brown eyes, or perhaps she imagined it because she wanted it to be there.

Why are you here? she wanted to ask. But she remained silent.

<><><>

29.8.305

I went outside.

Outside the air moves hot and quick. Energy collectors shine in unbearable sunlight, drinking in the power of the distant sun by day and the fury of the storm at night. The white bubble of the garage burned its shape into my retinas so I still saw the image when I closed my eyes. For the first time I understand why we casually call Sanctuary "the dome," even though it is more than one and more than one shape.

Leaving the biome isn't forbidden; but I don't know anyone who's done it, except the techs for maintenance. Still, the act has the quality of being forbidden. According to the records, samples from outside used to be collected, but that stopped long ago. I would like to revive the practice.

Remembering the thrill, my heart again beats hard as if I had sprinted around the habitat until I dropped. We think of outside as a barren place, but it is not. I saw signs of animals. I saw remnants of plants that I think are dormant with the season. That is a guess. We are disconnected from the planet's natural cycle.

Somewhere in the distance—I wasn't sure which direction to look—is the cave Nevran described in his recordings. He took shelter there. I can't even image being outside in the storm for an entire night.

* * *

14.9.305

I've been secretly studying Nevran's genetic code. I've made detailed suggestions for its use, everything from cloning to transplanting specific DNA sequences into other genotypes to supplant weaknesses. I add my notes below this passage. I dare not share them with anyone. I understand we must be careful so no harm is done. But as our capacity to sustain ourselves dwindles, I fear caution has already placed us in jeopardy.

* * *

25.9.305

Ambrose threatened to dismiss me for my "dangerous philosophy." It's really my success that intimidates him. My munch is thriving. I've submitted proposals to incorporate sections of its genetic material into existing crops to make them more nourishing and productive. As punishment, he assigns me to run errands that keep me out of the lab.

I'm trying to build a foundation for my ideas so they won't seem so radical in the future when Senior Student Manuel is advanced. Time is an enemy, and subtlety is not one of my virtues.

Medstat is treating a young man with a savage growth. Ambrose ignores the possibility of a genetic defect and will not allow anyone but himself to investigate.

Tonight I walked around and around the prairie until the lights dimmed for evening. I'm battling generations of Ambroses, men and women who only know how to follow the known path. We are as tame as the drowsy herd animals who do not so much as lift their heads in curiosity when I go past.

Jeremy put down his pen and switched off the light, rubbing his aching eyes. The translations he and Janvian had completed earlier in the evening were now transferred to his own journal, and the slates could be erased. Janvian slept amid the notes cluttering his bed.

In the earliest entries the Lorchan was a literal equivalent of the Amersan. Janvian would shake her head at the unintelligible butchering of her language. Jeremy had reminded her the passages were actually Amersan translated to Lorchan that they were now translating back to Amersan. As the writings progressed, the Lorchan became closer to natural, making it easier for Janvian but more difficult for him.

The work and pregnancy made Janvian sleepy, and she drifted off whenever her body told her to. Jeremy found pleasure in seeing her curled up on his bed, her hair a red tangle on the coverlet.

In the dark Jeremy closed his manuscript. With each word he was an intruder in another's secrets, taking them as his own. He no longer thought of the geneticist as a teacher or a senior as when he'd known her. Now she was truly Marla.

Marla, he thought, *what will you tell me next?*

<><><>

The cave entrance, double Lnez's height, was blocked by a wall of snow. He held the torch while Uz climbed the white barrier, using crevices carved into the surface for that purpose.

"This one be jammed good," Uz said.

Lnez handed him a long stick to loosen the fresh flakes clogging the small passage at the top. The wood crunched against powder and ice. Uz leaned an elbow on the ledge he'd made the time before and stretched his other arm to work at the spot. A wisp of cold rushed in. The gray light of morning painted a dull patch on the stone wall.

"Might have to get one of the little ones up here to squirm through if it gets any thicker." Uz sniffed loudly and squinted. "Wet."

Lnez enjoyed making the rounds with the burly man. He was only taken to those that were not secret, but that satisfied him. Large openings like this one had been barricaded with brush then packed with snow to prevent the wind from stealing their warmth. The vent had to be checked daily to prevent suffocation.

Breathable air balanced against warmth was of increasing concern. Now fires were only permitted in a few rooms with natural chimneys. The community pulled closer together as their wood, food and spirit dwindled. For Lnez, hunger was a familiar companion. He had learned to ignore it during many fasts, although those had been chosen.

"More coming," Uz said. "Wind be calling it down. Sky looks like an old rag. You wouldn't be leaving soon even if you had the provisions." He looked over a shoulder, raised his eyebrows and shrugged.

When he turned back, Lnez practiced the eyebrow and shoulder movement. His lack of physical communication confused people. There had been no need for it in the Unity. He was learning to use facial and body expressions. Uzec and Ham provided constant examples. The complexity and variety of their twitches and grimaces overwhelmed him.

He was equally fascinated by the connected caverns. Some of the passages were formed by great cracks leaving tilted floors. Others showed the axe marks of miners. Slim gaps often expanded into low-ceilinged pockets like cozy rooms.

Some walls were slick as ice, as if rock had melted then quickly frozen. Torchlight danced across the polished surfaces. The effect unnerved Uz, and he would rush through those stretches. Lnez savored them as the only brightness in a sunless world. They reminded him of the tunnels the Unity used to move in and out of the fortress as they pleased, the corridors deeper and older than the labyrinth.

We don't study our own land, Lnez thought. *We live with the sand and the storm, rocks that push themselves straight out of the ground, caves that spread like vines and we don't ask how they came to be.*

He took a deep, cleansing breath. Through the gemstone he stretched across the craggy cliffs he could not see. The emptiness was refreshing. He had lived in a closed community similar to this most of his life, but mystics were as one person. Living with the press of separate people was a strain. Increasingly he was forced to put up barriers to protect himself from their collective depression, frustration, and worry at being where they did not want to be.

The thieves were supposed to be south. That was all he knew. No one said why they were here instead—not in his presence anyway. He had no right to touch their minds for an answer.

Helping Uz with this task was his escape, giving him a chance to flex his mind and body, if only for a little while.

Lnez felt a flicker. And again. A presence moving slowly, painfully. "Someone's out there."

"You be doing that mystic stuff?" Uzec asked. "Gives me the creepy-crawlies, it does, to know you're poking about. Don't be poking at me or I'll poke right back." He jabbed the stick at the air to illustrate and jumped down from his perch.

"Are you expecting anyone?" Lnez asked. Breaking his own rule, Lnez touched the mind. "One person leading an animal. Disoriented. This one will never find the way without help."

"Amud be expecting supplies two quarters ago. But snow bows to no one's will but its own. Only a frozen fool would try to reach us in this." Uz ran a hand over his balding scalp. "Guess I'll have to go out fool hunting."

"I can lead him in," Lnez said.

Uz fidgeted and twisted his mouth. "You know it be a 'him'?"

"I usually can't tell gender, but this man has certain thoughts that—"

Uz held up a hand and scrunched up his face. He didn't want to hear what rolled around in another's mind. "All right, rogue, toss out a line and pull the fish in."

Lnez knew the path of their daily rounds. "I can get him to the crevice two stops from here."

"We'll hurry on and make sure it's open for the poor soul."

Lnez handed Uz the torch. "You'll have to guide me. The man needs my strength."

The ruddy cheeks blanched. "You be sure? Maybe the fish can swim it alone if you just send out a bit of a worm."

"It'll take much more than that."

Uz juggled the stick and the torch then put a hand under Lnez's elbow. "Well then, let's haul it in and thaw it out."

Uz led the way along the tunnel, muttering about fools and fish. Lnez concentrated on the wanderer.

The man was beyond cold, beyond knowing why he continued to march through the bitter wind, beyond remembering why he tugged at strips of leather clutched in his hand. He stumbled, unable to feel the ground under him.

Disjointed thoughts clashed against Lnez's efforts for order. He took Uz's idea of a worm and set a fire before the man, warm and beckoning. Friends waited, Lnez told him. Familiar faces drifted through the delirium. There was Amud, hooded brown eyes disapproving.

Lnez grasped the image of the thief and changed the expression to one of joy at welcoming a comrade. The man staggered toward friends and fire. His eyes were sightless in the glaring white. Lnez stumbled, blind. The strips of leather jerked from his hand and were gone. Failed. He'd failed. The path slid under numb feet. A thick wetness smothered him, and he lay still, accepting death.

~

CHAPTER
NINETEEN

Tremors shook the traveler. He lay near the fire, cheeks burned white. Frost on his eyebrows, hair and beard made him seem ancient. A woman spooned hot mash between the discolored lips. Others took stones heated at the edge of the fire, wrapped them in cloth and tucked them under the heap of blankets covering the man.

Across the flames Lnez huddled in a trance, echoing the violent shivers. Oktria fastened the mystic's mended cape at his throat so the shaking would not slide it from his shoulders.

"He'll recover," Oktria said softly. "You can let go." It seemed correct to whisper when saying something she did not believe. Lorcha was unforgiving of mistakes. She had witnessed comrades dying from great gushing wounds and from trickling ones. She had seen them fade from thirst and starvation, watched them give in to the cold after being rescued and placed near a warm fire. She expected the man to die and hoped Lnez would not be pulled from life with him.

The man had trudged a slippery mountain path to bring food to his friends. Good should be rewarded, not punished, by the elements. The old god Cyran-ozel should bestow riches on those who risked themselves for the benefit of others. They should be given health and easy paths.

Let the evil and the selfish meet frozen death, and soon.

Oktria felt a chill. If the selfish were struck down, who among them would be left standing? Her hand went to the pouch in her tunic. She knew what position she would be in. Horizontal.

She could not explain why she hoarded the small bundle. Despite her hunger, she had eaten nothing from it. Perhaps it was that as long as the cache remained hidden, there was hope.

Uz brought a steaming mug. "Maybe you can get Lnez to drink this. It be only water. Not my favorite, but we've plenty of it and that be in its favor. There be extra meat, if you don't mind it came to us on its own hooves. The beast be dead before it got here and just didn't have the sense to know it. And if the smell of baking bread drifts by your deprived nose, it be no dream. Today we feast."

Oktria pulled the horded pouch from her tunic and opened it. She took a piece of dried fruit and dropped it into the mug. "This will add sweetness and a soft treat to look forward to."

Uz swallowed tightly and rubbed a hand across his mouth. For days the camp had survived on rationed clobben meat and a mash made from grain and melted snow.

Oktria took the mug from Uz and put the pouch in his hand. "A feast needs fruit."

Uz held the pouch as if it contained gold. A clever reply seemed balanced on his tongue, but he clamped his lips together before it fell out.

<><><>

A cluster of entranced youngsters gathered around an older child who read from a tattered book. Flame from a thick candle illuminated the reader's expressive face. She held the manuscript at an angle so all could see the words and drawings. "Noalgaz, the little moon, called to his larger sister, 'Come, Pypeed, let us dance around the world.' So they took hands and circled the sky."

Rozel leaned against the wall a short distance away and listened. She knew the story well. For the anniversary of a kin's choosing day, she had copied it on crisp paper, adding her own illustrations, and had bound it with heavy thread as a gift.

The camp's morning bustle had settled into a slower pace. In the crowded cavern a group planned the rotation of work assignments. Others collected clothing and carried them off to the chamber set up as a laundry, trailing a sharp odor of soap. Amud reviewed the food rationing with the cooks. The new supplies had revived them, but two animals loaded with goods had collapsed on the trail. Only one-third of the expected provisions had arrived.

The brave man who had brought them survived and was able to talk. He did not know the mountains well enough to find shelter when needed, he said. Under Rozel's questioning he relayed that the trail was manageable—if you did not become confused by the way snow disguised the rocky features. And if no new snow fell. And if you had a strong animal. And if your mission was worth risking your life. There was more the man told Amud privately.

Rozel listened to the child read and chewed on her situation. When Lnez broke contact with the man, the mystic had been spent but had quickly regained his strength. Now he seemed fit, even rejuvenated by the experience. The man Lnez had rescued gave enough hope of success to chance traveling.

Amud had promised that when supplies arrived, Rozel

could take the minimum for the trip to replace those given to the community, a more than fair exchange when balanced against what they had already eaten. So few provisions had reached them that none could be spared.

Frowning, Uz came up beside her.

"You don't like the story?" she asked.

"Don't need to read to enjoy a good tale." The men of the camp had let their hair and beards grow. Uz's thick beard was trimmed to hug the jawline. He scratched at it with a broken fingernail. "That be Amud's doing, setting up a school. As if thieves had anyone to impress with learning."

Rozel said nothing. After her experience with the boy, she was careful not to think of this community as having the same opportunities as a clan. It became increasingly difficult to limit her thoughts. As she did her share of the work, she saw more similarities with her own life. And now a school, just like a clan. A starving clan.

Those two clobben frozen on the trail loaded with food might as well be in Aerrion City for all the good it did anyone here. This was a strange place to spend a winter.

"Uzec, why are you here?" Questions were impolite, and unwise when the alternative was a snowbank, but Rozel could not shake the feeling that important information silently moved around her.

Uz did not seem offended. "I'll wager that one be brewing a long time in your barrel."

"I shouldn't have asked," she said.

"I don't hear you taking it back." Uz chuckled and Rozel grinned at his teasing. "You'd know the whys and such if you hadn't be romping about in the high mountains playing clan games since Rojelon's death." He led her to an alcove that offered privacy. His joking tone masked something serious. He motioned for Amud to join them. Rozel saw an exhausted leader who'd been pushed into tough choices.

"You best tell her," Uz said to Amud.

"Why are you in the mountains?" Rozel asked.

"For the same reason you can't leave." Amud sat on the alcove's natural ledge spread with a blanket. "Traveling south from Aerrion City, we were ambushed by raiders in Joach armbands, but they weren't clanners. We recognized them from the city. Someone was recruiting in the taverns. Fat pay for dirty work and all the loot you could snatch. Only scum take an offer like that. Aerrion was clogged with them.

"We swung east. Then east again to avoid the same raiders. This time they were masquerading as Walbask. At a village we learned that travelers, caravans, even villages were being attacked. We knew about these caves and decided they were the safest place for a while. We didn't expect to get trapped here."

Mercenaries blaming their attacks on two different clans. Rozel sat down beside Amud. "Do you know who did the hiring?"

"I be approached myself," Uz said, "by a soul I'd lifted a few tankards with. But I figure he be a low player. Don't know who sits at the top."

"According to our friend who brought the supplies, things have gotten worse," Amud said. "Every clan's been blamed for something except the Felcon, which makes them look pretty guilty. But rumor is the funding is Tskant. That doesn't make sense."

Rozel closed her eyes and slammed a fist into her knee. Skaln and Calliud—or rather, the woman's indulgent parents. The brain and the money.

She opened her eyes and found Amud studying her. "So, it makes sense to you."

"That's why you can't leave," Uz said. "Weather aside, it not be safe."

Rozel rubbed her knee. A shame to suffer a bruise along with her other problems. She had to make her petition and show Skaln that he would not get his way unopposed. She would make it clear that she was challenging him, not her sister. Others might think her a traitor, but Skaln would know her true intention. "Your friend got through."

"Two others with him were killed," Amud said. "They sacrificed themselves so he could get away with the three loads of food."

Rozel needed soldiers to get down the mountain, a group small enough to move quickly and large enough to stage a good defense if attacked. But they could not be Drueten.

The men and women in the cave had no clan ties, but they had honor and lor to one another. Not like the dregs Skaln hired. She needed fighters like Amud, Ham and Uzec. But she did not have a wealthy lover to provide the necessary coin, and the family coffers were closed to her.

The young reader ended the story. Children whooped at the merry caper of the two moons. Another reader took her place. Rozel recognized the boy she had hurt with her thoughtless remark. The children shouted names of their favorite books. The boy selected a set of bound pages from a pile, his choice drawing cheers. If only he could apprentice in an honorable trade. Rozel knew master tailors. Perhaps there was one who would not question the lineage of an eager lad brought by the sister of the monarch.

Benoc would not approve of what she was thinking. But he would not know until spring. Maybe he would not have to know at all.

"Amud," Rozel said, "you need more food, and I need to be

about my business. Your friend said getting down the mountain was possible."

Uz leaned against the alcove wall. "If—"

"I know all the ifs," Rozel said. "You're planning to go after the two loads left on the trail, aren't you?"

Amud seemed surprised at what she had guessed. "Yes," he admitted.

"Then the rest of the way should be easy," Rozel said.

Amud shook his head. "Scum will pick you off the moment you reach the foothills."

"Then I need more fighters," Rozel said. "I want to hire some of your company."

"The risk is too great." Amud got up to leave.

Rozel stepped into his path. "Amud, what crime did you commit to be cast out of a clan?"

He measured her for a moment. "No crime. I was born a thief. And my parents before me."

"Uz, what clan where you born to?" she asked boldly.

"No clan," Uz said. "I flow from a long river of thieves."

"You live the penalties for the crimes of your ancestors," Rozel said. "And your children after you. I offer a way out for some. Unfortunately, not for all. I'll not make promises I can't keep."

"Rozel," Amud said, "we aren't thieves by choice, but we've all committed crimes. It's how we get what we need. It's how we live. None of us is innocent. There is no way for us within the law." He put a hand on her arm to brush her aside. "You have your clan," he whispered. "You don't need us."

Rozel grabbed his wrist and felt his pulse rage. She would not be moved. "I'm going to Aerrion Fortress. Before the Baerryns, I'll make my petition to be monarch. Lnez and Oktria stand with me, but by acting against my sister I'm a traitor. No other Drueten will join me."

Uz laughed. "Any soul with the brain of a tweeting doph know you be no traitor."

"We stay out of clan matters," Amud said.

Rozel knew she was a breath away from being struck to the ground. "When the monarchy is decided, Janvian will be on the throne, or I will. Either way I'll be in a powerful position. Drueten Clan is prosperous with many crafters. I can place your children with them as apprentices. No one will question the niece to the tarryn and sister to the monarch."

"Or monarch herself," Uz muttered, impressed.

The children were quiet while one voice read a key passage in the tale. Rozel released Amud's wrist. He let his hand fall from her arm. "How many?"

"I don't know," Rozel admitted. She wanted an honest trade not a hollow deal. "I can't guarantee a number. And I can't say how quickly it'll be done."

"One. Can you promise one?" Amud asked.

"Yes. One." "Two. Can you swear it will be two?"

"I swear it will be at least two," she said, "and more with time and luck."

Uz broke between them. He hugged Rozel in his big arms and spun her around. "Each apprentice be a master some day and a master trains many others in a lifetime. I'm with you. Even if it only be one, even if the one not be my own. It be like planting a tree. It'll branch as it grows. Our ancestors put us here. I'd like to be an ancestor what got some out."

The others noticed them and laughed. Someone whistled a dance tune. Uz set Rozel down and grabbed another partner.

Amud did not share the mood. "This affects the whole band. I'm not a tarryn. The decision isn't mine to make. We'll meet and discuss it. Whatever the band decides will be for all."

"I'm getting off this rock, Amud, if I have to wade through every snowflake and fight every raider on Lorcha by myself."

Rozel found him handsome now that his hair touched his shoulders and his beard had some substance. For several days she had thought about acting on that attraction. As far as she could tell, he did not have a current romance. If she made her feelings known now, he might think she was trying to influence him. She walked away. It was a bad idea.

"Rozel."

She turned. The unguarded warmth in Amud's eyes caught her breath.

"Can you really find apprenticeships for the children?" he asked.

"Yes." Her uncle might order her to clean animal stalls for the rest of her life for bringing in thieves. That would be nothing compared to the punishment he would devise if he found out what she was about to do now.

Rozel walked back toward Amud.

<><><>

The collection panel wobbled in the constantly moving air. Dougal adjusted the brace against the support and put the fastener he'd made in place. He unsealed a pocket in his jumpsuit and pulled out a tool. He'd had to make that too, but he'd enjoyed figuring it out.

"Hold it still," Dougal said.

The rectangle tilted over Jeremy's head. He planted his feet in a wide stance for stability and reached up to grasp the edges. His one-piece coverall was sealed along the front and at the wrists and ankles. A cap shadowed his eyes with a wide brim that narrowed as it circled to the back of his neck, but he still needed a visor to protect his eyes.

Dougal twisted the fastener. The sharp end of the scored cylinder worked its way through the brace and the support.

Jeremy saw the logic of what Dougal was doing, but he doubted he ever would have thought of it himself. "When did this idea hit you?"

"The fastener I found as an example of something or other in some old records on teaching physics. The thing to manipulate it I made up myself."

"Teaching what in physics?"

"I didn't notice."

Farther down the bank of panels Janvian examined the structure. Jeremy watched her stretch and touch, bend and stare, step back and look, step close and look. Her curiosity was insatiable. She seemed as fascinated with mechanical devices as Dougal was. The coverall she wore accentuated her growing abdomen. She liked the cap but found the visor awkward. Merede would be furious if she knew Jeremy had given in and let her come along. After the baby was born she would leave. Increasingly, as they spent hours translating the journals, Jeremy realized he did not want her to go.

Janvian rarely spoke of her dead spouse. She mourned privately, as was her right, and he did not intrude. She did not share much of the life she had left. Perhaps she had little to return to. Or perhaps he only hoped that.

In the passage they'd just finished converting to Amersan, Manuel, the senior student, had been moved to the agriculture station. Ambrose had been forced to advance Marla into the vacant position. Jeremy was anxious to tackle the next section, but he'd promised Dougal he'd assist with repairs.

"The table parts glow," Janvian said. She knew that wasn't exactly the right way to put it.

"The collectors," Dougal said. "They do that in the morning until the energy gets drained off."

At first they'd relied on solar power. Then the settlers, while they still had the engineering ability to do so, had switched to storm power. With aging collectors, Dougal was promoting a partial return to the old source, so they would have a combination of the two. The techstat team was not very receptive.

Dougal was taking his time with the brace. Jeremy tried not to waver. A knot developed between his shoulder blades. "How come I always end up helping you, but you don't help me."

"I looked at that horse with you."

"Yes, but you weren't much help."

"Animals don't like me." Dougal tested his work and gave it a satisfied rap with the tool, sending a dull clunk across the desert. "You didn't need me to tell you they're the same. You could see that for yourself. Besides you're helping me because this is our fault."

Jeremy released the panel. It held steady. "What?"

"Remember climbing on these girders when we were kids? Swinging and hanging upside down and pretending the sand was the sky? Well, I figure we're the reason the adhesive gave out." He slapped a beam above the spot he'd just patched. "Centuries of withstanding the elements and all it took to bring it down was two kids looking for an adventure."

Jeremy laughed. "The 'centuries of elements' probably had something to do with it too."

Dougal walked in the shade of the panels, checking stress points, connections and insulators.

"Have you ever wondered why we were the only children who snuck outside?" Jeremy asked.

"No," Dougal said.

❧

CHAPTER

TWENTY

The riders entered Aerrion City through a section well known for operating at the edge of clan law. Bundled figures who moved slowly along a street rutted by a cycle of freezes and thaws watched them carefully. The frigid air could not hurry those who had no pressing place to go, and the newcomers might be worth a look. Some peered from the shadows of hoods, judging the quality of clothes, weapons and animals. Some openly stared, their faces hard, slick, and sly.

Oktria, Rozel and Amud met the scrutiny first. Behind them Ham, Uzec and Lnez urged on weary clobben.

Uz affected a sneer and straightened his posture, showing his wide build. "Remember we be thieves among thieves. Let them think we be at least as cutthroat as they."

Rozel noticed her meran drew much attention, too rich a mount for this part of the city. Were any of these Skaln's spies? She kept her hair tied up under a scarf and hid her uneasiness behind an arrogant mask. This was not the first time she'd been here. She knew the value of a good bluff. Her favorite gambling den was only a stroll away. The colorful excitement of unruly streets that she relished was gone, replaced by a stench as cutting as the wind that caught their steamy breath.

The company dismounted before the Split Hoof tavern. Rozel was relieved to reach the end of a tough journey. Here snow was a light dust scattered across the ground. At times it seemed Alchorel was a conscious thing toying with the creatures it supported to pass the time during the routine exchange of seasons.

On the third day of hard pushing after leaving the caves they had reached the stiff carcasses of the abandoned clobbens, frozen sacks still lashed to their backs. Amud had brought extra people to manage the supplies. Worriedly Rozel had watched the little band climb back up the trail with their burdens. She had been suddenly reluctant to go the other direction.

"No one can reach Nept without my people knowing about it," Amud had said. "They'll send word if they see anything."

He had meant to reassure her. The farther Rozel got from Benoc, the more she felt she moved away from her duty instead of toward it—duty as she saw it, not as Benoc decreed.

She had tried to return Amud's kind words. "We cleared a good trail, and the sky shows relief for a day at least. Propaulnem and the others should have an easy trip."

The six of them had continued on. The temperature had grown milder with the decreasing altitude, but the signature of full winter hung in frosty script from barren branches. If Benoc needed her, she could never reach him in time to help.

Assuming she was in a position to do so. She might be too occupied with protecting herself to be able to rescue anyone else.

As they had worked their way toward the city, Lnez had guided them around the raiders. Rozel was furious at the invaders' penetration deep into Drueten land. With more fighters she would have punched a hole in their brazenness. But three thieves for three apprenticeships, plus surveillance of the trail leading to Nept, was the best deal she could manage.

Amud was a tough negotiator, not influenced by their activities of the previous evening. And Rozel was unwilling to pledge beyond her means, even to put additional soldiers at her back.

At least she'd gotten the specific one she'd wanted and the two he trusted most. Amud stayed removed from her when they were with others but was affectionate when they were alone. He'd proven to be a considerate lover. Despite the circumstances of their meeting, she found she trusted him more than most of the other men she had shared a bed with.

They were not a large enough company to harass the mercenaries. Rozel had been unable to do more than warn the villages they'd passed. Ham, Uzec and Amud had surprised her by putting on Drueten armbands. She had grown accustomed to seeing their sleeves unadorned.

The insignia no longer guaranteed a clankin welcome at the clusters of thatched huts. Villagers were suspicious of every stranger, and with good cause. Rozel's red hair and small stature, well-known clan traits, had gotten them hot meals and tales of attacks.

The Split Hoof was a long building that sagged in the middle as if an invisible giant sat on the roof. A tall structure tacked to one end held multiple floors of rooms to rent, each layer added with little concern for matching the corners and edges of the preceding one.

The tavern owner met Amud's request for a room with a grin. She wiped dirty hands on a towel slung around her neck. "It be good to see regulars, customers what know how to behave themselves in a respectable establishment, if you know what I be saying." She freed a key from a large hoop jangling at her waist and handed it to Amud. "No animals in your room. Stable the beasts next door at the Bale and Troth. Say I sent you."

The room was dirty but sufficient. Rozel dumped her bedroll in a corner. "The longer I wait, the greater the chance Skaln will discover I'm in the city. I have to speak to the Baerryns immediately."

Rozel left Lnez at the tavern with Ham and Uz. Arriving with the former Speaker, now turned rogue, was not the way to gain the mystics' favor.

Oktria and Amud accompanied Rozel to the fortress. No rope waited to help with the climb up the cliff as it had when she last used this route. She scowled at the towering stone, watching for detection from above. She wished they could have rested for a day or two. She wished the daylight was not so bright, but they dare not attempt the climb at night. Mostly she wished she did not have to enter the fortress at all. Wishes were sand for all they mattered.

They progressed slowly, using ropes where they could. The thorn tree arch put the wooden door in shadow. Rozel released the lock as Janvian had taught her. The door growled on its hinges. A darkness deeper than night greeted them.

They had no torch. Rozel led the way, her fingertips following the etched trail of circled arrows. The symbols were smooth, as if centuries of fingertips had brushed them. Between markings the stone was gritty and damp. She felt Amud and Oktria close behind her. The air did not stir except from their movement.

As they went, Rozel counted the circles. A junction with the main tunnel was ahead. Their breath and the rustle of cloth echoed strangely in her ears. Footsteps bounced back to her. Something was different.

Rozel found the next carving. It assured her she had

reached the main tunnel. She kept her fingers pressed against it and stretched her other hand forward. It jammed against a barrier. She explored the obstruction and found fresh mortar sealing newly placed rock. The way was solidly blocked.

<><><>

18.11.307

As always, life is a mixture of advancements and setbacks. Through each there is opportunity.

One of the incubation units failed again, and we lost a batch of chickens. We shouldn't be expending our resources cloning chickens! They are the classic example of reproduction through fertilized egg, and that's how we should be doing it. It requires some snipping and splicing, and accurate genetic tracking, but it would take some strain off the duplication equipment.

Because of munch, we've been able to increase the goat and sheep herds. Zoostat wants to try a larger animal in the prairie. It requested a specimen within the parameters of UC588 and UC595. Basically it would be a long-lived, manure producing herbivore, similar to but different from the ones we used to have years ago that stopped thriving and died.

Ambrose's health is failing. As Senior Teacher, I will manage and execute the project under his supervision. I've retrieved the hidden genetic material. I'm going to clone a horse.

* * *

6.12.307

Ambrose grows less able to function almost daily. Despite the differences in our philosophies, he has been a dedicated and conscientious teacher, even a kind and dear man at times. He accepts whatever I say with childlike trust, then promptly forgets the conversation. Yet he recalls details of gene segments he worked with over thirty years ago.

I have come to rely on Student Nicholas to help me correct his errors and make excuses for him. We can't hide the deterioration much longer. I feel guilty every time I take advantage of his condition. By the time the horse reaches maturity, he will not remember what such an animal looked like or that he told me to destroy everything that might provide its code.

The origin of Ambrose's ailment might be environmental or the result of a fall that seemed minor at the time. Neither is likely.

Nicholas compiled a list of those who were built using snippets of Ambrose's genetic material, a disproportionately large number over the years. The geneticist was like an ancient god, creating in his own image. Fortunately, we do not clone humans. People are composites, not exact duplicates as with plants and animals. We have identified some defects and removed them from the active bank, but we can never be sure there are not more undiscovered, waiting to ambush us.

Tomorrow I will notify medstat. I will accompany Ambrose to the consultation and turn over the list. Those who might suffer the same degenerative disease Ambrose experiences will be notified. I wonder if they should be spared this knowledge. Surely they'll be happier not worrying about something that might not happen, and that they can't stop if it does. This is blasphemous I know. But much of my thoughts—and many of my actions—are blasphemous of late. I dare write them only in a language no one else can read.

"The individual has absolute and exclusive control over personal or inherited sperm or egg, tissues, and genes; and further has access to all information known concerning ancestry and health. These rights shall not be altered, abridged or circumvented by any individual or group of individuals including any governing organization, formal or informal."

Our ancestors stole a Tynat craft because of belief in this sacred doctrine. They fled the tyranny of those who would violate these rules.

But in this case what purpose does "all information known" serve? You might die from an undignified disease that slowly destroys your mind or you might not. We don't know which it will be, but we'll tell you if we notice you showering in the waterfall.

This scars my joy at seeing my long-sought goal approach its conclusion. Besides Ambrose, there are a few others old enough to remember the visitor. They might notice that the horse looks remarkably like the visitor's meran. I can put them off with genetic jargon. People have limited curiosity and accept simple answers when they should not. How sad for us.

The citizens of the dome lack vision and inventiveness. We need the aggressive nature of the Alchorelians. Our ancestors must have had those qualities. The complacent do not steal starcraft and launch into the unknown because of a philosophy. Perhaps it was necessary that we lose those qualities to live confined by metal and vacuum. But we don't need to do that anymore. We must reinstate those qualities and reach beyond the bubble that is as much a prison as protection.

We must truly become Alchorelians.

<>‹›‹›

A merchant wheeled a pushcart from the main road onto the sloping approach to the fortress. A Felcon guard halted the man and interrogated him while another searched the late delivery. The man was allowed to pass. He labored up the incline with his load, cart wheels clattering on the bridge.

At the gate to the courtyard more soldiers poked through the goods and asked questions. Carpenters, sweeps and other workers moved around them, hurrying home before the early winter sunset. A mystic stood against the stone wall.

A short way down the road leading to the city Amud, Rozel and Oktria watched from a decaying hut. "A check point before the bridge," Oktria said. "I've not seen that before."

"I don't have to get inside," Rozel said, "just close enough to a mystic to request an audience. Then I'm under the Baerryns' protection."

Amud saw she had little tolerance for such a passive entry. She would not make a good thief. He knew that and more about her before their encounter in the mountains. Knowledge of clan leaders and those around them was necessary in his profession. He could not say exactly when his interest in the monarch's younger sister had turned personal. He only knew he had been in love with her since the night of the summer festival when she had joined the other costumed revelers in the taverns and gambling dens.

"No doubt that's what the guards on the road are supposed to prevent," Oktria said. "What if the council won't give you an audience?"

Rozel shrugged. "Then we're faezad bait."

Amud thought the situation intriguing. "You've both lived in the fortress under Felcon security. How can we use the system to our advantage?" This was more challenging than going through a secret tunnel, which obviously was not so secret or it would not have been barricaded.

"I found many ways to slip out," Rozel said. "But I just went back in through the gate. The guards knew who I was and never questioned me. You don't have to sneak in when you're expected to be there."

Every good thief knows that, Amud thought. Maybe there was hope for Rozel after all. "You could pretend to be a merchant. But you'd be recognized even with your hair covered."

"I'd shave my head and wear a portrait of Skaln if it got me into the fortress," Rozel said.

"I don't think that'll help." Oktria folded her arms and frowned. "They're sure to know me by sight too. Amud, I'll wager you could bluff your way as far as the mystic and do the requesting for Rozel."

"I might have gotten away with sending a messenger in my place if my sister was still physically close to the throne," Rozel said, "but I'll get no special treatment now."

Amud noted where the soldiers looked, who they spoke to among themselves, and who did the questioning. "I've some experience getting into places where I wasn't invited." Rozel held a keen intelligence, but she missed the obvious implication of her own words. "Let's give them what they expect."

~

CHAPTER

TWENTY-ONE

The eipy cowered among the rafters, refusing to come down and do tricks for the patrons no matter how it was coaxed or sworn at. The tavern keeper slapped a mug before the stooped old man. "The little thing just showed up, it did, all by itself." Brown beads splashed across bleached rings that looped the table like twisted rope. "Don't know where Konel be, if he be anywhere." She leaned over conspiringly, keys a jingle, dirty towel around her neck wreaking of stale liquor. "Lots of folks disappearing, and I don't much like them what takes their place."

The Sage rescued his mug before a ragged tendril dipped into it. "Business looks good." He took a bitter swig. The abbey brewed a civilized vintage that slid across the tongue like liquid moonlight, as different from this as gold from sand. Sometimes sitting on a cushioned chair before a fine woven cloth flowering with delicacies, he craved this roughness on his pampered pallet.

"Oh, the place be full every night. But it be too quiet." The owner pointed at the furry patch huddled overhead like a gray spirit. "Even a little creature knows it."

The Sage surveyed the room over the dented curve of his mug. Patrons sat in tight fists. Loners leaned against scarred walls, protecting their backs. Surely some of them were Skaln's hired cutthroats in the city to give their reports and get new orders.

The Sage counted on the independent thieves not being able to resist taking an unauthorized respite at the Split Hoof. He needed information about their forces, who fought with whom wearing what armbands, which roads were clear and which were not.

More urgently, he hoped to hear a rumor or a speculation or the fragment of a tale that would lead him to the Speaker turned solitaire who dared intrude in affairs beyond his station. His presence outside of the Unity was a gash that would not heal. The Sage suspected, but had no evidence, that the traitor was responsible for the mystic escorting the mock Janvian to be dismissed, eliminating the only source of information about Benoc's movements.

But that was only a shadow of the threat the rogue Speaker posed. With what he knew, suspected, and could guess, he might destroy the Sage's carefully constructed plan.

Success was close. Chances were good that a mystic would be born to the throne, preparing the way for the monarchy to be swallowed up by the Unity. Janvian had made it possible through her own actions without direct influence from him. That was the elegance of it, create a situation that makes certain occurrences inevitable then step back and let them happen.

Beyond the Speaker's meddling, it was unlikely he would keep the community's secrets now that he was no longer within it. The search for him drained the Sage's resources. Mystics who should be tending to other matters were scattered across the country hoping to trace him. He might be with Benoc in the mountains or on his own quest to follow Janvian. Or he might be nearby, watching for opportunities to disrupt what was in motion.

At one point the Sage had thought the matter ended. In Joach land a hidden mystic had been discovered. But it was the young son of a farmer. The widow could not bear the heartache of sending her only child away to an abbey, though it would have been for the boy's own good. When confronted by the Sage's agents, the boy had refused to leave. He was not an immediate threat, but he could not be allowed to live as a solitaire. Death had been simple and swift.

The mood in the Split Hoof was grim tonight, more conducive to combat than a friendly exchange of rumors. The Sage gave the tavern keeper a wink. "What if old Orioph takes away the quiet, eh?"

The fish eagerly jumped at the dangling bait. "Free ale the night long, if you can do that," she said.

The Sage chuckled. The woman was sure she would not have to carry through with the promise.

Stiffly the Sage climbed upon the table and sat on the edge, dangling his feet. His patched boots bound with rags barely reached the bench. A scarred hand disappeared inside a worn tunic and emerged clutching a stick.

The flute, slim as youth and unpretentious as age, had been carved not by a master but by a herder more skilled with melody than blade. The Sage put the twig to his cracked lips. His breath became a pristine breeze cutting the sour air. The first notes explored, weaving through the instrument's range. They tugged at ears and turned heads toward the freshness. He slipped into a charming tune.

"What bird screeching be this?" The sharp words clashed with the sweetness. Mumbles and laughter echoed agreement.

The Sage stopped the flow. The discord faded to an uneasy hush. Only the eipy chattered noisily as it scampered across the rafters. His mistake was offering sparkling mountain air when the preference was sewer stench. He would entertain them with something more akin to themselves. He piped a simple tune, ignoring shouts about his ancestry and creative uses for the flute that had nothing to do with music.

Above him the furry creature gripped the beam with its sharp claws and thrust a pointed nose at the sound, the weight of its head and chest balanced by its tail. It cautiously sniffed the notes. The music was different from its owner's whistling, yet the same. It swung its head back and forth with the rhythm, clicking its teeth; its tail served as counterpoint.

Coarse shouts urged the eipy to come down, causing the creature to pull back its nose in fright. The Sage mentally cursed them by the name of an ancient god he did not believe in. They were fools, their thoughts as complex as piss and just as useful. The eipy showed more intelligence. At least it instinctively recognized danger, which was more than these thinking animals did.

He sent a mental scan to the tiny brain. The double threads of fear and confusion wound through a longing for its owner. The man had been mostly kind, and the animal did not understand the abandonment. This tavern was the only refuge it knew, although it recognizing that the place was not completely safe. It was drawn by memories the music evoked but not brave enough to investigate. Too much had happened. Too much had changed.

Through the gem securely sewn inside his shirt over his heart so it could not be stolen again, the Sage spread the soothing salve of the flute's tune into the little mind until it blocked everything else. The sound was no longer a flute but the familiar whistle. The eipy ruffled its fur in joy, gave a squeal and leaped from the sagging rafter. It hooked a beam with its tail and swung vigorously.

Hard-faced criminals cheered and left their tables to tightened around the Sage and the dangling fur ornament. The eipy would have disappeared, but the Sage kept the whistle in its mind. Lured by the illusion, it dropped to the table and raised its long body on stubby hind legs. It shifted back and forth in a stiff dance, tail curling and uncurling above its head like feathery smoke.

The Sage watched the gaping, sweaty faces pressed around him. They would have met his questions with angry stares, or worse. Now with a few more tunes and tankards they would shove one another aside to tell him everything they knew. This was easier than probing their minds and it left no suspicious trace.

He ended the song and held the eipy with a thought. The eager crowd waited. As if oblivious to their presence, the Sage drained his mug. Squinting in the mottled light, he rolled the flute across his palm as if admiring the flaws. He puckered his lips around the reed. He wiggled his fingers against the knobby wood and flapped his elbows, shifted his shoulders and wrinkled up his nose. Bodies bent toward him.

A slow, melodic wisp wound through the dusky room. It gained speed and became a whirling tune. Whoops swung into the booming tale of wealth gained and lost; sex for love and for pleasure; and lor pledged, betrayed and lamented. The eipy capered on sharp claws.

Smiling, the tavern owner elbowed through the raucous crowd with a full tray. Singing patrons quickly became thirsty patrons. The melancholy might drink to forget their troubles, but the joyful bought ale for one another and counted their change less closely. The first mug she plunked beside the Sage, while others tugged at her wet sleeves, eager to spend their few coins on drink when they had a more odorous need for strong soap.

The Sage observed the rowdies. Their ale-clouded eyes were no longer fixed on him. They barely brushed him with a glance as long as the eipy danced. The swaying forest creature captured their attention. That was as it should be.

Across the room a tall man stood up on a bench to see over the crowd. Back straight, hands tucked into loose sleeves, he did not shift for balance on the narrow plank but held steady as if flat rock stretched in all directions.

The stance was familiar. The Sage knew he should recognize it; but it was out of context, dressed in a different disguise. While the others stared hypnotized by the little dancer, the stranger's unblinking gaze locked on him, taking his measure. The unwavering gray-blue eyes striped away his beggar's rags and pretense.

The Sage had never seen the former Speaker before. He only knew the mystic in a limited way, having little use for contact with those below the Prism.

Vibrations pulsed through his gemstone in rhythm to the flute's light measure and the eipy's prancing feet. At a distance it would not be noticeable, but this close a mystic powerful enough to be the Speaker of the Baerryns might feel the use of energy.

Who did the silver-haired watcher think the man with the flute was? Perhaps another rogue? Certainly not the mighty Sage, whom he had once approached with such awe that he could scarcely choke out respectful thoughts of thanks for his new position as Speaker. The disruption he'd caused had echoed through the community long after. This was no longer that timid soul, quickly—possibly too quickly—raised through the ranks.

How fortunate, and how ironic, that the Sage had searched the five territories when all he'd had to do was wait for the rouge to deliver himself to this very tavern. Now he could smother the flame himself and know the job was properly done.

He finished the melody then moved into another. Hands clapped and feet pounded the creaky floor. The little performer was comfortable now, enjoying the familiar routine. He mentally released it to caper on its own.

Would curiosity at the old man using a jewel to control an eipy be enough to lure the rogue to a secluded place?

Figures rippled low, flanking the former Speaker. The two stood, their solemn faces catching the firelight. The rough man and the pockmarked woman! They'd been with the fool when he'd stolen the crystal, and now they were with the rogue. An interesting alliance.

He knew the thieves would have killed him right there if they could have gotten away with it. Revenge was a poorly caged animal prowling inside them. They would not be cautious, and the noble Speaker would not let his new friends confront a mystic alone.

He finished the tune. The eipy bounded onto his shoulder and back into the rafters. The crowd pounded the furniture and one another with delight. Laughter turned to protests as he tucked the flute into his tunic. "Ah, that be enough for an oldster like me." Any information they had would have to be collected later. "Don't have the wind for it, I don't."

Stiffly he climbed from the table. A dozen hands reached to make his descent easier, and offers of full mugs abounded. He declined with a crooked grin and hobbled to the door, turning to acknowledge the friendly slaps on his bent shoulders.

He shuffled into the cold without a glance at the rogue or his companions. They would follow without prompting, and he would soon be rid of them.

<><><>

More frequently, Jeremy found himself rereading passages from Marla's journals. He shared them with no one but Janvian, not even Dougal.

* * *

20.3.309

Ambrose has been moved to medstat and is under constant care. My advancement to Senior Geneticist is official. Although I've been performing the duties for some time, the title is a bulky coat that's uncomfortable to wear. I'd hoped to achieve the position, but I'd envisioned the announcement being made at the party celebrating Ambrose's decision to retire into a tutoring role. I'm finding it hard to balance the guilt and the joy.

The native plant and animal samples Nicholas collected on his most recent outing have some intriguing elements. Our protocols for safely bringing them into the dome seem to be effective. We understand the danger in what we do. And the danger if we don't do it.

Analysis of all active human genomes is alarming. Ambrose—and, it appears, the senior before him—relied on the same segments so frequently that the current population represents a limited range. See my regular journal for full list of conclusions.

The threat of Ambrose's ailment in multiple subjects and

the possibility of defects we haven't yet identified heightens my concern. If—when—we lose the ability to build individuals in the lab, our isolated community may not be able to survive with such a small gene pool. This must be corrected. I have most of genstat working on a plan to activate more of our genetic catalog.

* * *

2.10.309

Today when I visited Ambrose, he didn't recognize me. He lives in a world that is one moment long. The past and the future do not exist.

I'm taking credit for nature again. Plant specimens P47 and T78 are doing splendidly. Specimen L26 did not thrive and was terminated. Nicholas is the only one who knows I did not create them by patching together archived genes. Which is more unethical—to do less than I can to revitalize the ecosystem or to do all that I am able and lie about my methods?

It is late. No answer tonight.

The horse continues to do well. Privately I've named it Spirit. I would like to make another large animal, but zoostat is still collecting data on the effects of the first one and is not ready to move forward.

"Halt, merchant." The guard hoped this cart would be the last one of the night. The sun was almost down, and thunder growled in the west. Noalgaz was ready to rise full, signaling the end of Smernt and the beginning of Boniskal, the third month of the year.

The woman let the squeaky single-wheeled pushcart rest on its supports and rubbed her hands together for warmth. Her long dark hair was braided in Joach style. A cap tilted over her face. "Two kegs of fine wine for Tarryn Skaln."

The guard observed the muscular merchant while his partner rapped at the barrels to be sure they were not filled with something other than drink. The woman's easy stance did not hide the trained fighter in her. Not the owner of the winery then but one hired to guarantee that the kegs reached the proper destination. Merchants were fearful of late, with raiders on the roads. To stay in business, they spent their profits on personal soldiers like this one and the silent one just before her bringing sacks of flour.

"Too cold for duty out here in the open," the woman said. "And no supper, I suppose, until the gate closes for the night."

"That be right," the guard grumbled.

"I don't suppose the two of you have empty cups nearby that could use a splash."

The guard quickly looked around. The soldiers at the gate were talking to the man with the flour sacks. The only other person nearby was a little carpenter bundled in a cloak, wearily struggling along the city road on the way home from the fortress, clanking tool bag on her back.

His partner grabbed cups from a pile of gear. The guard licked his lips as the woman filled them with liquid sparkling with the last of the day's light. He gratefully took the cup she offered and sipped. The sweetness was cool, but it went down warm. With a wink the woman picked up the handles of the cart and pushed up the bridge toward the fortress.

The carpenter squatted in the road, leaning over a spilled bag. The guard drained his cup and tossed it with the other gear. The wine made him feel friendly. Maybe the crafter would appreciate some conversation while collecting the tools.

"Carpenter!"

The guard was about to say that very word, but the voice came from behind him. He turned to see a man hurrying down the slope from the gate. Despite the weather he wore no cloak. His shirt sleeves were rolled to a Felcon armband as if he had rushed outdoors on an urgent errand.

"Hold, carpenter!" he called. "You're needed a moment longer at the stables."

The figure finished collecting the tools, hoisted the bag, and shuffled back across the bridge. Now the guard would have to talk to his partner if he wanted conversation, and he was tired of the woman's prattle about her skill at cards and her spouse's lovemaking and her children's cleverness.

Shouts came from the archway. In the fading light the guard saw the gate soldiers, the shirt-sleeved man, the wine hauler, and a glint of weapons in shuffling confusion centered around the little carpenter. Suddenly the scene was still. A tingling hit the guard. He felt calm and relaxed, as if he floated in a warm bath. At first he thought the wine had a hidden potency, but his slowed brain told him the sensation was a spell cast by the mystic at the gate.

He was pleased the mystic protected the poor little carpenter, although he wished the feeling was from the wine instead.

〜

CHAPTER

TWENTY-TWO

Skaln made an undignified sprint to the Baerryns' balcony. The mystic who'd been scanning his meal for poison had known what was happening but had not warned him. It had stood silent, shielding him from one danger while another walked through his gate. He would not have known except for his own soldiers.

The storm rumbled and flashed across the marble floor. Rozel, flanked by two other Druetens, addressed a semicircle of hooded figures.

"I have not given permission for these people to enter the fortress," Skaln shouted.

The center mystic spoke in the multiple voice. "Rozel asked audience. We granted it. The matter is not your concern."

Skaln was certain now that the Speaker was new and shorter than the previous one. He'd noticed other changes in the mystics at the fortress since Rojelon's death. "I am responsible for fortress security," he said.

"We guarantee they will do no harm while within these

walls," the Speaker said. "Just as we guarantee that they will come to no harm while under our protection."

Skaln regretted his emotional display. The Speaker seemed impressed with its own power and pleased by the opportunity to give the Felcon tarryn a subtle reprimand.

"I'm grateful for your assurances," Skaln said. "Rojelon's death and the unsettling occurrences since—"

"We understand," the Speaker said.

Skaln smiled. It understood all right. He didn't have to remind it the Baerryns were at fault.

"Rozel of the Druetens," the Speaker said, "we will continue with your petition."

Petition. Skaln's smile fell. Rozel was exceptionally thin. Her gaunt face showed the lines and deep moons of little sleep and rough travel. She wore riding clothes with muddy hems. The two with her were similarly clothed and also showed signs of fatigue. He recognized Oktria. The other was a stranger. He tried to dismiss the man as a simple soldier, but his look was that of a leader not a mere follower.

Perhaps she was here to plead for an extension to the time limit imposed on Janvian. That must not happen. Mentally he prepared an objection. Sanctity of the Baerryns' decision, something like that. He must be firmly on the throne when the *skyship* returned or the envoy would not deal with him.

"I, Rozel of the Druetens, great-granddaughter of the monarch Nevran, claim the throne for the good of Lorcha."

The argument caught in Skaln's throat. Rozel challenging her own sister! With the tarryn's most trusted soldier at her side! Could the Druetens be so divided?

No. It was a ploy. Benoc's hand was in this. The only surprise was that Rozel had agreed to it.

"Your petition is accepted," the Speaker said in its choral voice that spoke for all. "The Baerryns hold the ruling of

Lorcha in regency. The selection ceremony will be held at sunset on the last day of the year 401 of the Age of Order. We will name a new monarch from among the candidates. You must present yourself to us at that time to be reviewed for suitability. The merit of your claim will be judged against those of the other petitioners. If you are not in attendance, we will assume you have withdrawn your claim, or that you are dead and therefore unable to perform the duties of monarch."

Skaln hid a chuckle. He had thought mystics were incapable of humor. Or perhaps the Speaker was so involved in the formality that it had not recognize the absurdity of its own words.

The Speaker continued. "As an accepted petitioner, it is now your right to reside in the fortress, if you so choose, until the day of declaration. While in the fortress, we will ensure your safety. However, we cannot do so should you leave the gated walls."

The Baerryns filed out through their private arch. A robed figure, as tall as Skaln and exceptionally square-shouldered, appeared. He did not know mystics could be that wide. They were always slight, as invisible as the furnishings of a room, relying on mental powers rather than physical prowess. Rozel's personal protector seemed to possess both. Was this a not so subtlety message from the new Speaker?

"So, the little sister turns on her clankin," Skaln said. "What a glorious day for the Druetens."

Rozel took the sting with a flip of her head, her face flushed with defiance. "Any Drueten on the throne is preferable to the wrong Felcon."

"If you're referring to me," Skaln said, "you slash at the air. I haven't petitioned the Baerryns, although my lineage, too, goes back to Nevran. My lor is to Rojelon's child and Felcon

Clan. I'm no traitor." What was her real mission? And who was the stranger at her side?

Gently he led Rozel away from her companions and the mystic. Cautiously, she allowed it. He leaned over her as if this were a tender moment and noted that the strange man stiffened. "Should the baby tragically die before reaching the fortress, and its mother with it, then I would be forced to claim the monarchy for myself."

Rozel's intense blue eyes chilled him like the depths of the labyrinth. "You are too self-sacrificing, Skaln. You must learn to act more for yourself. Forget the heavy responsibility of the throne. The wealth, the power. Whisk Calliud away to a hut in the woods where you can happily raise gaegils for the rest of your lives."

A vision of Calliud in her jewels and white fur cape chasing fat, squealing animals sent him into laughter. He had missed someone to banter with during the past months. If he thought Rozel were a true traitor, he would offer her a tempting future. Imagine, ruling Lorcha with this fiery creature beside him!

The stranger was suddenly at Rozel's shoulder, his silent stare more menacing than a drawn sword. Skaln refused to give him more than a glance. This was a private skirmish. The fool should stay in the background where he belonged. Or did he have an interest here?

For a moment Skaln had forgotten his purpose for this conversation. He had learned one of the things he wanted to know. He could not resist one more poke with a sharp stick. "Why, Rozel. I'm touched by your concern for me. But you should be thinking of your own safety. Remember, you're only protected within the fortress. If you leave, you'll not find it easy to return."

<>‹›‹›

Janvian skimmed ahead in the journals, catching random phrases. Descriptions of scientific procedures were incomprehensible to her while Jeremy found them fascinating. He sat at his desk and bent over the pages of their latest translation, absorbing every drop.

She paced, book in hand. Sitting for long periods caused her back to ache. She was interested in Marla's comments on the dome's society. They gave her insight into how this world functioned and how Jeremy saw life.

As often happened despite her efforts to guard against it, thoughts of Rojelon were suddenly with her. The two of them had had only four years together. She sat heavily on Jeremy's bed and concentrated on the journal to keep away the tears.

* * *

18.10.309

> *Another day on minimum power. We are not used to this kind of conservation. All of the experiments have been terminated to direct genstat's ration of energy to the developing food stuffs. We won't be able to maintain all of them beyond another twenty hours. I've set up priorities based on agristat's capacity to take a crop once it's reached viability. I'm most worried about the citrus fruits.*
>
> *I can tell when the orbiting craft clears the curve of the planet. If it is day, the lights dim because the shields must be turned on, drawing energy from the storage units. If it is night, the shields are already on and the lights fade because the collectors must be turned off and protected from the ship's prying sensors.*
>
> *I wonder about the people who look down. What have they become in the centuries since the Sanctuary broke away? Do*

they search for remnants of those fugitives as we fear they do?
Or are we forgotten?

* * *

25.10.309

The storage units are back to full capacity and rationing has ended. Unfortunately, the environment in a bank of growth modules dipped below acceptable parameters. The organs are no longer suitable for transplants. As long as there are no emergencies or setbacks, we should be able to generate replacements before they are needed. I may need one myself. Every time the lights flicker my heart stops.

The Sage hobbled through the street in his hunched disguise. Noalgaz, its fullness signaling the end of one month and the beginning of another, was blocked by buildings. Stray light from cracks in shuttered windows striped the street. He ignored the annoyance of the cold and scanned. The souls in the Split Hoof were still a jumble. The rogue and the revenge-fevered thieves were not following him. Not yet. They needed no nudging. In a moment they would prance after him like three little eipys.

The Sage chuckled to the wind. The former Speaker was inexperienced and weak on his own. No doubt he had spent all but the first few inconsequential years of his life in the Unity. He had not practiced olax as the Sage did. It was amazing he had not gone mad in the isolation. And with his gemstone in fragments scattered across sharp rocks.

His mind had drifted. Ahh! The three were exactly where

they should be. The weather had emptied the night of opportunists. There would be no witnesses. Tomorrow the bodies would be found, throats neatly sliced in noble Lorchan fashion. Nothing mysterious about the deaths, not in this part of the city. And he would have the satisfaction of doing it himself.

Hard-soled boots crunched behind him. He shuffled into a narrow street suitable only for foot traffic. Thick smoke from the hovels on each side twisted against the red flashes overhead. The storm propelled heavy clouds toward the mountains to belch out their loads, leaving the city with wind but sparing it the worst of the snowfall. A child wailed as if it had been born to a life of winter.

A tent had been here until the frozen ground had forced its owner to find other accommodations. The wall of a third building closed off the end, making a shabby alcove. The Sage straightened from the feigned stoop. He blasted fear through the narrow channel.

Screams came from the bordering shanties, ripping the quiet fabric of night. A cry almost escaped his own lips as the backwash flowed over him.

The emotion dissipated. The cries faded. The alley was empty.

He scanned and found no trace of his prey. And yet, back in the street a curtain hung in the furry evening. He stifled a chuckle. The mental blanket was poorly blended at the edges, making it easy to define once he knew it was there. It redirected the flow of light but it was not protection. Vision was blocked from both sides. He could not see or detect them. They could not see or detect his movements.

Knife drawn, he crept toward the illusion. Ready to strike, he tore down the drape, revealing only cobblestones and diffused moonlight.

Tricked! How could that be?

They surrounded him. Enough of the game. He sent a paralyzing grip to their minds. It slammed against a barrier. The rogue had a gemstone!

Someone grabbed his wrist and twisted his knife-hand behind his back. A larger blade pressed against his throat. Mentally he reached out to halt the edge. Another force slowed his thoughts, and a thin line of pain etched his skin. Wetness trickled into his collar.

Minds were hard to kill, but bodies were easy. He had no illusion about his own mortality, but his plan must flower and bear fruit before he died. A mystic would sit on the throne. That mystic would become a Sage. And the Sages to follow would rule all of Lorcha by superiority, not accident of birth. It was his legacy. His gift.

He sensed the facets and symmetry of the rogue's crystal. The cut was beautifully balanced like his own, but it was not a perfect stone. A flaw, thin as a spider web, pierced its heart. He grabbed the vibration it produced and sent a shock through the jewel.

The blade fought to press deeper into his neck. He pulsed heat through the knife and the arm and into the brain. An anguished screech shattered his ear and he was suddenly free.

The knife fell with a thud. He swept it up and slashed. The body crumple into the dirty snow. He gave a kick to the mind for the sticky blood and the new scar he would have. The body convulsed then stilled.

Around him the hovels swayed like wrecked ships in murky water. He scanned but found only a single drunk too muddle-minded to find the way home.

～

TWENTY-THREE

"Good morning, Cousin Calliud of the Tskants." The woman nodded and smiled. The man beside her repeated the greeting like the reverberation of a sour bell.

Calliud could not ignore them on the narrow, winding stairs. At first she thought the two were servants and expected them to step aside. Now she looked at their faces and recognized them. Walbask armbands covered the cheap fabric of their sleeves. Although she felt no obligation to remember their names, they were cousins, yes. But not clankin and not important.

Calliud clutched the message in the pocket of her riding cape. She was not in the mood to waste time exchanging formalities with people she did not know or want to know. She had purposely avoided the main staircase so she would not encounter Rozel. But no place was free of the rabble who invaded the fortress.

The Baerryns let in any pretender who claimed a convoluted blood tie to the monarchy. Few could prove the lineage. The ridiculous petitions were accepted anyway. Like these Walbask cousins, the "heirs" strutted about the fortress, assessing its contents as if planning to sell the furniture.

Calliud granted the two a nod and a "hmm" as she pushed past, pulling aside the embroidered hem of her cape. In the close space the fine fabric still brushed against overly perfumed cloth. She hurried by the mystics who followed them —one for each. The flowery stench combined with the downward spiral and her haste unbalancing her.

Most of the ruffians traced their line to the monarch Corella, who was Felcon. The woman had an outrageous number of children. Five live births! The four younger siblings had grown and married, choosing their spouses' clans. Her own aunt had wed a Walbask man with a blood tie to Corella, which accounted for the ones who dared to call her cousin.

Only one of Corella's flock ever sat on the throne—Nevran. Only his descendants were true heirs. That lineage, although it forked into several streams, flowed to Skaln. She wished he would make his petition soon.

She understood his strategy. He must maintain the illusion of lor to Rojelon's unborn child as long as possible. The swarm of superficial candidates clogging the complex showed the country was dangerously divided. He did little to stop the disgusting displays of their own inferior qualities. By simple comparison, Skaln was the superior choice. He was a unifying leader that the Baerryns could not ignore.

Calliud reached the main floor out of breath. She understood, but she did not like the ambiguous position it placed her in.

The paper crackled in her fist. He must make his petition. She would demand so after this other matter was settled with her parents. She would ride to the estate now and tell them to order the caravan from Bask to continue to Aerrion City. Extra guards must be sent as escort.

Whatever the cost, the irefs, amicysks, gaedennen and other gems must arrive in time to be incorporated into the design of her wedding dress and to be sewn in place. Both tasks required great skill and could not be rushed. It was already the third quarter of the month of Jastayn. Almost spring. Then summer, then harvest and the new year.

She would go home and set this right. And she would be free of the ruffian-filled fortress for the day.

Around the corner laughter and shouts rattled against the stones. Calliud stopped, ready to turn back, but that hall was the quickest path to her escape. She straightened her shoulders and continued on.

"What be the bet?" someone bellowed.

Calliud's breath caught at the sight of rabble flipping knives into the polished surface of a priceless parquet wall hanging. The circular pattern formed by fitted pieces of dark and light woods had been crafted before Corella's reign. Now it was pitted from the tips of drunkenly tossed blades.

"Barbarians! Sand born!" she yelled.

The gamblers turned startled faces toward her in a tableau of surprise. In unison they erupted into mocking laughter and set up wagers for the next round.

"Fetch some wine and we'll let you join the game," a scaly reptile in a Joach armband brazenly called, "if you've got your own blade."

Calliud would not tolerate being treated like a servant. "Go play in the manure pile where you belong."

The reptile grinned with stained teeth. "Now be that the way to speak before the future monarch?"

Calliud jammed her fists into her hips. "And which of you is that?"

The reptile shrugged. "Bound to be one of us. At least we all be legitimate petitioners, accepted by the Baerryns themselves. We've a right to be here." His tone clearly said that she did not.

"I am Calliud of the Tskants." It took all her strength to keep her lip from quivering.

"That counts for spit around the old fortress these days," the reptile said. "You be nothing but a child of rich parents dressed up pretty. A decoration, worth as much as this fancy wood slab." He sent a fat blade into the soft wood.

Calliud trembled. She rushed through them and away from the viciousness, tears stinging her eyes.

Behind her the wagers continue. "Next flip for the treasury. Winner takes it no matter what of us be monarch."

"That be a good one. Nati, you have a go first."

Calliud's meran waited in the courtyard. A cowering groom held its reins. At least some people knew how to show respect. She mounted and urged it through the gate at a gallop, past startled servants and swearing soldiers. The animal charged over the bridge and down the steep road.

She felt she would suffocate in the slow pace of crowded city streets. She took a series of paths that skirted the populated areas, kicking the meran's sides for more speed. As she often did when she needed comfort, she imagined it was Foam's reins she held and Foam's gait under her.

The cloud-white beauty had been as quick and light as tumbling water. When she was a child, a thousand times she had thrown her small arms around the meran's neck and pressed her cheek against its muzzle, feeling the warm breath ruffle her hair.

At night she had smuggled Foam into her room, defying her parents and tricking her nurse. The animal had slept quietly on the woven rug next to her bed. Sometimes she'd curled up beside him. Or she'd stayed in her own bed, one arm dangling over the edge to stroke the silky coat, so the adults who'd controlled her life would object less.

But a white meran was too valuable to be a child's pet.

One morning Foam was gone. Her parents had explained he'd been sold to finance an important business opportunity. And think of all the pretty clothes they would buy her next year when the new venture brought a large profit. And wouldn't Calliud be glad that mama and papa were so successful.

She'd cried every night and continued to hang a hand over the edge of her bed. Nurse replaced the woven rug with a soft fur for her to touch so she could sleep.

When Calliud was old enough—well, perhaps a little young, but in control of some of her own money—she had tried to find Foam. The beautiful animal had died of a lung infection years earlier.

She stopped trembling. Guiltily, she let the meran find its own pace. So what if she was a decoration? Ornaments were highly prized—fine embroidery, sculpture, jewels, a white meran.

When she finally stood on the dais in the hearth hall, the Tskant lightning bolt in gold encircling her arm, the barbarians would choke on the memory of their cruelty.

She would be Lorcha's jewel, shining from the throne for all to admire. Then her parents would know her true value and would be proud of her.

Brick and wood, the estate of Trillege filled the horizon. Calliud sped home. Servants could fetch her things later. She would not enter the fortress again until her wedding day.

<>-<>-<>

Medic Richard traced around an irregular oval floating on the machine's monitor, his hand a rich brown against the flat black and white. "This picture is drawn by sound."

Janvian watched politely. The doctor was boring to listen to but interesting to observe. He tried so hard to communicate that his actions became comical. Although he said he had never been outside the dome, his skin appeared darkened by an unyielding sun. Individually his nose, mouth and eyes seemed enormous to Janvian; yet they fit into his wide face in an appealing manner.

There were others similar to him in a general way. Merede's skin was almost as dark, but her features were very different. It seemed as if each person claimed a separate ancestry. Nevran had told her, "They have many faces but are one clan." Now she knew what he'd meant.

Only a few could masquerade as Lorchan. Jeremy might pass for Walbask. Tamaki could pretend Tskant lineage, but his green eyes would arouse suspicion.

Richard would be challenged no matter what armband he wore. "See?" he said, tapping the screen. "Already the baby is very large."

Janvian nodded and hid a sigh. How could sound draw? The image was supposed to be the baby growing inside her, but it looked more like milk swirled in muddy water. Janvian had seen babies that were born before their time. Tiny creatures that fit in the palm of the hand, they looked nothing like what Richard showed her.

He rotated the oval. With his finger he drew an invisible line from a white mass on one side of the murky baby to a mirror image on the other side. "And you are very small from here to here." He wagged his finger back and forth, back and forth.

Janvian did not need a healer to tell her that. Drueten women's hips were close together and sometimes did not widen as they should for childbirth. It complicated delivery. Janvian had witnessed tragic results.

Richard pointed to the oval. "The baby must work very hard to be born." He pointed to her. "And you must work very hard. Too hard." He tapped his chest. "There is a strain. Very dangerous for the baby and for you. That is why we will remove the baby early. Cut, cut," he made a gesture she did not understand, "and the baby is out. Very easy for you."

She nodded. It was not easy. Blood loss was a greater threat than a weak heart. She had already decided how her baby would be born. Her mother and her mother's mother had survived natural births of healthy children. Janvian was willing to take the risk that she could too.

Richard smiled with his wide mouth and big teeth, obviously pleased with his communication skills. He spoke slowly and emphatically. "When it is time for the baby to be born, when it is time for the operation, Jeremy will bring you here. Yes?"

"Yes," she said. *Never*, she thought.

The table was bare except for tankards of ale, a poor substitute for wine. The best vintage came from a strip of mountains along the ocean in Joach territory, and no lumbering wagons filled with barrels had survived the journey since the raids began.

Artulk hid his nervous hands in the folds of his robe. It was not the lack of wine that bothered him. The cellar held many kegs. He would send a servant to fetch a decanter as soon as the guests left. It was the lack of sweets. Rich flavors helped him concentrate. Without them he had to use great willpower to follow the conversation around the table.

The Joach merchant, Yajed, ignored the drink. "My business has stopped, as the quality of the refreshments before you testify. In addition to wine, I can't get grain and cloth into the city, and I can't get finished goods out."

"I'm sure you mean no offense to our hospitality." Diakt, as was her way, stood behind the chair set for her. It was positioned between Artulk and the Felcon merchant Lucetra in an oblique show of combined power. "We each suffer."

Yajed leaned into the hard, spindled wood of her chair. She had brooded since her arrival. Grain was usually transported to market as soon after harvest as caravans and boats could move it. This year much of it was still stored in bursting Joach barns near the fields where it had been cut, blocked from buyers by raiders.

"I've noticed some merchants suffer less than others," Yajed said. "Diakt, Artulk, your businesses seem to have shelves that magically replenish themselves with goods at premium prices."

"I've noticed as well, and wondered," said Emullian, the Walbask merchant, positioned between Yajed and Lucetra. "Perhaps this meeting is to share the Tskant secret." The sharp-eyed man wore a finely woven robe draped at the shoulders with fur. But the dealer in gems was without several rings he had worn for many years.

Artulk heaved his thick body in a shrug. "This is Tskant land. Our warehouses are here. But I assure you, they're growing pitifully empty. Pitifully."

Diakt had orchestrated the meeting to illustrate that very point. Which was why there were no sweets, and only two servants quietly moved in and out of the room. They must appear as affected by the unrest as the others. Artulk wondered if their illusion was as transparent as Emullian's false show of wealth. Perhaps Emullian, Yajed, and Lucetra were aware of the large quantities of goods quickly brought to the city before the raids began. Perhaps that was what creased Yajed's face.

To Artulk's left, Gozax was uncharacteristically grim. She wore her office differently from the other tarryns. She joked and cajoled her way through difficult situations so that some thought her incapable of handling serious matters. They failed to see that she battled anger and resentment with good-natured banter and that she resolved heated disagreements so both sides felt appeased. But she did not need to rely on friendly phrases. She was a tarryn. Her word was law.

She could easily guess the true purpose of this meeting. Artulk expected her to be the most difficult to convince. As the tarryn who controlled Lorcha's commercial center, they needed her support.

The discussion was not advancing to Artulk's satisfaction. Nor to Diakt's. He saw it on her calm expression. He shifted in the stiff chair. A heaviness thumped against his thigh. He slid a hand into his pocket and touched the comforting key. He leaned a bulky arm on the table. "Think how quickly wectulk would completely destroy the structure of commerce we have all worked so hard to create."

"War?" Drops of ale slipped from the momentarily forgotten mug in Emullian's hand and splashed on his robe.

Artulk could tell Diakt was pleased by the reaction. She would not be pleased if she knew about the key. Artulk rubbed his thumb back and forth along the shaft. His mouth watered thinking of the scrolled box carved with plia blossoms that it unlocked. Thinking of the click as the latch released the lid, allowing a pleasing fragrance to escape. Thinking of waving his plump fingers over the private cache of delicacies, changing his mind several times and finally plucking a confection and plopping it onto his tongue. Thinking of the disapproval of his spouse if she knew of the outrageously high-priced luxury he indulged in behind closed doors for personal pleasure and not in public as a symbol of wealth.

Diakt strolled around the table as if she walked through a garden and the most pressing matter on her mind was to enjoy bird song. "There'll be war if the Baerryns' choice for monarch is not acceptable to the clans."

Emullian set down his mug and pushed it away. "Surely the baby will be chosen with Janvian as regent."

"Where is Janvian now?" Lucetra's voice was quietly deceptive. Artulk was certain he could speak of dismemberment and make it sound as if he commented on breakfast. "She's abandoned her responsibility to the country. Her own sister challenges her claim. Perhaps Rozel knows Janvian has no intention of fulfilling her obligation."

Yajed gripped the arms of her chair. "Perhaps you think Skaln is a better choice?"

"Skaln keeps order while your own clans are in chaos." Lucetra gave Yajed a narrow smile. "It wasn't Felcon raiders who burned a Walbask village."

A blade appeared in Yajed's hand, point toward Lucetra's throat.

Emullian grabbed Yajed's wrist in restraint, but his eyes were on Lucetra. "My clankin were attacked. My clankin died. If the Joach are responsible, then blood lies between Yajed and me and is none of your concern, Felcon."

Lucetra's smile never wavered. "I never meant to imply otherwise."

Emullian released his grip. He and Yajed exchanged looks that said if their positions had been reversed, the actions would have been the same.

Artulk hid a sigh. There was no stronger force than allied enemies. Lucetra knew better than to meddle in matters between other clans but had no self-discipline about such things. He was a child perpetually looking for a weak branch to jump on to see if it would break. No matter that when the wood snapped, he would fall with it.

The blade vanished so quickly that Artulk could not tell where it was concealed. Yajed bowed to his hosts. "My apology for drawing metal in your home. But I don't apologize for saying what I've seen. Your commerce flourishes while ours dies. Your caravans trickle through while ours are attacked before they cross out of our own borders. And now you want to use us to maneuver Skaln and your daughter into the monarchy."

"If you think my parents control the raids, you're mistaken." A disheveled Calliud stood in the doorway. Strands of yellow hair dark with sweat stuck to her wind-chaffed cheeks. Her boots dripped mud onto the patterned brick floor.

She strode to the table, leaving a wet trail, and waved a crumpled letter before her father. "I have it memorized. 'Dearest Daughter of Our Hearts, we received a message from the caravan carrying the jewels for your wedding dress. The master feels it is too dangerous to leave Bask. So sorry, Darling, but we have to agree. The cargo is too valuable to risk, and we cannot in good conscience order him to proceed. Your Loving Parents.'"

Diakt put a hand on her daughter's shoulder. "Don't allow yourself to be upset."

The young woman's anger became tears. "Mother, force the caravan to continue. Threaten to reduce the commission. Send extra guards. I must have those jewels or the wedding will be ruined."

The old nurse cowered outside the door in the tow of another servant. Diakt deposited a sobbing Calliud in the woman's arms. With a gesture Diakt directed the floor to be mopped, then she returned to the table.

Artulk was appalled by Calliud's disgraceful behavior, yet pleased. Diakt had been right not to let this particular cargo through. But even she could not have arranged a scene better than the one provided by their emotional daughter.

"Yajed," Artulk said putting a plump hand to his brow as if crushed by his child's distress, "I wish I had the influence you suggest, if only to make my sweet Calliud happy. But I'm at their mercy as much as you. That's why we must all band together."

"All?" Gozax broke her silence. "I see only four clans represented here."

"We don't need to be told to our faces that no Drueten will support Skaln's claim." Lucetra took a sip of ale. He was the only one enjoying the drink.

"Your tarryn hasn't petitioned the Baerryns," Gozax said.

Lucetra rolled the tankard between his palms. It was beautifully made of dull silver. "Then we must urge him to do so. For the good of Lorcha."

Lucetra was a fool. Artulk watched Gozax rise slowly from her chair and dreaded what was to come.

The tarryn's gray hair was pulled tight against her skull and gathered high on the back of her head. Loops of embroidered ribbon hung among the coarse strands. Her arms were loose at her sides, tense strength in every muscle. "Lor demands that we support the blood heir. To speak of anything else is treason, and I will give traitors what they deserve."

She did not show metal. There was no sign that she carried a knife. The Tskant tarryn had a more brutal weapon. With a single command she could revoke the permits of merchants conducting business within the city. Artulk and Diakt's legitimate enterprises would fail. They would be forced to increase their black-market activities, with enormous risk and with high capital investment that would strain their cash.

Worse, if Gozax interpreted this meeting as promoting treason, she could expel Artulk and Diakt from the clan and their riches would be but a memory.

Artulk resisted brushing beads of sweat from under his fringe of hair. "We explore options only," he said. "The intent is to unify support for a stabilized leadership so the present unfortunate situation will not escalate."

Gozax fixed her hard, gray eyes on each merchant in turn. "Then it's agreed that our first loyalty is to the babe. Whatever else is spoken of here is only if the baby is not presented to be named monarch."

Whatever the private opinions, all wisely voiced agreement. Gozax sat and resumed her silent posture.

Artulk pressed the key into of his fleshy palm. A disaster averted. The sweets would be a well-deserved reward. "I propose that, should Rojelon's child not appear to take its rightful place on the throne, we express to each of our tarryns our united support for Skaln as monarch." He gave a nod to Gozax, who stared at a far point on the wall.

Diakt turned to Lucetra. "Perhaps Skaln could be prepared to make a petition, should unfortunate circumstances occur."

Lucetra waved a hand helplessly. "I'll do my best to persuade him. But he is absolutely dedicated to the blood heir and has great hopes for the child's arrival."

"As do we all," Artulk said, wishing Lucetra had expressed this attitude earlier as they had rehearsed. He directed the discussion back to the original script Diakt had worked out and watched his spouse's pleasure as their guests unknowingly played their parts well. The key never left his palm. "Then if there are no further concerns to address—"

There were none.

~

CHAPTER
TWENTY-FOUR

Jeremy struggling with a series of journal entries. Janvian had tactfully made it clear that she wished to be alone during her free shift. He had been pressing her too hard, he knew, forcing his obsession on her. She was probably visiting Fujin and Spirit.

There were questions about the identical animals. He had assured the mayor he was researching it. Eventually he'd have to reveal Marla's subterfuge. He wasn't sure what the repercussions would be. Most likely, he'd be told to do an audit of all stored genetic material. He might be ordered to purge anything not original to Sanctuary. Munch had proven its value and would be exempt. So would some other flora and fauna well incorporated into the ecosystem. But their source material would probably be destroyed.

Cradle six failed completely. Jeremy had another conversation with Merede about the need for an alternative. Janvian's growing abdomen had the medic thinking human incubation, with all of its risks, might be feasible. Jeremy knew it would be necessary eventually.

Dougal hauled the dead machine to his workshop for parts. All of the carts were in service, so he used a broken one he'd striped down to wheels and an open box. He pulled it by a handle he'd attached. He called it the Conestoga. Jeremy didn't know the reference. Dougal thought it was a clever name and promised to explain it later.

In Janvian's absence Jeremy was forced to struggle through the new language on his own. He missed her laugh at his pronunciations, and their discussions about the subtle meanings of words. And he simply missed her.

His command of written Lorchan was superior to his spoken. Although he worked slowly, he could now decipher the bulk of a passage. Years after her death, Marla continued to be his teacher, but he was learning things far different from what he'd expected.

A series of records had its own numbering system. No year was given. It started with 1.1, indicating the timeline of a project rather than a day and month. There was an apology for the exclusion of important details. As soon as he understood what Marla had done, he raced through the entries.

* * *

24.10.0

Alpha was born today. Healthy and vigorous. 294 days after the first cell division. I had difficulty hiding my emotions as I watched the medic assist the parents in removing her from the cradle. Her cries are strong and encouraging. What a joy it will be to watch her grow. Her vital signs are all within acceptable parameters. Statistics included below.

* * *

28.11.1

Beta. Gamma. Born two days apart. Both healthy and vigorous. Statistics included below.

* * *

12.4.6

I see no physical characteristics between the three and the images of Nevran. That's not surprising. They are composites not clones. The outsider contributed most, but not all, of the source material. I have documented that they are more active than the average five-year-old and four-year-old. Their independence scales are above average but not alarming. They are above average in problem solving.

They ask 24% more questions than their peers. I predict this will decrease. The adults around them subtly discourage their curiosity. Alpha, perhaps because she is older, has started to self-censor. It will be interesting to see if the others follow that development.

Alpha structures her own learning activities. This seems to be related to questioning and the adult responses she receives (see above).

Beta is less social than his peers. He is inclined toward non-linear thinking.

Gamma is ambidextrous. He is highly above average in hand-eye coordination.

I'm planning Delta, but may do no more than that for now. I don't want to become like Ambrose, infusing too much of one vision into the population. There are many sequences stored away that should be revived. My goal is to achieve a balance.

<><><>

The warmer spring weather had yet to penetrate the tower of rooms attached to the Split Hoof. A fire illuminating the hearth took the chill from the room. Uz brought up a plate and a mug for Lnez, and a mug for himself. "The service be slumping like the roof. Odd since there be no customers for days 'cept us and a few locals."

Lnez took the food and drink and sat by the fire. "Locals?"

"A one-legged man what waves his crutch at the barkeep when he wants his tankard filled and that furry creature what lives in the rafters," Uz said. He sat on the splintering floor. "The tavern be hugely empty. I don't like scum, but it feels unnatural without them. No one complaining about the lousy way the Baerryns be running the country. No cursing over the prices."

Lnez pushed greasy liquid and over-cooked vegetables across his plate with a bent spoon. It seemed as if he had been eating the same stew for months. Maybe he had. "We're almost locals ourselves, we've been here so long. Did you see Rozel today?"

"No," Uz said. "They kept me in the kitchen washing up after the cooks." He pointed to Lnez's plate. "The work be lousy, but I don't have to come back here and eat that slop. Don't know how many heirs the fortress be feeding now. More than guards lately. They're hungry all the time."

"You still haven't found out where the guards have gone?"

"No one remembers them leaving," Uz said. "Oh, a groom says one went here to do this and a servant says two or so went there to do such. No one saw more than a few ride out the gate at a time. Not enough to account for empty corrals and bunks. I see guards about the fortress as often as before, but they always be the same ones."

"So they left in disguise or at night or by secret doorways," Lnez speculated. "And those remaining are trying to hide their absence."

"And they be gone where?" Uz asked. He yawned, tired from his labor.

Lnez chewed a mushy lump of starch but no revelation came. "Where everyone else went."

Uz held a mug but was too exhausted to drink. "That be a lot of everyone in the same place."

"You've got to talk to Rozel about it tomorrow," Lnez said, setting aside the plate. He pulled out a pouch and offered it to Uz. "Despite the city's sudden decline in population, I did well today."

"You shouldn't be on the streets."

"I was careful."

The large man batted away the pouch, pretending to be insulted. "I'm the one with the honest job."

"But I make more as a thief," Lnez said. He dropped the pouch beside the discarded plate. The day had been lonely and he was glad to have company. Their roles had reversed in less than a year. He had resided in the fortress as the Speaker, and Uzec had made his way as a thief. Now Uz held a job behind the gate and he create distractions while lightening pockets, and someone else was Speaker. Lnez wondered who.

Uz laughed and pounded the floor so the pouch jingled and the plate bounced. "You're not much of a fighter, but you snatch coin like a master. You be almost as good as—" Uz sobered. "I be going to say Yadul. Then I be going to say Ham." He traced the mug's rim with his thumb. "He'll search until he finds us."

The same thought kept Lnez sleepless. The Sage. Yes, it was the Sage. The man had a presence, an identifying signature. It had crackled as he'd ripped the power from Lnez's gemstone. It had shocked the air as he'd gloated over Ham's dying body.

Lnez should have cooled Uz and Ham's insane need to avenge Yadul's murder, but their lust had been infectious. He hadn't been prepared for the emotions that swept through him. He'd been wronged by mystics too, he'd reasoned. This was his chance to stop the Sage and get a dab of satisfaction. Only it hadn't worked out as planned. Ham was dead and Lnez had a scar to remind him of his folly.

Mystics prowled near from time to time. He and Uz would have moved to another tavern, but a messenger would seek them at the Split Hoof, so here they must stay.

"You'll explain it to me someday, won't you?" Uz asked. "When you trust me more. Who the ancient man be and why the Baerryns be about his dirty business for him?"

Lnez did not answer. During the past two months his wound had healed, but for both of them the memory still bled. It was not a matter of trust. He could not explain some without revealing all. And that seemed wrong.

Lnez felt a tug at the scan he maintained. "Uz!" He closed his eyes to concentrate. A figure climbed the stairs.

The large man grabbed a sword from under his bedroll and was at the door a moment before the knock came.

"Uzec," the hoarse voice whispered. "It's Jianerk."

Uz let the woman in. They listened to her breathy story. A large fighting force marched into the Drueten mountains. Villagers prepared to assault the invaders along the way, but they were outnumbered and had limited weapons. They could hope to do little more than slow the army's progress.

"They switch bands like changing hats," the woman said. "The weather be calm of late, so I be watching in the low hills. When I see the trouble, I didn't go back to the cave but come straight here as Amud told me to save time. The next up the trail had the job of warning the camp. Can't say how close the raiders be to Nept by now. Depends on the sky and the villagers along the way."

Lnez grabbed his cape. "Rozel has to know immediately."

Uz shook his head. "With hard riding and a fair wind we still be eighteen, maybe twenty days away. And Rozel best not leave the fortress."

"That's for her to decide," Lnez said.

"You can't go. The Baerryns'll grab you in a flash. They might not feel all your mystic stuff, but they're sure to know what you look like."

"You'd never get in," Lnez said.

"Neither'll you," Uz said.

"I don't have to."

"Just crouch in the slush outside the walls and do your twitchy thing and hope they don't notice?"

"Something like that."

The messenger didn't understand the details of the argument, but it ended as she suspected it would. Uz and Lnez left together.

The mayor's office looked on to the stream. "This isn't like the cradles," Richard said. "This is nature." That obviously gave him nightmares.

Jeremy sat cross-legged at the oblong table. The stated purpose of the meeting was to make sure Janvian would be prepared for the upcoming birth. They all seemed just as in need of preparation. On his left, Tamaki attentively leaned forward. On his right, Bartholomew folded his chin into his neck and closed his eyes in concentration—or sleep. Perhaps not everyone was equally concerned about the event.

Richard rubbed a hand against his bristly hair as if the static electricity could generate better answers than the ones he had. "I don't know exactly when the baby should be born because I don't know the date and time of fertilization. I'm working from a limited sample of physiology. One, to be exact. The gestation period might be longer or shorter than ours. I'm basing delivery date exclusively on the development of the fetus. Since the incubator is physically similar to us, I am using standard norms. The baby is viable and could be removed from the womb now. However, I prefer to be cautious."

"For clarity," Sasha said, "it would be helpful if we all referred to Janvian by name or as the mother, rather than as an incubator."

"The mother is not my area of expertise," Richard said.

Jeremy was called on to report. "There are no discernable genetic defects in the fetus. Analysis shows nothing that requires correction or that might need treatment. There could be an environmentally triggered reaction at birth. Given the compatibility of the mother, it seems unlikely." He wanted to state that he knew for certain Alchorel genes could dwell comfortably within the dome, but this was not the time.

Merede spoke about Janvian's health. "She is strong enough to continue carrying the child." Bartholomew confirmed that he observed no distress or interference with her work. "Except that she has to urinate frequently." Merede made note of that.

"Let's set a date," Sasha said.

"I can schedule surgery for first shift two quarters from tomorrow," Merede said. She'd performed the simulation multiple times and achieved certification. The instructional guides were ancient but detailed.

Richard agreed with the timeline. Tamaki confirmed

Janvian's language skills continued to improve and she understood the procedure.

"A birth from a human," Tamaki said. "This is really going to happen!" He turned to Jeremy. "Has she talked to you about being second parent?"

Jeremy shook his head. His blond stubble had grown into spikes at the crown. He'd noticed others had longer hair too. Perhaps Janvian's tresses were causing a style change.

Tamaki slouched with disappointment. "She hasn't? I'll go over that lesson with her again. If she doesn't say something, you have to volunteer. A child needs two right from the beginning, even a barbarian must understand that."

Fifteen days. Jeremy could barely think beyond the number. "She's not a barbarian." Fifteen days then everything would change.

Bartholomew gave a mock scowl. "Janvian is on the roster for second shift that day. Very inconsiderate of you, taking my most efficient worker." He chuckled. "Could use more like her."

Sasha asked Jeremey to stay behind as the others left. He'd been dreading this.

"Have you pursued the research question I proposed?" she asked. Her cloudy gray eyes had less than perfect sight and could no longer be corrected.

"I'll have a formal report for you soon," Jeremy said.

"I look forward to that. Perhaps you could give me a summary now."

Jeremy took a deep breath. "My summary is yes. Combining sperm and egg from a dome donor and an outsider donor has over a ninety-nine percent probability of producing satisfactory results."

"And genetically?"

Jeremy helped her rise from the cushion. Her bones were thin and fragile. Her back bent with the weight of her years and responsibilities. This was the perfect opportunity to tell her that Alpha, Beta and Gamma dwelled with them. Who were they? Adults now, he might brush by them or work beside them or laugh with them every day. Marla had been careful not to include identifying details. The few notes about their personalities were not enough, and he hadn't found any physical descriptions. He could narrow the possibilities based on when Marla was senior. Beyond that, without specific dates he could only guess.

How much of Nevran's material had Marla incorporated into her special offspring? He wondered if he had unknowingly passed those genes along to another generation through his own selections. He might have already come close to doing what the mayor had asked him to investigate.

The cloudy eyes held him. He decided to stick to the mayor's question. She understood he was limited in how much of the genome he could analyze. "From what I can determine, the single sample I examined has a below average number of undesirable predispositions. However, it's not only possible, it's probable that samples from other individuals would show traits—common ones and rare ones—that would produce undesirable outcomes if incorporated into the dome's genetic bank. I would need samples from across families and generations before I could even start to build a workable data set."

Sasha nodded, satisfied. She didn't explain her reason for wanting the information.

"How do you feel about Janvian?" Sasha asked.

Jeremy searched for a noncommittal reply and found none.

The mayor brushed aside his silent discomfort with the wave of a frail hand. "Unfair of me to ask something so personal. I apologize. It's just that she fits into our community very well. Although she's said little about it, she's obviously in considerable jeopardy in her homeland. Some of us have talked informally. At the next meeting the council will consider offering Janvian and the baby permanent residence. I expect the result to be unanimous approval. Since you've developed a close relationship with her, perhaps you'll convey the invitation, using whatever persuasive arguments you're comfortable with."

A rider leaned from the back of a winter-starved clobben and spoke to Villet. They were on the northern slope just beyond the village. Benoc did not recognize the woman. She had gotten past the guards posted along the road, yet she was not from Nept. A messenger would have gone to the barricade at the valley entrance. Important information would have been relayed to a soldier, not a child.

Why did they converse on the slope? During the past three days, spring had spread patches of green among the snow, but the wind held a sharp bite. A traveler risked being caught in a late storm. Why not come into the village to get food and shelter and visit with clankin.

Benoc did not enjoy sitting in a box. Whenever the weather permitted, which was more often as the days passed, he walked the circumference of the village. The increase in sunshine and rise in temperature felt good on his creaking joints but laid trouble on his mind. Bad weather was an ally; good weather was an enemy unlocking mountain passes. The question was not if an attack would come but when.

The rider could be a spy, quizzing young Villet on the number of soldiers. The youngster, although still with much of the child about her, had a healthy wariness Benoc admired. She was not likely to give away secrets.

The woman reined her animal back onto the mountain trail. Villet ran down the slope toward the stonecutter's as if her feet were on fire. Benoc cut his own path straight to Tlorieger's shop. His boots splashed through rivulets of melted snow. Villet danced over boulders and puddles. She reached the shop door first and was quickly inside.

When Benoc entered, the apprentice was choking out whispers. Tlorieger had his hands on the girl's shoulders to steady her. They turned startled faces to the tarryn like discovered conspirators.

The master put a protective arm around his apprentice. "Raiders climb the mountains. A large number of them. A troop. They look like trained soldiers."

"Who told you this?" Benoc asked Villet.

Tlorieger squeezed the girl's shoulders and answered for her. "A herder from a lower valley."

Benoc felt the lie as clearly as he recognized the warning concealed within it. He should not ask questions he would not like the answers to. He could not lift his eyes to the old master's. Of all the kin in Nept, of all the blood on Lorcha, he could not bear to doubt Tlorieger's lor.

"How long?" Benoc asked.

"Fighters from the villages along the way will slow them down," Villet said.

Benoc spoke quietly to calm the girl. "How long if they don't?"

Villet trembled. "Six days."

Benoc nodded and tugged at his beard. With a little help here and there, each day of travel could stretch into many more in the mountains. The raiders would learn how long a six-day journey could be.

~

TWENTY-FIVE

Dark clouds rolled and folded together in the overcast sky. Benoc smelled the threat of rain and advancing enemies. He stood on the barricade that blocked the entrance to the valley and checked the slopes on each side of the gorge. Archers with longbows crouched, ready to spring up and release death at his signal.

The stone, dirt, and wood barrier connecting the rock slides that formed a narrow entrance to Nept was stable but too low, barely head high. It was the best they could manage in the few days since spring began its slow arrival at this altitude. A clobben could not get over it, but his scouts told him the raiders had four strong meran. The animals could jump it easily. To prevent such a breach, shafts protruded from the top and were linked with wire.

Benoc crooked an arm around one of the posts, contemplating the flaws in his own defenses. It was too late for more fortifications.

Riders entered the gorge.

Exhausted Druetens had delayed this moment as long as

possible. Farmers, crafters and herders from here to the foothills had taken up what weapons they had and ambushed the invaders along the trail. They'd killed their scouts. At night they'd liberated their camps of food and animals. They'd blocked the roads with fallen trees and rubble. Where the snow had hung in great glistening shelves, they'd caused avalanches.

The tactics had turned each day's travel into a battle of its own, stretching six days to twelve. The price had been high. Fearless and fearful had died. The rest were worn to the bone and could barely raise the weapons in their hands.

And now the beasts pounded at Nept's door. The Druetens were outnumbered. Benoc recited a favorite poem.

> *Name no gods to me.*
> *Blood is deity;*
> *Metal serves the soul.*
> *Death's a worthy goal.*

He leapt from the wall. Placing a hand on a shoulder, giving an assuring nod, he went among the soldiers. At the other end of the village Kaul directed a fist of troops around a low house built against the mountain, and an unseen knot of selected warriors around a cottage. Oktria should have had that command. The apprentice tarryn lacked the experience, but he was the best leader here—after his father. If the fighting reached him, the battle was already lost.

Riders filled the gorge, some animals carrying two figures. Benoc signaled the archers. Shafts flew with deadly accuracy. Bodies fell. Bow strings sang again and again in harmony. Attackers cascaded over the peaks but could not reach the mountaineers in their protected perches.

A wave of riders deposited their extra passengers at the

barrier. The soldiers pressed tight against the wall and looped a rope around one of the poles. Together they pulled.

An arrow toppled a mercenary from a meran. The animal reared in confusion. Another rider snatched its reins. Abandoning her clobben, she vaulted onto its back. A spike on the barricade tilted and fell. She charged the wall, soaring through the breach.

The soldiers dug at the barricade, widening and deepening the gap. Another post crashed to the ground. A cleft appeared, low enough for a clobben to jump. Attackers, some mounted and some on foot, swarmed through the openings. The defenders struggled to stop the flow.

Benoc signaled his own riders positioned in the village streets to move forward. His mount appeared beside him. He took the reins from the herder who was now part of his troops and swung up into the saddle, sword drawn with an unconscious sweep. He sliced raider after raider. His meran was slain from under him. He rolled free and angrily shoved his blade into the nearest enemy.

He deflected blows and countered with his own. Metal on metal and cries of pain roared in his ears. Beside him a villager gurgle from a wound, red foam on his lips. The overcast sky bent to the ground and swirled clouds into his lungs, making him choke. Fire licked along a row of roofs.

The assault moved toward the fortified building at the end of the valley. Fallen Druetens formed a bloody carpet leading to it. On the porch a tight battle raged.

Benoc fought his way to the left. He almost lost his blade in a falling body.

The door of the house stood wide. A scar-faced mercenary stepped from the interior to the gray sunlight, bloody sword held across her chest. The place was nothing but an empty burrow. She scanned the village. Now she saw the pattern of the ruse in the formation of a final defense around a tiny cottage tucked unassumingly to the side.

The commander redirected the raiders. Kaul could not hold against so many. Benoc ordered the remaining troops to intercept them. He dodged through a maze of clashes.

He had to help his son. He had to reach Hannen. As long as she remained alive, the deception kept Janvian safe.

A blow to the head staggered him. Hannen and Janvian merged into a single thought. The world tilted. The ground smashed against his body. He tasted warm blood and cold grit.

The shop was smashed open, the last defense breached! The scarred commander dragged a raging red-haired woman into the street. Benoc tried to stand, tried to move, tried to force a hand through icy mud toward a distant sword.

Hannen was off balance from the roundness of pregnancy, but her reflexes were sharp. A wrist blade sprang into her hand. She stabbed her captor upward under the rib cage, piercing a lung. The mercenary pitched forward, a curtain of surprise drawn over the death. Hannen grabbed a fallen sword and shoved it at another attacker. Behind her a raider swung his weapon, splitting her skull with a dull crack.

Benoc screamed. He reached for Janvian as she fell, but he could not catch her.

The part of the quarry closest to Nept had been stripped of useful stone years ago. Master Tlorieger had set up a shelter of sorts where the young apprentices could go when they had free time or when they got on his nerves. He kept old tools and odd chunks of wood and rock there for them to play with.

From its entrance Villet watched her clankin being slaughtered. The twenty-three children in her care huddled behind her. Even the twins were quiet and still. This was one of a number of hiding places outside the village for the too young and the too ill or crippled. With all her heart, she'd wanted to stay with Master Tlorieger, but he'd flatly forbidden it. She would have disobeyed, but Tarryn Benoc wanted only strong fighters in the shop protecting the red-haired woman, who was probably not Janvian. The meran she'd arrived on was certainly not the famed animal that had belonged to Nevran.

The woman had been very appreciative of the cup of tea Villet had brought her. It was made with a mixture of leaves that were especially soothing for late in pregnancy. Villet came from a line of healers. Although it was not her chosen work, she was often asked to assist at births. With the woman's permission, she had placed a hand on the bulging belly and felt the baby's movement. She'd judged labor would begin soon.

Villet made the children stay away from the doorway so they couldn't see. The raiders attacked the house Benoc had set up as decoy. When they didn't find their prey, they searched for another target. She sobbed quietly, hiding her tears, as they battered their way into the stonecutter's shop. The red-haired woman was dragged into the street where all could see. She fought with every bit of strength she had but was struck down by a cowardly blow from behind that most surely killed her.

Villet cursed. Smoke billowed from the shop. "You're in charge," she shouted to the next oldest. She drew her dagger and ran with all her might toward the battle.

<><><>

The pain began as a dull ache in the lower back that nagged then receded only to reappear at regular intervals. Janvian stretched to ease the tightness. She took a deep breath and brushed a wisp of hair from her moist forehead. Then she stuck the probe into the nutrient solution between the clusters of tangled roots.

Around her the activities of agristat provided a comforting routine. The ache was easier to endure with a task to occupy her mind. Birth should still be far off. The longer she waited, the less time in which she would be missed.

Sudden pain rippled across her enlarged abdomen. Janvian fought the surprised cry clawing at her throat. She clutched the table's raised edge, leaving the probe to bob freely in the liquid.

"If you're not able to do your job, you should leave," Senior Student Rasch said.

Janvian wiped perspiration from her upper lip. "The baby is just playing."

"You should go to medstat," Rasch said.

Janvian searched Rasch's scrunched face for a sign that she was teasing. Movement was often vigorous at this late stage. The woman's eyes were serious. Pregnancy was considered unnatural here. Some people were fascinated by the condition and wanted to touch her. Others, like Rasch, were repelled by it and kept their distance as if she had a disease. Healers were no better. They behaved as if a woman were incapable of understanding her own body.

A tremor pushed away Janvian's breath. Too soon. Too soon. But it might not be. Six days ago she'd had aches and discomfort. She was certain the baby had turned in the womb into the head-downward birthing position. "Yes. I'll go there."

"I'll call for a cart," Rasch said.

"No," Janvian said too harshly. "Walking is good for me." This was not going well. She was relieved the baby had decided to arrive before the day of the surgery. She did not know how long she could have hidden from the unnecessary procedure. But she had expected time to make excuses for her absence.

Rasch took Janvian's equipment and watched until she cleared the airlock and was no longer the responsibility of agristat.

Janvian held her composure as long as she could. Another pain struck. Too soon. Too soon.

Dear child, she thought, *after all we've been through together, give me a little more time.* The baby answered with an adamant demand to be released.

<>\<>\<>

The musical splash of the waterfall had not changed, but Jeremy sat beside it in the central court of the habitat and heard a difference in its song. He could not let go of the transcribed pages in his hand, and so he read them again.

* * *

20.4.6

Alpha was found gently bobbing among the strands of kelp in the pool below the waterfall, blue eyes staring into nothing. Her parents are inconsolable. I am crushed. She was my daughter too. She belonged to all of us and the entire dome mourns.

Her death is my fault. I placed a child drawn to the thrill of a rocky climb among adults who couldn't anticipate such a dangerous act. Our environment of contentment was as toxic to her as poison air.

There will be no Delta. The experiment is over.

My child is dead.

Beta and Gamma must be closely watched.

* * *

Journal pages slipped from Jeremy's grasp and fluttered to the floor. He sat on stone at the edge of the pool and watched kelp tendrils roll with motion from the cascading stream. He imagined them framing a small face with empty eyes.

Five-year-old Alpha. The product of an unethical experiment, yet a most precious resource, was suddenly gone. He would be able to identify her now. With almost a full year before a replacement could have been born, her death would have left a six-year rift in the population. He cringed at his analytical thoughts. No one could be "replaced." Not Alpha. Not Marla. Not Nicholas. What they knew and thought and were had evaporated with them, leaving the dome a drier world.

For Jeremy, it would be the same when Janvian left. He delayed asking her to stay because he knew what her reply would be. And because he was unclear of his own motive.

Did he want her to stay for the changes she could bring to the dome? Or so she could continue helping him translate the journals? Or because when her mourning for her dead husband was over, he wanted to be standing beside her ready to declare his affection?

Whatever the council wanted and whatever he wanted, Janvian had a right to know the options. Individual choices were respected and allowed when possible. Dougal's activities proved that every day. The tech's excursions into the desert were not restricted. He wasn't encouraged to collect ore samples and experiment with them, but he wasn't prevented from doing so.

Jeremy was used to seeing diagrams for new styles of energy collectors, carts adapted for use on sand, and variations of shield generators decorating the walls of his friend's room.

Dougal wanted to build them all. He grappled with how to turn his wild ideas into reality, while devoting most of his time to repairing the real, failing equipment in front of him. If he'd been born a generation earlier, he might have prevented the genstat accident. Marla and Nicholas would still be alive and so much would be different.

Jeremy dipped his hand into the pool and let the cool liquid wash through his fingers. The room was suddenly hot. The enviro units must be malfunctioning again. He pulled his hand from the water and rubbed it on his shirt. He gathered the fallen pages of the journal, again reading the translation written in his own script.

Active. Independent. Excels at problem solving. Ambidextrous. Highly above average hand-eye coordination.

Jeremy suddenly no longer had to guess at the dates of the journal entries. He knew the exact time of Gamma's birth. Gamma was Dougal.

The pages trembled in Jeremy's hands. The lines writhed as if alive. Beta and Gamma. Born two days apart.

He heard his name and remembered where he was. Rasch from agristat apologized for interrupting. "I don't know if anyone told you. Janvian went to medstat. Something was happening with the baby. Richard might need a translator."

"How long ago?" Jeremy demanded.

"She left agri about half-way through second shift."

Over three hours. Jeremy shoved everything into his bag and pushed past Rasch. Medstat seemed impossibly far away.

<><><>

The ground rumbled. Blackness paled to gray as Benoc regained consciousness. He burned and shivered, skin damp, throat dry. Victorious whoops sounded around him, and he knew. Failure. Drueten Clan defeated.

He tried opening his eyes and found one swollen to a slit. Janvian's body lay in his sight and he was incapable of turning away.

No, it was not Janvian but Hannen, brave to the last and her babe with her.

∼

TWENTY-SIX

Villet knelt in gore. Swords clashed around her. Red soaked her clothes and covered her arms. Crimson dripped from the bundle she cradled. She cleared the tiny mouth of muck with a stained finger and willed it to breathe. It wailed, its first taste of life its mother's blood.

Benoc's skull vibrated. Shouts and metal striking metal. Burly mountain rasks danced past with swords. Raiders fell.

Kaul appeared, sword swinging. His son, alive and in command! This surely must be a dream. Red hair flashed amid the dull sheen of blades. Prisoners were led past. The painful task of sorting the wounded from the dead began around him.

"Benoc, Uncle."

Hands rolled him to his back and lifted his head. Janvian's face looked into his. No, not Janvian. Rozel, a scarlet crescent on her cheek. She knelt in the mud and held his head in her lap.

He lacked the strength to wrap his arms around her and pull her close. "I ordered you to stay at the fortress," he whispered then drifted back into midnight.

<><><>

Houses, shops and stables sent out smoky tendrils. Nept was in ruin and would take many summers to rebuild. The ambitions of so few affected so many across generations. Tonight both Pypeed and Noalgaz would rise but they would not touch. This day would be marked not for cosmic reasons but for what people had done to one another.

Rozel had Hannen's remains cleaned and dressed in finery. The gash of forennton, done hastily in a battlefield, was stitched closed. The body and the living child would be delivered to her spouse with care and respect.

Hannen was young to have a child, but it had suited her. She had spoken of the baby with joy while she and Rozel had been sequestered together. Rozel had given the woman the attention she wished she could give Janvian.

"She understood taking the monarch's place might lead to this," Amud said.

"You knew my sister wasn't here?" Rozel said.

"It was suspected. We couldn't live in these mountains, even for a little while, without having friends nearby," Amud said.

They surveyed the damage. Rozel noted the repairs that would need to be made immediately. "Your company joined the battle knowing this was a ruse and there was no blood heir here to protect."

Amud looked at the gray sky, deciding how much more to reveal. "We were already in it. Propaulnem and the others picked off raiders and snatched supplies all along the way. Those friends I mentioned, they're here."

Rozel removed the iref ring from Hannen's lifeless hand. The water-blue stone seemed heavier each time she carried it. The smoldering village reminded her of a poem Benoc was fond of quoting.

> *Others set the flames.*
> *We scurry to keep those we love*
> *From burning.*

Reluctantly she once again placed the gem onto her own finger.

The usalasia tea numbed the pain, but the pressure was constant. Janvian leaned against the warm box, legs wide, knees bent in the birthing position. Not on her back. Not with the child being cut from her by one who was not kin.

A hill and bushes sheltered the spot from the rest of the prairie biome. Fujin and Spirit snorted encouragement. Their presence provided comfort. They would serve as her clan. Although supporting arms would be better.

Hair stuck to her face in damp waves. The loose, oversized shirt clung to her with sweat. It was the closest she'd found to an appropriate gown. Like the pallet of soft bedding next to her and the canister on the box that warmed the tea, it was not correct, but it would do. The knife within reach was stolen from agristat. Meant for delicate cutting, it was not long enough to be a proper blade, but it would cut the baby's cord. And Janvian knew how to inflict shallow slices that would deter an enemy. She would have her child on her feet, defending the crib.

The improvised items had been easy to obtain. Nothing was secured. She had systematically stored the goods during her frequent visits to Fujin.

At first the baby had been eager to join the larger world. Janvian had tried to hold back the contractions until after she'd collected food, water and other items from her room that needed to be fresh and could not be left in the stash.

When the place was prepared with brewed tea, a make-shift mattress and blankets, water for cleansing, and a meal for after the birth, the baby had lost interest. Or perhaps courage, not a good sign in a monarch. Janvian had paced and chewed taynsea root to strengthen the contractions.

The white sky had darkened in imitation of the night outside while she had measured the space with her steps again and again. She'd accepted the delay as a good sign. It was the twenty-second day of Mareyn. Tonight Noalgaz would rise full and pull its larger reflection behind it. Both moons would light the sky. It was a strong time to be born.

Finally the contractions had taken on a rhythm.

"Rojelon of Felcon Clan, Judsant of Felcon Clan, Taznia of Felcon Clan, Nevran of Felcon Clan, Corella of Felcon Clan." Janvian whispered the succession of monarchs between pants. It was difficult to stay quiet but necessary. Not everyone worked and relaxed on the same schedule. Even this late there might be others in the shell.

Agony shot through her exhausted body. A cry escaped her control. Fujin whinnied and stomped the floor. Spirit reared and bolted. The pounding faded as he raced away.

Janvian cursed him for his faint heart and his desertion. She cursed Rojelon for dying. She cursed herself for letting her body become soft.

A cadence of hooves rumbled as Spirit stampeded a sleepy herd of grazers. The muffled storm rumbled above.

The meran reappeared followed by Jeremy, Richard, Merede and more! Had the entire dome come to intrude on her private moment?

"Sand-blasted traitor meran!" Janvian shouted at the animal in Lorchan. She grabbed the blade and dared them to touch her.

Jeremy's voice pleaded, but she did not understand the words. "Janvian, let us help you."

She pointed the weapon at him, unable to speak in any language except pain.

The pressure grew more severe with the baby's struggle to be born. She thought the agony could get no worse. She was wrong. The image of Jeremy, outstretched hand frozen by her rejection, wavered to a blur and darkened to a scream.

<><><>

"You shouldn't have left the fortress," Benoc said. The room was small but private with a real bed, the best Nept could manage for its tarryn when some buildings were ash and so many wounded rested on floors. He was propped up by a sagging feather pillow belonging to the town's alder. One eye was a swollen bruise of color. Bandages cushioned a gash on the back of his head. A blanket hid a mangled leg. The fussing over his injuries seemed to annoy him almost as much as his niece's disobedience.

Rozel sat on a stool beside him, Amud behind her. "I'm glad you're feeling better."

Uz stood at the end of the bed. "In case you be too dazed from that poke in the eye to remember, she saved your ass."

"Uzec." Oktria stood beside him and gave him a warning look.

The large thief folded his arms stubbornly. "He not be *my* tarryn, and somebody's got to talk straight to the squawking old bird."

"You're wearing a Drueten armband," Oktria reminded him. "Hero or not, show respect or keep your mouth shut."

Her response was as much a message to Benoc as to Uz. Allowing the thieves to continue wearing the rask insignia on their sleeves was a difficult concession for the tarryn, especially with the purple strip above it to mourn those who had died. It was almost as difficult to accept as being rescued by them—with his niece as leader. "Where's Kaul? I have to tell the boy who he should post for the watch."

"He's no boy," Rozel said, "and he's made guard assignments before. You should be proud of him." The room smelled of alcohol, the disinfecting kind and the pain-killing kind. Rozel twisted the blue stone around her finger. The tarryn second had explained the deception to the alder and the crafters council. Some of them had recognized Hannen, or suspected. "Kaul put out the story that the troops I brought were recruited from the ocean side of the mountains." Benoc seemed to approve but did not say so. She had not expected him too.

"Perhaps Master Tlorieger will add substance by 'recognizing' several of them," Benoc said.

Rozel fought an impulse to glance at Amud. Was the suggestion a simple one based on Benoc's trust in the stonecutter? Or was Tlorieger one of the friends Amud mentioned and Benoc knew about the connection? Rozel decided to let the bottom of that rock go unexplored. Some secrets were best kept. "I'll see to it," she said.

Benoc's face clenched at a wave of pain.

Rozel tried to redirect his thinking. "One of the captured soldiers is a Felcon from the fortress. And Amud and Uz identified some of the prisoners as mercenaries."

"Nasty ones," Uz said. "Swords to the highest bidder, willing to change employer if a more jangly deal comes along."

"The Felcon is proof that Skaln ordered the attack," Rozel said. "We can take that to the Baerryns." If only she'd been able to get here sooner.

Benoc's good eye closed, shutting him into his own world. "This was for nothing if you're not at the ceremony. It'll take an army to get you back in the gate."

"She has one," Amud said.

Rozel motioned for Amud, Uz and Oktria to leave.

"It will be told that Janvian died here," Benoc said. He opened his undamaged eye. "Skaln will use that to his advantage, even if he doesn't believe it. Now he'll move toward the throne with determination. You must do the same. Drueten Clan officially forgives you for your momentary transgression and gives your petition its support as reward for rescuing Nept. Have Kaul write the document and I'll sign it. Then get back to the fortress. Take every soldier healthy enough to travel." He managed a tired smile. "You're legitimate again. You don't need the thieves anymore."

Rozel tried to smile back, hoping he could not tell how weak it was. She touched a kiss to his damp forehead and stood to leave. A hand caught her arm.

"Your tarryn is mad as a whirling daeva at you for disobeying," Benoc said, "but your uncle's grateful you 'saved his ass.'" His shaking hand sent tremors along her arm. "The thief?"

"Do you ask as uncle or tarryn?"

"Uncle first, tarryn second."

That was a switch in priorities. "Then to my uncle, we'll

discuss it when you've healed. And to my tarryn, I have strong reason to trust him."

"Will this trust completely drain the Drueten treasury?"

Rozel slowly drew away her arm. She wanted to explain that Amud's thieves were not mercenaries. She wanted her uncle to understand that they lived like a clan. But to Benoc, blood was everything.

The thieves had no shared line. They were outcasts, their veins tainted with broken lor. Benoc would never allow what she had promise. Let him think the payment was in coin.

"Their price is reasonable."

Benoc's eyelids flutter in pain. He'd had wounds before but never this severe. Defeat pressed against his chest like an iron plate. He twisted his bruised face. "Rozel, you know your duty."

The raiders had wrecked the stonecutter's shop. The debris and blood stains had not yet been cleared away. Lnez huddled by the hearth. Villet returned from placing Hannen's baby with the twins' mother. She put a shawl across his shoulders. He accepted it although the tremors that shook him were not from the cold.

Tlorieger rolled the milky stone from palm to palm and sighed. He tugged at his beard. He studied the sphere by candlelight, carried it to the window and held it against the sunshine then sighed again.

"Blast it to sand," Uz said, leaning against the workbench, "stop blowing air and tell us if you be able to cut it or not."

Tlorieger raised his eyebrows. "I can cut anything."

He put the rock on the bench and covered it with a cloth.

Then he pulled a stool to the fire and sat facing Lnez. "Where is the other one?"

Lnez pulled the empty cage from a pocket. "Dust. You knew about the flaw. Maybe you put it there on purpose. A friend died because of it."

"Perfection is risky," the stonecutter said.

Lnez tried to blink away vertigo. He had gone to the stream where he'd found the first jewel and followed it toward its source. Far ahead in the winding creek and up into the mountain, gemstones had shouted to him like unruly children. One sang so loudly it was deafening. Uz had carried the stone for him.

What was the crafter saying?

"I cut it to make it controllable."

Lnez shook his head and suffered nausea. "This one must be perfect and as strong as your skill can fashion."

Tlorieger cupped Lnez's face in his large hands. "Look. See the jewel inside the stone. Know what it will become if I do as you ask."

Lnez swallowed in a dry throat and touched the stonecutter's mind. A globe of pure mountain ice burned white and wild. With this gem one would always wonder who was master and who was servant. "It will be flawless?"

"Yes."

"I need it."

"The most dangerous things are those we think we need," Tlorieger said.

<><><>

Richard sternly ordered Janvian to stay in bed. As soon as he left the room, she pushed aside the senior student's tentative restraining arms and swung her feet to the floor. She took a few halting steps. Her sore muscles rebelled against movement, but they would stiffen if she followed the medic's dictates.

Slowly she executed a series of elementary training exercises. Her thighs trembled from having held the birthing position for so long. The senior student covered his eyes at the immodesty of her med gown and voiced protests but kept his distance.

The fragrance of usalasia tea masked the strange smell of medstat. Against everyone's wishes, Janvian continued to drink the brew. It numbed the burning between her legs and added a familiar aroma to the sterile surroundings.

With the student's help, Janvian climbed back into the strange bed so far off the floor. "Bring me the baby," she said.

He smoothed the blanket and twisted a lip, uncertain what to do. Janvian could tell he was not used to getting orders from anyone except his teachers. "Richard told me—"

Janvian grabbed the neck of his shirt and pulled his face close to hers. "Bring me the baby," she said slowly with a smile, "or I'll twist this cloth until your head pops off."

The student's face blanched. He thought he might faint from fright. He had been with Jeremy, Richard and Merede when they'd discovered her. He'd seen the scalpel. Although he hadn't understood what she'd shouted, he'd clearly comprehended what she would do with the blade if they came too close.

As the moment of birth had distracted her, Jeremy had grabbed her wrist and taken the instrument from her. Richard and Merede had completed delivery while Janvian railed at them in her native language.

She was in full command of Amersan now. The student bobbed his head in agreement. She released him. He straightened his coveralls and his dignity. He lifted the tightly wrapped bundle from the crib, cautiously placed it in his patient's arms, then quickly stepping out of reach.

The door opened slightly and Jeremy's head poked through the gap. "Can I come in?"

"No," the senior student said.

"Yes," Janvian said.

The medic rubbed his neck. "I guess it's all right." He looked at Jeremy with sympathy. "If you need me, I'll be just outside."

Janvian loosened the blanket around the baby. She and Rojelon had a son! She checked him again to make sure he was still wonderful. And he was.

"All that work for something so small," Jeremy said. He peered at the pinched-faced, bald-headed child. "He's beautiful."

Janvian uncovered a breast for the baby to suckle. Tamaki had given her a lesson on bottle feeding. She'd corrected that right away and explained the vocabulary she required.

Jeremy fidgeted but said nothing.

~

CHAPTER

TWENTY-SEVEN

The guard had forgotten how this much standing made his feet hurt. Still it was better than cleaning slop buckets. His nose still burned from the stench and his fingernails harbored reminders in the cracks. Better to be here at his old post, pacing the mouth of the road leading to the fortress, than slinging excrement.

One tiny mistake and it seemed that his soldiering career was as good as gone. Again he puzzled over the incident that had caused his banishment to the latrine trench. How had Rozel switched places with the little carpenter directly before his eyes? How had her partner gotten into the fortress to call her in? His superiors had asked him those questions from sunset to sunrise. Now months later he could give no better answers than he had then. He simply did not know, but he was sure it was someone else's fault and not his own.

He hid a chuckle from the stern woman who stood watch with him—and over him. Truth be, best mistake he ever made. While he'd endured punishment, his company had been secretly ordered off somewhere. He'd not been so much as a thought in his commander's mind, so he'd been left behind.

With most of the troops gone so quickly, there'd been many positions to fill to keep up appearances and few to staff them. The guard had been back at his old post within days—with Stern Face to keep him from drink and disaster. He passed the time plotting small forms of revenge on her for the dry duty.

Four cloaked riders approached. Stern Face blocked the bridge as if to hold them back with her ample physical presence. The guard stepped to the side. He knew better than to place his soft body in the path of hard hooves.

The point rider halted the group and pushed back his hood so his face was visible. A strand of brown hair waved across his forehead and multiple braids cascaded over a shoulder.

"I am Ianz of Joach Clan, apprentice to Tarryn Melaph. Has she arrived yet?"

"She has," Stern Face said, not very stern-faced when she looked into the deep brown eyes of young Ianz. "You be the last." She questioned the handsome apprentice tarryn about the clankin with him without granting a glance to the others. He smiled and leaned toward her from the saddle with his answers.

The guard ran a sleeve across his nose to hide his disgust. The boy must be blind and stupid to treat the prickly old burr as if she were a blossom. *He* tended to duty and examined the riders.

The fortress was a nervous place. Rumor said Janvian and the unborn child were dead, killed by the renegade Rozel. A generous reward awaited the soul who delivered the traitor to Skaln. No questions would be asked about the condition of the body. The guard was not interested in rewards. They brought promotion and responsibility. He would have none of that.

Ianz he knew by sight, but he did not recognize the others. Their hoods were loosely draped about their heads, so he could see only part of their faces. A large man had double braids hanging over his left ear, and a large woman had double braids hanging over her right ear. He supposed the braid placement signified something or the other. Both had their cloaks thrown back, showing Joach armbands.

The fourth was bundled into the cloth as if cold in the early summer day, showing only a little of her face and no armband. A clasp with the Joach insignia of bound grain stalks entwined with a river snake gleamed in bronze at her throat, and a brown braid twisted out of the hood and across a breast.

Another glimmer caught his eye. It was not a sparkly ornament and not a shiny ribbon woven into a dull braid. A single strand of red light twisted against dark cloth. Or so it seemed.

He studied the woman. She was small like the little carpenter, but so were many others and shortness was no crime. She was pale for a Joach and blue eyed instead of brown, but she could have married a southlander and chosen that clan for herself if she pleased.

He scratched at his coarse britches and thought out his options. If he challenged and was wrong, it was back to the slop. Just the thought filled his nose with the stench. If he challenged and was right, he would be dead or rewarded. Neither path a joyful one.

If he did not challenge—

That was too much thinking. He opened his mouth to call to Stern Face. Let her have the honor of raising the alarm.

"Pass through, Apprentice Tarryn Ianz of the Joachs," Stern Face said.

The many revenges the guard had planned against old Stern Face were grains of sand compared to the opportunity before him. He clamped his mouth shut. He was not the one who had questioned the riders; he had not given the word to let them pass. If slop buckets were to be cleaned for this, he would not be the one with the rag.

<><><>

Ianz was last to enter the meeting. He nodded to Skaln and the other tarryns and seconds. He passed by two mystics—two when there was usually one—then took a chair beside his mother. The long table was lined with tense faces. Every clan was represented except the Druetens. At the head of the rectangle Skaln relaxed against the back of the padded chair, Rojelon's chair.

Melaph gave her son a disapproving frown for being late. Then she gave him a closer look. "What happened to your braids?" she whispered. "And get rid of that vengeful grin."

Ianz sobered and pushed back the cluster of braids that contained half its usual number of woven strands. A layer of hair chopped off at the nape stuck out in undisciplined curls. "I'll explain later."

"You most certainly will," his mother said.

Skaln rose. "You've all heard the sad and most horrifying news. Janvian is dead."

"Rumor only," Gozax said loudly. "And so it stays until I hear the truth from Benoc."

"Benoc may have his own reasons for inventing another 'truth,'" Skaln said.

"Just as there're those at this table who may have their own reasons to promote rumors," Melaph said. She spoke lightly but her weighty intent was felt.

"And is it rumor or truth that each of you has been challenged from within your own clan?" Skaln asked. "That some of your kin have declared war on their neighbors without your consent? That Lorcha is a breath away from wectulk?"

"They don't mean to be treasonous," Paulian said, brushing a pale brown lock from his forehead and inadvertently revealing a new scar at the hairline. "After almost a year without a monarch, they're just—uncertain."

Ianz was repelled by Paulian's gentle acceptance. The Walbask tarryn, and the others, should not just be looking to their own people. They should be outraged at the Baerryns' unwillingness, or perhaps inability, to squelch the renegade attacks. There was much to be admired in the man; unfortunately, they were not the qualities that made a great leader.

"You can end their uncertainty," Skaln said. "You can show them you are in control. That you lead your clan away from war and back to prosperity."

Prosperity as in commerce, as in business. There was no surprise on the tarryns' faces. Ianz realized his mother was not the only leader to be pressured by clan merchants. That implied an agreement among the wealthy traders that went across families. A deal had been struck based on coin rather than blood.

His stomach clenched into a fist. Suddenly he felt as naive as Paulian for not suspecting the alliance. His mother had said nothing to him. This was one of her lessons then. He was supposed to have recognized it on his own. They would have a lengthy discussion about it later. Right after the one about his hair.

"For the good of Lorcha," Skaln said, "I petitioned the Baerryns with my own claim to the throne. They most graciously granted it. You all know my lineage. I'm as much of the royal line as Janvian was."

The Felcon tarryn spoke as if he'd received confirmation of

the death and not just rumors. Other than Skaln, Ianz was the only one else in the room who knew it was true. Rozel had told him of her sister's murder. He'd been preparing himself for that possibility, but it still struck his heart.

"As close as Rozel," Gozax said.

Skaln seemed pleased someone else had brought the Drueten into the discussion. "She's proven herself a traitor. She probably also planned and executed the raid that killed her sister and the blood heir. She may even have driven the blade into Janvian herself. Stories of it are all over the city."

Ianz moved to stand and confront Skaln. Years of training made him pause at the light touch of his mother's hand on his arm. She did not look at him but at Skaln.

"Accusations are easy to make," Melaph said. "I could start a tale that a piece of Pypeed fell out of the sky and killed Janvian. There'd be people who'd believe it, but that wouldn't make it true. Do you have any proof?"

Skaln calmly gave the Joach tarryn a menacing look. "Not yet. When it comes, it will disqualify her. I have prepared a document for each clan declaring support for my petition. It requires only your signature and seal. With this assurance I will begin at once to end the raids and make the trade routes safe. You can return to your people and tell them that their lives will soon be back to normal."

The double doors burst open. Rozel strode in flanked by Oktria and Amud. Purple edged their Drueten armbands for the deaths at Nept.

"Traitor!" Skaln pulled a knife and hurled it toward her.

The blade's path curved, and it stuck in the wall, deflected by the mystics. Oktria and Amud were frozen before their hands reached their hilts. Baerryn power was strong in the room.

Rozel did not reach for a knife. Instead she pulled out a paper, the weapon of diplomats, and tossed it on the table. It slid along the smooth surface to the center. "My tarryn sends you this."

When no one made a move, Paulian tentatively reached for the document. Since it did not snap at his hand and no one stopped him, he dutifully picked it up.

Skaln locked Rozel in a furious gaze. "How did you get in here?"

"I'm a sanctioned heir," Rozel said. "I've a right to be here."

Skaln pounded the table. "You raised a blade against your clan."

Rozel came armed as a diplomat, but her tongue was not used to the role. "You believe your own lies. And blame others for what you set in motion."

Paulian cleared his throat for attention. "This says raiders attacked Nept. Prisoners are being questioned to discover their identities. Rozel, leading Drueten troops, arrived in time to save the village." Paulian rustled the paper. "It says 'Our clankin Janvian and the blood heir she carried did not live through the battle.'" His eyes blurred with tears. "Janvian is truly dead."

The room was quiet as a tomb. Rozel realized there had been some hope and she had taken it away. Benoc had worded his statement carefully so it was not a lie. Janvian had not lived through the battle because she had not been there to experience it. Still, he'd have difficulty explaining that subtlety later.

Rozel would remember Paulian's sorrow and tell Janvian. Despite the action of the previous Walbask tarryn, his clan would be treated with consideration by the new monarchy.

Paulian took a deep breath and continued reading, his

voice shaking. "'For her courage and lor, placing clankin and country above personal ambition, Drueten Clan supports Rozel, great-grandchild of Nevran, in her claim to the throne of Lorcha.' It's signed by Benoc and stamped with the Drueten seal."

Skaln snatched the sheet from Paulian and held it to candlelight to read for himself. The Walbask tarryn took the insult silently.

Ianz crossed his arms and gazed at his own reflection on the polished table. Rozel wished the young man would show more grief at the sudden announcement of his beloved's death. Instead it seemed to be an old wound. He might barely fool the others but not his mother. Melaph looked from Rozel to her son and knew how the rebel and her companions had gained entrance to the fortress.

"Baerryns!" Skaln waved the paper at the robed figure against the wall.

A multiple voice came from one of them. "Rozel of Drueten Clan presented the document to us and it was examined. We found it to be authentic. The signature is truly Benoc's; the paper carries his essence."

Skaln silently rubbed his clean-shaven jaw for a long moment. He tossed the paper on the table as if discarding an unimportant issue. "This changes nothing," he said. "Rojelon's child is dead, and I'm the logical heir. Tarryns, I am one of you. I understand the responsibilities of leadership. I ask that you sign these statements of support." Nervous servants distributed the affidavits and provided pens and ink. "I'll be the first." Skaln signed, giving Felcon support to himself. "Gozax, will you be next?"

The Tskant tarryn kept her gaze low, away from Rozel, and scribbled her name.

"Melaph?" Skaln prompted.

The tanned woman shrugged. "The blood heir's death is a great shock. I see no need to rush into a new loyalty. The ceremony is over three months away. All petitioners' qualifications will be reviewed before the Joach pledge their support to one."

Paulian was visibly upset. Walbask land bordered the Joachs and the Bewailed Wilde and no other land. Clashes were frequent between the two clans. Rozel hoped he would take the safe path, mirror the Joachs and stay neutral. But she could only guess at the pressures Paulian experienced from his own kin and the other clans. He had been tarryn for less than a year. The Walbasks were targets of anger over Rojelon's murder at the blade of Paulian's predecessor. Backing the favored horse in this race might give his clan an advantage in future land disputes if Skaln became monarch.

Wordlessly Paulian took the pen, his hand burdened by the weight as if the sharpened reed were made of crawood. He signed.

Skaln laid the three papers on the table. Felcon, Tskant, Walbask. They looked formidable compared to Rozel's lone Drueten declaration. "Mystic," Skaln said, "inform the Baerryns of these documents."

"It is done."

Skaln nodded to all except Rozel and her companions then left the room.

Melaph approached Rozel. Her many braids were twined into other braids to form one long rope of rich brown. "Don't confuse my son's impulsive behavior with Joach support," she said. "He acted on his own. Although I may be proud of him and might have done the same thing, I'm responsible to an entire clan and must consider their welfare. Janvian knew how to rule. As much as I find you more amiable than Skaln, and perhaps more just, you're not Janvian." Melaph walked away. Ianz trailed behind her.

She's right, Rozel thought. *I'm a pretender, no better than the drunks in the hall. I'm not Janvian.*

Sister, she pleaded, *don't force me to become you.*

TWENTY-EIGHT

Sound traveled forever. Light was sharp and real. Dry air whisked moisture from Janvian's cheeks. She gently bounced the baby in the sling that held him to her chest. How could the dome's people spend their lives under fabric and strange wood that was not wood when a giant sky curved above and the horizon was an enticing thread beyond reach?

Children scurried about the sand collecting pebbles and chipping rock samples from formations that poked through the shifting gold. A child pointed tClick here mound. "Who piled the sand here? Did you, Dougal?"

The younger ones speculated.

"I bet an animal did it, with huge claws."

"And a long, flat tail."

The veteran of other outings put her hands on her hips in disgust. "Don't you know anything?" she said. "The wind blew it there."

Dougal laughed and batted at the wide brim of the veteran's cap, knocking it over her eyes. "And maybe the wind has huge claws and a long, flat tail." He gathered the children around him. With edstat's reluctant approval, Dougal conducted these trips on his personal time to enrich the more adventurous children's general education, if their parents allowed it. Not all children were; not all parents did.

From his pack the tech pulled a contraption of metal and thick paper. "Wind is like the air currents in the dome, only it can have more force." He anchored the device in the mound. The wind pushed against the paper, causing it to swing backward. A wire pivoted along a curved scale. "This shows how fast it is moving."

Janvian listened to the lesson but kept her eyes on the land as she worked through a series of exercises. She was determined to put the quickness and accuracy back into her muscles. The baby seemed to love the movement. Close by, the garage airlock was a bubble floating on hot liquid. There were no hostile riders. No threats to the child who cuddled against her.

Dougal directed the six children of various ages to scoop up handfuls of sand. The youngest stared at the ground without touching it until the oldest picked up a fistful of grains and placed them in the boy's hands for him. In unison the children tossed them high. The wind caught the flowing particles and feathered them away.

A simple clan village supported at least five times as many children as Janvian had seen in the dome. Jeremy had explained that few were born, but they rarely died of disease or accident. Janvian watched the untroubled faces, bright caps shading them from the sun's harshness. Their lives were enormously different from those of clan children. The most threatening thing in their world was a handful of sand. They existed without weapons or the need for them. Their survival was guaranteed.

As these children grew they would select their own futures, not ones they were born to. Any of them could choose to be a scientist like Jeremy, a leader like Sasha, a tech like Dougal. They could pursue whatever their abilities and hard work led to.

She imagined her own child growing among them. He could have a life without the fear of assassination that Rojelon had lived and died with. He could be the machine user Nevran had wished to be. He could be safe.

She wondered what her life might be like here. Few situations called for diplomatic skills. There were no complicated trade agreements to negotiate, no land treaties or disputes, but she could learn to be a leader here.

She could continue in agristat while studying machine skills from Dougal. Nevran's passion might become her own.

Jeremy translated most of the journal entries himself now, but he still needed her assistance occasionally. He'd stopped asking her to do long passages a while ago. She'd thought he'd worried that it was too tiring for her. They'd all behaved as if a pregnant woman were a fragile ornament, like a lace portrait, instead of a real woman. Lately she wondered if he didn't want her to know the content. He should realize he could trust her. If there was one thing she understood, it was the necessity of secrets. She already held some that were of great importance to Jeremy, why not all?

She watched him ride a nervous Spirit in a circle. She had taught him to sit balanced in the saddle and to use the reins with authority. They had practiced in the prairie. On the first journey outside the dome, the meran was disturbed by the unusual smells and the unfamiliar feel under its hooves. It snorted and shook its head. It was not as smart as Fujin. The beast needed a great deal of direction to repeat a simple pattern.

Jeremy awkwardly dismounted. The ons and offs needed more work. He walked over to her, fingering the reins. Lately he seemed as skittish as the meran.

"Have you named the baby?" Jeremy asked without looking at her.

"It's hard to decide," she said. "He'll be called by it for a very long time."

"What about Nevran?"

"He was a monarch. It's not right to give his name to another." She almost said "to another monarch" but stopped herself. She must not be careless.

"Janvian," Jeremy said, his eyes on the ground, "you don't have to leave."

His statement so paralleled her own thoughts that she was startled.

"The council wants you to stay." He dug at the sand with the toe of his light shoe. "We all want you—and the baby—to stay. If you want to, that is. No one would ever force you."

These gentle people, and Jeremy, were not capable of forcing her to do anything. She was not completely surprised when he kissed her and she did not resist.

Jeremy offered love and safety. She wanted both, for herself and her child. The kiss and the man were part of the dome's seductiveness. It threatened to divert her from her duty and the fulfillment of her child's destiny.

Rojelon was alive in her heart. The new year was only two quarters away. The baby was strong, and she felt he was fit to travel. She gently pulled away.

Jeremy captured a strand of red hair dancing on the breeze and smoothed it behind her ear. "You'll need supplies. I'll arrange whatever you want."

<><><>

"Go away," Rozel shouted at the mystic following her. The fortress was thick with them. Their presence prickled her skin like the threat of inland lightning. She did not want it hovering outside her room, but she knew it would not obey. She slammed the heavy door but did not lock it. Stark furnishings filled the narrow space. Skaln had delighted in apologizing for the plain accommodations. Her previous room, lavish with brocades and carpets, had been given to another petitioner shortly after she'd left, he'd told her. Unfortunately, this was the best available. A private room at least.

Rozel cared little about the bare walls and the lack of carved legs on the single table. She slept well on the adequate mattress—too well in the silence of the fortress interior. The room had no window.

No window. No escape from the deceit of diplomacy, save one. Amud. Throughout the fatigue of her captivity, the pleasure they shared was her only freedom.

She put the necessary candle on the simple square of wood supported by plain spindles. Under a layer of ash, coals glowed dimly in the tiny fireplace. She stirred the embers and coaxed them to life with fresh fuel. The day's heat never penetrated this far into the stone structure.

Plotting and planning. Planning and plotting. Rozel was sick of it. She pulled off her boots and collapsed on the bed, wishing she were with Lnez and Uzec at the edge of the Bewailed Wilde waiting for Janvian. The quilt covering was village made, scars of uneven stitches held together scraps of fabric to form an unpatterned pattern. She traced the irregular boundaries, feeling the varying qualities of cloths.

The meeting with Benoc left her exhausted. All aftnoon and into the forenight they'd reviewed the list of petitioners. Drueten spies had collected volumes of information on them.

Around the gathered facts and rumors Benoc had created grounds for challenging each claim.

Rozel had rehearsed the exact phrasings of the objections. Benoc had drilled her on order, protocol, and inflection. The accusations were petty and boring—doubtful tradings, gambling debts, minor transgressions—making them difficult to remember. Rozel had been guilty of most of them herself at one time or another. Benoc had no patience with her when her attention slipped.

She'd suggested invented scandals that were far more interesting. The purpose was more to take up time than to eliminate candidates, so accuracy seemed unnecessary. "No lies," Benoc had insisted. "The challenges must wear the mark of genuine mire."

Benoc had limped around the table in the room Skaln generously allowed him to use for clan business. His wounds required more healing, but the end of the year was not something that could be postponed until he was completely fit. Only the old gods had that power. His injured leg stiffened if he remained still too long. As all Druetens did, he continued to wear purple above his armbands. The moons had done a lot of cavorting since the slaughter and it was past the usual time to mourn, but they would keep that tragedy an open wound.

He had massaged his temples. The headaches were less frequent and less severe now, except when he battled with his niece. "Repeat the order," he had said.

Rozel had recited the names of the petitioners in the sequence in which Benoc had decided she should challenge them. Spring had warmed into summer and summer had ripened into harvest. The last day of the new year was less than a quarter away. And no Janvian. "Skaln last," Rozel had said, finishing the list. She could not resist adding, "Or when Janvian arrives to pronounce the objection herself."

Benoc had massaged harder. "You might become monarch," he had growled. "Get comfortable with the idea."

Rozel put the session out of her mind. She heard a familiar whisper and smiled, frustration transforming into a more delightful tension.

Amud slipped in and bolted the door. She rose to greet him with a kiss. Together they toppled onto the bed. Each day she relied on him more to keep whatever it was that made her Rozel from getting lost in the labyrinth of fortress intrigue. She thought of him as the weed she clung to against Benoc's effort to cultivate her into the governmental garden, where the residents were more scratchy thistles than soft petals. And wouldn't her poetry-loving uncle be impressed by that metaphor!

Benoc allowed Amud and some of the other thieves to stay because Rozel insisted her deal with them held, and because of the shortage of fighters after the wounds and deaths at Nept. To the tarryn, Amud was no more than a hired sword, necessary but still a thief. He reacted to his niece's taking Amud as a lover the same way he had to her previous liaisons, with disapproval at her inappropriate choice of a partner. He refused to recognize this relationship was different from the others.

Rozel played with thoughts of marriage, knowing Benoc would forbid such an inappropriate union. If she defied him and wed anyway, her uncle would banish her from the clan. She could become monarch, rule the entire planet, and her tarryn would still have some authority over her. Benoc had made that plain in a handful of ways throughout their rehearsal today. Her duty was to sit on the throne, and his duty was to ensure she acted worthy of the honor.

Rozel broke the embrace and put a hand to Amud's cheek. "Let's leave."

"To have a few tankards at the Split Hoof?" Amud asked, puzzled. "To gamble at the Red Bone? You know you can't."

"Let's run away," she said. "We'll join your people. I'd enjoy being a thief. I've proven I have skills at disguise and at getting in and out of places. I've gotten into the fortress twice when it was most heavily guarded."

"Oktria and I helped you get in the first time and that swaggering young Joach devised it the second."

"I got us out by myself when Lnez sent me the mind message about the raiders," she said.

Amud propped himself up on an elbow. "A window and a rope are not inventive by thief standards."

"Then you'll teach me." It felt right, as if this were the move she'd been preparing for her whole life. It was the action she should have taken long ago when she'd realized she was not the refined, by-the-rules clankin she was expected to be. "I'm an accomplished gambler and street scrapper. I'll show you thievery as an art form."

"The Monarch Thief is it?" Amud said. "And how would you arrange for apprenticeships then?"

"Isn't our being together more important?" she asked.

"You're playing a game, aren't you," Amud said, searching her face for confirmation. "You wouldn't break your promise to me and you wouldn't abandon Benoc when he needs you most."

Rozel felt her breath halt. There was no air. People were always putting her into places with no air—the heavy veil and mourning clothes, the tent on the way to Nept, this room.

Candlelight flickered across Amud's worried face, tanned to the brown of harvest grain. Rozel breathed on her own and pushed him playfully. "Of course it's just a game. I couldn't leave now." She had lied to lovers before with an honest smile on her lips, but it had never hurt this much. She placed their being together above everything and everyone else. Apparently her lover did not.

He untied her shirt and folded back the cloth from her breasts. "You're in strange humor tonight. Maybe you're too tired for love making."

Rozel pulled him against her and rolled in the sagging bed until he was under her. Her hair cascaded like a burning waterfall. "We'll see who's tired when I get done with you." She kissed him fiercely. If leaving meant leaving alone, so be it.

A red blob marred the symmetry of the circular image. Dougal sat before the screen. With one hand he tapping a flat surface studded with coded lights. With the other he twisted tangled circuitry. Many of the machines in his shop were a similar combination of sleek controls and exposed guts.

At irregular intervals the blob changed position. Janvian watched in anticipation of the shifts. The tech explained the dark circle crossed with bright grid lines was a map of the sky, and the glowing blob was a starcraft.

Janvian refrained from plaguing him with her skepticism. How could the machine see an object so far away? When the *skyship* had been here a year ago, she'd searched for it from the height of the fortress walls and had seen nothing. She had tucked its existence into a far crevice of her mind, thinking it the smallest of her worries. It and its foreign ambassadors had been sent away. Yet here they were again. Had Skaln issued his own invitation, expecting to be in a position to negotiate treaties by the time they returned?

The shields were in constant operation to deflect any prying eyes from the sky. Power was rationed. The monitor provided the only light in the room. The greenish illumination carved gullies along the creases in the mayor's face. "You're certain they can't detect the tracking system?"

The screen blinked and the blob shifted. Dougal made a notation on a board like the ones in agristat. "The system uses a fringe frequency and is cloaked by its own centralized mag. At random intervals the mag goes off for the minimum number of microseconds to send a burst. Then it goes back on. Then it goes off to receive the bounce and send another burst. It keeps doing that and zap! We get a picture. At night the air is pretty charged, so there's some interference. If their equipment registers the fluctuation, they'll probably think it's a malfunction or a byproduct of the storm."

"I wanted you to see for yourself," the mayor said to Janvian.

Janvian watched the blinking red dot. She didn't understand Dougal's explanation, but she understood the threat. If the shields were turned off for her to exit, the Tynat craft might detect the dome. Even if she managed to sneak out, the ship might wonder where she had suddenly appeared from and decide to do an extensive search. She could only leave when it was on the other side of the planet.

Janvian had explain that she couldn't set out across the Wilde any time she chose. She needed a full day to reach the cave. It worried her that she would be traveling against the sun, instead of with it as on the journey here. Heading east she would lose daylight sooner. She had thought to counter that by making the trip at least seven days before the new year. Sunset would not be as shortened by the season, and she would have time to sneak into the fortress and gain the Baerryns' protection.

"Our ancestors fled from the society that produced the people on that ship," Sasha said. "They stole the most advanced vehicle ever developed and a most precious cargo. The Tyllur Nations will see us as fugitives and criminals."

"Or perhaps as Lorchans," Janvian said.

Sasha smiled. "Perhaps."

"You rule here," Janvian said. "You can forbid me to leave until the ship is gone."

The older woman shook her head. "You're not a child incapable of comprehending the consequences of actions. You're an adult. You can see where your choice leads."

"And what if my choice endangers the dome?"

"So be it," the mayor said. "This is our heritage. If we say we'll follow our principles tomorrow but not today, then we'll soon be fleeing from ourselves."

The red blob blinked to another spot. Janvian admired the woman's dedication but rejected her philosophy. It worked well within the dome's dependent structure where necessity merged individual needs and community needs. The inhabitants did not seem capable of making selfish, personal choices that threatened the welfare of the dome; but Janvian was.

Her goals were not their goals. Her needs turned counter to the pattern of their lives. She was as much a red light blinking through the circle's well-ordered grid as the craft.

"You know I need to leave at a sunrise. When will it be safe?" Janvian asked Dougal.

Numbers and graceful curves scurried onto the board from the tech's pen that was not a pen. "Can't say. This ship's not following the usual course. When it settles into an orbit, I'll be able to estimate how long it'll take to arc out."

Janvian marveled at his incomprehensible answers. She wished she could take his brilliance back with her, so he could teacher her child to delight in machines.

Lately the drawings and confiscated inventions hidden

below the fortress were in her thoughts. Again she wondered, what had Lorcha not become because of their suppression? What would the country be, or not be, a century from now because of a fear so old that the memory of its birth was lost?

These people gave her shelter and treated her as if she were blood. They extended *sanctuary* and all its privileges to her. They showed her another life.

"I'll wait—for now," Janvian said.

The mayor closed her eyes in relief. She moved her lips to whisper gratitude.

Janvian stopped her. "I must leave in four days' time. No later." She was serious when she called them Lorchans, for that's what they were. Born to the planet for generations past, they owed the same lor to the monarch as the other clans, pledged or not. Whether good or ill, Lorcha's future was their future.

"We'll find a way," Sasha said. "And I have a request. I ask that you take Jeremy with you."

Janvian kept her eyes from darting to him. Since the kiss in the Wilde, he'd stiffly distanced himself from her. "It isn't necessary. I can make the journey by myself."

"I volunteered," Jeremy said.

"You would have to understand the reason," Sasha said. "I'll explain."

~

TWENTY-NINE

Lnez watched.

The violent lightning play of last night was fresh in his thoughts but a distant memory to the sand. The Wilde was smooth and peaceful, as flat as the sky and just as endless. No telltale thread of dust announced a rider to the eye. No disturbance in a scan betrayed a presence to the mind.

He leaned against a slab that had shot out of the ground last night beside the crescent-shaped campsite. The lamprock glowed brightly. Bewaks strutted in and out of the sheltered space, eating crumbs from the midday meal that Lnez had sprinkled for them. Uz slept, oblivious to a fat, speckled bird that pecked at an exposed toe. There had been little rest for him last night amid the crashing and thrashing of the storm. He had fallen asleep at daylight then awakened long enough to share a meal before dozing off again.

Having lived in the fortress, Lnez was used to the noise, and as a mystic he was enriched by the energy. Through the haze of sleep, he'd felt his strength intensify with the fury. He'd dreamt his power had boiled and distilled, like a potent drink.

He'd floated in it and melted into it until he was the energy and the energy was he. He'd bolted awake to daylight and Uzec's snoring, surprised to find himself flesh and blood.

In the late harvest heat, he wore a light shirt and loose breeches tucked into short boots. The packed sand was too hot to go barefoot. From under a pile of stones he took out the perfect sphere and cradled it in his hands. The boulders in this spot dampened mystic abilities and the gemstone's intensity. The natural property was known in the Unity. He wondered if particles of it scattered across the desert affected his range and accuracy. He used a little cache he'd made out of it to protect himself from the jewel's fierceness.

Standing in the center of the clearing, he held the orb before him. Exposed, the facets gathered and fractured light from all direction, making rainbows. He experimented with a tight scan across the gentle waves of heat. The crystal alternated between resistance and seduction, pushing him away then coaxing him in. He fought both. The towering rocks at his back and sides vibrated with a faint echo of his effort when he got sloppy and let the force slip. At best he achieved a coexistence, stretching control for longer periods of time. The sameness of the sand helped him concentrate.

He was not so intent on the crystal that he forgot why Rozel stationed him here, nor the great trust it implied. Benoc would not approve; he approved of so little. Who better to trust as a watcher than someone who has known Janvian's hiding place all along?

These people's lives were so short. They worked toward a future they would never experience. Blood and ancestry ruled them. There was always a great hope for the next generation. And so they would accept a baby with the right blood and the right ancestry as their monarch.

It was not surprising they viewed mystics as a mistake of

nature. Lnez and his kind were aberrations, unable to reproduce. Their bloodlines withered and were gone forever.

If born a mystic, Janvian's child would rule for a long time but would have no heirs. When that was discovered, which belief would prove the stronger: right of ancestry or abhorrence at the sterile freak?

Lnez knew little about babies. There were children in the Unity, ones as young as four, but not babies. Mystic characteristics were usually not noticeable until three or later. Kin often ignored the signs for years hoping they were mistaken, subtly teaching the child to hide its abilities. By age four the tendencies were too strong. Parents were too exhausted to continue the pretense. Clankin were too afraid to ignore it.

Parents often wept at the gate when they finally delivered their child to one of the few abbeys that were known to the clans. Lnez had never understood the tears. There should be no grief in placing the young mystic where it belonged. It would be trained to use its gifts, and it would be happy. Yes, he had been happy in the Unity.

The thieves' camp had given him a different perspective. He was beginning to understand the sorrow of parents being separated from their children. He wondered what it was like to be a parent. He wondered if his parents had wept at the abbey gate.

A rainbow of colors folded over him. The sphere was no longer in his hands but surrounding him. He touched the sparkling wall, smooth and cold. Through it he saw Uz turn in his sleep, sending startled bewaks flying. This was his own fault. He had become distracted and the crystal had taken him. Now he was trapped.

He pounded at his prison. Panic rose in his throat and became a cry.

The sphere would not let him go.

<><><>

Janvian sat on the floor in the garage airlock, leaning against piled provisions. On a blanket at her side the baby slept. It would be daylight soon. Fujin and Spirit stomped about. Once saddled they were eager for an outing.

Dougal entered from the dome. After three days of the same routine Janvian found it impossible to raise her eyes to look at him.

"Not today," Dougal said. "Sorry. I'm sure your family will understand if you're a day or so late."

"I'm leaving at sunrise tomorrow," Janvian said.

Dougal squatted and peered at the sleeping child. "How's little what's his name?"

Janvian gave him a tired smile. "Healthy. Active. A good eater. If you don't object, I'd like to call him Dougal."

The tech blushed and pushed a knuckle into the floor to steady himself. "After me? I'm not even dead yet. I've never heard of a baby being named for someone who's still alive."

"It's unusual in the families too," Janvian said, "because it might cause confusion. But sometimes it is done. And the two of you will be living in different places. According to custom, I need your approval."

Dougal stroked his namesake's tiny hand. "I'm honored! It makes me feel immortal, like passing on my DNA. Can I help you store stuff away and carry Baby Dougal back to your room?"

Janvian nodded. Jeremy always took care of the merans. He had gotten them ready then disappeared. If the starcraft had been on the other side of the planet, she would have left without him.

298

<><><>

Exhaustion drained away panic. Lnez held bruised hands to his chest. The jewel encircled him; its pulse became his heartbeat. The curved wall distorted the view of the shelter in the rocks and the Bewailed Wilde. Uz slept in bright sunlight.

Lnez closed his eyes and saw the world, the moons, the sun, orbiting planets, a glittering galaxy. His free existence had been confining; this imprisoned one was so free.

But still a prison, the result of his mistake and not of his own choosing. He had made more choices for himself during the past year than during all of his previous 378. And he liked it. This gem would not take that from him. Not without a fight.

He thought of his dream and his waking to Uz's snore. He pulled back step by step. Galaxy to planets to the white sun to Alchorel. How beautiful! How sparkling and patched with colors. How like the crystal. He and the mystics and the clans huddled on such a small bit of it, as if in a tiny boat in a vast ocean.

And there *were* oceans. Huge ponds that cradled other lands within them.

He focused on the inhabited land. On the Wilde. On the crescent camp site. On one sleeping thief befriended by strutting birds.

Lnez breathed to the cadence of the rumbling snore, felt the itch in the small of his back where sand had sifted through a poorly mended tear in his shirt. A bewak pecked at his toe—

Lnez stood in the clearing holding the sphere before him in both hands.

Uz snorted but did not wake.

Lnez put the crystal back under the pile of protective rocks. He walked to the opening in the semi-circle of vertical slabs. His knees buckled, refusing to hold his weight. He leaned against the glowing monolith and slid to the sand. The plain waved with heat like ripe grain. Although immense, it now seemed so small.

Lnez watched.

Nearby, sheltered by towering rocks, another watcher searched for a telltale thread of dust to the eye and scanned for a disturbance in the mind.

<><><>

The peaks of the little fortress reflected the sun's last slow touch as it slid low behind the riders. A tilted triangular slab continued to shine as the sun set. It glowed with the remnant of the previous night's energy.

Janvian kept her eyes on the pinnacles and ignored the thunder that chased the pounding of Fujin's hooves. The shadow racing before her turned bloody with the gathering storm. For two days she had pushed the meran until its coat steamed, its mouth foamed, and its lungs neared bursting. Still the rocks mocked her with their distance, and the green land hid behind their border.

The baby whimpered in the sling against her chest. She had waited too long and would fail because of it. Her journey from west to east had shortened the day. They would be caught in the full force of the lightning. She had tried to explain it to Jeremy. Dougal, who watched the trail of an orbiting starcraft, understood.

A voice called over the growing rumble but she rejected the plea. "We've got to find shelter."

Twilight washed the monotonous landscape. Fujin slowed. Savagely she dug the heels of her frustration into his sides. The meran trotted then walked. The baby cried in long wails. The little fortress was in sight. How could it still be so far away?

The meran took her down into the sand. The fissure sunk below the plain. Another cave! The hard, uneven floor would make an uncomfortable bed, but it was shelter.

Jeremy dismounted, weak with relief. His mind was numb. He couldn't think through the last two days, and he had no idea what the next one would be. In the dome he had a daily schedule. At present he had nothing beyond a vague plan to collect genetic samples—with permission of the donors—and take them back to Sanctuary. He wasn't sure he could get back.

He gathered glowing pebbles from the entrance and brought them farther in to provide light. He watched Janvian tend the baby while he removed the worn saddle and bridle from Fujin and the Dougal-designed, dome-crafted gear from Spirit. She had not explained where she had to be or why she had to be there at a certain time. He had stopped trying to ask casual questions that might give him a hint. He knew it was about family and it was important, which wasn't much. To Janvian, everything about family was important. Wherever it was and whatever it was, it was tomorrow and they weren't there yet.

~

CHAPTER

THIRTY

The hearth hall blazed with torches and candles. Although outside the sun skimmed the horizon, in the windowless room at the center of the fortress it was perpetual night. Other parts of the structure always suffered a chill, but this space housed some even-tempered wind that left the cavernous fireplace unused much of the time.

Rozel tugged at the waist of the overlay. An embroidery of small birds decorated it, matching the blue-green of the robe. The thick lining felt like the tree bark the birds perched on. Under the heavy garment the fine cloth of the robe bunched. No matter how she adjusted the pleated sleeves and high collar, the clothing didn't fit. "I feel silly. I'm in the wrong place. Give me a sword, not a debate."

Benoc had dismissed her bright red gown as unsuitable for its color and lack of protective layers. Instead he had brought her some of Janvian's ceremonial attire to choose from. She'd eliminated all the others as too ornate or too boring and was left with this one.

"You'll need skills in both to survive this crowd," Oktria said. The warrior appeared only casually interested in the gathering. But she carefully observed the mood and movement in the room.

"Stop fidgeting," Benoc ordered.

Amud seemed comfortable and handsome in borrowed clothes, as if he often dressed in formal robes and attended ceremonies with tarryns and wealthy merchants. "You look wonderful," he said.

Rozel almost punched him in the ribs for his being amused by her nervousness. She should slug him anyway for not escaping with her. Instead she turned to her uncle to banter away some of her agitation. "Tarryn Benoc, I'll get even with you for this."

"I'm sure you will." Benoc would not be jarred from his solemn cloud. He stood with his weight on his healthy leg and surveyed the hall.

The gathering was small for such an important ceremony. Tarryns and their kin stood in tight fists, dividing the enormous space as they did the land. Mystics marked the walls like fence posts. Skaln strolled the territory, visiting the encampments, avoiding the Drueten stronghold. Under the guise of safety, he had limited those allowed into the fortress to only the most necessary through power and influence. With the rekindled memory of Rojelon's death a year ago despite the presence of mystic protectors, the Baerryns had not objected nor pretended to be insulted by the implication.

Benoc and the other tarryns were each allowed only three escorts. One of the Drueten positions was taken by a surprise for Skaln and would be of no value in a fight. The others were battle-honed soldiers, valiant but still only two. Beside them three prominent Drueten merchants appeared mild in embroidered cuffs and collars, but they were trained fighters and knew what was expected of them.

As a petitioner Rozel was permitted a limited entourage. That added Amud and Oktria, making nine clankin plus a thief against the many Felcon patrolling the building.

Rozel knew Benoc did not count Amud. She was sure her uncle mentally prepared a lecture about her relationship with him. She was spared that argument until this matter was settled. By then she might not be around to hear it. And it might no longer matter.

The carved double doors of the hearth hall stood wide. She couldn't help glancing at the opening again and again, hoping to see her sister. Others watched it too, awaiting the arrival of the Baerryns.

Instead a brilliant statue posed in the doorway. The sculpture moved, molten sunlight rippling with miniature stars. Calliud paraded into the room clothed in an elaborate gown scattered with jewels. A wedding gown. A monarch's wedding gown worked in gold.

Gasps ripple across the gathering. Majestically Calliud toured the room, nodding graciously to startled guests as if they were here at her invitation. She settled between her red-faced parents. A low buzz rumbled into an explosion of whispers. Her intended husband frowned at her from a knot of Felcons.

Benoc whispered a long and descriptive oath. Oktria muffled a chuckle. Rozel's nervous tension evaporated. The outrageous display was far more entertaining than the purple gown at Rojelon's viewing. It was so inappropriate and so uniquely Calliud that Rozel was no longer concerned with her own performance.

A pleasant, aromatic silence drifted through the hall, hushing the crowd. A pathway cleared through the center of the room, although Rozel was not aware that anyone moved. Her attention was gently turned back to the gaping doorway.

Single file, the nine Baerryns entered. The rustle of their robes instilled awe as they moved in procession to the dais. They formed a curve on the platform. Anonymous in their shrouds, they looked no different from other mystics; but the atmosphere held a unique intensity that demanded respect.

Rozel tapped her foot and concentrated on other things to shake off the influence that penetrated the air like incense. Last night she had pushed Amud out of her bed after their love making with the excuse that she needed undisturbed sleep to be alert today. Perhaps he had realized it might have been their last time together. He had kissed her and left, saying nothing.

She had not called him back and had not allowed the tears to last more than a moment. During the past days, she had done her own plotting and planning. She knew her sister well. Janvian would move the Wilde itself to get to the ceremony. But maybe the Mirage Clan had not been as delighted to shelter Nevran's clankin as the old man had expected. Maybe they held Janvian captive.

If Skaln was named monarch, her life was spit and her promise to the thieves worth about the same. If the Baerryns had the poor judgment to give her the golden armband, she could fulfill her promise to Amud, but she could never have him. She would be tied to affairs of state, without the freedom to act on her own.

In the tiny room that never quite warmed, she had stared into the flames swaying across the brick fireplace. She would give Janvian as much time as possible, but she would not wait for the Baerryns to choose between mistakes. If her sister did not arrive, she would ride across the Wilde and find her.

In the crowded emptiness of the hearth hall Rozel moved her arm to press lightly against Amud's. He kept his face turned toward the dais, but she felt a gentle pressure in response. Knowing that a pack and riding clothes were stashed in the stable near her meran gave her more comfort than his touch.

Blast him to sand, she thought wearily. *Blast him for placing his duty to a thief clan before his feelings for me. Blast him for being so like Benoc. Will I ever get my own life back?*

Another line of mystics entered. Each of the five figures carried a cushion draped with an armband showing a clan insignia worked in gold. Attention went to the embroidered cloth, making the bearers almost invisible. The cushions seemed to float to the dais and arrange themselves behind the nine. A petitioner gapped as the glittering symbol for his clan passed him, hoping beyond reason that it would be his.

Felcon soldiers closed the double doors with a solid boom that sounded like the final toll of fate. Rozel continued to expect Janvian to push open the wood at any moment, but she felt like the gasping petitioner who hoped without reason.

In a multiple voice the Speaker began the proceedings. "Relacav brought this land from the wectulk of the Lost Years into the stability of the Age of Order. As he decreed, we serve as protectors of the monarchy. In his name, we guide the peaceful transfer of leadership. We do so for the good of Lorcha."

"For the good of Lorcha," the group echoed, open hands rising to shoulders in salute.

"On this last day of the year 401 of the Age of Order, we gather to choose the successor of Rojelon of the Felcon Clan, whose reign will begin when Pypeed and Noalgaz, full with the roundness and prosperity of harvest, share the center of the sky and embrace in joy to signal the new year. Sanctioned petitioners, step forward."

Benoc gave Rozel a nudge. She pulled her eyes from the carved doors and stepped before the dais along with the others. Skaln took the center position. Calliud elbowed her way to the front of the observers and stood behind him smiling and sparkling.

Two Walbask petitioners fought over a choice spot near Skaln, but not exactly next to him for fear of comparison. Rozel stayed to the side. There were twenty-two petitioners, mostly Walbask, which reflected badly on Paulian. Others had been granted a claim, but the more cautious had withdrawn as the Drueten and Felcon rivalry had become clear and clan tarryns had chosen sides.

Those that remained defied their leaders. Rozel's previous crime seemed less severe and more forgivable compared to them. She was the only Drueten. Other kin had been accepted. Not all were strong in the practice of lor when a throne was the prize, and she had not set a good example. To their credit, they had only petitioned after they believed Janvian was dead. But they had done so despite Benoc's granting support to Rozel. The tarryn's quiet discussions with them before the ceremony had caused them to change their minds. He would have preferred to keep them all to add to the Drueten numbers here, but he wanted no surprises from kin seeking opportunities for themselves.

Likewise, the multitude of Felcon petitioners previously encouraged by Skaln had discreetly vanished, and he was the only wearer of the phianj armband to stand before the dais.

The Speaker continued. "Only those sanctioned petitioners within the walls of Aerrion Fortress can be considered for the monarchy. Tarryns, although we are not bound by the opinions of those beyond ourselves, it was Relacav's wish that you be consulted in the selection of your ruler. We now allow your statements of support for any of the petitioners before us."

Skaln bowed. "Felcon Clan supports my claim."

"Drueten Clan supports Rozel," Benoc called out.

Paulian attempted a squeaky start, cleared his throat and tried again. "Walbask Clan, kin and merchants, supports Skaln of the Felcons." Rozel heard the private message and appreciated the distinction Paulian made. The tarryn did not agree with his own words, but the economic forces within his clan overpowered his personal belief.

"Tskant Clan's first loyalty has always been to the blood heir of our slain monarch Rojelon," Gozax said, her loud voice easily heard. She was flanked by Calliud's parents, an intimidating pair, perhaps meant to be so for the tarryn's benefit. "With our Drueten neighbors and all of Lorcha we mourn the loss at Nept. That said, the Tskant Clan supports Skaln of the Felcons." Artulk and Diakt showed minute signs of relief. Gozax had not been easily persuaded into making that proclamation.

Despite Benoc's efforts to gather allies, the Druetens stood alone. Rozel took a deep breath and kept her posture proud. She wanted to shove a handful of animal dung into Skaln's false smile of humility.

Ianz's mother was last to declare. "Joach Clan supports"—Melaph paused as if struggling with the decision—"Rozel of the Druetens."

Murmurs of surprise sprang up and were quickly squashed. Rozel almost whooped for joy. They were not alone. Skaln's smile slipped. Rozel wanted to laugh. He looked as if a handful of dung *had* been shoved in his face. Melaph might soon regret her pronouncement, but for now Rozel was enjoying the results. Maybe this ceremony would be interesting after all.

"Petitioners," the Speaker said. "Do you accept one another as equal candidates?" It stood as if it were a dead tree flanked by other dead trees. Rozel found it hard to believe that Lnez, who was so involved in their lives, had once been that detached.

"We do." The petitioners' joint response rang discordantly in comparison to the harmony of the Speaker's multiple voice. Some bellowed, others stammered, a few barely managed a sound from parched throats. But all answered—except Rozel.

"Challenge!" Rozel said in her boldest, most confident tone. Benoc had rehearsed her in procedure, had given her the words and inflection, and had schooled her to conduct herself as Janvian would. But he was somewhere behind her now. She stood before the Baerryns as Rozel, and Rozel she would be. She would let them know the woman they considered for the throne.

"Name whom you challenge," the Speaker said.She heard the whisper of "Skaln" flow like the rush of water. "Natirut of the Walbask Clan," she said. The crowd buzzed with shock. Natirut's face flushed in disbelief. She was the least likely to be selected, hardly worth the attention.

The Speaker gave no sign of surprise. "State your objection."

"Natirut wagered her claim in a game of point," Rozel said.

"Gambling with one's legacy might not be wise," the Speaker said, "but it is not a crime."

"That isn't my grievance," Rozel said. "I challenge her petition because she didn't win. By continuing with her claim, she is reneging on a gambling debt. I submit to you that the lost bet and her refusal to honor it disqualifies her."

"Natirut of the Walbask Clan, what is your response?" the Speaker asked.

"It was just a friendly game," Natirut said. "No one took it serious like."

"Did you wager your claim to the monarchy?" the Speaker asked.

"I suppose I did," the woman said. "I'd had a few tanks by then."

"Did you lose?" the Speaker asked.

"Not through my own fault," Natirut said. "My knife be bent for sure. Didn't win a round all night."

The Speaker was silent. Rozel clamped her lips together to keep a straight face. The Baerryns must be having an interesting conversation over this one.

The Speaker said, "We have examined the challenge and found it to be of merit. Natirut of the Walbasks is removed from candidacy."

Natirut shrugged good-naturedly at Rozel and stepped back into the crowd.

"Petitioners," the Speaker said, "do you accept one another as equal candidates?"

"Challenge!" Rozel called. She wondered how the Baerryns would react to this one.

<><><>

The Visionate drifted naked above her simple pallet. Clothes were weighty; they strained her energy. The border of white that framed the thick drape covering the narrow window faded slowly, too slowly.

Her west-facing cell in the fortress was stale. She craved air, but it was still daylight. And so she floated, collecting the report of a spy outside the gate. Felcon troops patrolled the road and bridge. Druetens were secluded nearby. No Janvian. No blood heir. No Sage. Or should she call him Orioph, for that was probably the disguise he dwelled in. He was hidden even from her when he was in olax.

Her spy in the hearth hall told her nine mystics stood on the dais. Traditionally the Speaker and any eight represented the Unity during the selection ceremony. The true deliberation was conducted by the Prism, with counsel from the Sage and the Visionate. Its members could be anywhere and were often scattered at various abbeys. The session was open to the entire community so everyone could observe and learn.

This time the Sage had pushed his authority too far and had bound them all in absurd restrictions. The mystics acting as protectors and armband bearers were to keep their thoughts within the room. The members of the Prism were physically present on the stage, even though it was unwise to place the high-ranking mystics in a potentially volatile position. Under the pretense of avoiding distractions that might interfere with the vital task of selecting a new monarch, their minds were sealed from all but one another. The Visionate was not included. The Sage was not available for consultation.

Did he suspect she had interfered with the previous Speaker? Did he want the decision makers isolated so he could manipulate them without the scrutiny of the entire Unity?

The agreed upon plan was for the Prism to declare Rojelon's child monarch and itself regent. The wording would be different. The clans didn't know the Baerryns had an internal hierarchy. It would be presented as if the whole of the Unity, with all its joined minds, would guide the country until the delicate babe reached adulthood.

The Visionate knew the Sage's real intent. She saw it in several futures and could guess which one the Sage imagined for himself. Janvian dead. The blood heir cradled in his arms formally presented and accepted. His logical and compelling proposal that *he* and he alone serve as regent and rule the country. It was close enough to the original blueprint that the Prism would agree. The former Speaker was a fresh example of what happened if one questioned.

Again she saw the Purge that followed those futures. Each one depended on the timely arrival of the blood heir, which may not happen.

The absence of Rojelon's heir triggered other disturbing probabilities. Since arriving at the fortress, she'd been plagued by the visions. Without her counsel, the Prism would make a grievous mistake that would destroy any hope of mystic rule and would irrevocably alter the country.

The Visionate shivered. Her withered legs ached in the damp cell. She wished she were back in the abbey floating in the hot mineral pool. She saw futures where the Sage did not return from his solo journey. Then the clans would not be the only ones with a new ruler. The position might come to her. It was one of several possibilities. If it came to be, it might be too late for her to correct her predecessor's errors.

The oblong border around the shade-covered window bloomed from white to rose. Carefully the Visionate lowered herself to the course cloth covering her bed. She dragged her legs over the edge and lifted her weight onto the stunted limbs, cursing her humanness while grateful for the ability, unique to herself, that allowed her to defy torturous gravity.

Unless she broke the order of isolation, the Prism's choice would send them toward disastrous futures. Interfering meant shattering every rule, promise, edict, and code governing the separation of responsibilities within the Unity. She lacked the courage. She could not bear the same fate she had imposed on the former Speaker. She dared not act as long as the Sage lived.

～

CHAPTER

THIRTY-ONE

In the distance the disturbance looked like a tight swirl of smoke. Lnez hoped it was sand thrown into the air by animal hooves and not a whirlwind. He scanned. "Two riders."

Uz rocked from foot to foot and squinted into the afternoon sun. "Two? Can't be two. Unless the young monarch be quite the prodigy."

"Two adults." Lnez strained for greater detail. "A baby." Yes, a healthy child strapped against one of them. "The new ruler of Lorcha, Uz."

The thief wrestled with the puzzle of double riders. "She didn't go alone then, that be the answer. She took someone with her."

Lnez smiled and gave him another possible answer. "Or she's bringing someone from the Mirage Clan with her."

Uz had no idea that yesterday his slumbering presence had rescued Lnez from within the gem's power. He'd awakened shaking off a strange dream but remembered nothing specific.

"You think she found it then and there really be people living in the sand?" Uz asked.

"She's been somewhere," Lnez said. "I don't know anything about child birth. Could she manage having a baby and finding food and water on her own?"

"It be done. Maybe by mountain folk sometimes. And a lone thief can't be asking for help. It be a tough thing though. Better to have someone." He shaded his eyes with his hands. "They be drifting north."

"I'll guide them here." Lnez stood in the heat, clear of the jagged rocks and their obstructing property. After several nights at the edge, he felt strong. He sent out a mental beacon to draw them in.

The smoky line continued to bend to the right. Another vibration called the riders. Lnez examined the pulse. He recognized the shape and knew the mind that powered it.

He ducked back into the safety of the rock shelter, mouth dry. "The Sage." The terror of the disastrous attack that had gotten Ham killed shook him.

"No mistake?" Uz asked.

Lnez shook his head. The thin swirl became plumes. The curve northward was more pronounced. The riders were probably unaware they'd shifted course. "He's pulling them."

Uz's balding head had turned red from the sun. He rubbed it as if it were a talisman. "Maybe that's you what moved them and you just don't realize it. Maybe you do this sort of thing out of habit."

Lnez could not tell if Uz teased or was serious. The absurdness of the remark helped him swallow down the fear. "It's him."

"I'll go after them," Uz said. "You ride for Kaul."

Lnez was ashamed of his behavior. The thief was giving

him a way out, but he could not take it. "Kaul can't help. We have to do this ourselves."

Uz shrugged. That was no different from what he was used to.

Lnez instructed Uz to ride out and head them off. They quickly saddled one of the merans granted to them because of the importance of their task.

"What of the old man?" Uz asked.

"He'll try to control you too, if he gets the chance. I'll make him put all his focus on me. When that happens, Janvian will correct her course, but she might not be headed for this exact spot. Bring her here. That's important. Get her off the sand into these slabs as fast as you can." Lnez pressed a ring into the thief's hand. "Even with an armband she won't trust you. Show her this. It identifies you as acting for Rozel. Then take her to Kaul. Be careful. There're sure to be Felcons patrolling the countryside."

"Take your own advice," Uz said. "He killed Yadul and Ham. That be enough to lose. I wanted revenge once, but no more. I only want what be left of my friends alive. That fancy sparkle of yours better work." Then he was off.

From under the pile of rocks Lnez retrieved the gemstone. It called to him with frightening recognition. He put it into a pouch and tied it at his throat with a cloth strip. It was a crude replacement for the elegant golden chains and oval cage, but it was functional. He fastened his shirt closed over the bulge. The sphere tugged at him with tidal force. He felt as if he carried a moon.

Lnez moved northward along the line of rocks forced from the ground by centuries of lightning. According to the old tales, once there were hundreds of clans and no desert and no storms. He watched Uz race toward the two riders while he climbed to a precipice.

In the Unity he'd felt part of something larger and more important than himself. He'd thought the Baerryns were peacekeepers. Then he'd discovered they were enslavers and manipulators. He'd needed a new mission and he'd found it. He had to see this through.

A short, round figure stood on another rise. He sent a chill through the man, making his presence known. With a slow assurance the Sage turned. No hesitation. No searching the cliff to find the source of the irritation. His eyes went straight to Lnez.

"I only want the baby," the Sage thought to him. "I have no use for the mother. She can do as she pleases." He sounded reasonable. He grinned. "Take her to her clan. She'll be happy with them."

Yes, he only wanted Janvian to be happy. That was all. Didn't the smile prove that? Lnez wanted that too. The thought drifted through his mind like blossoms. He would take Janvian home where they would be happy. They would all be happy.

Lnez brushed away the filmy web. He'd expected an assault, not a charming delusion.

The Sage frowned. "I'm not that easy to dismiss. Know that you cannot beat me. Know that there is no help for you within the community. Know that I am the only one who will enter the fortress with the child monarch."

A tempest struck Lnez. How dare he challenge the Sage! He was a rogue, the lowest of creatures. Selfish. Insane. Betrayer of the shared oneness of the Unity. Alone. How did he presume to alter what must be!

Lnez fought back. He was a rogue, but not alone. It was the Sage's vanity that subverted the Unity. He deflected the attack with his gem and felt his opponent's surprise.

"Another!" the Sage thought. "I should like to know where

you find these rare delights. When I've finished and your brain is like porridge, I'll rip that knowledge from you."

The sphere shuddered and rang like a bell as the Sage probed it, searching for a flaw. Lnez cried out as if he again clung to the open balcony awaiting the plunge to his death.

He staggered and slipped on the slanted slab. Gravel carried him downward. He flung out a hand, grasping for a crevice. Sharp ridges scraped his fingers but did not halt his fall. He wrapped a fist around the pouch to protect the jewel. A chip or crack would destroy his only weapon.

The shale split and crumbled. Chunks tumbled over him in their haste to reach the ground. The fabric strip ripped, and the pouch was loose in his hand. He abandoned hope of stopping his descent and wrapped his arms around his head.

He thudded face down in rubble. A landslide crushed him. The ground quaked then was still. A trickle of pebbles pelted his back.

The Sage laughed. "Another gemstone gone? Unfortunate but necessary. It was a formidable piece."

The Wilde spread before the Sage like fine golden cloth. "Your friend joins the others," he thought. "I know that one. Should have killed all of them that first night. Sand blasted thieves. They've been a burr in my breeches ever since. That's what I get for being benevolent. I won't make that mistake again. Not with him or with you."

Lnez lay numb and half buried. He didn't know if the sphere was still in his hand. He squeezed. Pain jolted through him and he choked on tears. But he felt the moon, whole and full. It must be covered by shielding rocks.

The rhythm of hooves heading toward the Sage vibrated in his skull. How much time had passed? Perhaps he'd lost consciousness.

Slowly he dragged his damaged hand from the scree,

crying out at each inch. He worked the jewel free of the pouch. He pressed the cool brilliance against his forehead. The crystal gathered him into its heart. He went willingly.

In his mind Lnez formed the teardrop his friends had described to him. Elongated facets sparkled like spring water. From the encounter in the alley he knew its character and the uniqueness of its pulse.

He reached for it and enclosed it in his thoughts. The gem shook with ferocious rage. He clutched it tight. A tiny fracture marred the core. He twisted all his anguish at betrayal and abandonment into the crevice. The size and weight of his own despair shocked him. He no longer needed the misery or wanted it. He released the fury.

The silver shaft shattered. An angry cry, like the loss of life itself, rang long then ended empty.

Black light. Cold heat. Lnez dwelt in the heart of the stone. He was the stone. He was black light. Cold heat.

From another place words chanted in his ear. A baby cried. Lnez wept a tearless river. The child was how he had come to belong and what he belonged to. In that other world he had a country, a clan, friends, a name.

The crystal encased him in pristine isolation. He did not choose this. He would not choose this. The gemstone could never be his existence.

A woman's voice hushed the child with soothing coos. Lnez opened his eyes, trying to awake from the nightmare.

"Open your hand, man!" Uzec gently pried at his fingers. "Open!"

Lnez realized he had heard the insistent chant for some

time. He looked at his fist. A knot of ice sparkled between battered knuckles.

"Uz." Lnez was shocked at how weak his own voice sounded. He licked blood and salt from cracked lips and swallowed dust. A jagged rock pressed into his bruised back. He leaned against the wall, unable to lift his head.

Uz looked at him with a face beaten from the inside with worry. On the outside his cheek showed the mark of a blow beginning to swell and discolor. "Open your hand, friend."

Lnez relaxed the muscles and tried to obey but found that the hand would not respond. Uz slowly unfolded the fingers. The jewel glowed crimson and gold with a captured sunset.

Uz carefully lifted the gem between thumb and forefinger as if it smelled foul. "You left us for a blink or two." He dropped it into the cloth pouch, gritty with pulverized rock. "You clutched it like it was your soul. And with your hand all busted up too."

"Only part of my soul," Lnez said. He had the thief fasten the small bag around his neck with a fresh strip of cloth.

Uz moved stiffly, favoring one leg. "Thieves knot. It'll never come loose on its own."

Lnez scanned his injuries. Crunched hand with several broken bones, a lump at the back of the head over a thin skull fracture, a gash on the forehead, assorted swollen bruises.

A young man in strange clothes gave him a sip of water and bandaged his hand. Serious and intense, he spoke a few words of Lorchan but mostly uttered sounds Lnez didn't understand.

"This be Jeremy," Uz said. "Funny name, but it's what he's called. That be all I know. Can't talk and ride hard at the same time. Not that talking would do much good anyway. He not be wearing an armband, but he be no thief. Something be wrong with his arms. His wrists and elbows be stiff, like they never be trained right. His face tells everything he be thinking, so he's probably not a gambler."

A woman spoke to Jeremy in the same language. Janvian sat cross-legged, a bundle to her bare breast.

Lnez pushed himself forward and suffered the consequences of moving too fast. "Where—?"

Uz held him back with token pressure. "Old Orioph be no worry now." He tilted his head at a lifeless mound a short distance away. "He had the touch on us for sure. I would a sworn we rode straight toward where we be camped, but we ended up right at his feet. Thought it was the end of us 'til his sparkle exploded. I'm guessing you know something about that. Burst like it'd been smacked by lightning. He staggered around like a daeva possessed him, bleeding where shiny bits stuck in his neck. Went mad, he did, if he been't so before. But he still held us. Getting off that meran be like throwing myself at an invisible wall. I took a tumble and smashed my leg. Managed to get to him and slit his throat. For Ham and Yadul and you too. I be glad to make the slash myself with my own blade. Then we found you buried in the rocks like you be dead."

"The baby?" Lnez asked.

Janvian brought the bundle to him. Even with the strain of travel the woman looked strong and fit.

The blanket framed a round face. The creamy skin was smooth with the absence of worry. The eyes were almost closed in contentment. Yes, this was the child he had touched in the womb.

Are you a mystic? Lnez thought. But the answer to that was years away.

"Healthy," Lnez said.

"Thanks to Jeremy's people," Janvian said, cradling the child. "He says your hand is badly damaged, and he doesn't know how serious your head injuries are. If you can't ride, you can stay with him and our brave clankin here until I can send help. Uz skipped the part where he wrestled with the traitor until he could get a blade into him. He insisted Jeremy take care of you first. I can guess some things about the man you call Orioph. I don't have time for explanations right now, but I'll expect them later."

She looked from Lnez to Uz. "I don't know either of you. I'm grateful for your help, but I'll want to hear your lineage. If you hadn't brought this," she held up her hand and showed the ring back where it belonged, "I would have thought you were enemies, despite your armbands. You wear mourning strips for a clankin's death. I'll need to know about that too."

"And the sparkles," Uz said. "You'll want to hear about them."

Janvian nodded. "It's on the list."

"Kaul is waiting with soldiers to get you into the fortress," Lnez said, shakily getting to his feet. "I'll take you to him. Uz, I'll need your meran. When you're patched up, take Jeremy back to our camp to get our supplies and the other animal. "

"You must stay here and have Jeremy tend to your injuries," Janvian told Lnez.

"I can take care of my wounds," Lnez said.

Janvian pursed her lips as if she added that to the list. "You'll slow me down. Tell me where Kaul is. I can find him on my own."

"By the furry rask on my arm, Janvian, you need him, well or ill," Uz said. He shifted his leg so Jeremy could examine it better.

Janvian seemed to accept his advice. She spoke to Jeremy in the other language. The young man left Uz and stood close to her while they talked privately. Lnez swung up onto the meran Uz had used then calmly waited.

Jeremy held Baby Dougal while Janvian mounted Fujin

then handed her the bundle. She tucked the child into the sling under her cape. He turned his back so he would not see her ride away. After the strange event with Orioph, who was now dead, he better understood she rode toward danger. The hoof beats faded behind him. His patient called. He didn't understand but the tone was jovial.

"Come, strange friend. While you fix my leg, I'll teach you a song in proper words so you'll at least be able to enter a respectable tavern.

~

THIRTY-TWO

Candles, once gloriously tall, now dwindled. Flames choked in their own reflective wax pools. The shortened light brought the hearth hall low to a stub of a room.

"Petitioners, do you accept one another as equal candidates?" Weariness shaded the Speaker's multiple voice.

"Challenge," Rozel said. She was tired too, but she refused to show it.

"Name whom you challenge," the Speaker said.

"Skaln of the Felcons."

The wilted observers thought they were beyond surprise but now discovered they were not. Rozel had objected in turn to each rival standing with her before the Baerryns. Nine had been successful, eleven had not. Although the charges themselves had often been entertaining, the investigations into them had been tedious. Explanations and questioning had ranged from a few select words to intense debate as Rozel had argued her positions and the candidates had countered.

The Baerryns' deliberations were sometimes brief but more

often were long ribbons of silence that had curled around the uncomfortable observers. Twice they had halted the proceedings and left the room. Even mystics required food and water and chamber pots.

Skaln was the only one Rozel had not yet tested. The whispered consensus was that even she dared not risk angering a candidate supported by three clans. Her action to the contrary shoved aside the crowd's drowsiness and hunger.

"State your objection to Skaln's petition for the monarchy," the Speaker said.

Rozel's feet hurt. The Baerryns had planned to announce their decision shortly after sunset but that was long past. Darkness engulfed the fortress. In the west the storm rolled across the Wilde. In the east slow Pypeed climbed the sky. By now guests should be celebrating the announcement of a new monarch whose reign would begin with the new year. She decided not to think about which side of the sand her sister might be on. She resisted hopping onto the dais and sitting cross-legged for the rest of the ceremony. The throne was pushed to the back of the platform to make room for the mystics. Being selected monarch might be the quickest way to get a chair. "Skaln executed a traitorous breach of lor," she said. "He designed and ordered the murders of my sister and the blood heir."

The gathering stirred like leaves in a whirlwind. Rozel turned toward the rustling, training prompting her to protect herself. Benoc, Amud and Oktria sheltered her back. The tarryn's soldiers were not with them. They had a task close by.

Hands froze on undrawn weapons as the mystics scattered against the walls performed their duty. Calliud wavered and leaned against her mother, too slight to bear the bulk of her gown through the lengthy proceedings.

The Baerryns stood in wordless consultation. Skaln folded

his arms across his chest and gave an amused smile. Rozel wondered how many of the cloaked blades halted by the mystics had been grasped for her and how many against her.

The Speaker said, "In your voice we hear that you do not believe your sister is dead."

You fraud, Rozel thought hard at the Speaker, not knowing if it received the message. *You heard nothing. We both know Janvi wasn't killed at Nept because she was never there.*

The Speaker continued without reacting. "This may be a natural denial of loss. You believe Skaln is guilty of executing a plot against the blood heir. However, belief is not evidence."

Rozel met Skaln's smile with steady certainty. "Examine his mind, and you'll know that it's true."

"An outrageous accusation," Skaln said calmly.

"We do not touch minds without reason," the Speaker admonished.

"I give you reason," Rozel said.

Benoc signaled. From a corner of the room his two soldiers escorted a figure wrapped in a cloak. This was the surprise he had brought into the fortress as one of his three, leaving him short a fighter. He unfastened the cloak and pushed it to the floor. The drugged man wore a Felcon armband. Despite the stubbled chin and crumpled clothes, some in the crowd recognized him as belonging to the Felcon troops.

"This man was a leader in the attack on Nept," Benoc told the Baerryns. "Under questioning, he confessed that he acted according to his tarryn's orders and that the goal of the assault was to kill Janvian and the blood heir."

"The man lies to hide his own crimes," Skaln said, seemingly unconcerned. "When the country was most in need of loyal fighters, he deserted clan and kin to become a mercenary. The Felcons cast him out. We curse him and memories of him. He's a traitor. He shouldn't be listened to and he doesn't deserve to live."

The words were even and void of passion. Rozel hoped the Baerryns *could* hear the unsaid in a person's voice so they could recognize the deceit in what Skaln proclaimed.

"Candidate Rozel," the Speaker said, "we will take custody of the man presented and examine his mind. Then we will determine how to proceed. For this, we require the solitude of our own room. Therefore, we pause in the administration of this ceremony. We will inform petitioners and witnesses when we are ready to resume."

Clouds boiled angrily over the Bewailed Wilde. Light flared and died in random patches. But while the nightly storm strafed the sand, the sky over the fertile land was darkly clear and alive with stars. Constant Pypeed and fickle Noalgaz sailed across it like round boats. Their bright glow placed a false pattern of sure ground and shadowy holes before the riders.

Janvian and Lnez rode hard. They could be stealthy or they could be fast, but not both. Fujin ran with a strained gait but no hesitation, as if the scent of home was so powerful that the imperfect light made little difference. Lnez's animal was fresh and eager, but he guided it poorly. Swollen right hand useless, he grasped the reins in his left.

Lnez did not lie to himself by thinking he had tamed the gemstone. It was not a thing to be conquered. For the moment they had an alliance. Using its energy, he blocked the distracting pains in his hand, back and legs. Later, when he could concentrate, he would accelerate the healing. Mostly he scanned. Full moons facilitated their speed but placed them in easy view of the many other riders he sensed. He and Janvian outpaced two of them on slower animals. More were ahead. Friend or foe, he could not tell.

The western branch of the Aerrion River flowed south from the bend where it protected the fortress gate. They neared the bank. A rider washed in double moonlight patrolled the far shore. Spying them, it spun its mount and headed north toward the city.

Upstream the placid water bordered a sleepless town. Fires burned along the docks. Lnez's mind told him souls huddled in groups around the flames. What should be a night of celebration was one of silence. Uncertain of the future, they watched the moons, and they watched the tower for the light that would tell them a new monarch ruled.

With his mind Lnez followed the scout racing through the streets, startling docksiders. Soon Skaln would know they were near.

He scanned a stand of trees and bent their course toward it, wishing he could tell which clan waited there and hoping the plan still held. He ducked under the shelter of spreading branches and smelled ripening nuts. He felt the movement of many around him. "It's Lnez," he said to the trees. "And Janvian."

Drueten soldiers and thieves wearing rask insignias drifted from leaf-shadowed hiding places. Amud's people out numbered clan.

Kaul greeted Janvian. He grasped Fujin's bridle and led the animal into the clearing at the center of the copse. The meran nuzzled him in recognition. Janvian noticed the young apprentice tarryn had changed some from a year ago. His beard had grown fuller and his blue-gray eyes seemed more direct. In the speckled light he seemed a larger version of his father. "The tower?" she asked.

"No signal yet," Kaul said. "Rozel promised to keep the

ceremony lively until you arrived. By now she's probably exhausted all the tricks she'd planned and is trying to juggle burning candlesticks."

"Rozel's doing what?" Janvian asked.

Kaul stroked Fujin. "I'll explain later. She sends a message, 'You can't return the way you left. The path is blocked.' I don't know what it means, but she assured me you do."

Janvian nodded solemnly. "Yes, I understand."

Lnez urged his animal forward so he was beside Kaul. "Uz is injured," he said. "We left him at the edge with one named Jeremy. Can you send someone to help him?"

Kaul shook his head, dark hair like curled leaves about his shoulders. He had the look of a serious commander now, not a boy unconvinced of his own authority. "They'll have to wait. We can't spare anyone. Our numbers are low, and from Rozel's message I presume we'll have to fight our way through the gate." Kaul looked to Janvian for confirmation.

"I can think of no other option," Janvian said. The bulge under her cape moved with a soft noise. She pushed aside the cloth and gently bounced the child to soothe him. The baby gurgled and stretched.

Rough fighters and seasoned thieves quietly closed a circle around the mother and child. Clankin put hand to shoulder in salute.

"See what you fight for," Janvian said. A rosy face topped with wisps of red hair squinted at the stars. "Rojelon's son. The blood heir. He needed a fresh name that carried no history of clan squabbles or wars. He is called Dougal."

Kaul ran a finger along the smooth cheek, a light brush, no more. He turned away and swiped at his own cheek, then he signaled.

Clobben appeared and the company mounted. Kaul took the lead. Lnez and Janvian were placed in the middle of the formation. As they rode, the fortress grew before them. The stones burned with moonlight. The mystic presence was strong within the walls. Lnez felt it even at this distance. A concentration of power radiated from the structure as if it were the very sun. He knew it was The Prism.

<><><>

Benoc refused the offer of luxury, clearly stating he preferred the reassurance of hard wood. Despite his protests, Rozel maneuvered him in front of a lounge puffy with plump cushions. Oktria gave him a one-arm shove. He teetered on his good leg then fell into the pillows. It never would have happened if he'd had two healthy legs.

The thief Amud had the good judgment not to laugh. He arranged a stool opposite the tarryn and lifted the injured leg onto it, careful of the bandage under Benoc's robe.

Rozel pulled up a chair for herself and plunked into it. She stretched her legs and wiggled her toes, closing her eyes to drink in the full pleasure of the act.

Benoc watched, amazed at her ability to ignore the seriousness of the situation. How could she think of personal comfort when the monarchy was a fingertip away? "You didn't follow the plan," Benoc admonished her.

Rozel kept her eyes closed. "I made it more interesting so no one would fall asleep. Especially me."

Coded rapping saved Rozel from a sharp lecture. Oktria went to the door and collected a tray of food and drink, and a message. "Skaln still won't allow any but his own kin on the battlement, and he's sealed off the rooms with any useful windows. We can't receive a signal from Kaul, and we can't check the moons' paths ourselves. Noalgaz must have risen by now and begun its move toward Pypeed. Hard to say how far off their joining might be."

Benoc thought through what the break in the ceremony might mean. Lnez had told him the mystics wanted the baby to be named monarch. Then they would declare themselves as regent. Would they dare do that if the mother, with her own claim to the throne, stood with the child on the dais? They'd been tolerant of Rozel's interruptions but had done nothing to stretch them out. This delay was first sign that they expected the baby to appear before they were forced to make a decision.

"Examining the Felcon traitor is not enough," Benoc said. "The mystics should be probing Skaln's mind as well."

Amud put food and a mug on a table close to Benoc before he served himself. "They don't want to know what Skaln's been involved in. As long as they have no evidence, he isn't guilty of anything. They want him to remain a viable candidate."

Benoc agreed but made no effort to show it to the thief. At least his niece had chosen an intelligent outcast. "A Drueten must have the throne."

Rozel tugged off her boots. "But not the wrong Drueten!"

Benoc pierced his niece with a stern eye. "You'll do your duty." His wound throbbed and he had difficulty banishing the ache. "If it takes a year or a lifetime of years, you'll hold the monarchy for your sister."

Rozel had developed an immunity to Benoc's misplaced parental looks. She chucked her boots into a corner and thought only of her pack stashed in the stable.

<><><>

Disruptions crashed together like squabbling children, making it impossible for the recently installed Speaker for the Prism to think clearly. He was embarrassed for himself and for the rest of the nine, which made the disturbance among them worse. They might as well be urinating through their robes in public.

He stepped from the private room onto the balcony and into the embrace of the storm, hoping for comfort. The smell of lightning was strong tonight. Facing west, he had no view of the moons that would soon join as the new year began.

Speaker. For the Prism. There had never before been such a role or the need for one. Likewise, the nine had never physically been in the same place together until now. Lesser mystics had always performed the tedious task of representing the members of the elite group before the clans; a minor voice had communicated their decrees.

It seemed the Sage had gone mad, mandating they travel. Actually traverse in carriages to Aerrion Fortress. They had threatened to defy the order. But here they were, their minds managing the frailties of their bodies so they could endure the ordeal.

Far worse was the barrier the Sage demanded they keep between the Prism and the rest of the Unity while dealing with the whiny petitioners seeking the monarchy. They had no access to the Sage, no knowledge of the baby who was supposed to become monarch under their care.

Even the Visionate was excluded from their thoughts at a time when they desperately needed her counsel. The Speaker privately believed the Sage did not want them to know of the possible futures. Not for the first time, the Speaker wondered if the Sage worked toward a different plan, a different outcome, than the one they had agreed on.

The situation was obviously not what the Prism had hoped for. How badly had things gone wrong? He sent a worm wriggling through the solitude that enclosed them. He was not a fetch and carry mystic. He was of the hierarchy and had power of his own. He would face the Sage for his defiance, if it came to that. Right now he needed to contact the Visionate.

His probe made no progress. How many mystics were assigned to keeping the isolation intact? He would persist. One of the guardians was sure to make a mistake.

He ruffled a blanket of calm across the Prism. The youngest of them reported on her examination of the captured Felcon. "The man acted under Skaln's order."

"Did he receive instructions from Skaln himself?" the Speaker thought.

"No, they were given through another, now dead."

The Prism absorbed the information and deliberated.

"Do we examine Skaln?" They had recognized indicators of lies when he'd spoken of the captured clankin. If they did so and found evidence to support the Drueten charges, they must declare him guilty of treason and reject his petition.

A discussion swirled through the Prism's linked minds.

Without Skaln, Rozel would remain the only viable candidate. The rest of the rabble lacked the most basic qualifications and had less impressive lineage.

She was too headstrong but not personally ambitious.

She had only the Druetens and the Joachs behind her, geographically an impossible coalition.

Skaln was in a better position to prevent fighting among the clans. He would be a tyrant, but there would be something close to peace.

War would be a better catalyst for the future we strive toward.

"We are being too cautious," several voices thought. "We could fulfill our plan now, without the child monarch as transition."

The Prism Speaker had expected that bubble to surface. They'd managed the country for the past year. The Sage had promoted the strategy and it had seemed a logical step toward their goal, but it had been a mistake. Continuing to rule without the blood heir would not be well received.

The Speaker shuttered. Standing on the dais in the hearth hall making such an announcement, they would be easy targets for angry clanners. With so many mystics in the room an attack on them would fail. Probably. But it would start a fire not quickly extinguished. Had the Sage anticipated such an event? Was that why he'd ordered them to face the petitioners themselves instead of leaving the task to surrogates?

The Speaker hushed the many voices. He'd allowed them to avoid making a decision. No more.

"Now we will choose."

Her body a heavy burden, the Visionate ascended from the bleak cell to a higher room. Someone important slept here, someone deemed worthy of smooth sheets and the large westward windows that drew her here. No doubt the woman was below in the hearth hall, where the Visionate was not allowed to go. On the Sage's orders, mystics guarded the doors and blocked her from communicating with any of the Unity. Her spies were useless. Her gift was her only source of information.

She opened the panes and floated in the frame. Here, so close to the Wilde, the storm tasted wonderfully mad. Lightning clawed the sky. She reached out to the future.

Multiple streams wavered before her, telling her no decision had been made in the chamber below. She probed for clues to the present.

Otherworlders strolled through Aerrion city. Machines stalked the streets. Skaln must still be a candidate. He was the link to that possibility.

War spread like a disease. That future was always there and told her nothing new.

Peace reigned. Almost as common as war.

A strange clan rose up. This thread was stronger than a year ago when it first formed.

Clans disappeared. She'd been seeing that one since she'd been a child and still puzzled to understand it.

Fires purged the mystics to ash. The threat was often there. It seemed more vivid tonight, fanning out in different ways.

Mystics ruled. But not through the Sage's efforts. He was not there.

She searched snaking tendrils and did not find him.

The streams froze. Futures vanished as if a desert wind drank them dry.

The Visionate reeled from the emptiness.

CHAPTER

THIRTY-THREE

The Druetens watched the fortress from a safe distance. Above the stone tower the moons arced toward their meeting point. Armed figures paced the battlement. Torches blazed at the gate. Guards—some on foot, many mounted—patrolled the slanted road and its bridge over the river. Soldiers blocked the junction where the slope met the route from the city.

Kaul surveyed the defenses. "They've increased the troops since I was last here."

"According to lor, the heir can't be kept out," Janvian said, "but I doubt those Felcon are stationed to uphold the law. She had planned to get in through the hidden passage she'd used before. Rozel's message had told her that was impossible. The other secret entrances she knew of were difficult and slow. She could not risk trying one only to find it sealed as well. "There must be mystics. We can use their protection."

Kaul raised an eyebrow at Lnez. He knew how the mystic came to be with them but Janvian did not.

"We need the Baerryns, but it's best to be cautious," Lnez

335

told Janvian. This was not the time to explain that the highest level of the Unity had arranged Rojelon's death. Mystics who were not part of the governance would be unaware of the plot and could be approached. If he delivered Janvian and the baby to low-ranking guardians before witnesses with clan at their side, they should be safe. Then he could disappear before any discovered who he was, using the power of his new gemstone to accomplish the escape.

"There should be mystics at the gate," Kaul said, "but I see no hooded figures."

Lnez scanned and detected none near the bridge. On the battlement he found one behind a cloak. The illusion parted slightly so the being within could look with eyes and mind. The watcher was more skilled than those usually stationed at the gate. Was it under the Sage's orders or placed there as a single sentinel because many mystics were needed for the ceremony? If contacted, would it assist them or alert the Felcon guards?

"Will we have to fight our way in?" Kaul asked Lnez.

"A moment," Lnez said. A straight attack without support was insane. He searched for Oktria's mind, for Rozel's mind, for Benoc's mind. "We are here," he tried to tell them. "We need your help." His pleas echoed back. He sent the messages in sharp daggers, propelling them with all the power he dared demand of his gemstone, but they blunted against an impenetrable barrier. The force vibrated as if he'd struck a gong. His presence was known now and there was no reason for secrecy.

Lnez called to the mystic on the moon-shadowed battlement. There would be no mercy for him, he was a rogue and would not be treated gently, but perhaps the watcher still held to his honor-bound duty to protect the monarchy. "We bring the child of Rojelon and the babe's mother," he thought into the warm harvest night. The mind was surprised at being discovered. It absorbed the message but gave no response. He tried again. "It is your obligation, above all others, to protect the blood heir." His plea reached emptiness.

Lnez turned to Kaul and shook his head. Although she might wonder, Janvian did not ask what had occurred.

"To the bridge then," Kaul said. The apprentice tarryn gave tactical instructions to his troops. They rode unchallenged to the midpoint over the Aerrion River.

Lnez had expected to be struck by a blow from the Unity. Perhaps an attack could not be made from within the shroud encasing the fortress. Good. He would make use of it. He leaned close to Janvian. "When the battle begins, stay near me."

A line of guards, no doubt alerted by the watching mystic, blocked the gate. A Felcon too large for the clobben under her separated from them and rode slowly to the fortress side of the bridge where it met the cobblestones to the gate. Moonlight glinted off the metal clasps on her leather vest that showed she had rank. "Come no farther if you value your lives."

"We demand entrance," Kaul said. "We escort the blood heir, child of Rojelon."

"No one crosses the bridge."

"The babe shares Felcon and Drueten blood. He is as much your clankin as mine."

"Rojelon himself couldn't get through the gate tonight." Her hard eyes searched among the Druetens as if she knew the one she sought. Janvian's russet hair was not hard to find.

"To deny the heir entrance is to defy lor," Kaul said.

"Consider it defied." The Felcon grinned, showing wide white teeth. "No one crosses."

From among the sword-wielding warriors, a single rider came forward onto the bridge carrying a torch. Too late Lnez understood. He sent a freezing wind through the soldier's mind. The man shivered, dropping the burning shaft. Fire sparked and rolled into a dark line of dead vines that wove across the worn wood.

Thick flames spiraled up into the night, forcing the Druetens back toward the road. Attackers came from the rear, mercenaries without clan insignias. Their slashing blades blocked escape from the spreading fire. Lnez's meran reared and spun. Unable to separate friend from foe, he didn't dare send out a freezing blast. Choking on thick smoke, he clung to the reins with his uninjured hand. Heat crackled around him. His confused mount collided with Janvian's. Fierce determination on her soot-smeared face, she swung a sword blocking a blow from a hired fighter. In the sling tucked under her cape, the baby cried, like the wail of the wind against the clank of metal on metal.

Lnez sensed a rider intent on Janvian. He saw firelight streak the face and glint along the weapon. Shaking off the chaos, he sent a false vision into the intense mind. The man's blade swept empty air.

Trapped between fire and mercenaries, there was no way to reach the gate. Lnez knew another route. He'd dismissed it as holding the greatest peril. Now he saw it in his thoughts as clearly as if it had been placed there. Peace in the midst of turmoil. A calm center in the whirlwind.

He touched Janvian's mind. Contact came smoothly, as it had a year ago on the balcony when she'd asked for the Baerryns' assistance. *I tried to help then, and I'm trying now,* he thought. Janvian's willing response made the connection dangerous. He must not hold it too long.

Lnez maneuvered to the side of the bridge where land supported the wood. He jumped his meran over the low railing, feeling Janvian plunge down the steep embankment behind him. The animals slipped on damp grass and slid to the rocky river bank. He guided them under the structure, which formed its own kind of night. Dirt and sparks sifted through spaces between the boards, pelting them like falling stars. Here the river rushed deep, swift and unforgiving. A burning plank fell, barely missing them. It smacked the water with a hiss and swirled away.

Mentally Lnez examined the ground under the current. He found the narrow, twisting island of sand and rock slashing diagonally from shore to shore under the dark liquid.

Above them the bridge groaned with the weight of fighters and stomping mounts. Lnez jumped from his meran and tugged Janvian from hers. He put his good hand around her. Together they splashed into the river. As the water churned to her waist, Janvian clutched the baby to her but did not resist the mystic's guidance. Her foot slipped. The bundle dipped into the stream, and the baby shrieked louder.

As if in response, the creaking overhead became a crack. Hooves clattered from the danger. Lnez plunged for the far shore, dragging Janvian. They reached a rise free of the current and pressed against a stone wall. The ramp collapsed in a fiery rain. Steamy plumes rose from the river. Jutting boards hung smoldering.

In the ragged shelter of the broken bridge Lnez let Janvian fall to a patch of wet gravel. He released her mind but she stayed tangled in his thoughts. Exhausted, he collapsed onto the silt beside her. He splashed icy liquid on his face and swiped at the droplets with a dripping sleeve. With effort he pushed away her mind and shook free of the contact, feeling a strange relief at the aloneness.

Janvian ignored her crying child and stared at the silver-haired man. "I know you."

<>＜><>

Yellow light fell in soft pools from glowing lamprock hung in cages. Veins of pale ore in the walls reflected the illumination. A faint hum seemed to come from far away. Across the polished floor Lnez and Janvian left wet trails from soaked boots and drenched clothes.

Janvian ran a hand along the smooth contours as she hurried through the wide passage. The child was quiet now, sleeping while others fought to place a world in its small hands. "Carved through solid rock," she said. "Machine made." She sniffed the air. "Dry. Clean. Too warm for this far below ground. Perhaps heated by the device I hear?"

"This tunnel is older than the fortress," Lnez said, "older than the secret passageways the monarchs use. It's best if you ask no questions about it." He'd guided Janvian through the false image of mud and rock under the damaged bridge and into the tunnel while quickly confirmed what Janvian had already determined from their mental contact, that he'd been the Speaker of the Baerryns when they'd met on the balcony but he was no longer of that community.

What else she'd learned through the link and how much she'd guessed, Lnez could not tell.

"We're so close," Janvian said. "We must beat the moons. Are there guardians near by? Can you alert them so they'll delay until we arrive?"

How could he explain that as a rogue, a solitaire, he was an intruder with no right of passage here? This seemed the only path open to them, but it might prove more dangerous than the flaming bridge.

"The guardians will find us." Lnez stopped, realizing his own stupidity. This was far from the public place he'd hoped for, with Drueten kin and witnesses around them. If they died here, no one outside of the Unity would know. In the confusion he had accepted the refuge of the tunnel as his own idea. Now he recognized the signature of an imprint. The touch had been cleverly done by an experienced mind, but he should have questioned a solution he'd rejected as too perilous.

A hooded figure appeared in the center of the tunnel as if a curtain had fallen. Janvian pulled back in surprise.

"You are expected," the mystic said.

CHAPTER
THIRTY-FOUR

Stubby candles had been replaced by fresh tapers, filling the hearth hall with eager flickers. Refreshed from the recess in the ceremony, tarryns, merchants and petitioners faced the dais and watched the mystics reform the pattern of Baerryns and armband bearers. In contrast to wilted gowns and robes, eyes gleamed with nervous excitement.

Rozel shared none of their emotions. The new moons closed together, so said a rumor that was probably no more than a guess. No one was allowed near a window to confirm or refute it. The world outside the stone walls moved toward midnight and a new year, but this place seemed exempt from time.

My daeva has brought me here, Rozel thought. *I'm to spend eternity arguing with faceless mystics. Benoc arranged this punishment for me.*

Behind her Amud stood with Benoc, Oktria and the other Druetens. Arms folded across his chest, feet set wide to balance his weight, he looked confident and commanding. Rozel decided that he should be a candidate for monarch instead of herself and the other petitioners remaining after her challenges.

The hopefuls spread themselves before the dais, keeping a cushion of space from one another. Most sent quick glances to each side, still evaluating the competition. Rozel ignored all but one. Skaln avoided her gaze. He seemed stiff, afraid to turn or blink for fear of what the motion might become. He was a step away from being named monarch or traitor. Glory or doom was his depending on the decisions of the Baerryns.

The Speaker did not gesture or make a sound but somehow demanded Rozel's attention. Everyone's eyes fixed on the robed figure.

"The Felcon prisoner has been examined," the Speaker said. "There is evidence that the targets of the raid were Janvian and the blood heir and that the traitor believes he acted on the orders of his tarryn."

An eruption of shouts was muffled by mystic influence. Rozel felt her elation suppressed. The Baerryns were determined not to let her enjoy more than a sweet drop of revenge.

"This is only the traitor's belief however," the Speaker continued. "The order to attack Nept was issued through another, now dead, who claimed it came from Tarryn Skaln. The prisoner admitted that he did not know for certain if this was true. No evidence was found to establish an unquestioned link with the Felcon tarryn. Therefore, we have no reason to examine him. Skaln's claim to the throne remains."

Rozel heard Benoc's gruff protests swell then fade. Skaln returned to life. He turned his head slowly to face Rozel and gave her a smile.

"Petitioners," the Speaker said, "do you accept one another as equal candidates?"

Rozel felt the center of the room shift and all eyes turn to her. The battle was over. She had no more barbs to toss and no more petitioners to poke. Disappointment drained away her energy. She was not sure she could stand up long enough to hear a new monarch proclaimed. At this point she almost hoped it would be her, so she could finally sit down.

Something in her could not let the moment pass. Rozel opened her mouth. The room held its breath. She yawned, a large, bored yawn that summed up her feelings about the entire ceremony.

Amud and Oktria laughed the loudest. Rozel was sure Benoc frowned disapprovingly. She did not turn to check.

The Speaker continued as if the formal proceedings still held some dignity. "According to the laws established in the reign of Relacav at the dawn of the Age of Order, we will now choose the new monarch of Lorcha from those petitioners assembled."

The mystics stood immobile as if consulting among themselves. Rozel felt the pause was traditional, to make the ceremony more exciting. She did not believe they had waited until now to discuss such an important decision. What else had they been thinking about all day?

"We, the Baerryns, declare the new monarch of Lorcha, successor to Rojelon's throne, to be"—the Speaker froze as if suddenly elsewhere, as if the robe was empty, just cloth held in place by custom.

Skaln jumped onto the dais. "Finish it!" The Speaker was oblivious to his command. From a cushion Skaln snatched the Felcon armband worked in gold. He held it over his head like a triumphant banner, displaying the glittering phianj with wings spread and talons flexed. Cheers were mentally calmed. Only confused murmurs rippled across the gathering.

The huge double doors burst open from the force of a whirling wind that swept the room. Candles were snuffed out then violently flickered into great torches. The mystics stationed along the walls bowed low.

In unison, the Baerryns on the dais widened the semicircle. The cushion bearers joined the crescent, aligning themselves toward an invisible spot. Skaln was pushed from the stage by unseen hands and staggered to his previous position with the petitioners.

The wind spun to the dais and spiraled at the focal point of the mystics' arc. A tiny robed figure appeared and the air calmed. "We are the Visionate," the raspy collective voice said. It was almost a whisper, yet all heard it clearly. Rozel found it hypnotic. "The graveness of the situation demands our attention."

The robe swayed slightly. There seemed more cloth than body. From her position on the floor Rozel thought she saw unobstructed light flow between the hem and the wooden boards of the platform as if the swaddled figure floated before her. Mystic tricks, she decided, done for effect like the wind and the voice. Still, she was awed. Not much was known about the structure within the Baerryns. One often seemed the same as another. Except this time Rozel felt she stood at the feet (if there were feet) of a leader.

"Tarryn Skaln," the Visionate said, "you used your authority as defender of the fortress to keep our observers from the walls. But we have other ways to watch." It sounded displeased without voicing anger. "A Drueten presented the blood heir and asked for the right of entry. By your orders it was denied."

"My sister?" Rozel grasped the edge of the platform, afraid to believe yet wanting to with every muscle. The room rumbled with the news and was quieted by mystic force.

The golden armband now hung at Skaln's side from his clenched fist. "A lie to get Drueten soldiers into the fortress," he said. He pointed at Rozel. "So they could put her on the throne by force."

Benoc shouted protests and demands, citing this law and that law. Rozel tugged at her wrist blade, determined to show Skaln something he understood. The sharp metal stubbornly refused to leave its sheath.

"Silence," the Visionate said. And was obeyed. "The battle outside the fortress between Felcons and Druetens has ceased by our intervention. Through our power we bring the blood heir."

Lnez strode in. Grime streaking his silver hair and accentuating the creases around his mouth and eyes made him appear ancient. The crowd murmured their confusion.

Rozel held her breath. A woman entered, her red hair disheveled and dulled with soot. Water stained clothing askew, she seemed an illusion in a mirror, showing Rozel how battered she felt.

But the woman was real. And the baby she held before her, unwrapped for all to see, was real. The child blinked at being in such a curious position.

Rozel didn't try to fight her elation and the tears that came with it. Startled cries fanned across the room. Felcon, Drueten, Tskant, Walbask, Joach eyes flicked from neighbor to neighbor. Some reached for weapons hidden in their clothing but were prevented from drawing them.

Rozel rushed with Oktria and Benoc to form an escort as Janvian marched to the dais. She fell into step beside her sister. "Don't ever do this to me again," she said in greeting. The three, joined Amud and Lnez, placed themselves between the crowd and the dais as Janvian climbed the stairs to the platform and faced the gathering. The child squirmed in her arms. "I present the son of Rojelon."

"That could be any brat," Skaln said. The crumpled

insignia seemed to be sliding through his fingers. He didn't notice the mystic that snatched it up and carrying it away. The crowd rumbled. Some in agreement, some in protest.

"Bring the child to us," the Visionate commanded.

Janvian stepped into the semicircle. She stood a head taller than the tiny Visionate. It put a hand on the baby's forehead. The bony white flesh veined with blue looked as old as sand. The child ceased squirming.

Rozel had never seen a mystic make physical contact with anyone before, except Lnez. The rogue leaned on Amud's arm. Now that his task was accomplished, his strength had dissolved.

On the dais the Visionate sucked in a long, irregular breath like the flutter of dry leaves. Its contact with the child seemed to require great effort. Rozel shrugged away a feeling that its purpose was to discover more than the child's parentage. An infant had little to tell about the past. Could a mystic with the title of Visionate divine a soul's future? Slowly, reluctantly, Rozel thought, the mystic withdrew its hand. "We see the child is from the union of Rojelon and Janvian," it said.

Benoc raised his voice. "Visionate and Baerryns, Drueten Clan supports the blood heir and pledges lor to the new monarch."

Gozax pushed her way through a knot of clankin to the dais, using her elbows for leverage. In a formal robe and finely embroidered overlay the Tskant tarryn presented a formidable presence. Her gray hair was tied back in a decorative ribbon from her large, handsome face. She addressed the mystics, but she faced the crowd. "The blood heir is now present. The Tskant Clan supports Rojelon's child and regrets its former declaration."

Pale and weeping in her golden gown, Calliud sagged

against her parents. From other parts of the room the Joach tarryn and the Walbask tarryn added their support.

"Does the Felcon Clan wish to declare?" the Visionate asked in its eerie multiple whisper.

Skaln said softly. "Felcon Clan supports the blood heir."

"He is called Dougal," Janvian told the robed figure.

Mystics carrying the Drueten and Felcon insignias came forward. The Visionate took an armband in each hand and draped them over the baby. "We declare Dougal, child of Rojelon of the Felcons and Janvian of the Druetens, monarch of Lorcha. Until such time as a choice is made, the child is kin to both clans."

Rozel led a cheer for her nephew and gave the hand to shoulder salute. The Druetens had a ruler on the throne that was not her. She felt satisfaction and relief in that, but she looked at her sister, safely home, and knew the real joy of the moment.

The gathering suddenly quieted. "With our mind we see the moons touch," the Visionate said. "A new year begins; a new monarch has been declared. Because a babe cannot perform the duties necessary to rule a country, we name a regent to act in his place and to guide him in his training until such time as it is determined that he is fit to govern for himself. As regent we name Janvian of Drueten Clan. Further, to safeguard the child, Aerrion Fortress is given into the care of Tarryn Benoc."

Cheers for the regent erupted across the room. Skaln heard them, but they were far away. For a moment the monarchy had been his, as it was meant to be. He discovered his hand on the hilt of his concealed knife. It slid smoothly from the sheath, and he felt pleasure in the motion. His mind told him his action was unwise; but the weight of the blade was sweetly overpowering, and the anger that burned in his heart urged him on.

He lunged at Janvian, determined to gain what her cunning had snatched from him, not wondering how this was possible in the presence of mystic protectors. He would be monarch. He would wear the golden armband and sit on the throne. Tarryns would salute him as he had saluted Rojelon for many years. So many years. It would be as he'd dreamed from his youngest days. And he would marry Lelian. She would be beside him always.

A knife was suddenly in Janvian's hand. She dodged, deflecting the blow with her blade.

Skaln misjudged the force of his rush. The momentum carried him beyond his target, exposing his back. The hilt of Janvian's weapon slammed into the base of his skull, and he sprawled across the dais.

He pushed onto an elbow and flipped his knife, feeling the sharp tip between his fingers. He locked Janvian's water-blue eyes in a deadly stare and raised the weapon. He shifted his gaze to the infant in her arms to show her his real target and to freeze those liquid pools.

The blade flew. Janvian pivoted and sent her own stiletto soaring. Skaln rejoiced, certain his knife tore into the baby's soft flesh. The thrill caught in his throat. He put a hand to cold metal and warm blood. His enemy's knife had skimmed his thick collar and lodged in his neck. His head rolled heavy. He fell back with a bone chilling crack. He wondered if Lelian had felt this same calm shock spread through her body as she lay dying.

The candlelight faded. He heard his name called in a child's voice. He expected Lelian to reach out to him from the smoky ceiling, but the air turned musty and unbreathable.

The dark stretched before him and behind him. No lamp.

No torch. No candle. Skaln touched a damp wall for balance and took cautious steps along the labyrinth. A stir told him an opening to a side tunnel was near. He shrank from it, fear as paralyzing as the trickle of sweat on his neck. He had to go on, blindly, step by step.

A child's laugh echoed around him. A small hand grasped his sleeve and pulled him deeper into oblivion.

<><><>

The overlapping circles of Noalgaz and Pypeed made the balcony bright as day. The smaller, quicker brother and the larger, slower sister released one another to take their own paths through the new year.

Facing west toward the red storm, the Visionate sat uncomfortably in a cushioned chair, her mind too weak to take the strain from her frail body. The theatrical display of power had drained her. Some of it had been remarkably simple. Declaring the moons joined—she had guessed at that, not bothering to check with her spy on the battlement. No one in the room knew if that was accurate.

Other effects were more complex. Wind, the illusion of invisibility, and controlled influence over the assembly required skill and energy. The Prism had assisted but she'd carried the burden of the action. At her direction the others of the Unity had been occupied with squelching the ridiculous battle at the fortress bridge and getting the mother and child to the hall.

Prodding Skaln to attack Janvian might have been a mistake. But his dealings with the *skyship* envoy made him too dangerous to live. The Visionate would manage the repercussions, just as she would deal with the issue of the former Speaker turned rogue.

Lightning crackled across the sand. The gemstone at her forehead drank deeply, but a single storm was not potent enough to penetrate her aches of mind, body and spirit.

Futures again spread before her. They held a different flavor than before. It would take time to explore them. With Skaln gone, otherworlders still walked in some of them, but not many. The former Speaker was prominent in some and absent in others. These new people concerned her. The Mirage Clan. They dwelled in many futures, tied more strongly to the return of machines than the foreign traders were.

Tremors shook her withered limbs. The Prism and the Unity mourned the Sage's death. She did not. Nor would she be concerned when her own came. Shortly she would be installed to take his place, giving her command of the Unity, making her the most powerful mind on the planet.

And still she did not know. She had touched the child, searching for a spark of mystic ability and found none. Was it not there? Had their efforts to create one of their own kind who would rule the clans failed again? After decades of manipulation this had been the closest they'd come to fulfilling the plan. Perhaps their research had not discovered a critical factor. Perhaps exposure to the storm did not produce a mystic after all.

Or was the ability simply dormant in the baby, as with naturally occurring mystics, undetectable until the child developed?

She did not know, and none of the futures told her.

A thousand roads each had a thousand branches. As time passed they would mingle and join. She would watch them for signs so she would be prepared for whatever the child came to be.

For now, she would be patient.

<><><>

A light placed in the tower window announced the selection of the new monarch. Drueten and Felcon banners flew over the fortress. A temporary bridge was quickly constructed. The tarryns sent messengers to their homelands with the news.

On the dais in the hearth hall a cradle rested beside a single chair. Both were empty. Quickly washed and freshly robed, Janvian stood on the platform before the gathering, reluctant to sit alone where once she had shared a double throne with Rojelon. On her sleeve a Drueten armband edged in gold signified her position as regent.

At her side Great-uncle Benoc bounced the baby in his arms. "You should be asleep, little one," he crooned. "Ah, you have the handsome features of the Druetens."

Janvian laughed. The baby had been slumbering peacefully until Benoc had insisted on holding him. She held a goblet adorned with the insignias of the five clans.

Servants delivered wine about the room in preparation for the traditional toasts to the new year. Death had interrupted Rojelon's. She would mourn him for the rest of her life, but she would not let grief keep her from living. She would not hide from the world, neither here nor anywhere else. She would not place herself inside a bubble, like Jeremy and his people.

Clankin, friends and enemies held cups waiting for her words. She found it difficult to separate them neatly into those categories. Artulk smiled at her, Diakt confidently at his side. Their daughter was absent. Skaln's successor stood grim. Having only recently been allowed to assist at Aerrion Fortress, she suddenly found herself a new tarryn surrounded by Drueten guards, the only Felcon allowed in the room.

Rozel had changed into her red dress. She moved through the guests like a giddy dancer, her long hair flying. A brown-haired man wearing an earring identical to Oktria's watched her every move. Although he wore the Drueten insignia, Janvian did not recognize him. He mostly spoke to Oktria and the rogue Lnez.

The man behind the mystic was another stranger dressed in kin garb. He wore a hat that was completely out of place at a formal ceremony. She could not see his face. It seemed her clan had suddenly grown.

She held out her goblet to the gathering, candlelight catching the curved rim. "Welcome, Lorchans. Good fortune to you in the new year, Age of Order 402." There were wounds to heal. A united Lorcha remained a dream. The child gurgling in Benoc's arms would be the healer, and the dreamer who'd shape the world's path. She would begin the change, guiding her child, Rojelon's child, to the future she and Rojelon had planned together.

"Join me in a salute to Relacav who brought us from chaos to order, who showed us we are strongest together, who placed before us a standard by which we measure all our actions: For the good of Lorcha." She sipped the bitter-sweet wine she had chosen. Clankin, friends and enemies drank with her.

She lowered her goblet and looked to her sister. Rozel nodded and tilted her cup toward Janvian. She responded back in kind, a silent toast of their own. On the dais she could not complete it with a sip. Rozel assumed that role for both of them by draining her goblet. She grinned at Janvian, then pulled the stranger with the hat from behind Lnez.

Jeremy! He adjusted the neck of his borrowed shirt and smiled at her. She held his gaze for a moment. He was part of her hope for the country. And perhaps part of what she hoped for herself.

Janvian again raised her goblet. "To Monarch Dougal and the future of Lorcha!"

AUTHOR'S NOTES

What fun to build two environments!

The planet is modeled on Earth (not surprising, since humans live there) with modifications important to the plot. Snow I already knew about. The desert took more research, since I have little experience with great sandy expanses. I found lightning fascinating. I took a bit of liberty with it on Alchorel but not beyond the possible.

The dome is a big slice of world crammed into a small space. Instead of running on seasons, it maintains a consistent climate. That makes it easy to choose what to wear every morning. You don't have to check the weather reports for the heat index or the wind chill. Instead, your daily vigilance goes into maintaining the habitat.

Each environment has its own delights and its own demands. Each takes a certain skill set for survival.

If you had the chance to live in one or the other, would you choose the steady, consistent life inside a bubble that requires your constant care, or the uncertainty of nature that runs by itself, needing nothing from you and owing you nothing?

MEET THE AUTHOR

DANITH McPHERSON writes science fiction, fantasy, and mysteries. In keeping with her Scottish heritage, she is a kilt maker and proudly wears McPherson tartan.

In her fantasy novel *Blade of Mad Vision*, a brother and a sister are separated on a strange planet. When they finally reunite, they must wield their swords to try to save that world.

Her short stories have appeared in *Asimov's Science Fiction Magazine, Amazing Stories,* and other places. You can find some of them in *Roar at the Universe*. The collection includes "Roar at the Heart of the World," which was selected for *The Year's Best Fantasy and Horror, Seventh Annual Collection.*

Her mystery novels feature sleuth Cassie Windom solving murders in Minnesota lake country.

amazon.com/author/danith

goodreads.com/danith

facebook.com/DanithMcPherson

If you enjoyed *Monarch of Lightning*, please leave a review on Goodreads and Amazon through the links below. Like most authors, I depend on reviews to help readers find my stories. Thank you for reading!

At Goodreads, click on "Write a review."

At Amazon, scroll down to "Review this product."

You might also like—

Blade of Mad Vision

Fencing is just a sport for Austin and Skylar, until they find themselves on a strange planet and discover how dangerous swordplay can be.

Austin would do anything to find his missing sister Skylar.

When a stranger appears claiming he's been sent by her, Austin is suspicious. But he is forced to follow the man to another world where sword fighting is more serious than the fencing Austin knows.

Scan to buy from Amazon

A young artist who is being hunted for making dangerous art, joins them as they seek Skylar. Her drawings predict that the brother and sister will do battle against a powerful enemy.

Scan to buy from Barnes and Noble

Austin only wants to rescue his sister and return home, but Skylar, held captive by a desperate lord, is determined to take care of herself and to help her new friends save their planet from destruction.

You might also like—

Roar at the Universe

Enjoy these speculative tales of people in crisis, fighting to survive, that span time and space. The collection includes "Roar at the Heart of the World," selected for *The Year's Best Fantasy and Horror, Seventh Annual Collection.*

Scan to buy from Amazon

AVERTED VISION

A Cassie Windom Mystery

Sometimes you have to look away to see murder clearly.

After a frightening tornado, a figure floats on the surface of Beauty Lake. Cassie swims out, desperately hoping the person is still alive.

If not, well, this isn't her first dead body.

Haunted by the vicious murder of her best friend by an abusive lover, Cassie Windom abandons her career in Los Angeles and flees back home to Minnesota.

She hopes to leave behind the guilt of a gruesome secret and to reshape her life. But escape is not as easy as changing geography, and a quirky small town is not the quiet retreat she expected.

Buy from Barnes and Noble

Buy from Amazon

www.ingramcontent.com/pod-product-compliance
Lightning Source LLC
Chambersburg PA
CBHW051202190726
48288CB00006B/1778